HADES
ALEXANDRA ADORNETTO

www.atombooks.net

FOR EVERYONE WHO'S BEEN TO HELL AND BACK

ATOM

First published in the US in 2011 by Feiwel and Friends, an imprint of Macmillan
First published in Great Britain in 2011 by Atom
This paperback edition published in 2012 by Atom

A CIP catalogue record for this book
is available from the British Library.

ISBN 978-1-907410-78-9

Printed and bound in Great Britain by
Clays Ltd, St Ives plc

Papers used by Atom are from well-managed forests
and other responsible sources.

MIX
Paper from
responsible sources
FSC® C104740

Atom
An imprint of
Little, Brown Book Group
100 Victoria Embankment
London EC4Y 0DY

An Hachette UK Company
www.hachette.co.uk

www.atombooks.net

*How art thou fallen from heaven, O Lucifer,
Son of the morning!*

—Isaiah 14:12–15

*The Devil went down to Georgia, he was
lookin' for a soul to steal.
He was in a bind, 'cos he was way behind;
he was willin' to make a deal.*

—Charlie Daniels,
"Devil Went Down to Georgia"

{ Contents }

The Kids Are All Right

WHEN the final bell sounded at Bryce Hamilton, Xavier and I gathered our things and headed out onto the south lawn. The weather forecast had predicted a clear afternoon, but the sun was fighting an uphill battle and the sky remained a cheerless, gunmetal gray. Occasionally the watery sunlight broke through and fingers of light danced across the grounds, warming the back of my neck.

"Are you coming over for dinner tonight?" I asked Xavier, linking my arm through his. "Gabriel wants to try making burritos."

Xavier looked across at me and laughed.

"What's funny?"

"I'm just thinking," he said. "How come in all the paintings, angels are depicted guarding thrones in Heaven or taking out demons? I wonder why they're never shown in the kitchen making burritos."

"Because we have a reputation to uphold," I said, nudging him. "So are you coming?"

"Can't." Xavier sighed. "I promised my kid sister I'd stay home and carve pumpkins."

"Shoot. I keep forgetting about Halloween."

"You should try and get into the spirit of it," Xavier said. "Everyone around here takes it very seriously."

I knew he wasn't exaggerating; jack-o'-lanterns and plaster headstones already adorned every front porch in town in honor of the occasion.

"I know," I said. "But the whole idea creeps me out. Why would anyone want to dress up as ghosts and zombies? It's like everyone's worst nightmares coming to life."

"Beth." Xavier stopped walking and took hold of my shoulders. "It's a holiday, lighten up!"

He was right. I needed to stop being so wary. It was six months now since the ordeal with Jake Thorn and things couldn't have been better. Peace had returned to Venus Cove and I'd grown more attached to the place than ever. Nestled on the picturesque Georgia coastline, the sleepy little town in Sherbrooke County had become my home. With its pretty balconies and ornate shopfronts, Main Street was so quaint it could have been an image on a postcard. In fact, everything from the cinema to the old courthouse exuded the Southern charm and gentility of a long-forgotten era.

Over the past year the influence of my family had spread and transformed Venus Cove into a model town. The church congregation had tripled in numbers, charity missions had more volunteers than they could handle, and reported incidents of crime were so few and far between that the sheriff was forced to find other things to occupy his time. Nowadays the only disputes that happened were minor, like drivers arguing over who saw a parking space first. But that was just human nature. It couldn't be changed and it wasn't our job to try and change it.

But the best development of all was that Xavier and I had grown even closer. I looked across at him. He was just as breathtakingly beautiful as ever. His tie hung loose and his blazer was slung casually over one shoulder. I could feel his taut body occasionally brushing against mine as we walked side by side, our footsteps falling in time. Sometimes it was easy to think of us as one entity.

Since the violent encounter with Jake last year, Xavier had hit the gym even harder and thrown himself into sports more vigorously. I knew he was doing it so he'd be better equipped to protect me, but that didn't mean I couldn't enjoy the perks. Xavier had more definition in his chest and washboard abs. He was still slender and perfectly proportioned, but I could see the muscles in his arms rippling beneath the fine cotton of his shirt. I looked up at his refined features: his straight nose, high cheekbones, and full lips. In the light of the sun, his walnut-colored hair was streaked with gold and his almond-shaped eyes were like liquid blue topaz. On his ring finger he now wore the gift I'd given him after he had helped me recover from Jake's attack. It was a thick silver band etched with three symbols of faith: a five-point star to represent the star of Bethlehem; a trefoil to honor the three persons of the Holy Trinity; and the initials IHS, an abbreviation of *Ihesus*, the way Christ's name was spelled in the Middle Ages. I'd had an identical one made for me and I liked to think they were our special version of a promise ring. Another person who'd witnessed as much as Xavier had might have lost all faith in Our Father, but Xavier had strength of mind and spirit. He'd made a commitment to us and I knew that nothing could persuade him to break it.

My train of thought was broken when we bumped into a group of Xavier's friends from the water-polo team in the parking lot. I knew some of them by name and caught the tail end of their conversation.

"I can't believe Wilson hooked up with Kay Bentley," a boy named Lawson snickered. He was still bleary-eyed from whatever misadventure had taken place over the weekend. I knew from experience it probably involved a keg and willful damage to property.

"It's his funeral," someone muttered. "Everyone knows she's done more miles than my dad's vintage Chrysler."

"I don't care so long as it wasn't on my bed. I'd have to burn everything."

"Don't worry, man, pretty sure they were out on the back lawn."

"I was so wasted, I don't remember a damn thing," Lawson declared.

"I remember you tried to hook up with me," replied a boy named Wesley in his lilting accent. He contorted his face into a grimace.

"Whatever . . . it was dark. You could do a lot worse."

"Not funny," Wesley growled. "Someone posted a picture on Facebook. What am I gonna tell Jess?"

"Tell her you couldn't resist Lawson's ripped body." Xavier thumped his friend on the back as he sauntered past. "He's really built from all those hours on the PlayStation."

I laughed as Xavier pulled open the door of his sky blue Chevy Bel Air convertible. I climbed in, stretched out, and breathed in the familiar smell of the leather seats. I loved the car almost as much as Xavier did now. It had been with us from the very beginning, from our first date at Sweethearts Café to the showdown with Jake Thorn at the cemetery. Though I'd never admit it, I'd come to think of the Chevy as having a personality of its own. Xavier turned the key in the ignition and the car roared to life. They seemed to move in sync—as if they were attuned to each other.

"So have you come up with a costume yet?"

"For what?" I asked blankly.

Xavier shook his head. "For Halloween. Try to keep up!"

"Not yet," I admitted. "I'm still working on it. What about you?"

"How do you feel about Batman?" Xavier asked with a wink. "I've always wanted to be a superhero."

"You just want to pretend you drive a Batmobile."

Xavier gave a guilty smile. "Damn it! You know me too well."

When we reached number 15 Byron Street, Xavier leaned across and pressed his lips against mine. His kiss was soft and sweet. I felt the outside world fall away as I melted into him. His skin was smooth beneath my fingers and his scent, fresh and clean as ocean air, enveloped me. It was mingled with a touch of something stronger—like vanilla and sandal-wood combined. I kept one of Xavier's T-shirts, dowsed in his cologne, under my pillow so that every night I could imagine he was with me. It was funny how the goofiest behavior could feel perfectly natural when you were in love. I knew there were people who rolled their eyes at Xavier and me, but if they did, we were too absorbed in each other's company to notice.

When Xavier pulled away from the curb, I snapped back to reality, like someone waking from a deep sleep.

"I'll pick you up tomorrow morning," he called out with a dreamy smile. "Usual time."

I stood in our tangled front yard watching until the Chevy finally turned off at the end of the street.

Byron was still my haven and I loved retreating there. Everything was soothingly familiar, from the creaking steps on the front porch to the large and airy rooms inside. It felt like a safe cocoon away from the turbulence of the world. It was true to say that while I loved human life, it scared me sometimes. The earth had problems—problems almost too large and too complex to fully comprehend. Thinking about them made my head spin. It also made me feel ineffectual. But Ivy and Gabriel had told me to stop wasting my energy and focus on our mission. There were plans for us to visit other cities and towns in the vicinity of Venus Cove to expel any dark forces residing there. Little did we know they would find us before we had a chance to find them.

Dinner was already underway when I got home. My brother and sister were out on the deck. They were each engaged in solitary activities; Ivy had her nose in a book and Gabriel was deep in concentration, composing on his guitar. His expert fingers massaged the chords gently and they seemed to answer his silent command. I joined them and knelt down to pat my dog, Phantom, who was sleeping soundly with his head resting on his giant, silky paws. He stirred at my touch, his silvery body as sleek as ever. He looked up at me with his sad, moonlight eyes, and I imagined his expression to say: *Where have you been all day?*

Ivy lay semi-recumbent in the hammock, her golden hair flowing down to her waist. It looked resplendent in the light of the setting sun. My sister didn't quite know how to relax in a hammock; she looked too poised and reminded me of a mythical creature who had somehow found herself unceremoniously plonked in a world that made no sense to her. She was wearing a pastel blue muslin dress and had even set up a frilly parasol, to protect her from the fading sunlight. No doubt she'd found it in some vintage shop and couldn't resist buying it.

"Where did you get that?" I laughed. "I think they went out of fashion a while ago."

"Well, I think it's charming," said Ivy, laying down the novel she'd been reading. I took a peek at the cover.

"*Jane Eyre?*" I asked dubiously. "You do know it's a love story, right?"

"I'm aware," said my sister huffily.

"You're turning into me!" I teased.

"I highly doubt I could ever be as swooning and silly as you are," Ivy replied in a matter-of-fact tone but her eyes were playful.

Gabriel stopped strumming his guitar to look over at us.

"I don't think anybody could outdo Bethany in that department," he said with a smile. He put down his guitar carefully and went to lean against the railing, staring out to sea. As usual

Gabe stood arrow straight, his white-blond hair pulled back in a ponytail. His steel gray eyes and his sculpted features made him look like the celestial warrior he was—but he was dressed like a human in faded jeans and a loose shirt. His face was open and friendly. I was pleased to see that Gabriel was more relaxed these days. I felt as if both my siblings were less critical of me, more accepting of the choices I'd made.

"How is it you always get home before me?" I complained. "When I take a car and you walk!"

"I have my ways," my brother replied with a secretive smile. "Besides, I don't have to pull over every two minutes to express my affection."

"We do not pull over to express affection!" I objected.

Gabriel raised an eyebrow. "So that wasn't Xavier's car parked two blocks from school?"

"Maybe it was." I tossed my head nonchalantly, hating how he was always right. "But every two minutes is a slight exaggeration!"

Ivy's heart-shaped face glowed as she broke into a laugh. "Oh, Bethany, relax. We're used to the PDAs by now."

"Where did you learn that?" I asked curiously. I'd never heard Ivy use abbreviated colloquialisms. Her formal speech usually sounded so out of place in the modern world.

"I do spend time with young people, you know," she said. "I'm trying to be hip."

Gabriel and I burst out laughing.

"In that case, don't say *hip* for starters," I advised.

Ivy leaned down to ruffle my hair affectionately and

changed the subject. "I hope you don't have plans for this weekend."

"Can Xavier come?" I asked eagerly before she'd even had a chance to explain what she and Gabe had in mind. Xavier had long become a fixture in my life. Even when we were apart, it seemed there was no activity or distraction that could keep my thoughts from straying back to him.

Gabriel pointedly rolled his eyes. "If he must."

"Of course he must," I said, grinning. "So what's the plan?"

"There's a town called Black Ridge twenty miles from here," my brother said. "We've been told they're experiencing some . . . disturbances."

"You mean demonic disturbances?"

"Well, three girls have gone missing in the last month and a perfectly sound bridge collapsed onto passing traffic."

I winced. "Sounds like our kind of problem. When do we leave?"

"Saturday," Ivy said. "So you better rest up."

Co-Dependent

THE next day Molly and I sat with the girls in the west courtyard, which had become our new favorite hangout. Molly had changed since the loss of her best friend the year before. Taylah's death at the hands of Jake Thorn had been a wake-up call for my family. We had not foreseen the extent of Jake's powers until the day he'd slit her throat to send us a message.

Since then Molly had drifted away from her old circle of friends and out of a sense of loyalty, I'd gone along with her. I didn't mind the switch. I knew Bryce Hamilton must now be full of painful memories for Molly and I wanted to support her in every way I could. Besides, our new group was more or less the same as the old one. These were girls we'd hung out with on occasion but never become close with. They knew all the same people and gossiped about the same things, so becoming integrated into their group was easy as pie.

Things were strained in the group that had once included Taylah, and I knew Molly couldn't really relax with them. Occasionally, out of the blue, conversations would come to an awkward halt. The kind of pause where you knew everyone was thinking the same thing: *What would Taylah say right now?* But no one had the courage to speak her name out loud. I had a feeling things would never be quite the same for these girls. They'd tried to make things go back to normal, but most of the time it felt as if they were trying too hard. They laughed too loudly and their jokes sounded rehearsed. It seemed that whatever they said or did, they were constantly reminded of Taylah's absence. Taylah and Molly had been at the very core of the group, self-appointed authorities on so many things. Now Taylah was gone and Molly was completely withdrawn. The other girls had lost both their mentors and were completely adrift without them.

It was hard watching them struggle collectively with their grief; a grief they couldn't articulate for fear of unleashing emotion they couldn't control. I so badly wanted to tell them not to see death as an end but as a new beginning and explain to them that Taylah had simply crossed to a new plane of existence, one that was unencumbered by physicality. I wanted them to know that Taylah was out there still, only now she was free. I wanted to tell them about Heaven and the peace she would find there. But, of course, sharing any of that knowledge was impossible. Not only would I be breaking our most sacred code and exposing our presence on earth, but I'd also be instantly kicked out of the group for being a lunatic.

Our newly adopted friends huddled around a cluster of carved wooden benches beneath a stone archway that they'd claimed as their own. One thing that hadn't changed was their territorial nature. If any outsiders accidentally strayed into our area, they didn't linger long. The glaring looks of disapproval that flew in their direction were usually enough to drive them away. Gray clouds rolled ominously overhead, but the girls never went inside unless there was absolutely no alternative. As usual they sat with their hair perfectly coiffed and their skirts hitched up, soaking up the weak rays of sunlight that dipped and wavered behind the clouds, washing the courtyard in a soft, dappled light. Any opportunity to work on their tans could not be missed.

The Halloween party on Friday had served to lift everyone's spirits and generate a lot of excitement. It was being held at an abandoned estate just out of town that belonged to the family of one of the seniors, Austin Knox. His great-grandfather Thomas Knox had built the house in 1868, several years after the Civil War ended. He was one of the town's original founders and although the Knox family hadn't visited the place in years, historical landmark laws protected it from demolition. So it had remained vacant and uninhabited over the years. It was a run-down, old country homestead with deep porches on every side, surrounded by nothing but fields and a deserted highway. The locals called it the Boo Radley House—nobody ever went in or out—and Austin claimed he'd even seen his great-grandfather's ghost standing at one of the upstairs windows. According to Molly, it was perfect party material; nobody ever passed that way except for people who'd taken a wrong turn on a road trip or the occasional trucker. Plus, it was well enough away from town that nobody could complain about the noise. It had originally started out as a small gathering, but word had somehow gotten out and now the whole school was talking about it. Even some of the better-connected sophomores had managed to score an invite.

I sat next to Molly, whose titian curls were wound on top of her head in a loose bun. Without makeup she had the face of a china doll with wide sky blue eyes and rosebud lips. She couldn't resist a slick of lip gloss, but aside from that, she'd pared everything back in her attempt to win favor with Gabriel. I'd expected by now she'd be over the hopeless crush she had on my brother, but so far her feelings for him only seemed to have intensified.

I preferred Molly without makeup; I liked the way she looked her age rather than someone ten years older.

"I'm going as a naughty schoolgirl," Abigail announced.

"In other words you're going as yourself?" Molly said with a snort.

"Let's hear your great idea then. . . ."

"I'm going as Tinker Bell."

"As who?"

"The fairy from *Peter Pan*."

"This isn't fair," Madison whined. "We made a pact to all go as Playboy Bunnies!"

"Bunnies are old." Molly tossed her head. "Not to mention trashy."

"I'm sorry," I interrupted, "but aren't the costumes supposed to be scary?"

"Oh, Bethie," Savannah said with a sigh. "Have we taught you nothing?"

I smiled sheepishly. "Refresh my memory?"

"Basically the whole thing is just one massive—," Hallie began.

"Let's just say it's an opportunity for us to mingle with the opposite sex," Molly cut in, shooting Hallie a sharp look. "Your costume needs to be scary *and* sexy."

"Did you know Halloween used to be about Samhain?" I said. "People were really scared of it."

"Who's Sam Hen?" Hallie looked baffled.

"Not who . . . what," I said. "It's different in every culture. But essentially, people believe it's the one night of the year when the world of the dead meets the world of the living; when the dead can walk among us and possess our bodies. People would dress up to trick them into staying away."

The group stared at me with newfound respect.

"Oh my God, Bethie." Savannah shivered. "Way to freak us all out."

"Do you remember when we had that séance in seventh grade?" Abigail asked. The others nodded enthusiastically as they recalled the event.

"You had a what!" I spluttered, barely able to disguise my disbelief.

"A séance, it's when you . . ."

"I know what it is," I said. "But you shouldn't mess around with that stuff."

"I told you, Abby!" Hallie exclaimed. "I told you it was dangerous. Remember how the door slammed shut?"

"Yeah, only because your mom shut it," Madison hit back.

"She couldn't have. She was in bed asleep the whole time."

"Whatever. I'm thinking we should try it again on Friday."

Abigail waggled her eyebrows mischievously. "What do you say, girls? Who's in?"

"Not me," I said resolutely. "I'm not getting mixed up in that."

The looks they exchanged suggested they were unconvinced by my refusal.

"THEY'RE so childish," I complained to Xavier as we walked to French class together. Doors slammed, announcements rang over the loudspeaker, and chatter flowed freely around us, but Xavier and I were locked in our own world. "They want to hold a séance and go dressed as bunnies."

"What kind of bunnies?" he asked suspiciously.

"Playboy, I think. Whatever that means."

"That sounds about right." Xavier laughed. "But don't let them talk you into anything you don't feel comfortable with."

"They're my friends."

"So what?" He shrugged. "If your friends walked off a cliff, would you do it too?"

"Why would they walk off a cliff?" I asked in alarm. "Is someone having problems at home?"

Xavier laughed. "It's just an expression."

"It's silly," I told him. "Do you think I should go as an angel? Like in the film version of *Romeo and Juliet*?"

"There would be a certain irony in that," Xavier said, smirking. "An angel posing as a human posing as an angel. I like it."

Mr. Collins glared at us as we arrived and took our seats. He seemed to resent our closeness and I couldn't help but wonder whether his history of three failed marriages had left him a little jaded about love.

"I hope the two of you will descend from your love bubble long enough to learn something today," he sniped cuttingly and the other kids snickered. Embarrassed, I ducked my head to avoid eye contact with them.

"It's all right, sir," Xavier replied. "The bubble's been engineered to allow us to learn from within it."

"You're very amusing, Woods," Mr. Collins said. "But the classroom is not the place for romance. When it all ends in heartbreak, your grades will pay the price. *L'amour est comme un sablier, avec le cœur remplir le vide du cerveau.*"

I recognized the quote from the French writer Jules Renard. Translated it meant: "Love is like an hourglass, with the heart filling up as the brain empties." I hated his smug certainty, as if he knew for a fact our relationship was doomed. I opened my mouth to protest, but Xavier touched my hand under the table and leaned across to whisper in my ear.

"It's probably not the best idea to get fresh with the teachers who'll be grading our final papers."

He turned back to Mr. Collins, putting on his best class-president voice. "We understand, sir, thanks for your concern."

Mr. Collins looked satisfied and went back to writing subjunctive verbs on the blackboard. I couldn't resist poking my tongue out at his back.

Hallie and Savannah, who were also in my French class, caught up with me at the lockers. They looped their arms affably through mine.

"What have you got now?" Hallie asked.

"Math," I replied suspiciously. "Why?"

"Perfect," Savannah said. "Walk with us."

"Is something wrong?"

"We just want to talk to you. Y'know, have a girl-to-girl chat."

"Okay," I said slowly, wracking my brain to think what I might have done to warrant this strange intervention. "About?"

"It's about you and Xavier," Hallie blurted out. "Look, you're not gonna like hearing this, but we're your friends and we're worried about you."

"Why are you worried?"

"It's just not healthy for you guys to spend so much time together," Hallie said expertly.

"Yeah," Savannah chimed in. "It's like you're joined at the hip or something. I never see you apart. Wherever Xavier is, you're right behind him. Wherever you are, he's there . . . *all the frigging time*."

"Is that that a bad thing?" I asked. "He's my boyfriend; I *want* to spend time with him."

"Of course you do, but it's too much. You need to get some *distance*." Hallie emphasized the word *distance* as if it were a medical term.

"Why?" I looked at them dubiously, wondering if Molly had put them up to this or if it truly was their personal opinion. I'd been friends with these girls all through summer, but it still felt a little early for them to be dispensing relationship advice. On the other hand, I'd only been a teenage girl for less than a year. In some way, I felt I was at the mercy of their experience. It was true that Xavier and I were close, any fool could see that. The question was, were we *unnaturally* close? It didn't feel unhealthy given everything we'd been through together. Of course, these girls could never know about our struggles.

"It's a researched fact," Savannah broke through my train of thought. "Look, I can show you." She reached into her bag and yanked out a well-thumbed copy of *Seventeen* magazine. "We found a quiz for you to take."

She opened the glossy cover and flipped to a dog-eared page. The image showed a young couple sitting in chairs facing opposite directions but bound together by chains around their waists and ankles. The expression on their faces was one of confusion and dismay. The quiz was called, "Are you in a co-dependent relationship?"

"We're not that bad," I protested. "It's about how we feel, not how much time we spend together. Besides, I don't think a magazine quiz can measure feelings."

"*Seventeen* gives pretty reliable advice—," began Savannah hotly.

"Okay, don't take the quiz," Hallie cut in. "Just answer a few questions, okay?"

"Shoot," I said.

"What's your favorite football team?"

"Dallas Cowboys," I said without hesitation.

"And why's that?" Hallie asked.

"Because it's Xavier's favorite team."

"I see," Hallie said knowingly. "And when was the last time you did something without Xavier?" I didn't like the way she sounded like the prosecutor in a court case.

"I do plenty of stuff without Xavier," I said dismissively.

"Really? So where is he right now?"

"He has a first-aid training session in the gym," I said brightly. "They're going over CPR, but he already learned it in ninth grade during a water-safety program."

"Right," Savannah said. "And what's he doing at lunch?"

"He has a water-polo meeting," I replied. "They have a new junior that Xav wants to train to play defense."

"And dinner?"

"He's coming over to make barbecue ribs."

"Since when do you like ribs?" The girls raised their eyebrows.

"Xavier likes them."

"I rest my case." Hallie put her face in her hands.

"Okay, I guess we do spend a lot of time together," I said grumpily. "But what's wrong with that?"

"It's not normal is what's wrong with it," Savannah declared, enunciating every word. "Your girlfriends are just as important. "It's like we don't even matter to you anymore. All the girls feel the same, even Molly."

I stopped short. Finally the fog lifted and the purpose of this discussion became clear to me. The girls were feeling neglected. It was true that I always seemed to be declining their invitations to go out in favor of spending time with Xavier. I'd always thought I just preferred spending downtime with my family, but maybe I had been insensitive without realizing it. I valued their friendship and on the spot vowed to be more attentive.

"I'm sorry," I said. "Thanks for being honest with me. I promise I'll do better."

"Great." Hallie beamed. "Well, you can start by joining in the girls-only event we've got planned for the Halloween party."

"Of course," I agreed, eager to make amends. "I'd love to. What is it?" I had the sense even before I'd finished the question that I was on the brink of falling into a trap.

"We're going to commune with the dead, remember?" Savannah said. "No boys allowed."

"A séance," Hallie said brightly. "How awesome is that?"

"Awesome," I reiterated flatly. I could think of plenty of words to describe what they had in mind, but *awesome* just wasn't one of them.

Unholy Night

FRIDAY came around faster than I expected. I wasn't especially looking forward to the Halloween party. I'd much rather have spent a night at home with Xavier, but I didn't think it fair to impose my reclusiveness on him.

Gabriel shook his head in surprise when he saw my costume, which consisted of a white satin sheath dress, gladiator sandals borrowed from Molly, and a pair of short, fluffy synthetic wings I'd rented from the local costume shop. I was a parody of myself, and Gabriel, as I'd guessed, was unimpressed. It must have seemed like some kind of sacrilege to him.

"It's a little obvious, don't you think?" he asked wryly.

"Not at all," I replied. "If anyone suspected us of being super-human, this should throw them off the scent."

"Bethany, you are a messenger of the Lord, not a detective in a B-grade spy movie," Gabriel said. "Try to remember that."

"Would you like me to change?" I sighed.

"No, he wouldn't," Ivy said, patting my hand. "The costume is lovely. After all, it's just a high school party." She gave Gabriel a pointed look designed to bring the discussion to a close. Gabriel shrugged. Even though he spent his days disguised as a music teacher at Bryce Hamilton, it seemed the machinations of the teenage world were beyond him.

When Xavier arrived he was dressed as a cowboy in faded jeans, tan boots, and a checkered shirt. He even wore a leather cowboy hat.

"Trick or treat?" he said with a grin.

"No offense, but you don't look anything like Batman."

"Ain't no need to be nasty now, ma'am," Xavier said, adopting a heavy Texan accent. "Are you ready to go? Our ride's awaitin'."

I laughed. "You're going to keep this up all night, aren't you?

"Probably," Xavier said. "I'm driving you wild with desire, aren't I?" My brother coughed to remind us of his presence. He was always uncomfortable with outward displays of affection.

"Don't stay out too late," Ivy said. "We're leaving for Black Ridge early tomorrow morning."

"Don't worry," Xavier promised. "I'll have her home by the time the clock strikes midnight."

Gabriel shook his head. "Must the two of you embody every cliché in the book?"

Xavier and I looked at each other and grinned. "Yes," we replied.

It was a half-hour drive to the old abandoned homestead. The black stretch of highway was dotted with the headlights of other partygoers, and nothing but open fields surrounded us. We were strangely elated that night. It was an odd feeling, like the whole world belonged to the students of Bryce Hamilton. The party marked the end of an era for us and we had mixed feelings about it. We were all on the cusp of graduating and shaping our futures. It was the start of a new life and while we hoped it would be full of promise, we couldn't help but feel a degree of nostalgia for all we'd be leaving behind. College life with all its associated independence was just around the corner. Soon friendships would be tested by distance and some relationships would not survive.

The night sky seemed vaster than usual and a gibbous moon drifted between wisps of cloud. As we drove, I watched Xavier out of the corner of my eye. He looked so at ease behind the wheel of the Chevy. His face was free of anxiety. We were cruising now and he steered with one hand. Moonlight fell through the window, illuminating his face. He turned to look at me, shadows dancing across his even features.

"What are you thinking about, babe?" he asked.

"Just that I could do so much better than a cowboy," I teased.

"You are really pushing your luck tonight," Xavier said in mock seriousness. "I'm a cowboy on the edge!" I laughed, not fully understanding the reference. I could have asked him for an explanation but all that mattered was that we were together. So what if I missed the occasional joke? It made what we had even more intriguing.

We swung into the winding, overgrown driveway and followed a battered pickup truck full of senior boys calling themselves the "wolf pack." I wasn't sure what that meant, but they were all wearing khaki bandanas and had painted black war stripes across their chests and faces.

"Any excuse to get their shirts off," Xavier joked.

The boys were lounging in the back of the truck, chain-smoking and working their way through a keg. Once the truck was parked, they let out a wolf cry and leapt out, heading toward the house. One of them stopped to throw up in a nearby bush. Once he'd expelled the contents of his stomach, he straightened up and kept right on running.

The house itself reflected the Halloween theme. It was old and rambling with a creaking porch that stretched across the length of the front. The house was badly in need of a paint job. Its original white paint was cracked and peeling, revealing grayish weatherboards underneath and giving the whole place an air of neglect.

Austin must have enlisted the help of his female friends as decorating crew because the porch was brightly lit with jack-o'-lanterns and glow sticks, but the windows on the top floor remained in darkness. There was no other form of civilization in sight. If there were neighbors, they were too far away to be seen. I understood now why this house had been chosen as the party venue. We could make as much noise as we wanted and no one would hear us. The thought made me a little uneasy. The only thing separating the house from the highway was a collapsing fence that had seen better days. I could see a scarecrow propped on a stick in the middle of the yard about a hundred meters from where we stood. Its body was limp and its head lolled eerily to one side.

"That's so spooky," I whispered, drawing close to Xavier's side. "It looks so real." He wrapped a strong arm around me.

"Don't worry," he said. "It only goes after girls who don't appreciate their boyfriends."

I elbowed him playfully. "That's not even funny! Besides, the girls think it's healthy for us to spend some time apart."

"Well, I disagree." Xavier wrapped an arm around me.

"That's because you're such an attention seeker!"

"Watch out, I think he can hear you. . . ."

Inside the house was already crowded with guests. It had been vacant so long that the power had been disconnected and the whole place was lit with lanterns and candles. To the left was a sweeping staircase. It was obvious Austin's parents had let the house go because the stairs looked worn and rotted through in places. Someone had put a candle on the edge of every step and now the wax dripped down, pooling like frosting on the wooden boards. Empty rooms spilled off the wide hallway. I knew drunken couples probably occupied them, but the darkness was still unnerving. We made our way down the corridor, weaving past bodies all decked in various outfits. Some had gone all out in terms of costumes. I caught flashes of vampire teeth, devil horns, and plenty of fake blood. Someone really tall and dressed as the Grim Reaper glided past us, his face completely concealed beneath a hood. I saw Alice in Wonderland (the zombie version), Raggedy Ann, Edward Scissorhands, and a Hannibal Lecter–inspired mask. I gripped Xavier's hand tightly. I didn't want to ruin his night, but I found the whole scene slightly unsettling. It was like all the characters from horror stories suddenly coming to life around us. The only thing that took the edge off the eeriness was the constant flow of chatter and laughter. Someone plugged in an iPod dock and suddenly the house was filled with music so loud it shook the dusty chandelier above us.

We picked our way through the crowd and found Molly and the girls in the living room, ensconced in a faded tapestry club lounge. The coffee table in front of them was already littered with shot glasses and half-empty bottles of vodka. Molly had stuck with her original idea and come as Tinker Bell in a green dress, tattered at the hem, ballet flats, and a pair of fairy wings. But she had chosen her accessories carefully and in keeping with the spirit of Halloween. She wore silver chains around her wrists and ankles, and her face and body were smeared with fake blood and dirt. She had a plastic dagger protruding from her chest. Even Xavier looked impressed, his raised eyebrows indicative of his approval.

"Gothic Tinker Bell. Solid effort, Molls," he complimented. We took a seat on the divan next to Madison, who, true to her word, had turned up as a Playboy Bunny in a black corset, fluffy tail, and a pair of white bunny ears. Her eye makeup was already smudged so she looked as though she had two black eyes. She downed another shot and slammed the glass victoriously on the table.

"You two suck," she slurred as we squeezed in next to her. "Those costumes are the worst!"

"What's wrong with them?" Xavier asked, sounding as if he couldn't care less about her opinion but was merely asking out of politeness.

"You look like Woody from *Toy Story*," Madison said, suddenly unable to suppress an attack of the giggles. "And, Beth, come on! You could've at least come as one of Charlie's Angels. There's nothing scary about either of you."

"Your outfit isn't exactly terrifying either," Molly said in our defense.

"Don't be too sure about that," Xavier said. I smothered a smile behind my hand. Xavier had never liked Madison much. She drank and smoked too much and always gave her opinion when it wasn't wanted.

"Shuddup, Woody," Madison drawled.

"I think maybe someone should lay off the shots for a while," Xavier advised.

"Don't you have a rodeo or something to organize?"

Xavier jumped up, distracted from responding by the entrance of his water-polo team, who made their arrival known to everyone present by letting out a collective and uninterrupted war cry. I heard them greeting Xavier in the hall.

"Hey, man!"

"Dude, what's with the outfit?"

"Did Beth put you up to this?"

"Man, you are so whipped!" One of them straddled his back like a chimp and tackled him playfully to the ground.

"Get off me!"

"Yee-haw!"

There were a few more hoots of laughter and the sounds of a friendly scuffle. When Xavier surfaced he had been stripped of everything but his jeans. His hair, which had been smoothed back neatly when we walked in, was now ruffled. He shrugged at me as if to say he couldn't be held accountable for the behavior of his crazy friends and slipped on a fitted black T-shirt that one of the boys tossed him.

"Are you okay, Huggie Bear?" I asked, protectively reaching up to fix his hair. I didn't like it when his friends played rough. My attentiveness raised a few eyebrows among his friends.

"Beth." Xavier put his hand on my shoulder. "You have got to stop calling me that in public."

"Sorry," I said sheepishly.

Xavier laughed. "Come on, let's get something to drink."

After grabbing a beer for Xavier and soda for me, we headed out to the back porch and settled down on a deep sofa that someone had dragged out. Pink-and-green paper lanterns hung from the eaves, casting the withered yard in a soft light. Beyond it, the fields stretched out to the edge of the dense, black woodland.

Aside from the rowdy antics of the partygoers inside, the night was still and tranquil. A rusty tractor stood abandoned in the high grass. I was just thinking how picturesque it looked, like a painting from a forgotten time, when a lacy undergarment floated out of the side window coming to land at our feet. I blushed deeply as I realized there was a couple inside and they weren't engaged in deep and meaningful conversation. I quickly averted my gaze and tried to imagine what the old house might have been like in the days before the Knox family let it fall to rack and ruin. It would have been grand and beautiful back in the day when girls still had chaperones and dancing consisted of a graceful waltz played on a grand piano, nothing like the gyrating and thrusting going on inside right now. Social gatherings would have been stylish and tame compared to the havoc being wreaked upon the old house tonight. I imagined a man in coattails bowing before a woman in a flowing dress on this very same porch, although in my imagination it was polished and new and honeysuckle wound around the quaint posts. In my mind's eye I saw a star-studded night sky, the double doors flung open so the sound of music trickled out into the night.

"Halloween sucks." Ben Carter from my literature class broke through my reverie as he flopped down beside us. I would have answered him, but Xavier's strong arm encircled me and made it difficult for me to concentrate on anything else. Out of the corner of my eye I could see his hand hanging loosely over my shoulder. I liked seeing the silver faith ring on him—it was a sign that he was taken, unavailable to anyone but me. It seemed oddly out of place on an eighteen-year-old boy so beautiful and so popular. Anyone else seeing him for the first time would take one look at his perfect form, his cool turquoise gaze, that charming smile, the shock of nutmeg hair falling across his forehead and know that he could have his pick of girls.

They would simply assume that like any normal teenage boy, he would be out enjoying the perks of being young and attractive. Only those close to him knew that Xavier was completely committed to me. Not only was he breathtakingly gorgeous, he was a leader, looked up to and respected by everybody. I loved and admired him, but I still couldn't quite believe he was mine. I couldn't fathom that I had been so lucky. Sometimes I worried he might be a dream and if I let myself lose focus, he might fade away. But he was still sitting beside me, solid and secure. He answered Ben when it became apparent that I had zoned out.

"Relax, Carter, it's a party," he said, laughing.

"Where's your costume?" I asked, forcing myself back to reality.

"I don't do dress-ups," Ben said cynically. Ben was the sort of guy who thought everything was puerile and beneath him. He managed to maintain his contemptuously superior persona by engaging in nothing. At the same time he always turned up just in case he might miss out on something. "My God, they're sickening." He wrinkled his face in disgust at the lacy underwear lying on the porch. "I hope I never fall for someone so hard that I agree to have sex in a tractor."

"I don't know about the tractor," I teased. "But I'm betting one day you'll fall in love and there won't be a thing you can do about it."

"Not a chance." Ben stretched out with his arms crossed over his head and shut his eyes. "I'm too bitter and jaded."

"I could try and set you up with one of my friends," I offered. I quite liked the idea of matchmaking and was fairly confident in my skills. "What about Abby? She's single and pretty and wouldn't be too demanding."

"Dear God, please don't," Ben said. "That would have to be the worst match in history."

"I beg your pardon?" Ben's lack of confidence in my abilities was disappointing.

"Beg all you want." Ben snorted. "My decision is final. I won't be set up with a cooler-drinking, stiletto-wearing bimbo. We'd have nothing to say to each other except *bye*."

"It's good to know you have such a high opinion of my friends," I said crossly. "Is that what you think of me?"

"No, but you're different."

"How so?"

"You're weird."

"I am not!" I exclaimed. "What's so weird about me? Xavier, do you think I'm weird?"

"Calm down, babe," Xavier said, eyes twinkling with amusement. "I'm sure Carter means *weird* in the most flattering sense."

"Well, you're weird too," I hit back at Ben, realizing at the same time how petulant I sounded.

He chuckled and downed the rest of his beer. "Takes one to know one."

The sound of raucous voices coming from inside drew our attention. The screen door was thrown open and a group of boys from the water-polo team appeared on the porch. It was amazing, I thought to myself, how much they reminded me of young lion cubs, jostling and tumbling over one another. Xavier shook his head in gentle admonishment as they stumbled toward us. I recognized the faces of Wesley and Lawson among them. They were easy to pick out; Wesley with his slick, dark hair and low-set brows and Lawson with his white-blond crew cut and hooded blue eyes. They were a dull blue, I noticed, they didn't sparkle like Xavier's. Both boys were shirtless and striped with war paint. They acknowledged my presence with a curt nod in my direction and I thought fleetingly back to a time when men would click their heels and bow in the presence of a lady. I returned their acknowledgment with a smile. I couldn't bring myself to do what my friends called the "s'up nod"—it made me feel as if I were in one of those music videos Molly watched on MTV where men in hoods rapped about "homies" and something called "bling."

"Come on, Woods," the boys called. "We're headed to the lake."

Xavier groaned. "Here we go."

"You know the rules," Wesley called out. "Last one there has to skinny-dip."

"My God, they really have discovered the pinnacle of intellectual stimulation," muttered Ben.

Xavier got up reluctantly and I stared at him in surprise.

"You're not going, are you?" I said.

"The race is a Bryce tradition." He laughed. "We do it every year wherever we are. But don't worry, I never come in last."

"Don't be so sure," Lawson crowed as he leapt off the porch and pelted toward the woods at the rear of the property. "Head start advantage!" The rest of the boys followed suit, shoving one another unceremoniously as they ran. They went crashing through the overgrown shrubs and headed for the open fields like a stampede.

Once they'd disappeared, I left Ben to his philosophical brooding and went inside to find Molly. She and the girls had moved and were now huddled secretively in a little cluster by the foot of the stairs. Abigail had a supersize paper bag tucked under her arm and they all looked very serious.

"Beth!" Molly clutched my arm when I joined them. "I'm glad you're here; we're about to get started."

"Get started with what?" I asked with curiosity.

"The séance, of course."

I groaned inwardly. So they hadn't forgotten about it. I'd hoped the plan would be abandoned once the girls started having fun.

"You guys can't be serious?" I said, but they were looking at me with complete sincerity. I tried a different technique. "Hey, Abby, Hank Hunt is out back. He looked like he could really use some company."

Abigail had been crazy about Hank Hunt since junior high and hadn't stopped going on about him all term. But tonight, not even he could distract her from the plan at hand.

"Who cares about him," Abigail scoffed. "This is heaps more important—let's go find an empty room."

"No," I said firmly, shaking my head. "C'mon, guys, can't we find something else to do?"

"But it's Halloween," Hallie said, pouting like a child. "We want to talk to ghosts."

"The dead should stay that way," I snapped. "Can't you go and bob for apples or something?"

"Don't be such a party pooper," Savannah said. She got up and began to drag me up the stairs after her. The others followed eagerly. "What could go wrong?"

"Is that a rhetorical question?" I said, pulling away. "What *couldn't* go wrong?"

"You don't actually believe in ghosts, do you, Bethie?" Madison asked. "We're only trying to have some fun."

"I just don't think we should play around with this stuff." I sighed.

"Fine, don't come," Hallie snapped. "Stay down here by yourself and wait for Xavier like you always do. We knew you'd bail anyway. We'll have fun without you." She shot me a betrayed look and the others nodded in support of her. I wasn't having any luck impressing upon them the danger associated with their plan. How could you tell children they were playing with fire if they'd never had the experience of being burned? I wished Gabriel were here. He radiated authority and he'd know exactly what to say to change their minds. He had that effect on people. Here I was sounding like nothing more than a wet blanket. Some ministering angel I was turning out to be. I knew it wasn't within my powers to stop them, but I couldn't let them go without me. If anything happened, at least I could be there to deal with whatever they encountered on the other side. They were already climbing the stairs, clutching one another's arms as they whispered in excitement.

"Guys," I called out. "Wait up . . . I'm coming."

Crossing the Line

UPSTAIRS the house smelled musty and stale. On the landing the striped ivory wallpaper was peeling away in sheets from the rising damp. Although we could hear the party raging on below us, it was preternaturally still on the second floor as if in anticipation of some paranormal experience. The girls lapped it up.

"This is the perfect setting," said Hallie.

"I'll bet this place is already haunted," added Savannah, her face flushed with enthusiasm.

Suddenly my concerns seemed disproportionate to the situation. Was it possible that I was overreacting? Why was I always assuming the worst and letting my conservative nature bring down the mood of everyone around me? I scolded myself mentally for always jumping to dire conclusions—what were the chances of these fun-loving girls actually making a connection with the other side? It had been known to happen, but it usually required the guidance of a trained medium. Lost spirits generally didn't appreciate being called on as a source of teenage entertainment. Anyway, the girls would probably get bored when they failed to get the results they anticipated.

I followed Molly and the others into what had once been the guest bedroom. Its tall windows were opaque from a fine layer of accumulated dust and grime. The room itself was empty except for an iron bedstead pushed up against a grimy window. It had a rickety iron frame that had once been white but had tarnished to a buttery color over time. There was an equally faded quilt scattered with pink rosebuds. I guessed the Knox family didn't even visit the old country house much anymore, let alone invite guests down for the summer. The window frames looked weathered by the sun and there were no curtains to block out the moonlight. I noticed the room faced west and overlooked the woods at the rear of the property. I could see the scarecrow standing guard in the field, its straw hat flapping in the breeze.

Without needing any prompting the girls arranged themselves cross-legged in a circle on the threadbare rug on the floor. Abby reached into her paper bag carefully as if she were withdrawing a priceless artifact. The Ouija board she unpacked from its green felt cover was so well-worn it might have passed for an antique.

"Where did you get that?"

"My grammy gave it to me," Abby said. "I went to visit her in Montgomery last month."

She placed the board with exaggerated ceremony in the center of our circle. I hadn't seen one before other than in books, but this one looked more decorative than I'd expected. Around its perimeters, the alphabet was scrawled in two straight lines along with numbers and other symbols I didn't recognize. In opposite corners and surrounded by curlicues were the capitalized words YES and NO. Even someone who'd never seen a Ouija board before couldn't miss its association with the dark arts. Next Abby withdrew a fragile, long-stemmed sherry glass wrapped in tissue paper. She tossed the paper aside impatiently and placed the upturned glass on the board.

"How does this thing work?" Madison wanted to know. Aside from me, she was the only other participant not brimming with anticipation. I suspected it was more due to the lack of alcohol and boys in the room than any concern about our safety.

"You need a conductor like a piece of wood or an upturned glass to communicate with the spirit world," Abby explained, enjoying her role as resident expert. "Strong psychic powers run in our family, so I actually know what I'm talking about. We need everyone's combined energy for it to work. We all need to concentrate and each put our index finger on the base of the glass. Don't press too hard, or the energy gets clogged and it won't work. Once we make contact with the spirit, it'll spell out what it wants to say to us. Okay, let's get started. Everyone put your fingertips on the glass. *Gently*." I had to hand it to Abby. She was pretty convincing considering I was quite sure she was making everything up on the spot. The girls complied eagerly with her instructions.

"What now?" said Madison.

"We wait for it to move."

"Seriously?" Madison rolled her eyes. "That's it? What stops everyone from just spelling out whatever they want?"

Abby glared at her. "It's not hard to tell the difference

between a joke and a real spirit message, Mad. Besides, the spirit will know things, things no one else could." She tossed her hair. "I wouldn't expect you to understand. I only know because I've had a lot of practice. Now, are we ready to start?" she asked in a solemn voice.

I dug my fingernails into the rough carpet beneath me, wishing there were some way to slip out of the room unnoticed. When Molly struck a match to light the candles someone had arranged on the floor, I jumped. She brought the flame to the wicks and the candles sizzled to life.

"Try not to make any sudden movements during the séance," Abby said, glaring pointedly at me. "We don't want to alarm the spirit. It has to feel comfortable with us. "

"You know from experience or from what you've seen on the John Edward show?" Madison asked sarcastically, unable to help herself.

"The women in my family have always been very connected to the *other side*," Abby said. I didn't like the way she emphasized the words *other side*, as if she were telling a ghost story at school camp.

"Have you ever seen a ghost?" Hallie asked in a hushed voice.

"I have," Abby declared, deadly serious. "Which is why I should act as medium tonight."

I didn't know whether Abby was telling the truth or not. People sometimes caught flashes of the dead as they crossed between worlds. But most of the time ghost sightings were the result of a rampant imagination. A flash of a shadow or a trick of the light could easily be mistaken for something supernatural.

It was different for me—I could sense the presence of spirits all the time—they were everywhere. If I focused, I could tell who was lost, who had just passed on, and who was searching for their loved ones. Gabriel had told me to tune them out—they weren't our responsibility. I remembered when my elderly friend Alice had come to say good-bye after she'd passed on the year before. I'd seen her outside my bedroom window before she faded away. But not all spirits were as gentle as Alice; the ones that were unable to let go of their earthly attachment lingered for years, becoming more and more twisted, driven mad by the life around them that they could never be part of again. They lost touch with humans, came to resent them, and often acted out in violent ways. I wondered how keen Abby would be if she knew the truth about what was really out there. But there was no way of telling her, not without giving myself away completely.

The girls nodded in agreement, happy to relinquish rights to the role of medium. I felt Molly shiver beside me. "Now join hands," Abby said. "And whatever you do, don't let go. We need to form a protective circle—if you break the circle you set the spirit free."

"Who told you that?" Savannah whispered. "Doesn't breaking hands just end the séance?"

"Yes, and if it's a harmless spirit then breaking hands will send it back to rest, but if it's vengeful then we have to be careful. We don't know what we're summoning."

"Well, how about we just summon a nice friendly ghost," Madison said, prompting Abby to give her a contemptuous stare.

"What, like Casper?"

Madison didn't appreciate being mocked, but we all knew Abby was right. "I guess not," she conceded.

"Then it's luck of the draw."

I bit my tongue to refrain from commenting on Abby's fool-proof plan. Conducting a séance on the one night of the year when it was actually likely to work was stupid in the extreme. I shook my head and tried to banish my doubts. I reminded myself this was nothing more than a childish game; something most teenagers dabbled in for fun. The sooner we got it over with, the sooner we could go downstairs and enjoy the rest of the night.

Molly and Savannah, who were sitting on either side of me, each took hold of one of my hands and gripped them tightly. Their palms were clammy and I sensed a combination of fear and excitement. Abby bowed her head and closed her eyes. Her blond hair flopped inconveniently in front of her face and she interrupted her invocation to tether it into a loose ponytail with the Day-Glo hair tie she wore around her wrist. Then she cleared her throat theatrically, cast us all a meaningful look, and began to speak in a low voice that sounded like a chant.

"Spirits that walk the earth, we invoke you to come forward and dwell among us! We mean you no harm; we only want to make a connection. Do not be afraid. If you have a story to tell, we want to hear it. I repeat, we will not harm you; in return we ask that you do not harm us."

The room swelled with a deadly silence. The girls exchanged uneasy glances. I knew that some were now regretting expressing so much enthusiasm for Abby's project and wished they were downstairs drinking with their friends and flirting with the boys. I gritted my teeth and turned my thoughts away from the distasteful ceremony that was taking place before me. I had enough sense to know that disturbing the dead was not only unwise, but insensitive too. It went against everything I'd been taught about life and death. Hadn't they ever heard of the expression *rest in peace*? I wanted to pull my hands away and leave the room, but I knew Abby would be furious and I'd be wearing the label of *buzzkill* for the rest of the year. I sighed heavily, hoping they would soon get bored when no response was forthcoming and abandon the game. Molly and I exchanged dubious glances.

Five long minutes elapsed with only the sound of our breathing and Abby periodically repeating her incantation. Just as the girls were beginning to get restless and someone complained openly about a leg cramp, the crystal glass began to wobble. Everyone sat bolt upright, each girl's attention fully restored. The glass shook for a moment longer and then began to teeter its way across the board, spelling out a message as it went. Abby, as self-appointed medium, called out each letter the glass touched until it had spelled out a clear message.

Stop. Stop now. Leave this place. You are all in danger.

"Oooh, that sounds exciting," Madison said mockingly. The others looked at one another uncertainly, trying to determine the person in the group who was behind the prank.

With everyone's fingers on the glass, it was impossible to tell who was moving it. I felt Molly clutch my hand tighter as another message began to be spelled out.

Stop. Listen. Evil is here.

"Why should we believe you?" Abby asked boldly. "Do we know you?"

The glass now seemed to move in giant swoops, entirely of its own volition. It swam across the board and came to rest defiantly on the word *YES*.

"Okay, now I know this is a joke," said Madison. "Come on, own up. Who's doing it?" Abby ignored her protest.

"Shut up, Mad. No one's doing it," Hallie snapped. "You're breaking the mood."

"You can't honestly expect me to believe . . ."

"If we know you, tell us your name," Abby insisted.

For several long seconds the glass seemed to stall.

"Told you this is all a load of crap," Madison began, but no sooner had she spoken that the glass resumed its dance around the board. At first it seemed confused, lingering under some letters and then steering away suddenly as if to tease us. It seemed uncertain to me, like a young child, not entirely familiar with the process. It careered across the board spelling out *T-A-Y*. Then it stopped as if it were unsure what to do.

"You can trust us," Abby urged.

The glass slunk back to the middle of the board and slowly looped across to spell out the final three letters, *L-A-H*.

It was Molly who broke the uncomfortable silence. "Taylah?"

she whispered in a voice that came out sounding strangled. Then she furiously blinked back tears and glared around the circle.

"Okay, this isn't funny," she hissed. "Who did it? What the hell is wrong with you guys?"

Her accusation was met by a flurry of head shaking and protests. "It wasn't me," they each said. "I didn't do it."

I felt a chill run down my spine. Deep down I knew none of the girls would stoop so low as to bring their dead friend into the game. Taylah's death was still fresh, no one would dare joke about it. And that meant only one thing—Abby had made a connection, broken the barrier. We were treading on dangerous ground.

"What if it's not a joke?" Savannah suggested tentatively. "No one here would be that sick. What if it really is her?"

"There's only one way to find out," Abby said. "We have to summon her and ask for a sign."

"But she just told us to stop," Molly protested. "What if she doesn't want to be summoned?"

"Yeah, what if she was trying to warn us?" Hallie shivered.

"You're all so gullible." Madison rolled her eyes. "Go ahead and summon her, Abby, nothing's going to happen."

Abby leaned forward, bending low over the Ouija board. "We command you," she said, her voice deepening. "Come forward and show yourself."

Through the window, I saw a dark cloud drift across the sky, obscuring the moon and completely blotting out the silver light that had been filling the room. For a moment I felt Taylah's presence, radiating warmth as strong as the heat in the hand I held. But just as suddenly she vanished, leaving nothing but a cold space in the air.

"We command you," Abby repeated with heightened emotion. "Come forward!"

The windowpanes rattled as the wind started to howl outside. The room suddenly felt very cold, and Molly wound her fingers so tightly around mine she was almost cutting off my circulation.

"Come forward!" Abby commanded. "Show yourself!"

At that moment the window flew open and a harsh wind rushed into the room, snuffing out the candles in an instant. Some of the girls squealed and gripped each other's hands more tightly. I felt the wind on the back of my neck, like cold, dead fingers. I shuddered and hunched forward, trying to protect myself from it. Savannah whimpered and I knew she felt it too. These girls might be oblivious to most things, but anyone could sense that there was now a presence in the room and it was none too friendly.

I knew then I had to say something before it was too late.

"We have to stop this," I cried. "It isn't a game anymore."

"You can't leave now, Beth. You'll ruin everything." Abby's eyes darted around the room. "Is someone here?" she asked. "Give us a sign that you can hear me."

I heard Hallie gasp and looked down to see the glass drifting silently across the Ouija board. It came to rest on the word *YES*. Savannah's hand in mine was now slippery with sweat.

"Who's doing that?" Molly whispered.

"Why have you come?" Abby asked. "Do you have a message for someone here?"

The glass spun in a circle across the board and responded with the same message. YES.

"Who is it for?" Abby asked. "Tell us who you've come to see."

The glass slid down until it found the letter A. Then it loped gracefully from letter to letter as it began to spell out a name. Abby looked confused as she put the name together in her head.

"Annabel Lee?" she said puzzled. "There's nobody here by that name."

I felt a claw of ice fasten around my heart. That name might not mean anything to them, but it meant a lot to me. I could still remember him standing before the class and reading the poem in a voice like velvet: *"It was many and many a year ago / In a kingdom by the sea, / That a maiden there lived whom you may know / By the name of Annabel Lee."* I remembered the way his dark eyes had seared into mine and I'd felt then a terrible, burning uneasiness deep within me. That same feeling flooded back to me now, and I felt my throat go dry and my chest begin to seize up. Could it really be him? Had an innocent prank really summoned something so monstrous? I didn't want to believe it, but looking at the bewildered expressions around me, I knew there was no mistake. That message was intended for me and me alone. Jake Thorn was back and right here in the room with us.

My gut reaction was to instinctively tear myself away, but I fought against it. Protecting the others was the only thing that stopped me. I prayed we still had time to end the séance properly and return the evil we'd conjured back to where it came from.

"Tell us what you want," Abby said, swallowing hard, her voice several octaves higher than before.

What was she doing? Couldn't she see how out of our depth we were? I was about to take charge and demand that Abby stop when the doorknob began to rattle vigorously. It shook and twisted from side to side as if some invisible force were trying to get out. By all logical reasoning it was impossible— the door was unlocked. Such an unnatural occurrence proved too much for some of the girls to handle.

"Try to stay calm," I counseled in as level a voice as I could muster, but it was too late. Molly pulled her hands free and scrambled backward on all fours. In the process she kicked the board with her foot and sent it skidding across the floor- boards. The sherry glass flew into the air and landed beside me, splintering into tiny shards. At that moment I felt a rush of frosty air hit me in the chest, almost knocking the wind out of me. The bedroom door flew open, rattling on its hinges.

"Molly!" Hallie screeched as soon as she'd recovered from the shock. "What have you done?"

"I don't want to play anymore," Molly cried in a choked voice. She wrapped her arms around her torso, as if she could hug the warmth back into her body. "Beth was right, this was a stupid idea, and we should never have done it."

I got up and fumbled for the light switch, my stomach

twisting into a knot when I remembered the power at the house had been disconnected.

"It's okay, Molly." I put an arm around her shoulders and hugged her, trying not to let her see the panic that was welling inside me. Somebody needed to stay calm. I could feel Molly's body shaking uncontrollably. I wanted to tell her it was nothing but a stupid game and we could all have a good laugh about it later. But deep down, I knew this was no harmless prank. I rubbed Molly's arm and said the most comforting thing I could think of.

"Let's just go downstairs and pretend it never happened."

"I don't think it's that easy." Abby's voice was soft and ominous. She was still kneeling on the floor, picking up shards of broken glass, her eyes fixed on the mess before her.

"Stop it, Abby," I said angrily. "Can't you see she's scared?"

"No, Beth, you don't get it." Abby looked up at me and I saw all her condescension had fallen away. Her blue eyes were just as wide and alarmed as Molly's. "She broke the circle."

"So what?" I demanded.

"Whatever we summoned was trapped within the circle," Abby whispered. "We could have sent it back. But now . . ." Her voice was tremulous as she looked around the room uneasily. "Molly just set it free."

Highway to Hell

I stood on the landing watching my hysterical friends stumble down the stairs two at a time. It wouldn't be long before word spread that there'd been an actual ghost sighting on the night of Halloween. While no one had actually seen anything, I was sure the story would be embellished many times before the night was over.

A sudden wave of dizziness caused me to reach for the banister to steady myself. So far what had been planned as a night of fun had turned out to be anything but. I'd had enough of this party. It was time to leave. Now all I had to do was find Xavier and ask him to take me home. When the dizziness passed, I found my way into the kitchen where I was grateful to be greeted by a much more innocent Halloween activity. A group was taking turns bobbing for apples in a tin tub they'd dragged in from the barn and placed in the center of the room. A girl was on her knees practicing taking deep breaths before submerging her face in the water. The onlookers cheered her on. When she finally rocked back on her heels, her dark hair clung to her exposed neck and shoulders and a rosy apple was clenched triumphantly between her teeth.

When someone propelled me forward, I realized I had unwittingly joined the line to play.

"Your turn!" I felt a swarm of warm bodies around me.

I resisted by digging my heels into the floor. "I don't want a turn. I was just watching."

"Come on!" the voices urged. "Give it a shot."

I decided it might be easier to pick up an apple than try to fight their enthusiasm. Despite the voice in my head telling me to run, to leave this place, I found myself on my knees staring at my own reflection distorted by the movement of the water. I squeezed my eyes shut and forced the warnings out of my head. When I opened them, I saw something in the water that made my heart stop. Hovering just behind my reflection was a wobbly image of a wasted face, its skeletal features concealed behind a heavy hood. It clutched something in its crooked, clawlike hand. Was it a sickle? Its free hand reached out toward me and its abnormally elongated fingers seemed to curl themselves like tendrils around my neck. I knew it was impossible, but the figure was startlingly familiar. I'd seen its iconic black robes in books and paintings and I knew it from my teachings back home. It was a representation of death . . . a Grim Reaper. But what did it want from me? I couldn't be touched by death so it must be here for a different reason. It was an omen. But of what? I panicked and pushed my way roughly out of the circle and ran for the back door.

Outside I could still hear the muffled cries of protest at my alleged lack of participation. I ignored them and put a hand on my chest as if willing my heartbeat to steady. The cool air helped a little, but I couldn't shake the feeling that the phantom reaper had followed me and was lurking nearby, waiting for a chance to catch me alone and encircle my throat with its wafer-thin hands.

"Beth, what are you doing out here? Are you all right?"

I heard a strange sound and realized it was coming from me. I was taking long, gasping breaths. The voice was familiar but it didn't belong to Xavier as I'd hoped. Ben Carter got off the porch and came and stood beside me, shaking me gently as if I needed to be woken from a trance. The human contact made me feel marginally better.

"Beth, what happened? You sounded like you were choking. . . ." Ben's uncombed hair hung over his brown eyes, which now looked at me with trepidation. I tried to catch my breath but failed and began to fall forward instead. If Ben hadn't been there to catch me, I would have toppled facedown onto the ground. Ben seemed to be of the opinion that I had caused my own state of suffocation.

"What the hell are you doing?" he demanded, once he'd established that I wasn't dying. He peered at me closely. Beneath his apprehension I saw a new idea dawn. "Have you been drinking?"

I was about to vehemently deny such an allegation before realizing that it was probably the most plausible explanation I could offer for my erratic behavior.

"Maybe," I said, twisting out of his grasp and struggling to my feet. I backed away from Ben, fighting the urge to burst into tears. "Thanks for your help," I said rapidly. "I'm fine. Really."

As I walked away from him, one question kept sounding in my head, loud and clear. Where was Xavier? Something was wrong. I could feel it. Every celestial instinct warned me that we needed to get out of here. *Fast.*

I found a weeping willow in the front yard and leaned against its sturdy trunk. I could see Ben still standing by the front porch looking at me with an expression of concern mingled with confusion. But I couldn't worry about having offended Ben now. I had more important things to think about. Could it seriously be happening again? Could demons have returned to Venus Cove? I knew for a fact that there was no more evil in this place. Gabriel and Ivy had seen to that. Jake had been banished—I'd seen raging tongues of fire consume him. He couldn't be back. But why was every hair on my body standing on end? Why were chills coursing through my veins like tiny lightning bolts?

I felt as if I were being hunted. From where I stood alone on the gravel drive, I had an uninterrupted view of the back fields and the thick woodland beyond. I could see the scarecrow in the paddock, his head drooping onto his chest. I hoped Xavier was on his way back from the lake. I knew as soon as I saw him my fear would ebb away like a receding tide. Together we were strong and could protect each other. I needed to find him.

Just then, a gust of wind set the dry grass rustling. The scarecrow's clothing began to flap and its head snapped up, staring directly at me with its black button eyes. My heart somersaulted in my chest and I let out a piercing scream. I spun on my heels and started back toward the house.

I didn't get far before colliding with someone.

"Whoa, take it easy," said a boy, hopping lightly to one side. "What's up? You look kind of freaked out."

His speech was far too slurred for a demon's, and when I glanced up, I saw he didn't look like one either. He wasn't wearing a costume and I recognized him vaguely from somewhere. My panic subsided a little when I realized it was Ryan Robertson, Molly's former prom date. He was standing with a huddle of people who had gathered outside the front porch. A half-consumed cigarette dangled from his hand. The group regarded me with sluggish disinterest. There was a sharp, bitter scent in the air that I couldn't identify, but was strangely pungent.

I lifted a hand to my cheek, felt it burning hot, and was grateful for the cool night air against my skin. "I'm okay," I said, trying to sound convincing. The last thing I wanted to do was raise unnecessary alarm based on my own misgivings.

"That's good." Ryan closed his eyes dreamily. "I wouldn't want you to be not okay, if you see what I mean." I frowned; he wasn't sounding entirely coherent. Was it me, I wondered? Was I going completely crazy or was this bizarre party to blame?

I jumped when the screen door slammed. Molly appeared on the porch.

"Beth, there you are!" She seemed relieved to see me and leapt down the steps. "Way to freak me out! I didn't know where you'd gone." Her gaze swept disdainfully over Ryan and his cohort. "What are you doing with *them?*"

"Ryan was just helping me," I mumbled.

"I'm a helpful person," Ryan declared indignantly.

Molly caught sight of the hand-rolled cigarette in his hand. "Are you high?" she demanded as she thumped his shoulder.

"Not high," Ryan clarified. "I believe the term is *greened out*."

"You loser!" Molly erupted. "You're supposed to be driving me home. No way am I spending the night in this creepy dump."

"Quit your whining, I drive better high," Ryan said. "Sharpens my senses. By the way, I think I need a bucket. . . ."

"If you're gonna puke, don't do it near me," Molly snapped.

"I think we should call it a night," I said to her. "Will you help me find Xavier?" My suggestion was met with a swell of protest from Ryan and his friends.

"Sure," said Molly, rolling her eyes at them. "I doubt tonight could get any weirder."

We had just headed back toward the house in search of Xavier when the sound of a motorcycle tearing through the grass caused us to turn around. There was something urgent about the way it screamed to a halt in front of us, spraying gravel through the air. Molly shielded her eyes against the glow of the headlights. The rider slid off in one easy movement but left the engine running. He was dressed casually in a worn aviator-style leather jacket and backward baseball cap. I recognized the tall, well-built boy immediately as Wesley Cowan. Xavier and I passed his house every Friday afternoon on our way home from school. Wes would inevitably be crouched in his driveway polishing his dad's old Merc in preparation for a weekend of partying. Wes played on Xavier's polo team and I knew he numbered among his closest friends. Like Xavier,

Wes was one of the hardest boys to rattle. There was very little that succeeded in shaking his air of confidence. It was surprising to see him now with his shirt muddy and his face creased with worry.

Instinctively Molly reached out to grab his arm.

"Wes, what's wrong?"

His chest heaved as he struggled to get the words out. "There's been an accident at the lake," he gasped. "Someone call 911!"

Ryan and his friends sobered in an instant, collectively withdrawing cell phones from their pockets.

"No reception," Ryan announced after a few minutes of trying. He shook his cell in frustration and cursed under his breath. "We must be out of range."

"What happened?" Molly asked.

Before he spoke, Wesley threw me a strange look; it was almost imploring, like he was seeking my forgiveness.

"We dared him to dive-bomb from a tree but there were rocks in the water. He hit his head. He won't wake up."

As he spoke, his gaze never left my face. Why was he singling me out like this? I'd remained silent, but now a cold panic seized me, wrapping around me like icy fingers. It wasn't Xavier. It couldn't be Xavier. Xavier was the responsible one who had gone down there to keep an eye on the others. Xavier was probably down there right now, using his first-aid training until help arrived. But I knew my heart wasn't going to stop pounding until I knew for certain. Someone else asked the question I couldn't bring myself to utter.

"Who's hurt?"

Wesley's eyes looked guilt ridden and he hesitated a fraction too long, so I knew the answer before he spoke the name out loud.

"Woods." It came out as a bland statement of fact, devoid of emotion, which didn't strike me as odd until later when I replayed the scene in my head. But in that moment, all I could feel were my legs giving way beneath me. My worst fear—much greater than anything happening to me—was that any harm should come to Xavier, and now it had just come true. For a second it was too much to take in and I sagged helplessly against Ryan, who tried to hold me up, despite his own lack of balance. So this was what Xavier and I got as reward for spending time apart. I couldn't believe fate could be so cruel. The one night our paths diverged he ended up unconscious. Wes put his head in his hands and groaned.

"Man, we are so screwed."

"Was he drunk?" Ryan asked.

"Course he was," Wes snapped. "We all were."

In all the time we'd been together I'd never known Xavier to have more than a couple of beers. I'd never seen him touch hard liquor; he thought it was irresponsible. I couldn't reconcile the image of him drunk and reckless in my head. It didn't add up.

"No," I said numbly. "Xavier doesn't drink."

"Yeah? Well, there's a first time for everything."

"Shut up and call an ambulance!" Molly screeched. Then I felt her arm around my shoulder and her auburn curls brushed my cheek as she leaned her head against mine. "It's okay, Bethie, he'll be okay," she said.

Wesley watched us. His panic seemed to have transformed into a perverse delight in my distress. Others had gathered now and everyone had an opinion to voice on the best course of action. Their voices combined to create a meaningless babble.

"How bad is it? Should we try getting him to a doctor?"

"We're all screwed if we call 911."

"Oh, great idea," someone retorted sarcastically. "Let's just wait and see if he comes to by himself."

"How bad is it, Wes?"

"I'm not too sure." Wesley looked defeated. "He cut his head. There was a fair bit of blood. . . ."

"Crap. We gotta get help."

The image of Xavier lying on the ground bleeding spurred me to action.

"I have to find him!" I was already stumbling toward Wesley. "Someone show me the way to the lake!" Molly was suddenly by my side, her hands gripping my shoulders both restraining and comforting.

"Calm down, Beth" she said. "Can somebody drive her?"

"Don't be stupid, Molly, the lake's in the woods," Ben said. "You can't get there by car. Someone drive into town and call a friggin' ambulance."

I couldn't waste another second listening to their facile deliberations when Xavier was hurt and my healing powers could help him.

"I'm going," I announced, breaking into a run.

"Wait! I can take you." Wes had suddenly reverted back to his former concern. "It's faster than runnin' in the dark," he added weakly, as if he knew that taking me to Xavier would in no way exonerate his involvement in the accident.

"No," Molly said protectively. "You should stay here while we try and get a doctor."

"What about calling his dad?" someone suggested. "He's a surgeon, isn't he?"

"Good idea. Find his number."

"Mr. Woods is a cool guy, he won't report us."

"Yeah and how are you gonna contact him without reception?" Ben sounded exasperated. "Telepathy?"

I was struggling to keep my wings from bursting free and carrying me to Xavier. It was my body's natural reaction, and I didn't know if I could contain them much longer. I looked impatiently at Wesley.

"What are we waiting for?"

By way of reply he mounted the bike and offered me his arm so I could use it to wedge myself in behind him. The shiny motorcycle glinted like some alien insect in the moonlight.

"Hey! What about a helmet?" Ben asked churlishly as Wes kicked the bike into gear. He resented the school jocks and their daredevil antics. I could see in his face that he was also concerned about my safety given Wesley's questionable level of responsibility. I understood that Ben was only being protective, but right then I had only one objective in mind and that was to get to Xavier.

"No time." Wes was curt. He reached back to grab both my arms and positioned them securely around his waist.

"Hold on tight," he instructed. "And whatever you do, don't let go."

The bike spun around before careening down the driveway and out toward the black ribbon of highway.

"Isn't the lake the other way?" I shouted over the roar of the engine.

"Shortcut," Wes bellowed in reply.

I tried reaching out to Xavier to sense the extent of his injuries. But I drew a blank. It surprised me; I could usually sense his moods even before he did. Gabriel had told me I would know immediately if he were ever in trouble. But this time I'd missed it. Was it because I'd been too busy stressing out over a ridiculous séance?

Wes had just turned onto the highway and begun to pick up speed when I heard a voice calling my name from behind. Even over the din of the engine I knew it was a voice I loved more than any other and I'd been waiting to hear it all night. It revived me. Wes swerved the bike around, and I saw Xavier standing, washed in moonlight, on the side of the road. My heart lightened immediately. He looked perfectly healthy.

"Beth?" he repeated my name in a cautious tone. He was standing just meters away from us and I was so excited to see him in one piece that it didn't even occur to me that anything might be amiss. I didn't stop to wonder why Xavier looked so surprised to see us.

"Where are you guys going?" he asked. "And, Wes, where the hell did you get that bike?"

"Xavier!" I cried out in relief. "Thank God, you woke up! How's your head? Everyone's so worried. We need to get back and tell them you're okay."

"My head?" he asked, the consternation on his face deepening. "What are you talking about?"

"I'm talking about the accident! Maybe you have a concussion. Wes, let me off this thing."

"Beth, I'm fine." Xavier scratched his head. "Nothing happened to me."

"But I thought—," I began and then stopped short. Not only did Xavier look fine but there wasn't a mark on him and no evidence of an injury. He looked exactly the way he did when I'd left him, in jeans and a fitted black T-shirt. I saw Xavier's posture shift subtly into a more defensive stance. His ocean blue eyes darkened as understanding dawned.

"Beth," he said slowly. "I want you to get off that bike."

"Wes?" I tapped him lightly on the shoulder, suddenly aware that he hadn't spoken a single word for the entire duration of my conversation with Xavier. The bike was still vibrating beneath me and yet the person in front of me remained motionless, his gaze fixed ahead.

Xavier strained to take a step forward, but something prevented him and he remained rooted to the spot. He tried to keep his voice level, but I couldn't miss the undercurrent of urgency.

"Beth, did you hear me? Get off *now!*"

I planted both feet on the ground in order to appease Xavier, but when I tried to shift my arms from around Wesley's waist, he suddenly revved the engine and the bike shot backward. I had to clutch him even tighter to avoid falling off.

Until that moment I still thought the whole thing was an

elaborate hoax on Wesley's part that Xavier failed to find amusing. Then I saw Xavier run a hand helplessly through his hair and watched his forehead crease in anguish. I saw a look in his eyes I hadn't seen since that fateful afternoon in the cemetery when he'd been incapacitated and I'd been captured before his very eyes. He wore that same look now—the one that told me he was desperately searching for an escape, even though he knew we were cornered. It was as if he were facing off against a poisonous snake that might strike at any moment and the slightest wrong move could be fatal. Wes spun the bike in random circles, enjoying the anxiety he was causing. Xavier yelled out and tried to run forward but an unseen force held him back. He gritted his teeth and hurled himself against the invisible barrier blocking his way, but it was no use. The bike careered tauntingly in all directions.

"What's going on?" I cried as the bike finally stopped and settled into the dust. "Xav, what's happening?"

We were closer to Xavier now and in his eyes I could see deep pain, but also anger and intense frustration at his inability to help me. Now I knew I was in real danger. Maybe we both were.

"Beth . . . that's not Wes." The words chilled me to the core and filled me with defeat. I tried letting go of Wesley. I was ready to throw myself off the bike, but I couldn't move my arms. They seemed to be pinned by an invisible force.

"Stop! Let me off!" I pleaded.

"Too late," Wesley replied, only it wasn't Wes anymore. His voice was now slick and smooth, a polished English accent clearly detectable. That voice had haunted my dreams for so long, I would have recognized it anywhere. The body I had my arms wrapped around began to shift beneath my fingers. The broad, muscled chest and well-defined arms shrank to become leaner and colder to the touch. Wesley's broad hands became slender and turned bone white. The backward baseball cap flew off to reveal lustrous black locks that danced in the wind. For the first time he twisted his face around to confront me. The sight of him so close made me sick to my stomach. Jake's face hadn't changed a bit. Black shoulder-length hair contrasted sharply with the pallor of his face. I recognized the narrow nose that drooped slightly at the tip and the cheekbones carved out of rock that had made Molly once compare him to a Calvin Klein model. His pale lips parted to reveal small and dazzlingly white teeth. Only the eyes were different. They seemed to pulse with a dark energy, and as I looked into them I saw that they were neither green nor black as I remembered but a dull shade of burgundy. Just like the color of dried blood.

"NO!" Xavier shouted, his face contorted with despair. His voice was swallowed by the wind on the empty highway. "GET AWAY FROM HER!"

What happened next was a blur. I knew Xavier was somehow released from his immobility because I saw him sprint full speed toward me. My arms too became free and I tried to wrestle myself off the bike but felt a searing pain in my head and realized that Jake was now holding a fistful of my hair. He was maneuvering the bike singlehanded. I ignored the scalding sensation and struggled harder, but my efforts were useless.

"Gotcha," he purred. It was the sound of a contented predator.

Jake twisted the throttle hard and I heard the engine roar to life like an angry beast. The motorcycle bucked and lurched unsteadily forward. "Xavier!" I cried just as he reached us. We simultaneously outstretched our hands and our fingers nearly met. But Jake violently veered the bike so that it slammed into Xavier's side. I heard a heavy thud as the metal slammed into his body. I screamed as Xavier was thrown backward and rolled limply onto the side of the road. Then I couldn't see him anymore. The bike sped past, leaving him lying in a cloud of dust. Out of the corner of my eye I could see people starting to make their way up to the road, attracted by the commotion. I only prayed they'd find Xavier in time to help him.

The bike hurtled up the deserted highway that uncoiled before us like a black whip. Jake was driving at such breakneck speed that when we rounded a bend we found ourselves almost parallel with the ground. Every fiber in my body yearned to return to Xavier. My one true love. The light of my life. My chest constricted to the point where I couldn't breathe when I thought of him lying motionless in the dust. My pain was so all consuming that I hardly cared where Jake was taking me to or what horrors awaited. I just needed to know that Xavier was okay. I tried not to allow myself to consider the worst although the word *dead* rang in my ears, clear as a church bell. It took me a moment to realize that I was crying. My body convulsed with huge, wracking sobs, and my eyes burned from the scalding tears.

There was nothing else to do but call upon the Creator, praying, begging, pleading, bargaining—anything to make him protect Xavier. I couldn't have him ripped away from me like that. I could survive emotional turmoil; I could survive the most intense physical torture. I could survive Armageddon and holy fire raining down upon the earth, but I could not survive without him. A strange thought entered my head: If Jake had killed Xavier, Jake would have to pay. I didn't care what divine laws forbade it—I would seek retribution for my loss. I was willing to pardon any crime, but one against Xavier, and so help me, God, Jake would get his comeuppance. I wanted to scratch and tear at the body in front of me—to punish him for once again infecting my life with his black presence. I felt contaminated even being near him. I considered flinging my weight to the side and trying to topple the bike. I knew that at the speed we were traveling, we'd probably both end up smeared across the asphalt, but I was desperate.

Before my thoughts could rage further out of control, something happened—something I could never have imagined, not even in my most twisted nightmares. It should have terrified me; the very idea of it should have knocked me into unconsciousness. It was so unfathomable that I felt nothing but a sickening feeling that seemed to come from my core and spread like poison through my body. The highway defied gravity and suddenly reared up in front of us. A deep, jagged crack appeared in its center. The highway was splitting open. The crack widened like a hungry cavernous mouth, waiting to swallow us up. The wind that whipped my face grew warmer and steam rose from the broken asphalt. I knew instinctively what it was from the feeling of hollow emptiness that emanated from it. We were heading straight toward a gateway to Hell.

And then it was upon us.

I screamed again when the motorcycle hovered a moment in midair. Jake cut the engine just before we plummeted soundlessly into the void. I turned around to see the aperture close behind us, shutting out the moonlight, the trees, the cicadas, and the earth I loved so much.

I had no idea how long it would be before I saw it again. The last thing I was aware of was falling and the sound of my own ragged screams before the darkness consumed us.

Welcome to My World

I looked around, disoriented, and shivered in my flimsy satin shift. I remembered nothing about how I'd come to be here. My hair was damp with sweat and the fluffy costume wings I'd been wearing were gone. I figured they must have come loose and been wrenched off during the turbulent ride.

There wasn't anything about this place that was even vaguely familiar. I was standing alone in a dark and cobbled laneway. Fog swirled around my feet and the air was pungent with a strange odor. It smelled like decay as if the very air itself were dead. It looked like the derelict part of some urban landscape because I could see the smoky outline of skyscrapers and spires in the distance. But they didn't look real—more like buildings in a faded old photograph—blurry and lacking in detail. Where I stood there were only brick walls covered in crude graffiti. The mortar had fallen out in places, leaving openings that someone had stuffed with newspaper. I heard (or imagined I heard) the scuttling of rats coming from behind them. Overloaded Dumpsters were scattered around and the walls were windowless apart from a couple that had been boarded up. When I looked up, I found that there was no sky, only a strange expanse of darkness, dim and watery in some places and thick as tar in others. This darkness breathed like a living thing and was much more than the mere absence of light.

An old-fashioned lamppost shedding a milky light allowed me to identify a black motorcycle propped just a few meters away. Its rider was nowhere in sight. Seeing the bike made my mind reel and forced me back to my current predicament. I fought to make sense of what had just happened but memory failed me. Random images flashed through my mind in no apparent sequence. I remembered a rambling house off a highway, a grinning jack-o'-lantern, and the laughter and banter of teenagers. Then the harsh sound of an engine being revved and someone calling my name. But these images were like the pieces of a jigsaw puzzle that I'd only just begun to assemble. It was as though my mind were denying me access to the memories for fear I wouldn't be able to deal with them. It was dishing them out in fragments that made little to no sense. Suddenly one vivid image crashed through the barrier and the recollection caused me to gasp aloud. I was back aboveground, immobilized by fear, as a motorbike driven by a raven-haired boy recklessly pitched itself through a slash in the highway. How was that even possible?

I had the feeling I'd been standing in the deserted alley for a while and yet had no sense of how much time had passed. My thoughts felt thick and sluggish, and trying to navigate my way through them was arduous. I massaged my throbbing temples and groaned. Whatever happened had also taken its toll physically and my limbs felt shaky as if I'd just run a marathon.

"It takes a day or two to adjust," said a honey-smooth voice. Jake Thorn materialized out of the shadows to stand by my side. He spoke to me with such lilting familiarity, as if he and I had known each other long enough to dispense with formalities. His sudden appearance put my senses on high alert. "Until then you may experience some disorientation or a dry throat," he added. His nonchalant tone was astounding. Despite my confusion I felt like screaming at him, and if my throat hadn't felt as parched as a desert, I would have.

"What have you done?" I croaked instead. "Where am I?"

"There's no need for alarm," he replied. I wondered if he might be trying to reassure me, but he wasn't able to pull it off and only ended up sounding condescending. I looked at him not even trying to conceal my skepticism. "Relax, Beth, you're in no danger."

"What am I doing here, Jake?" It was more a demand than a question.

"Isn't that rather obvious? You're here as my guest, Beth, and I've taken care of everything to ensure your stay is a pleasant one." There was such an uncharacteristically expectant look on his face that for a moment I didn't know how to reply. I looked at him wide-eyed.

"Don't worry, Beth, this place can be a lot of fun when you're with the right people."

Almost to illustrate his point the ground beneath us began to vibrate. A song I recalled from last summer blared so loudly it ricocheted off the walls. It appeared to be coming from behind solid steel doors at the far end of the lane. They looked how you might imagine the entrance to a maximum-security prison. Only it wasn't a prison but rather a venue of some sort, indicated by a neon sign flashing above the doors. PRIDE. I saw the tail end of the letter *P* trail off across the roofline in what was meant to represent peacock plumes.

"Pride is one of our most popular clubs," Jake explained. "And it's the only way in. Shall we?" He indicated via a courtly flourish that I should walk ahead of him, but my legs seemed rooted to the spot and refused to cooperate. Jake was forced to take my arm and escort me. The fog cleared to reveal a young man and woman standing outside the doors. The woman was insect thin, pale, and dressed in nothing but sequined black shorts, a leather bra, and the highest platform shoes I'd ever seen. Fine silver chains hung via silver hooks from her bra down to her navel, creating a mesh curtain in front of her torso. Her platinum blond hair was cropped short, and a cigarette hung from black painted lips. I was surprised to see the young man was even more heavily made up than his female counterpart. His eyes were boldly outlined and there was black polish on his nails. He wore a leather vest over a bare chest and checkered pants that tapered at his ankles. Piercings were visible on every body part exposed. The woman traced the outline of her lips suggestively with the tip of her tongue on which I could see a silver stud. Her eyes had a hungry look as they traveled over my body.

"Well, well," she purred as we approached the entrance. "Look what the cat dragged in. It's a glow-in-the-dark doll."

"Good evening, Larissa . . . Elliott." Jake's greeting was acknowledged by a silent and simultaneous inclination of heads.

Elliott smirked and cast an approving glance in Jake's direction. "Seems someone took something that didn't belong to them."

Jake's face broke into a gloating smile. "Oh, I think she belongs to me."

"Well, she certainly does now." Larissa's laugh was low and guttural. She'd outlined her eyes so the liner curved upward, giving her a feline look.

The way they talked about me as if I weren't there was unsettling. It made me feel like some kind of trophy. If I had been less disoriented, I might have expressed my disapproval. Instead, I asked the only question that sprang to mind and my voice came out sounding childish and waif-like.

"Who are you?"

Elliott clicked his tongue disapprovingly. "She obviously don't get out much." That made me angry.

"It's really none of your business!" I retorted, causing the pair to break into peals of laughter.

"She's entertaining, as well," commented Larissa. They cocked their heads and continued to study me with an unsettling intensity. "What else can she do?"

"Oh, just the usual," I snapped back angrily. "Backflips, knife throwing, that sort of thing."

Jake sighed with sudden boredom. "Can we move this along, please?"

Larissa shrugged obligingly and bent down to look me directly in the eye. "You wanna know who we are, doll-face?" she asked. "We're the door bitches."

"Excuse me?" I was taken aback.

"We man the entrance. Nobody gets in or out without our say-so."

"But seeing as you're a VIP," Elliott jibed, "you can go right on in or should I say *down?*" The pair shared a conspiratorial chuckle.

"And what if I don't want to?" I said defiantly.

Elliott raised a quizzical eyebrow and waved his hand vaguely behind me. "Honey, can you see any place else to go?"

I had to admit he was right. Surrounding the alleyway was nothing but an oppressive swirling blackness, the kind that looked capable of devouring you. There was only one path with one door at the end of it. Only one direction any of us could take. As much as the idea of going through those doors made me feel queasy, I knew it couldn't be as dangerous as wandering through the blackness alone. I didn't know who or what was out there. I still didn't even know where I was. I felt Jake's warm breath behind my ear.

"You'll be fine," he murmured. "I'll look after you." It was strange how they all waited to see what my decision would be. As if I actually had a choice.

I squared my shoulders and stepped forward with bravado I didn't feel.

Larissa bared her teeth in a smile before grabbing a tight hold of my wrist and turning it upward. Her grip was cold and claw-like, but I tried not to flinch. She held my wrist faceup as Elliott pressed something down on the inside. I braced myself to feel pain, but when I looked, he'd only left an inky imprint behind. It was a stamp of admittance in the form of a smiley face.

Larissa pressed a buzzer and the heavy doors slid open. Jake ushered me into a vast carpeted foyer where flights of narrow corkscrew steps veered like a labyrinth in several directions. There was no time for closer inspection as he steered me swiftly toward the central steps. The pumping music grew louder once we started our descent underground. The sound was so over-powering that I looked hesitantly back toward the open door. Larissa appeared to read my mind.

"Too late to change your mind, sweetheart," she said. "Welcome to our world."

Then she slid the heavy doors shut behind us.

I followed Jake down the narrow stairwell until it led to an open dance floor, where a throng of bodies was pressed together, fists pumping the air and heads thrashing to the beat. The dance floor was a checkerboard of colored lights flashing on and off. I was surprised to see people of all ages on it. The sinewy, leather-clad limbs of the elderly contrasted sharply with the firm, exposed flesh of youth. I was startled to see a few children there too. They had the designated task of clearing the tables and refilling drinks. The one thing that united them all—young and old alike—was the vacant expression they shared. It was as if they were only physically present and some vital part of them had been erased. They were like sleepwalkers, consumed by mechanical movements that were only interrupted long enough to down another shot of liquor.

Occasionally under the masklike faces I detected a darting eye or nervous flicker, as if something dire were coming. The track playing was a computerized dance number made up of a single line that was repeated continually: "I'm in Miami, bitch." Light flashed across the polished concrete floor, casting shadows across the bodies moving in sync with the rhythmic beat. The mingled scent of cigarettes, spirits, and perfume was overwhelming.

I'd never stepped inside a club before so I had no point of comparison, but it looked surreal to me. The ceiling was illuminated by a myriad of tiny lights and the walls were lined with red velvet so they looked like upright couches. Scattered around the perimeters of the room were white cubes that served as tables, as well as low velvet couches that looked battered and well used. The tables had glowing, cone-shaped lamps on them and the bar that wound around one side of the club had been crafted to simulate the appearance of molten lava. Around the bar loitered black-suited security guards stonily nursing their drinks. A striking-looking woman behind the bar juggled shot glasses and threw bottles with the dexterity of a circus performer. Her woolly ringlets, flecked with gold, surrounded her face like a mane and she wore a figure-hugging red bandage dress with brass armbands. An asp tattoo wound its way up the burnished dark skin of her throat. She watched us distractedly and didn't avert her gaze even when someone ordered a drink.

As Jake and I inched our way through the press of bodies, the crowd parted to make way for us. They never stopped dancing, but their eyes followed our every move. When someone reached out a tentative hand to touch me, Jake made a low, hissing sound and threw a lethal look. The onlooker's curiosity shriveled instantly. Jake acknowledged the barmaid with a formal nod that she doubtfully returned.

"What can I get you to drink?" he asked. He had to shout over the music to be heard.

"I don't want a drink. I just want to know where I am."

"You're not in Kansas anymore." Jake chuckled at his own joke. I had a sudden urge to make him listen—to see how frightened I was.

"Jake," I insisted, grabbing his arm. "I don't like it here. I want to leave. Please take me home." Jake looked so taken aback by my touch he didn't answer right away.

"You must be very tired," he said finally. "How insensitive of me not to notice. Of course I'll take you home." He signaled to two bearlike men who were standing at the bar in black suits and sunglasses, which looked absurd given we were in a dimly lit club underground.

"This young lady is my guest. Take her to Hotel Ambrosia," Jake instructed. "Make sure she's safely delivered to the executive wing on the top floor. They're expecting her."

"Wait, where are you going?" I called out.

Jake directed his smoldering gaze at me and smirked, seeming to enjoy my dependence on him.

"I have some business to attend to," he said. "But don't worry, they'll take care you." He glanced at the bodyguards. "Their lives depend on it."

The guards' vacant expressions didn't alter, but they nodded almost imperceptibly. Then I found myself enveloped by rock-hard muscle as they shepherded me out of the club, roughly shoving aside dancers that got in our way.

Back in the underground lobby I peered past my escorts to see that Pride was only one of several clubs that wove their way underground like catacombs. From the murky depths of one stairwell I could hear muffled moans and soon two men in suits emerged dragging a disheveled-looking girl with a tear-stained face. She wore a lacy corset and a denim skirt that barely covered the tops of her thighs. Her struggle to free herself from their vise-like grip was futile. When her eyes met mine, I saw terror in her face. Instinctively I took a step forward, but my move was intercepted by one of the guards.

I brushed them off and tried to sound casual, doing my best rendition of the way the girls at school spoke. "What's up with her?" I figured the more alarmed I appeared, the less information I'd be given.

"By the look of it she just ran out of luck," replied one guard while the other punched numbers into his cell phone and muttered our location to the person on the receiving end.

"Luck?" I parroted.

"In the gaming room?" he replied as if the answer to my question was patently obvious.

"Where are they taking her?" This time he merely shook his head in disbelief at my ignorance and walked me toward a long car with tinted windows that had pulled up outside the club. It was strange to see a car indoors, but the underground tunnels, I realized, were wide enough to fit two cars side by side and were meant to serve as roads. The rear door was opened for me and the guards slid in on either side so I was ensconced between their bulky forms. The smell of cigar smoke clung to them.

We drove for a while through the winding tunnel that seemed to spiral into nowhere. Wandering partygoers shuffled out of the way when they saw us coming. Once we moved away from the club district I noticed that these people didn't seem to be celebrating. They drifted aimlessly around with staring eyes and vacant faces like the living dead. Looking at them closer, I saw their skin had a grayish tinge to it.

Finally at the end of a steep tunnel we came to a towering building that had perhaps been white, but had now faded to the color of yellowed parchment. It must have been at least twenty stories high and classical in style with plaster scrolls above the windows.

Revolving doors led us into a vast and opulent lobby. The hotel was designed so the rooms on every floor overlooked the lobby, giving the effect of looking up into a maze. The showpiece of the lobby was a curtain of tiny fairy lights. It hung from ceiling to floor illuminating a central marble fountain in which stone nymphs frolicked. Adjacent to the reception desk rose an ornate glass elevator in the shape of a giant capsule. Here the hotel staff were dressed in crisp uniforms and the mood was business-like compared to the seediness of the clubs. When I walked in, they all froze for a moment and fixed me with the eyes of vultures before resuming their duties. Despite their seemingly ordinary appearances, I could see something untamed in their gazes, something that made me squirm inside. I was grateful to be flanked by the two burly security guards, as I would not have liked to be left alone with them.

"Welcome to the Ambrosia," said the woman behind the reception desk in a light and airy voice. With her tailored suit and blond hair wound in a smooth bun, she was the picture of efficiency. Except for her unblinking, shark-eyed gaze. "We've been expecting you. Your rooms are ready." Her cheerfulness belied the sharp look in her eyes. Her long manicured nails made a soft, clacking sound as they moved fleetingly over the keyboard. "The penthouse has been reserved for you."

"Thank you," I said. "It's a beautiful hotel, but would you mind telling me where I am?"

The woman stopped short, dropping her professional demeanor for a moment.

"He hasn't told her?" She looked incredulously at my escorts, who exchanged looks as if to say *Don't ask us.* I was having trouble containing the feeling of dread growing in the pit of my stomach. It was spreading upward like a fungus. "Well, my dear"—the receptionist's eyes glinted darkly— "you're in Hades. Make yourself at home." She slid a key card in a plastic pouch across the polished counter.

"Excuse me?" I said. "By Hades you don't mean . . . you can't mean . . ." I faltered. Of course I knew instantly what she meant. I knew from my studies that the literal translation of the place meant "the unseen." But my mind refused to acknowledge it as true. Until I heard it spoken aloud I didn't have to believe it.

"Otherwise known as Hell," the receptionist said breezily. "But don't let Mr. Thorn catch you calling it that. He prefers the more classical name. And you know how pedantic demon princes can be."

I only caught part of what she said because I'd stopped listening. My knees began to tremble. The last thing I saw were the bodyguards lunging forward as the black marble floor came up to meet my face.

Underground

I woke to a deafening silence. A milky light filtered into the room and I rubbed my eyes to get a better look at my surroundings. The first thing I saw was a sitting area with a fireplace. The last embers were crumbling to a soft glow in the grate, casting shadows across the room and softening the edges of the furniture. The room was richly decorated in dark timbers, and a crystal chandelier hung from the decorative ceiling.

I found myself lying in an oak-paneled bed with gold satin sheets and a rich burgundy coverlet. I was wearing an old-fashioned nightdress with lacy cuffs. I wondered where my costume had gone? I had no memory of taking it off. I propped myself up and looked around, from the plush carpet to the heavy velvet drapes to the vast welcome basket that sat on a low glass table with gilt claw feet. A huge leopard-skin rug was laid out at the foot of the bed. The bed itself was covered in plump pillows and an inordinate amount of tasseled cushions. When I felt something cool and fragrant beneath my cheek, I turned over to see my pillows were scattered with red rose petals.

A huge marble vanity stood against one wall; its mirror encrusted with gemstones. Displayed on it was a mother-of-pearl hairbrush and a hand mirror along with an array of expensive-looking perfumes and lotions in blue glass jars. An ivory silk dressing gown was draped over the foot of the bed. Two wingback armchairs had been strategically arranged in front of the fire. The bathroom door was open and I caught a glimpse of gold taps and an antique tub. There appeared to be no consistent theme to the decor; it was as if someone had opened a magazine and randomly pointed to whatever suggested opulence and had it delivered to this room.

A breakfast tray with a pot of steaming tea and pastries had been left on the low table. When I tried the door, I found it locked. My throat felt dry and parched so I poured myself a cup and sat on the plush carpet to drink it while I gathered my thoughts. Despite the luxurious surroundings I knew I was a prisoner.

Someone had taken away the key card so there was no way out of the room. Even if I managed to escape and made it down to the lobby, it would be crawling with Jake's allies. I could try and get past them and make a run for it but how far would I get before being recaptured?

There was only one thing I knew for certain. I could tell by the stone-cold feeling in my chest that I'd been torn away from everything I loved. I was here because of Jake Thorn, but what was his motivation? Was it revenge? If so, why hadn't he killed me when he had the chance? Did he want to somehow prolong my suffering? Or was there some other agenda like there always was with Jake? He'd seemed so genuine about making me feel comfortable. My knowledge of Hell was sketchy as my kind never ventured here. I wracked my brains, trying to recall snippets of information that Gabriel might have shared with me, but I drew a blank. I'd only been told that somewhere, deep underground, there was a pit crawling with creatures so dark they were unfathomable to us. Jake must have brought me here as punishment for humiliating him. Unless . . . A new thought suddenly dawned on me. He hadn't seemed particularly vindictive; in fact there'd been a strange excitement in his eyes. Was it possible he actually thought I could be happy here? An angel in Hell? That only proved how little he understood. My only objective was to return home to my loved ones. This wasn't my world and never would be. The longer I stayed here, the harder it would be to find my way back. I knew one thing for sure: Something like this had never happened before. An angel had never been captured, plucked from the earth, and dragged into a prison of fire. Maybe this went deeper than Jake's bizarre attachment to me. Maybe something terrible was on the brink of being unleashed.

A row of tall windows stretched along the length of one wall, but they looked out onto a swirling gray mist. There was no sunrise here and daybreak appeared to be marked by a watery light that looked as if it'd filtered down through a fissure in the earth. The thought of not seeing the sunlight for a long time brought tears to my eyes. But I blinked them away and gathered up the silk dressing gown, wrapping it around myself. I went into the bathroom to wash my face and brush my teeth, then ran a comb through my hair to unravel the knots that had appeared. There was a suffocating silence in the hotel suite. Every noise I made seemed exaggeratedly loud. With a pang of longing I remembered what it was like to wake up in Venus Cove. I associated it with a cacophony of sound: music playing, birds singing, and Phantom loping up the stairs. I could picture in perfect detail my bedroom with its pockmarked boards and rickety writing desk. If I closed my eyes, I could almost remember the feel of my soft white bedspread against my skin and the way the canopy made me feel as if I were cocooned in my own little nest. Mornings there were met with a silvery predawn light that was quickly broken by streams of golden sunlight. It would wash over the rooftops and dance over the waves of the ocean, setting the whole town alight. I remembered how I used to wake to the sound of birdsong and the breeze tapping lightly against the balcony doors as if to rouse me. Even when the house was empty, the sea was always there, calling to me, reminding me that I wasn't alone. I remembered the mornings when I'd come downstairs to hear Gabriel's fingers lazily strumming his guitar and to smell the inviting aroma of waffles in the air. I couldn't remember the last time I'd seen my family or how we came to be separated. When I thought of Venus Cove, I felt a brief flutter of hope in my chest, as though I could will myself back to my old life. But a moment later it was gone, transformed into despair as heavy as a stone pressing on my heart.

I opened my eyes to see my reflection in the mirror and realized that something was different. Nothing had changed in terms of my features; there were the same wide brown eyes flecked with gold and green looking back at me, the small pixie ears, and the porcelain skin tinged with pink. But the expression in my eyes was that of a stranger. My eyes that had once sparkled with curiosity were lifeless. The girl in the mirror looked lost.

The room was set at a comfortable temperature, but I still shivered. I walked quickly over to the closet and pulled out the first garment that came to hand—a black tulle cocktail dress with puffy sleeves. I sighed and hunted around for something more appropriate only to find that there wasn't a single piece of practical clothing in there. The outfits varied from floor-length evening gowns to tailored Chanel suits with silk blouses. I settled on the simplest item I could find (a knee-length, long-sleeved dress in crushed moss green velvet) and some ballet flats. Then I sat on my bed and waited for something to happen.

I remembered Venus Cove and my siblings vividly, but I knew there was something or someone I was forgetting. It nagged at me, an insistent tug at the back of my mind, and trying to remember was exhausting. I lay on the bed and stared at the scrolls on the ceiling. I could feel a gnawing pain somewhere inside me, but I couldn't identify its source. I even wished Jake would show up in case talking to him provided the trigger for these lost memories. I could feel them stirring in the recesses of my mind, but every time I tried to grasp them, they slipped away.

The click of a key card startled me and a round-faced girl entered the room. She was wearing the standard housekeeping uniform: a plain taupe dress with the Hotel Ambrosia logo on the pocket, beige stockings, and comfortable oxfords. Her honey-colored hair was pulled back into a ponytail and held in place with a clasp.

"Excuse me, miss, would you like me to make up your room now or should I come back later?" Her manner was diffident, and she kept her eyes downcast to avoid eye contact. Behind her was a cart laden with cleaning products and piles of fresh linen.

"Oh, that's really not necessary," I said, trying to be helpful, but my suggestion only served to make her uncomfortable. She stood at a loss, awaiting further instructions. "Or now is fine," I said, moving to one of the wingback chairs. The girl looked visibly relieved. She moved with practiced efficiency, straightening the bedclothes and changing the water in the vase, even though she couldn't have been more than sixteen years old. Her presence was strangely calming. Perhaps it was the open candor of her face that was so at odds with these bizarre surroundings.

"May I ask your name?" I said.

"I am Hanna," she replied directly. I noticed her English was a little stilted, as if she hadn't learned it as her mother tongue.

"And you work at this hotel?"

"Yes, miss, I've been assigned to you." My face must have reflected my confusion because she added, "I'm your maid."

"My maid?" I repeated. "I don't need a maid."

The girl misconstrued my irritation as being directed at her. "I will work hard," she reassured me.

"I'm sure you will," I said. "But the reason I don't need a maid is that I'm not planning on staying here very long."

Hanna gave me a strange look and then shook her head vehemently. "You cannot leave," she said. "Mr. Thorn never lets anyone leave." She clapped a hand over her mouth, conscious of having said too much.

"It's okay, Hanna," I said. "You can say anything to me. I won't repeat a word."

"I'm not meant to speak to you. If the prince were to find out . . ."

"You mean Jake?" I snorted. "He's not a prince!"

"You mustn't say things like that out loud, miss," Hanna whispered. "He is the prince of the Third Circle and treason is a capital offense."

I must have looked completely baffled. "There are Nine Circles in this world, each one ruled by a different prince," she explained. "Mr. Thorn presides over this district."

"Which idiot gave him so much power?" I snapped and then, seeing the alarm on Hanna's face, quickly modified my tone. "I mean . . . how did that come about?"

"He was one of the Originals." Hanna shrugged as if those six little words explained everything.

"I've heard about them," I said. The term rang a bell. I was sure I'd heard my brother Gabriel use it, and I knew it dated back to the beginning of time and creation.

"When Big Daddy fell from grace . . ." Hanna began casting a furtive look at the door.

"I'm sorry?" I interrupted her. "What did you just say?"

"That's what we call him down here."

"Call who?"

"Well, I suppose you would know him as Satan or Lucifer."

I felt the pieces of the puzzle begin to fall together in my mind.

"When Lucifer fell from Heaven there were eight angels who pledged their allegiance to him . . . ," I continued the story for her.

"Yes." Hanna nodded eagerly in confirmation.

"Michael cast them out along with their rebel leader and they became the very first demons. Since then they've used whatever means they can to wreak havoc on the earth in retaliation for their expulsion." I paused to let the enormity of it sink in. I frowned as a paradoxical image came into my head.

"What is it, miss?" Hanna asked, seeing my expression.

"It's just hard to imagine that Jake was once an angel," I said.

"I wouldn't say hard; more like *impossible*." Hanna's words were so blunt that I had to smile.

Still, I couldn't shake the thought from my head. Jake and I shared a genealogy. We had a common maker. What he'd since become was so far removed from what he was originally created to be. I'd always known it, but I guess I was so eager to banish him from my mind that I'd never allowed myself to think it through properly. I couldn't reconcile that the Jake I knew, the Jake who had tried to destroy my town and the people I loved, had once been just like me. I knew about the Originals. They were the most faithful servants of Lucifer, the ones who'd been with him right from the word go. Throughout human history he'd sent them to occupy positions in the highest echelons of society. They had crept into communities on earth, enabling them to continue their corrupting influence on mankind. They had infiltrated the ranks of politics and law where they were able to destroy without consequence. Their influence was poisonous. They indulged man, preyed on his weaknesses, and used him to their own advantage. An appalling thought occurred to me. If Jake worked for a higher power, then who was really to blame for what had happened thus far?

"I wonder what Jake wants this time?" I murmured.

"That is easy," said Hanna in her funny, stilted English. She seemed happy to be of use, to impart some information I didn't possess. "He only wants for you to be happy. After all, you are to be his bride."

I laughed at first, thinking she was making some horrible, tasteless joke. But when I looked at Hanna with her round, childlike face and big brown eyes, I knew she was only repeating what she'd heard.

"I think I need to see Jake," I said, slowly trying to conceal my mounting panic. "Right away. Can you take me to him?"

"Yes, miss," she replied promptly. "The prince has asked to see you anyhow."

Hanna ushered me down the dimly lit corridors of Hotel Ambrosia, moving like a ghost across the thick carpet. Everything was eerily still, and if there were other occupants, there was no sign of them. We took the glass elevator, suspended in midair like a bubble. Once inside we could see all the way down to the central fountain in the lobby.

"Where are we going?" I said. "Does Jake have a special dungeon he likes to conduct business from?"

"No. There's a boardroom on the ground floor." I realized Hanna took everything I said at face value, so sarcasm was pretty much lost on her.

We stopped in front of a pair of imposing paneled doors. Hanna's reluctance to go any farther was obvious.

"It's safer if you go in alone, miss," she said pointedly. "I know he means *you* no harm."

I didn't argue with Hanna. I certainly didn't want to expose her to the vagaries of Jake's temper. I didn't feel frightened now that I was going to come face-to-face with him again. In fact, I wanted a confrontation, even if only to tell him what I thought of him and his heinous plans. He'd done his worst; there was nothing further he could do to hurt me.

Jake looked edgy when I walked in, as if he'd been kept waiting too long. There was a fireplace here too, and Jake was standing with his back to it. He was dressed more formally than usual in tailored pants, an open-collared shirt, and a deep purple dinner jacket. Light danced across his bone white skin. He looked just the same as I remembered, with strands of long dark hair falling across eyes that were glassy and reminded me of a shark's. When he saw me, he began pacing around the room, pausing to examine one detail or another. There was a vase of long-stemmed roses in the center of the table. Jake plucked one to inhale the scent and then twirled it idly in his hands. He ignored the thorns and trickles of blood that ran down his fingers as if he couldn't feel any pain at all. I realized he probably couldn't and the wounds healed a moment later.

An imposing table filled the boardroom, so highly polished it reflected the ceiling. High-backed swivel chairs were arranged around it. A giant monitor took up an entire wall. On it I could see scenes from the clubs. I watched in fascination the image of bodies shiny with perspiration dancing so closely together they were almost melded into one entity. Even though it was only on a screen, the scene made me feel light-headed. The image shifted suddenly to rows of statistics and numerical calculations, then back to the tireless dancers. It seemed to zoom in on individuals and tabulate information about them.

"What do you think of my club rats?" Jake boasted. "Damned to drink and dance for eternity! That was my idea." He held a tumbler from which he periodically sipped an amber liquid. A half-smoked cigarette hovered on the rim of an ashtray.

Someone coughed and I swung around to see we weren't alone. A youth who didn't look much older than me sat in the far corner of the boardroom, stroking a sleeping cat. He was dressed in a checkered shirt and pants so big they had to be held up with braces. His brown hair was cut jaggedly across his forehead as if it had been done with a pair of shears. He sat with his feet pointing inward the way a child might.

"Beth, meet Tucker. He's one of my assistants and he'll be keeping an eye on you. Tucker, stand up and shake hands,"

Jake barked at the boy before smoothly turning back to me. "My apologies for his boorish manners."

Jake seemed to treat him as some kind of pet that he was in the process of training. When Tucker stood up and came toward me, I saw that he had a discernible limp and dragged his right leg. He held out a large, calloused hand for me to shake. I saw a deep scar ran from his upper lip to the base of his nose. It pulled his lip up slightly so that he looked as if he were permanently sneering. Despite his size he seemed vulnerable to me. I tried smiling at him, but he only scowled darkly and averted his gaze.

Tucker's movement roused the cat, a Siamese and none too friendly. It arched its back and hissed ferociously at me.

"I don't think he likes competition," said Jake in a silky voice. "Enough with the temper tantrum, Faustus. How are you settling in, Bethany? I'm sorry your arrival had to be so *dramatic*, but I couldn't think of any other way."

"Really?" I retorted. "I would've thought over-the-top is just the way you like it, being the big drama queen you are." I tried to make my words as offensive as I could. I was in no mood to humor him.

Jake twisted his mouth into an O of mock surprise and clamped his fingers over it.

"My, my, we've learned to be catty. That's a good thing. You can't go through life always being Little Bo Peep."

Jake reminded me of a chameleon in the way he could alter his appearance to blend with his surroundings. On home ground he was entirely different from the way I remembered him at school. At Bryce Hamilton he had been self-assured but still an outsider. He'd his devoted clan of followers, but it was the subculture he represented that was his strongest attraction. He'd known he didn't belong and made no attempt to conceal it. Instead, he seemed to revel in drawing attention and when he worked his seductive influence over a student, it gave him a smug satisfaction. But he'd always been on the alert, prepared for any eventuality. On his home turf, Jake was entirely relaxed, his shoulders sloped, his smile lazy. Here, he had all the time in the world and his authority went unquestioned.

He rolled his head to the side impatiently and addressed Tucker. "Are you going to pour my guest some wine or just stand there all day like the oversize lump of uselessness you are?"

The boy hurried over to a low table and grabbed a crystal glass with clumsy hands. He filled it with crimson liquid from a decanter, and set it down gruffly in front of me.

"I don't want a drink," I snapped at Jake, pushing the wine away. "I want to know what you've done to me. There are things I want to remember, but my memories are blocked. Unblock them!"

"What's the point in remembering your past life?" Jake smiled. "All you need to know is that you were an angel, and now you're *my* angel."

"You honestly don't think you can keep me here without some consequences? Some divine retribution?"

"I'm not doing too badly so far," Jake chuckled. "Besides, it was high time you got away from that hick town. It was clearly holding you back."

"You make me sick!"

"Now, now, let's not squabble on your very first day. Please, do sit down." Jake's voice became suddenly inviting as if we were two friends reuniting after a long separation. "We have so much to talk about."

No Exit

"I'M not discussing anything with you until I get my memories back," I said through gritted teeth. "They weren't yours to take and there are things I need to remember."

"I didn't take away your memories, Beth," Jake scoffed. "Though it's flattering you think I'm powerful enough to do so. I may have buried them temporarily but dig deep and you'll find them. Personally, I'd let it go, make a fresh start."

"Will you show me how? I can't do it by myself."

"Give me one good reason why I should." Jake rocked back in his chair and pouted. "I'm sure you'll only twist things to make me look bad."

"I'm serious, enough with the games!"

"Bethany, has it occurred to you that maybe I'm doing this for your own good? Maybe you're better off this way."

"Jake, please," I said softly. "I'm not the same person anymore. I don't recognize myself. What's the point of having me here if I don't even know who I am?"

Jake gave an exaggerated sigh as if my request were a huge imposition.

"Oh, very well." In a single fluid movement he crossed the room to where I was standing. "Let me see what I can do."

Jake pressed two cool fingers lightly against my right temple. And that was it. The repressed memories cascaded like an avalanche. I had to reach out and steady myself by holding on to the edge of the table. I still remembered my peaceful life at Byron, but now the missing pieces of the puzzle were back. I remembered the core and center from which everything else stemmed. I saw the night of the Halloween party, only this time I wasn't alone. Someone with dazzling blue eyes, honey-streaked hair, and a smile so disarming it made me weak at the knees was by my side. Remembering Xavier's face caused an indescribable rush of happiness to surge through me.

But it was short lived. Seconds later another memory savagely blotted out the first. I saw Xavier's crumpled figure lying on the dusty road while a motorbike sped away into the darkness. The memory made me so heartsick I wished I could give it back and force it out of my mind. My whole body now ached with the pain of our separation and the sight of his lifeless form. I couldn't live with the knowledge that he might be gone. If I knew that Xavier was alive and well, I could even bear my exile to this God-forsaken wasteland. Without him, I wouldn't be able to muster the will to survive. I realized at that moment that, wise or foolhardy, all of my happiness came from one single source. If that source was cut off, I wouldn't be able to function; I wouldn't want to.

"Xavier," I breathed. I felt as if all the air had been

sucked out of the room. Why was it so stifling in here? The image couldn't be dislodged. "Please tell me he's all right."

Jake rolled his eyes. "Typical. I should have known your thoughts would go straight to him."

I was choking back tears. "Wasn't it enough to abduct me? How dare you hurt him! You're a vicious, heartless coward." Rage suddenly replaced my distress. My hands curled into fists and began beating at Jake's chest. He didn't try to stop me but simply waited for the anger to subside.

"Feel better now?" he asked. I didn't feel better, but I did feel a tiny sense of release. "Let's dispense with the melodrama," he said. "Pretty boy isn't dead—just a little worse for wear."

"What?" My head jerked up.

"The impact didn't kill him," Jake said. "It just knocked him out."

The relief I felt was resuscitating. I sent a silent prayer to whatever higher power had spared him. Xavier was alive! He was breathing and walking the earth, perhaps just a little more bruised than when I last saw him.

"I suppose things are better this way," Jake said with a wry smile. "His death might have started things off on the wrong foot between us."

"Do you promise never to hurt him?" I asked testily.

"*Never* is a long time. Let just say he's safe for now."

I didn't like the implication behind the words *for now*, but decided not to push my luck.

"And Ivy and Gabriel are safe?"

"They're a formidable force together," he said. "Anyway,

they were never part of the plan. I was only interested in getting you here and now that's done. Although for a while I wasn't sure I'd be able to pull it off. It's no easy feat for a demon to drag an angel into hell, you know. I'm not sure it's ever been done before." Jake looked pleased with his achievement.

"It sure looked easy to me."

"Well," Jake said, smiling indulgently. "I didn't think I'd be able to rise again after your holier-than-thou brother sent me back down here. But then those silly little friends of yours started summoning spirits right there in Venus Cove! I couldn't believe my luck."

Jake's eyes smoldered like coals. "It wasn't a very powerful incantation that girl recited. It only awoke some restless spirits, but they were more than happy to trade places."

"They weren't trying to summon demons," I said defensively. "Séances are only supposed to conjure spirits." I couldn't shake the feeling of responsibility. I had chosen to turn a blind eye when I should have done more to stop them, including smashing the board into tiny pieces and throwing it out the window.

"It's more of a lucky strike really," Jake said. "Who knows what you'll pull out of the ground." I glowered at him darkly. "Don't look at me like that, it's not entirely my fault. I couldn't have brought you here if you hadn't accepted my invitation."

"What invitation?" I said sarcastically. "I don't remember you asking if I wanted a pit stop in Hell."

"I offered you a ride and you accepted," Jake said smugly.

"That doesn't count, I was tricked—I thought you were someone else!"

"Too bad. Rules are rules. Besides, how naïve can you be? Didn't it strike you as a teeny bit odd that Mr. Responsible would dive-bomb from a tree into a river? Did you really think he'd ditch you to play frat-boy pranks? Even I didn't think you'd fall for that. You of all people should have known better, but it only took a second to break your faith in him. You sealed your own fate by accepting that ride. It hardly had anything to do with me at all."

His words hit me like blows. As the realization of my own stupidity sank in, Jake began to laugh. I'd never heard anyone laugh in such an empty, hollow way. He reached out and grasped my hands in his.

"Don't worry, Beth. I'm not going to let one little mistake change my opinion of you."

"Let me go home," I pleaded. Somewhere in the recesses of his mind I hoped there lingered a vestige of decency that would allow him to feel a hint of remorse, a tinge of guilt, anything I could beg or bargain with. But I couldn't have been more wrong.

"You are home," Jake said in a flat voice. He pressed my hands to his chest. His flesh felt as malleable as dough, and for an awful second I thought my fingers would sink right into the hollow cavity where his heart should have been.

"I'm sorry I can't be human for you," he drawled. "But you have a few irregularities of your own, so I don't think you can sit in judgment." He released one of my hands, allowing his fingers to hover over my retracted wings.

"At least I have a heart, which is more than I can say for you," I said. "It's no wonder you don't feel anything."

"That's where you're wrong. You make me feel things, Beth. That's why you have to stay. Hell's a whole lot brighter with you in it."

I wrenched my other hand free. "I don't have to do anything. I may be your prisoner, but you have no power over my heart. And sooner or later, Jake, you're going to have to accept that." I turned on my heel to leave.

"Where do you think you're going?" Jake demanded. "You can't just wander around here unchaperoned. It's not safe."

"We'll see about that."

"I really wish you'd reconsider."

"Leave me alone!" I yelled over my shoulder. "I don't care what you want."

"Don't say I didn't warn you." In the hallway I found Hanna waiting dutifully.

"I'm leaving this hellhole," I announced and headed in the direction of the revolving doors. The lobby looked unattended so perhaps I wouldn't be intercepted.

"Wait, miss!" Hanna cautioned, scuttling alongside me. "The prince is right, you don't want to go out there!"

I ignored her and flung myself through the revolving doors and out into the middle of nowhere. Surprisingly no one made any attempt to stop me. There was no plan in my mind but that didn't matter. I wanted to put as much distance between Jake and myself as I possibly could. If there were portals into this place, those same portals had to lead out. I only needed to find one. But as I ran into the smoky tunnels Hanna's words reverberated in my head. *There is no way out.*

Beyond Hotel Ambrosia the tunnels were deep and dark, littered with beer bottles and the burnt-out husks of old cars, charred from the inside out. They twisted all around me and the people that staggered past seemed caught in a daze, completely unaware of my presence. I could tell they were condemned souls by the hollow looks in their eyes. If I could find the road we'd taken to get to the hotel, maybe I could persuade the door bitches to let me out.

The deeper I ventured into the tunnels, the more I began to notice things, like the strange mist and the smell of burning hair that was strong enough to make me cover my mouth with my hand. The mist swirled around me, marshaling me forward, and once it cleared I saw that I was nowhere near Pride, the club through which I had first entered. In fact, I had no idea where I was, but I sensed a deep evil, like a chill in my blood. For one thing, strangers surrounded me. I wasn't sure what to call them, but I knew they had once been people. There was no way you could call them that now. They looked more like wraiths and they walked around aimlessly, vanishing in and out of the dark crevices. Their energy was still present even though they looked through vacant eyes and their hands clutched uselessly at the air. I focused on the apparition closest to me, trying to understand what was happening. It was a man smartly dressed in a business suit. He had a neat haircut and wore metal-framed glasses. After a few moments a woman materialized in front of him along with the domestic setting of a kitchen. The whole scene shimmered like a mirage, but I had the feeling that for those involved it was far more real. A heated discussion erupted between the pair. I felt ill at ease watching them as if I were intruding on a very private moment.

"No more lies. I know everything," the woman said.

"You don't know what you're talking about," the man replied in a tremulous voice.

"I know that I'm leaving you."

"Don't say that."

"I'm going to stay with my sister for a while. Until things get sorted."

"Sorted?" The man was becoming more agitated.

"I want a divorce." There was a resolve in her voice that made the man crumble and he made a low, moaning sound.

"*Shut up.*"

"I've had enough of you treating me like dirt. I'm going to be happy without you."

"You're not going anywhere." His body language was threatening, but she didn't read the signs.

"Get out of my way."

When she tried to push past him, he seized a carving knife from the set on the counter. Even though it wasn't real, the knife's blade gleamed and looked solid. He lunged forward and slammed his wife back against the counter. I didn't see the knife come up, but the next minute it was lodged firmly under her rib cage. Instead of remorse, the sight of blood unleashed a frenzy. He stabbed repeatedly, ignoring her shrieks until the opening he had made was a bloody pulp. Only then did he hurl the knife aside and his wife's limp body slipped from his grasp. Her eyes were wide and staring, cheeks flecked with her own blood. As soon as she hit the tiles on the floor, she vanished and the kitchen disappeared with her.

I cowered in a corner, my breath in my throat, trying to stop my hands from shaking. This was one scene I would not forget in a hurry. The man looked dazed, turning in circles, and for a dreadful moment I thought he'd become aware of my presence. But then the woman reappeared before him, whole and untouched.

"No more lies. I know everything," she said.

It was as if someone had hit replay on a movie. I realized the whole grisly scene was about to be repeated before my eyes. Those involved were doomed to relive it infinitely. The other figures scattered around me were each reliving their own crimes of the past: murder, rape, assault, adultery, theft, betrayal. The list seemed endless.

I'd always interacted with the concept of evil on a philosophical level. Now I felt as though it was all around me, palpable and real. I ran blindly back the way I'd come without stopping. There were times when I felt things brushing past me or catching at the hem of my dress, but I shook myself free and kept running. I only stopped when I thought another step would cause my lungs to collapse.

I knew I'd lost my way because the tunnels had vanished. I was now standing in wide-open space. In the ground ahead lay a crater-like opening rimmed with fiery embers. I couldn't see what was going on inside, but I could hear tortured shouts and screams. I'd never seen anything even remotely like it, so why did it feel so oddly familiar? *The lake of fire awaits, my lady.* Could this be the place referred to in the cryptic note I'd found jammed in my locker all those months ago? I knew I shouldn't approach. I knew the right thing to do was turn around and find my way back to Hotel Ambrosia, even if it was my prison. Whatever lurked in this place was not something I was ready to witness. So far Hades had been a surreal world made up of underground tunnels, shady nightclubs, and an empty hotel. But as I took my first tentative steps toward the fiery pit, I knew this was going to be different.

The indescribable wailing of the occupants reached me before I was even close. I'd always thought medieval depictions of Hell with its twisted bodies and instruments of torture were nothing but a device designed to frighten and control an ignorant populace. But now I knew the stories were true.

It wasn't easy to make out what was happening through the ruby glow that emanated from the pit, but there were clearly two distinct groups, the tormented and their tormentors. The tormentors wore leather harnesses and boots. Some wore hoods like executioners. The tormented were either naked or in rags. From the earthen walls hung an array of metal devices designed to inflict pain. My eyes traveled over the saws, branding irons, and rusty pliers. At ground level were vats of boiling oil, a dunking device, and hot coals. There were bodies chained to posts, hanging from rafters, and strapped into cruel devices. The souls writhed and screamed as the torturers relentlessly continued their devilish work. I watched them drag a naked man across the ground and force him into a brass coffin, bolting the lid shut. They slid the coffin into an oven and I watched as it slowly heated up, glowing orange and then red. From inside came muffled screams of agony, which seemed to amuse the demons. Another man was tied to a post with ropes, his eyes turned upward in supplication. At first I didn't realize that the yellow sheath flapping from his thigh like washing on a line was his own skin. He was being flayed alive.

The images that flashed before me were of blood and torn flesh and festering wounds. I could watch for only a few seconds before the bile started to rise in my throat. I threw myself onto the dry, cracked ground and covered my ears. The smell and the sound were both unbearable. I began crawling away on my hands and knees, not trusting myself to walk upright without passing out.

I'd only crawled a few meters through the dust when a boot crunched down on my hand. I looked up to see myself surrounded by three whip-wielding tormentors who had noticed my arrival. There was nothing recognizably human in their pitiless faces. There was a rattling of chains when they moved but closer inspection revealed them to be no older than schoolboys. It was incongruous seeing such cruelty on their perfect faces.

"Looks like we have a visitor," said one, prodding me with the heel of his boot. His voice was musical and laced with a Spanish accent. He moved his foot and used it to lift up the hem of my dress, exposing my legs. The tip of his boot was traveling uncomfortably high.

"She's hot," grunted his companion.

"Hot or not, it ain't polite to go wandering around restricted areas without an invitation," the third demon chimed in. "I say we teach her a lesson." His eyes glinted like marbles. He had a pouting mouth and spoke with a lazy drawl. His shock of fair hair fell over his eyes and sharp features.

"I get her first," the other objected. "When I'm done, you can teach her whatever you like." He flashed me a grin. He was stockier than the others and his copper bangs were blunt. He had a sprinkling of freckles across a porcine nose.

"Forget it, Yeats," warned the first boy who had a head full of black curls. "Not until we know who sent her."

Yeats brought his face level with mine. His small teeth reminded me of a piranha's. "What's a pretty little thing like you doing wandering these parts alone?"

"I'm lost," I said shakily. "I'm from Hotel Ambrosia and I'm Jake's guest." I tried to sound important but didn't dare meet his gaze.

"Damn." The blond one sounded annoyed. "She's with Jake. I guess we better not mess her up too bad then."

"I'm not buying it, Nash," Yeats snapped. "If she was really with Jake, she wouldn't be out here."

Suddenly my head was reeling. I didn't think my body could cope with much more. Yeats looked unimpressed.

"If you're going to throw up—do it over there. I've just had these boots shined." I felt my chest heave as I dry retched.

"Come on, get up!" Yeats hauled me to my feet. He looked triumphantly at the others as his arm encircled my waist. "What do you say we put you to good use? How do you feel about an audience?" His hands were rough as they struggled with the buttons on my bodice.

"If she does belongs to Jake and he finds out, who knows what he'll do. . . ." The boy called Nash sounded nervous.

"Shut up," Yeats said and turned to the first boy. "Diego, help me hold her down."

"Get your filthy paws off her," said a voice so menacing it could have cut through steel.

Jake materialized out of the shadows. His dark hair was unbound and, coupled with his furious expression, it gave him a look of animal-like ferocity. He appeared a good deal more dangerous than the others. In fact when they stood side by side, the three youths looked like amateurs or naughty schoolboys who'd been caught breaking the rules. In Jake's presence they lost their cockiness and looked paralyzed with fear. He seemed to tower over them and had an air of authority that made them cower. If there were echelons of power in Hell, this trio must have occupied one of the lower orders.

"We didn't know she was, uh . . . spoken for," Diego said apologetically. "We wouldn't have touched her otherwise."

"I tried to tell them she was . . . ," Nash began, but Diego stared him into silence.

"You're lucky I'm in a good mood right now," Jake hissed. "Now, get out of my sight before I put you on the rack myself." They scurried back to the pit from where they'd come like jackrabbits. Jake offered me his arm as he led me away. It was the first time I was actually glad of his presence.

"So . . . how much did you see?" he asked.

"All of it."

"I did try to warn you," Jake sounded genuinely sorry. "Would you like me to try and erase the memories? I'll be careful not to touch your old ones."

"No, thank you," I said numbly. "It was something I needed to see."

9

Lake of Dreams

EVERY day that passed without news of Venus Cove added to my misery.

I could think of nothing but what I was missing in the lives of those I loved. I knew they must be frantic with worry. Had they guessed where Jake had taken me or were they ready to file a missing person's report? I knew if I were held hostage anywhere on earth, the divine powers of my siblings would track me down. But I had no idea if their radars could reach deep into the core of the earth. When I thought about my family, I remembered the simplest things; the way my brother used to experiment in the kitchen, handling food as though it were art; the way my sister used to braid my hair with a skill only she possessed. I thought of Gabriel's hands and the way they could make any instrument bow to his will and Ivy's river of golden hair. Mostly I thought of Xavier; the way his eyes crinkled gently at the corners whenever he smiled; the smell of his car after we'd eaten burgers and fries in the Chevy overlooking the ocean. Although I'd only been gone a few days, I grieved for every moment that passed. Worst of all was that I knew Xavier would be blaming himself and I couldn't do anything to ease his guilt.

Time became my biggest enemy in Hades. On earth it had been so precious because I didn't know when it would run out, but here it was drawn out and immeasurable. The tedium was the hardest to bear. Not only was I a prisoner in Jake's soulless world, I was also an angel in Hell and treated with either scorn or morbid curiosity by its elite. Most of the time I felt like a sideshow freak. There was something about the place that seemed to eat at me from the inside like a cancer. It was easy to give into it—stop thinking, stop fighting—and I could I feel it happening to me. I was terrified by the idea of waking one day no longer caring about human suffering or whether I lived or died.

For days after stumbling across the lake of fire and its associated horrors, I fell into a deep depression. I had little appetite, but Hanna was patient with me. Jake's assistant, Tucker, had been assigned as my personal minder and was always around though he rarely spoke to me. Together they became my constant companions.

They were in my room one night as usual, Hanna trying to coax me into eating a mouthful or two of the broth she'd prepared and Tucker diverting himself by crushing paper into balls and tossing them into the fireplace to watch them ignite. I pushed away Hanna's offer of dessert and watched her face crease into a mask of stress. Tucker looked up and shook his head at her in tacit communication. Hanna let out a heavy sigh and set down the dinner tray while Tucker went back to poking the embers in the fire. I curled myself into a ball at the end of my bed. The old Bethany Church felt dead and buried. I knew I would carry the horror of what I'd seen around with me forever.

We all started when we heard the soft buzz of a key card and Jake let himself into the room. He was obviously so sure of his authority that he hadn't felt the need to knock and was totally oblivious to having impinged on my privacy. He seemed to believe round-the-clock access to me was wholly within his rights. I saw Tucker stand up and linger self-consciously, as if he should be making himself useful, but Jake ignored him and marched over to where I lay, regarding me carefully. Unlike Tucker, I made no attempt to get up or even turn my head to face him.

"You look awful," he observed. "I hate to say I told you so."

"I don't want to see you," I said dully.

"I thought you'd understand by now that there are far worse things in this place than seeing me. Come on now, you can't blame me for what you've seen. I didn't create this place even though I may have some jurisdiction over it."

"Do you enjoy inflicting pain and torture?" I asked in a hollow voice, looking up to meet his eyes. "Do you get off on it?"

"Steady on," Jake sounded offended. "I *personally* don't torture anyone. I have more important things to do."

"But you know it's happening," I insisted. "And you do nothing about it."

Jake shared a bemused look with Tucker, who was frowning at me as if he thought I were an idiot.

"And why on earth would I try to stop it?" he asked.

"Because they're people," I said weakly. It was always so exhausting talking to Jake. It left me feeling as if I were running in circles and getting nowhere.

"No, actually they're souls of people who were very bad in life," he explained patiently.

"Nobody deserves this—no matter what their crime."

"Oh, really?" Jake folded his arms. "Then you have no idea what mankind is capable of. Besides, they all had the choice to repent and they chose not to. That's how the system works."

"Yeah, well, your system stinks. It turns good people into monsters."

"And that," Jake said, wagging a finger thoughtfully, "is the difference between you and me. You insist on seeing man as inherently noble even when all evidence suggests otherwise. Humans—urghh!" Jake shuddered. "What's noble about them? They eat, they breed, they sleep, they fight—they're nothing but basic organisms. Look what billions of them have done to the planet; their very existence is polluting the earth and you blame us for it. If humans are God's greatest achievement, he seriously needs to review his design. Take Tucker, for instance. Why do you think I keep him around? It's to remind me of God's fallibility." Tucker's face flushed crimson but Jake seemed not to notice.

"People are much more than that," I replied, partly to cover up Tucker's humiliation. "They can dream and hope and love. Doesn't that count for anything?"

"Those are usually worse off because they're so delusional. Empty yourself of compassion, Bethany, it won't serve you well here."

"I'll die before I become like you," I said.

"I'm afraid that's not possible," said Jake breezily. "You can't die here. Only the earth entertains such ridiculous notions as life and death. Another one of your father's little quirks."

I was spared the effort of challenging Jake further when we heard voices in the hall and a woman sailed into the room with all the aplomb of a celebrity.

"This is supposed to be my room," I muttered. "Why do people think they can just barge in and . . ."

I stopped short when I gave the woman a closer look and remembered her instantly as the tattooed barmaid from Pride. It would have been hard to forget the annihilating look she'd given me then. She gave me a fleeting glance this time as if my presence were too immaterial to take up any more of her time. She was riled. I could see that in the fixed line of her mouth and the way she brusquely pushed past Tucker.

"So this is where you've been hiding," she chided Jake.

"I wondered how long it'd be before you'd show up," Jake said lazily. "You know you're getting yourself a reputation as a stalker."

"Shame a bad reputation don't mean jack here," the woman replied.

There was a derisive tone in the way he addressed her, but she seemed only amused by it. "Beth, meet Asia, my . . . very personal . . . personal assistant. She gets stressed if she doesn't know exactly where I am at any given time."

I sat up to get a better look at her. Asia was tall and striking like an Amazon. She was dressed provocatively in a gold halter top and a leather miniskirt. Her jet-black hair with the texture of spun wool surrounded her feline features. Her lips were exaggeratedly full, sticky with gloss, and permanently parted. The way she stood with her shoulders thrust back reminded me of a boxer, and her coffee-colored skin had a slight sheen as if it had been oiled. Her shoes were extraordinary, like works of art; fawn-colored, open-toed lace-up ankle boots with heels like ice picks.

"Jimmy Choo," she said reading my mind. "Divine, aren't they? Jake has them specially made for me every season."

There was a look in her smoldering eyes I was familiar with. I'd seen girls give it to one another at school when they wanted to issue a clear warning that said, "Hands off!" Asia didn't need to say anything to me; her look spoke volumes. As Jake's lover she was sending me a clear message that said he was off-limits to me if I valued my life. In order to make the status of her relationship patently clear, Asia slithered around Jake like an asp at his throat, rubbing up and pressing her bare flesh against him. Jake's hand traveled up her polished thigh, but in his eyes I was sure I could see boredom. Asia surveyed me from head to foot, decidedly unimpressed. "So, this is the little bitch everyone's talking about? *Small*, isn't she?" Jake made a clicking sound with his tongue.

"Asia—play nice."

"I can't see what all the fuss is about," she said, circling me now with a panther-like grace. "If you ask me, baby, I think you're downgradin'."

"Well, nobody asked you." Jake gave her a warning look. "And we talked about this; Beth is *special*."

"Are you saying I'm not?" Asia put her hands on her hips and arched her eyebrows flirtatiously.

"Oh, no, you're very special," Jake chuckled. "But in a different way. Don't think your talents haven't been appreciated."

"So what's with the Mary Sue outfit?" Asia asked, plucking at the frilly sleeve of my dress. "You got some fetish for Southern belles? It's very pure. That's what this is all about, right? But did you really have to dress her like she's twelve?"

"No one dressed me," I snapped.

"Oh, how cute!" Asia threw me a scathing look. "It talks."

"I was just explaining to our guest how things work down here," Jake said, steering the conversation in a safer direction. "I was trying to explain to her how life and death have no meaning here. Would you mind assisting me in a brief demonstration?"

"With pleasure," Asia agreed. She came to stand right in front of him and threw back her head, seductively sliding off her halter top until she stood only in a black bra, revealing the smooth milk chocolate skin of her torso. Jake's eyes traveled appreciatively over her body for a moment, before he spun around and seized a fire poker from its hook beside the grate. I realized his intention too late and the scream caught in my throat as he plunged the thick tip into her chest. I expected howls of pain or spurting blood, anything but what I saw. Asia only gasped then shuddered with pleasure and closed her eyes in ecstasy. When she opened them and caught sight of my horror-stricken face she dissolved into laughter. The poker was buried inches deep in her chest without the slightest hint of a wound of any kind. It looked as if it had molded to her body, as if it had always been a part of her. When she grasped it with both hands and wrenched it free of her flesh, it made a gruesome sucking sound. Seconds later the smooth skin closed over the puncture the poker had created.

"See?" Asia said. "The Grim Reaper can't touch us. He works for us."

"But I'm not dead," I blurted, unthinking.

Asia snatched up the poker from the floor where she'd tossed it. "Why don't we test that out?" she hissed. She sprang at me with animal speed, but Jake was faster and intercepted her, whipping the weapon from her tight grasp. He threw her onto the couch and crouched over her, the tip of the poker pressed menacingly against her throat. Asia eye's flashed with excitement. She bared and gnashed her teeth as she ran her hands along his hips.

"Bethany is not a toy," Jake said, as if he were scolding a naughty child. "Try to think of her as your baby sister." Asia held her hands palm up in defeat but couldn't repress her expression of deep disappointment.

"You used to be so much fun."

"Ignore her." Jake looked at me. "She'll get used to you in time."

That's if I survive, I thought bitterly. "It doesn't make sense," I said. "How can you torture souls when they can't feel pain?"

"I never said *they* couldn't feel pain," Jake explained. "Only the demons are immune. The souls, on the other hand, feel everything acutely. The beauty of Hades is that you keep regenerating only to go through it all again."

"The torture cycle's set on repeat," Asia said with a crazed look. "We can hack 'em up and by sundown they'll be whole again. The poor suckers look so relieved to know they're close to the end. You should see their faces when they wake up without a scratch and it starts all over again."

My face must have reflected the light-headedness I suddenly felt. I sank down into a chair, resting heavily on my elbow. Jake brushed Asia's wandering hands from his chest and came over to me. He lifted my chin with an icy finger.

"Tell me what's wrong," he said in a voice surprisingly devoid of sarcasm.

"I don't feel well," I said flatly.

"Poor baby's sick," Asia crooned.

"What can I do?" Jake asked.

My gaze wandered inadvertently to Asia. I knew it wasn't wise to make an enemy out of her, but her very presence was making me feel unwell. Jake looked at her flippantly over his shoulder. "Get out," he commanded without a second's hesitation.

"What?" She sounded genuinely surprised and even unsure of who he was addressing for a moment.

"NOW!"

Asia had clearly never been in a position in which she wasn't Jake's favorite and she didn't like it. She threw me one final venomous look before storming off. I breathed easier with her gone. The malice she projected was debilitating, as if she were feeding off my very life source.

"Tucker, pour us a drink," Jake ordered. Tucker sprang to life, moving to the dresser to pour whiskey from a crystal decanter into a tumbler. He handed it to Jake with an expression that suggested a mixture of fear and loathing. Jake held out the glass to me.

"Drink this."

I took some tentative sips of the warm, glowing liquid and felt surprisingly better. It burned inside me, but somehow the burn had a numbing effect.

"You need to keep your strength up," Jake said, putting an arm casually around me. Instantaneously I shook myself free. "You don't always have to be so defensive." He swung himself playfully around a bedpost and slid in beside me so deftly I barely had time to react. Although filled with a strange darkness, Jake's face was beautiful in the fading light. His lips parted in a slow smile and I could hear him breathing fast. His black eyes traveled unhurriedly over my face. He always had a way of making me feel exposed and vulnerable.

"You must make an effort to be happy," he murmured, trailing a finger along the inside of my arm.

"How can I try when I'm more miserable than I've ever been?" I said. There was little point in trying to mask my feelings.

"I understand you're pining for lost love," Jake said, in a voice that sounded almost sincere. "But that human can't make you happy because he can never truly understand what you are."

I edged away from him, but his grip on my arm tightened and he began tracing the network of veins beneath the translucent skin. I flinched, remembering how his touch had been accompanied by an uncomfortable burning sensation in the past. It felt different this time, almost soothing. I figured I was in Jake's domain now and he could manipulate things any way he chose.

When Jake left, I couldn't settle and Tucker loitering by the closed door only made me more uncomfortable. Instead of returning to the fire, he withdrew an electronic device from his pocket and began compulsively playing games to wile away the time.

"You can sit down," I suggested, remembering his lame leg, which must have been bothering him because he kept readjusting his position, shifting his weight from foot to foot.

He looked up for a moment, startled by my expression of kindness.

"I won't tell anyone," I added with a smile.

Tucker hesitated a moment, then relaxed enough then to slide down and sit with his back against the door.

"You oughta try 'n' git some sleep," he suggested. It was the first time I'd heard him speak or look at me directly. His voice wasn't what I expected. It was soft and mellow with a lilting Southern twang. The tone, however, was surprisingly world-weary for someone his age. "If you're worried about Asia, she won't bother you while I'm around." He seemed proud of his ability to keep watch. "She's a piece of work, but I ain't easily fooled, despite what y'all might think."

"I'm not worried," I reassured him. "I trust you, Tucker."

"You can call me Tuck," he said.

"Okay."

Tuck hesitated, and then looked at me with interest. "What makes you so sad all the time?"

"Am I that obvious?" I gave a small smile.

Tuck shrugged. "I can see it in your eyes."

"I'm just thinking about the people I love . . . ," I said, "and whether I'll ever see them again."

A pained expression crossed his face as though my words had triggered troubling memories of his own to resurface.

"You can see them again if you want to," he said. It was barely a murmur. Had I heard him right? All my hopes were suddenly roused, but I tried to keep my voice from trembling.

"Excuse me?" I asked slowly.

"You heard me," Tuck mumbled.

"Are you saying you know a way out of here?"

"I didn't say *that*," he snorted. "I said you could *see* them again."

This time he sounded mildly annoyed at having to explain what should have been patently obvious. It struck me suddenly that this lumbering boy with his crooked haircut might know more than he was letting on. Could his allegiance to Jake be merely pretense? Was it possible that here was one person in all of Hades with a vestige of conscience left? Was Tuck trying to tell me he was prepared to help? There was only one way to find out.

"Tell me what you mean, Tuck," I asked, my heart leaping with expectation.

"There's a way," he said simply.

"Can you tell me?"

"I can't tell you," he answered. "But I can show you." He brought a broad finger up to his lip in warning. "But we have to be careful. If we're caught . . . ," he trailed off.

"I'll do whatever I need to do," I said determinedly.

"There are five rivers in Hades. One is for forgetting your past life, but there's another that let's you return to it. Well, at least temporarily," Tuck said. "Drink from it and it will give you the ability to visit your loved ones whenever you like."

"Visit them how?"

"You'll be able to project," Tucker said. It seemed the more he spoke, the less I understood what he meant. I looked at him blankly, my previous expectation dwindling to disappointment. It was entirely possible that Tucker wasn't even in his right mind. The fact that I was attaching so much hope to what he had to say was a testament to my desperation.

Tuck read the mistrust in my face and tried to be clearer.

"There's things here you won't have read about in books. Drinking from the Lake of Dreams creates a trancelike state that allows your spirit to detach from your physical body. It takes skill, but someone like you should pick it up easy. Once you learn how to do it, you can go anywhere you like."

"How do I know you're not lying?"

Tucker looked dispirited at my lack of trust. "Why would I lie? Jake'll have me thrown into the pit if he finds out."

"Why help me then? Why risk your safety?"

"Let's just say I'm fixin' to settle a score," he said. "Plus, you look like you could really use a home visit." His lame attempt at humor made me smile.

"Have you managed to? Go home, I mean?"

A forlorn look came into his eyes. "By the time I worked out how there wasn't much point, everyone I ever knew had gone. But you could check on the people you care about 'cuz they're still alive."

The lake's potential filled me with hope.

"Take me there now," I begged.

"Not so fast," he cautioned. "It can be dangerous."

"How dangerous?"

"Take too much and you might not wake up."

"And how is that bad?" The words slipped out before I had a chance to think about them.

"It ain't if y'don't mind being in a coma for the rest of your life, watching your family day in and day out like they're characters on a movie screen but never bein' able to talk to them or reach them. Is that what you want?"

I shook my head although admittedly it sounded a darn sight better than what I had now.

"Okay," I said. "You're in charge of the dosage. But you've gotta take me there right now!"

10

Devil's Feast

WE were almost at the door when it opened with a muted clack and Jake unexpectedly let himself into the room. Tuck and I both started and tried to cover our confusion by moving in entirely opposite directions. Jake arched an eyebrow and looked at us quizzically. He was dressed in a charcoal dinner jacket and a red silk cravat.

"Good to see you're still up, darling," he said in that irritating formal manner of his, as if he were something out of a 1950s movie. "I hope you're hungry. I've come to take you to dinner. It's just what we need to lighten the mood around here."

"I'm actually pretty tired," I hedged. "I was planning on going to bed."

"Really? Because you look wide awake to me," he said, scrutinizing my face closely. "More than awake—I'd say you look excited about something. Your cheeks are all flushed."

"That's because it's always so overheated in here," I said. "Seriously, Jake, I was hoping to have an early night. . . ." I tried to speak in what I hoped was an assertive tone, but Jake cut me off by waving his hand irritably.

"Enough excuses. I'm not taking no for an answer, so hurry up and get ready." It struck me that he could be capable of such erratic mood swings. One moment he could be dark and threatening and the next as excited as a schoolboy. Suddenly his tone became more upbeat and he smiled. "Besides, I want to show you off!"

I threw Tucker an imploring look, but his face had returned to its previous expressionless mask. There was nothing he could say or do that wouldn't get us both into hot water.

"I just want to be left alone," I said to Jake.

"Bethany, you must understand that there are certain duties attached to your new position. There are important people who are anxiously waiting to meet you. So . . . I'll be back in twenty minutes and you'll be ready." It was not a request. He was almost out the door when he paused as if a new idea had just occurred to him. "By the way," he said over his shoulder. "Wear pink tonight. They'll get a kick out of that."

Dinner was held in a lavish underground dining room lit by a screen of fire at one end. In place of wall hangings the room had an array of weaponry, including Roman shields, spiked maces, and long blunt stakes—the kind Vlad the Impaler might've had in his fourteenth-century Romanian castle.

As Jake and I were the first to arrive, we stood in the flagged foyer as waiters served up finger food on silver platters and French champagne from tall flutes. Peals of frivolous laughter heralded the arrival of the other guests. Looking around I saw they were mostly made up of elite members of Jake's court. Everyone who approached Jake to pay his or her respects eyed me with unconcealed fascination. Most were dressed elaborately in leather and fur. In my powder pink dress with its scalloped neckline and full knee-length skirt, I felt distinctly out of place. I was relieved to find that I couldn't see Asia anywhere. I wondered whether her exclusion was intentional. I was sure it would only fuel her resentment toward me.

After a brief lapse of time a gong signaled the commencement of dinner and we were all ushered to our places at the long oak table in the dining room. As host, Jake was seated at the center. Grim-faced, I slunk into my designated seat beside him. Sitting directly in front of us were Diego, Nash, and Yates, whom I'd first encountered in the pit. With them were three strikingly dressed women. In fact, all the assembled guests were beautiful, both male and female alike, but in a strange and frightening way. Their features were perfectly crafted as if from glass and yet they looked so different from Ivy and Gabriel. I felt a pang thinking of my brother and sister, immediately followed by the sting of tears. I bit down hard on my lower lip to hold them back. I might be naïve, but I knew how unwise it would be to show vulnerability in front of company like this.

I studied the faces around me. They were rapacious, conceited, and sharp eyed. Their senses seemed accentuated, as if they could hone in on scents and sounds like wild animals programmed to hunt. I knew they could make themselves appear as seductive and tempting as ever when luring human prey. Although their beauty was striking, there were times when I caught fleeting glimpses as subtle as a passing shadow of their real features that lay beneath the masks of perfection. What I saw made me recoil. I could not suppress my shock when I realized that they merely assumed the guise of humans for outward appearances.

In their true form the demons were anything but perfect. Their actual faces were beyond horrifying. I found myself staring at a statuesque female with coils of chocolate brown hair. Her skin was milky pale; her almond eyes an electric blue. Her delicately hooked nose and round shoulders made her look like a Grecian goddess. But beneath the glamorous exterior she was an image of putrefaction. Her skull was misshapen, with a bulging forehead and a chin as pointed as a dagger. Her skin was mottled and bruised, as if someone had beaten her, and her face was covered in weeping sores and welts. Her nose was pushed up into her head so that it resembled a snout. She was bald apart from patches of thin, matted hair that hung around her face. Her real eyes were cloudy and red rimmed and her mouth was little more than a slot through which you could glimpse stumps of teeth and rotting gums when she threw back her head and laughed. I saw similar flashes all around the table and felt my stomach begin to churn.

"Try not to stare," Jake admonished in my ear. "Just relax and don't focus on it." I complied and found that once I took his advice, the flashes stopped and faces of the party returned to their cruel but beautiful masks. My lack of enthusiasm eventually drew their attention and was misconstrued as rudeness.

"What's the matter, Princess?" Diego asked from across

the table. "Our hospitality not up to your standards?" If the group had been holding back until then, Diego's comment served as a catalyst, encouraging others to voice their thoughts.

"My, my, an angel in Hell," chuckled a redhead I'd heard Jake address as Eloise. "Who would have thought we'd see the day?"

"Is she staying long?" complained a man with a fastidiously groomed beard. "She reeks of virtue and it's giving me a headache."

"What did you expect, Randall?" someone snorted. "The righteous ones are always exhausting to have around."

"Is she a virgin?" the redhead asked. "I haven't seen one of those down here in a while. Can we have some fun with her, Jake?"

"Oh, yes, let's share her!"

"Or sacrifice her. I hear virgin blood can do wonders for the complexion."

"Does she still have her wings?"

"Of course she does, you moron, she won't lose those for a while."

I sat up straighter, alarmed by the implication that I might soon be wingless, but Jake touched my elbow reassuringly and flashed me a look that said he'd explain everything later.

"You've outdone yourself this time, Majesty," pandered another guest.

The voices blurred together in an orchestra of babble. They were like a group of children competing to see who could draw the most attention. Jake tolerated their antics for a while before slamming his fist down on the table so hard the crockery rattled.

"Enough!" he shouted above the rising chatter. "Bethany is not available for rent nor did I bring her here to face an inquisition. Kindly remember that she is my guest." Some of the demons looked abashed about having unintentionally displeased their host.

"Exactly," concurred Nash in a fawning manner. He raised his glass. "Allow me to be the first to propose a toast."

For the first time my attention was drawn to the table, laden with all manner of delicacies. All the food on offer was rich and extravagantly prepared. Someone had gone to extreme lengths to set the table so that the linen napkins, the silverware, and the crystal were all accurately aligned. There was roasted pheasant, pâtés and terrines, wheels of soft cheeses on timber boards, and platters of exotic fruits. The dusty bottles of wine seemed to outnumber the people. The demons evidently didn't believe in self-denial and the deadly sin of gluttony was probably a desirable trait here.

I made no effort to touch my glass although they were watching me expectantly. Under the table Jake prompted me by tapping my foot lightly with his. His face seemed to say, *Don't embarrass me now.* But I had little interest in helping him save face in front of his entourage.

"To Jake and his charming new acquisition," Nash continued, giving up on waiting for me to participate.

"And to our eternal source of guidance and inspiration," added Diego, giving me a withering look. "Lucifer, god of the Underworld."

I don't know why I chose that moment to speak. I wasn't feeling particularly brave so perhaps it was sheer indignation that allowed me to find my voice.

"I wouldn't call him a god, exactly," I said flippantly.

There was an appalled silence during which Jake looked at me, astounded by my stupidity. His ability to protect me in Hades must have limits and I'd very possibly just crossed the line. Then Yeats broke the tension by clapping his hands and erupting into laughter. The others followed, equally eager to gloss over my faux pas rather than linger on it and spoil the evening. Yeats looked at me with amusement in his eyes, but the threat in his voice was unmistakable.

"I hope you get to meet Big Daddy soon. He's gonna love you."

"Big Daddy?" I remembered Hanna using the same absurd nickname. It sounded like something out of a gangster movie. "You can't be serious," I said. "You actually call him that?"

"You'll find we're not big on formalities down here," Yeats continued. "Just one big happy family."

"Sometimes we call him Papa Luce," Eloise chimed in as she downed the contents of her wineglass. "Maybe he'll let you too when you get to know him better."

"I have no intention of calling him anything," I proclaimed.

"That's a shame," said Yeats. "Seeing as you're here at his behest."

What did that even mean? I glowered at Jake to show him I demanded an explanation. He smiled at me wanly as he sipped his wine. He held my glass out to me, indicating I should do likewise.

"Why don't we talk about this later, darling," he said with an exaggerated sigh. He wrapped a proprietary arm around my shoulders and tucked a strand of hair that had come loose behind my ear. "Tonight's about having fun; business can wait."

The demons eventually lost interest in me and focused their attention on eating and drinking themselves into a stupor. Their appetites were voracious given their svelte forms. After an interval of several hours a few guests rose to excuse themselves. I saw them stagger and disappear behind a stone partition leading to an inner chamber. Sounds of retching and grunting followed by the sound of running water filtered out, but no one seemed to take any notice. Then the guests would return to the table, dab delicately at the corners of their mouths with their napkins, and resume eating.

"Where did they go?" I said, leaning in to Jake.

Diego overheard and answered on his behalf. "To the vomitorium, of course. All the best eateries have them these days."

"That's disgusting," I said, looking away.

Jake shrugged. "Many cultural practices seem disgusting to outsiders. Beth, you haven't touched a thing. I hope the vomitorium thing hasn't put you off."

"I'm not hungry."

Rejecting the food was a symbolic gesture, but I knew that I couldn't keep it up indefinitely. I was fading away and sooner or later I would need sustenance if I planned to survive. Jake frowned with displeasure.

"You really should try a little something. Are you sure I can't tempt you with anything?" He lifted a fruit platter and placed it in front of me. The fruit looked plump and delicious, like it had just been picked and drops of dew still clung to the skin. "How about a cherry?" He dangled one in front of me invitingly and I heard my stomach growl. "Or a persimmon. Have you ever tried one?" He cut one open with a knife, exposing the juicy yellow flesh inside. He slid a piece onto the end of his knife and offered it to me.

I wanted to turn my face away, but the scent was intoxicating. I was sure ordinary food didn't smell this tempting. The smell seemed to lodge inside my head, taunting me. Maybe one little mouthful of fruit couldn't hurt? I felt a dizzying sense of relief at the idea. But that wasn't normal. Food was supposed to serve as sustenance, as fuel for the body. That was how Gabriel had always described it. I'd experienced the sensation of physical hunger many times on earth, but this was like a craving. Hungry or not, there was no way I was going to share food with Jake Thorn. I pushed the plate roughly away.

"In time," Jake said, almost consoling himself. "You're strong, Beth, but not so strong that I can't break you."

When the feasting was over, the party wandered in a different direction to an open candlelit space where cushions and lounges were scattered across the floor. The mood seemed less languid now as the guests began to stroke and caress one another with growing urgency. There was no coupling off, just a press of bodies with the single intent of seeking gratification. One man leered at Eloise, who responded by tearing off his shirt with her teeth. I turned modestly away when she began licking his chest and he responded with moans of excitement. Jake and I were the only ones still seated.

"Not joining them?" I challenged him.

"Debauchery gets a bit old after two thousand years."

"Trying celibacy for a change?" My tone could not have been more caustic.

"No, just looking for something more." He gazed at me in a way I found disconcerting and almost a little bit sad.

"Well, you're not going to find it with me," I said sternly.

"Maybe not tonight. But perhaps one day I'll win your trust. I can afford to be patient. After all, I've got all of eternity to try."

Eventually my glumness proved too much even for Jake because he mercifully let me retire early and I was returned to the relative safety of Hotel Ambrosia via a limousine. Tucker was already waiting for me in the lobby, ostensibly there to escort me to my room.

"How do you stand it?" I fumed as we got into the elevator. "How does anyone stand being here? It's so horrible and empty." Tucker gave me a meaningful look and then pressed a button I guessed wouldn't take us to the penthouse floor.

"Follow me," he said simply.

We got out of the elevator and walked in silence through a deserted corridor until we reached a rich tapestry hanging on the far wall. The colored silk threads had been deftly woven to depict a flock of demons as feathered and clawed birds of prey, descending on a mortal man chained to a rock. Some tore at his flesh while others disemboweled him. Even through the fabric, the expression of agony on the man's face was so vivid that I shuddered. Tucker pulled the tapestry aside to reveal a flight of steps chiseled into the stone. They seemed to lead deep underground, into the very core of the hotel. The air smelled different here, musty and dank compared with the perfumed lobby. There were no lights so I couldn't see more than a hand's breadth in front of me.

"Stay close," Tucker said.

I descended after him, clutching the back of his shirt to make sure I didn't lose sight of him in the suffocating darkness. The staircase was narrow and winding, but we managed to find our way to the bottom. When Tucker stopped, a brazier on the wall flickered into life. We seemed to be in an underground canal, filled with murky, green water. A breeze swirled around my feet and if I pricked my ears and listened very carefully, I thought I could hear the sound of voices whispering my name. Moss covered the earthen walls and water dripped from the roof of the tunnel. I noticed a wooden dinghy was moored by a platform near the steps. Tucker untied it and tossed the rope aside.

"Get in," he said. "And try not to make any noise. We don't want to disturb anything." I didn't like the way he said "anything" rather than "anyone," and it unsettled me.

"Like what?" I asked, but Tucker focused his attention on directing the boat and refused to elaborate further. While the oars sliced silently through the muddy water of the canal I sat rigidly, my knuckles white from clutching the sides. I sensed movement far beneath us. Suddenly the surface rippled as though someone were skimming stones from the embankment.

"What's that?" I whispered in alarm.

"Shh," he replied. "Don't make a sound."

I obeyed but let my eyes wander back to the water. Bubbles appeared beneath the surface just as something pale and bloated became visible. Pale moonlike disks surrounded us, floating like buoys on the surface of the river. I leaned out of the dinghy, squinting to make out what the queer shapes were and clapped a hand over my mouth to stifle a scream when I saw they weren't buoys but disembodied heads. All around us cold, dead faces bobbed in the water, their hair fanning like seaweed, their vacant eyes staring straight at us. The one closest to me had once been a woman, but now her skin was puckered and gray like she'd spent too much time in the bath. The severed head knocked ghoulishly against the side of the boat. I swallowed back the questions on the tip of my tongue when Tucker threw me a warning look.

When he moored the boat near a flat outcrop of rock, I leapt out gratefully. We were standing in an alcove that was about the size of a small inlet. In the center was a body of water shimmering like diamonds. It flowed into several tributaries to an unknown destination. It was so clear I could see straight through to the pebbled floor. The rocks where we stood had been worn smooth as silk. I gave Tucker a questioning glance, unsure whether it was safe to speak yet or not.

"This is the place I was telling you about," he said. "This here is the Lake of Dreams."

"The one that will take me back home?" I asked, remembering our last conversation that had been cut short by Jake's arrival.

"Yes," Tuck said. "Not physically, of course. But you'll be able to go there in your mind."

"So what now?"

"If you drink a mouthful, you'll be able to see what your heart most desires. The water acts like a drug, only it stays in your bloodstream for ages. You'll be able to project anytime, anywhere."

I didn't need further encouragement. I moved quickly to kneel at the lake's edge and scooped the crystal-clear water into the palm of my hand. Without hesitating I raised my cupped hand to my mouth and drank eagerly.

A gentle hypnotic hum began in the air like the whirring of cicadas. I leaned in closer scanning the surface of the water for a sign. Looking into the lake made me feel disconnected from my body, as if I were falling under a spell. Suddenly I had a sensation very much like being hit in the chest with a punching bag. When I exhaled, I saw my own breath like a glowing orb. It hovered in front of me just inches from the water. Inside it, thousands of tiny balls of white light skittered furiously. I watched the orb descend slowly and disappear.

"Don't worry," I heard Tucker whisper. "The lake is reading your memories so it knows where to take you."

For a while nothing happened and there was only the sound of our combined breathing. Tucker was talking to me, but his voice was muffled. Then I couldn't hear him at all and realized why. I was looking down at him from above. The lake and its surroundings began to dissolve although I knew I was still physically there.

A panic began to rise as a new location formed around me. At first it appeared pixelated, like a photograph someone had tried unsuccessfully to enlarge. But when it came slowly into focus, I was no longer afraid.

Instead I felt a rush of emotion so powerful it felt like tumbling headlong into a whirlpool. I was going home.

11

Reunion

THE kitchen at Byron Street was exactly as I remembered it; large and airy with views of the frothy ocean on every side. I was standing in the middle of it with all my senses functioning and yet I knew I was only a spectator watching from the sidelines. I could move freely in the space and yet I wasn't part of it. It was like watching the opening of a movie from inside the screen. It was early morning. I could hear birdsong as well as the whistling of the kettle on the bench top. The French doors were open and someone was mowing the grass at Dolly Henderson's place next door. There was a tiered cake plate with iced cupcakes that I remembered Ivy baking some days before I'd disappeared. They hadn't been touched and looked stale now. A vase of wilting cornflowers also sat on the bench, a reminder of the cheerful place the kitchen had been just a few days earlier.

In the next second the scene burst into life. Xavier was sitting at the kitchen table with his head in his hands, just a few meters from me. His posture drew my attention because I'd never seen him slumped over like this before. He was wearing a familiar fitted gray T-shirt and sweatpants, but the stubble on his face suggested he hadn't made it to bed that night.

I willed myself to move closer to him and was excited to find I could do it without too much effort. The proximity was dizzying. I wanted so badly to reach out and touch him, but I couldn't. My ghostly self had no substance and my hand passed straight through him. Xavier looked different. I couldn't see his face properly, but his shoulders and the muscles in his forearms were tense. I could feel the sense of grief hanging in the room.

The scent of freesia wafted past me, a fragrance I knew only too well. My sister appeared in the doorway and looked at Xavier with concern. Ivy appeared as angelic and composed as ever, but the uncharacteristic crease in her brow betrayed her. I could see she was overcome with worry.

"Can I get you anything?" she asked Xavier gently.

"No, thanks," he replied. He sounded distracted, as if his mind were far away, and he barely raised his head.

"Gabriel's gone back to visit the Knox place," Ivy continued. "He thinks he might pick up some clues."

Xavier was too lost in his own brooding thoughts to reply. Ivy came to stand beside him. Reading his mood, she placed a tentative hand on his arm. He jerked at her touch, not allowing himself to be comforted.

"We mustn't lose heart. We'll find her."

Xavier raised his head to look at her. His face was paler than I'd ever seen it and there were circles under his bright blue eyes. His lips were pressed into a hard line. He looked forlorn, consumed by his grief. I wanted to reach out and take his face in my hands, to tell him that I was okay—trapped, lonely and miserable but otherwise unharmed. I might not be in his arms where we both wanted me to be, but I was coping. I was surviving.

"How?" he said after a long interval. He struggled to keep his voice even. "We have no idea where he's taken her . . . or what he's doing to her." That last thought proved too much and his voice cracked.

I felt a cold lump of dread rise in my throat. If they had no idea where I was, what hope did they have of ever finding me? Neither Gabriel nor Ivy had actually witnessed my disappearance so all they had to go on was Xavier's sketchy report of what he'd seen before Jake had run him down. As far as they knew I might be held hostage in some remote corner of the globe.

"Gabriel's working on it," Ivy said, trying to sound confident. "He's good at figuring things out."

"Shouldn't we be there with him?" Xavier said helplessly.

"He knows what to do, what signs to look for." There was an awkward lull in their conversation when all that could be heard was the ticking of the hall clock.

"It's my fault," Xavier said finally. Saying the words out loud seemed to offer him some relief. "I should have been able to protect her." His eyelashes looked wet with tears, but he brushed them away before Ivy could see them.

"No human stands a chance against that sort of power," said my sister. "You can't blame yourself, Xavier. There's nothing you could have done." Xavier shook his head adamantly.

"Yes, there is," he said through gritted teeth. "I could have stayed with her. If I hadn't been fooling around down at the lake, none of this would have happened." He curled his hands into tight fists and swallowed hard. "Don't you see? I promised I'd look after her and I let her down."

"You didn't know. How could you know? But you can help Beth now by not falling apart. Be strong for her sake."

Xavier squeezed his eyes shut and nodded.

"Gabe's back," said Ivy, way before the key even turned in the lock. Xavier rose from his chair and seemed to falter forward. Minutes later Gabriel appeared in the kitchen. Even though he was my brother and I knew him as well as anyone could, his radiance still made me gasp. His perfect, marble-sculpted features were severe. His silver eyes were solemn and his face grave.

"Any luck?" asked Ivy.

"I think I found something," Gabriel said hesitantly. "It *may* be a portal. I could smell sulfur on the highway near the Knox house."

"Oh, no." Ivy moaned and sank into the nearest chair.

"Why is that important? A portal? What's a portal? A portal to where?" Xavier asked his questions in rapid succession, but Gabriel answered in a measured voice.

"There are openings in this world," he said, "that lead directly into other realms. We call them portals. They can appear randomly or they can be conjured by someone powerful enough."

"What kind of realms? Where's Beth?" There was a rising panic in his voice. *I'm right here*, I wanted to call out but my voice failed me.

"The asphalt on the highway was burned," Gabriel observed, sidestepping the question. "And everything around it scorched. There is only one place that can leave behind marks like that."

Xavier took a breath as if to steady himself. I could see the moment when the truth behind Gabriel's words dawned on him.

"That can't be true," he said weakly, his rational mind still struggling to comprehend.

"It's true, Xavier." Even Gabriel had to turn his face away in order not to witness the effect he knew his words would have. "Jake has dragged Bethany into Hell."

Xavier looked as if his worst nightmare had been realized. The news hit him like a slap in the face. His jaw dropped and his eyes stared fixedly at my brother, as if he were waiting for him to burst out laughing and reveal the whole thing was a bad joke. He stayed that way for several long minutes, as though he had turned to stone. Then suddenly his whole body seemed to shudder with anguish. My ghostly self, as insubstantial as vapor, grieved alongside him. We made a sad and sorry pair—the human boy and the apparition he could not see but who loved him more than anything in the world.

Everyone it seemed was behaving out of character in my absence. Gabriel did something then I'd never seen from him before. He crossed the room and knelt down before Xavier, his hand resting lightly on his arm. It was a sight to behold— an archangel kneeling before a human in an expression of humility.

"I'm not going to lie to you," Gabriel said, looking him

directly in the eye. "I'm not sure how to help Bethany now." These were the words I most dreaded hearing. Gabriel never glossed over the harsh truth. It wasn't in his nature. What he was doing now was preparing both himself and Xavier for the worst.

"What are you talking about?" Xavier cried. "We have to do something! Beth didn't choose this. She was kidnapped, remember? That's actually a criminal offense in my world. Are you saying it's okay in yours?"

Gabriel sighed and replied as patiently as he could. "There are laws that govern Heaven and Hell that have existed since the beginning of time."

"What is that even supposed to mean?"

"I think what Gabe is trying to say is that we don't make the rules. We have to wait for instructions," Ivy said.

"Wait?" echoed Xavier, growing more frustrated at their lack of resolve. "You can wait till doomsday if you like, but I don't plan to just sit around."

"We don't have a choice," said Gabriel sternly. They could not have been more different, angel and mortal, polarized by their opposing views of the universe. Gabriel, I could see, was losing patience. Xavier's incessant questions were draining him. He longed for solitude in order to commune with the powers above. Xavier on the other hand was not going to feel better until he was offered a plan of action. He was applying the rules of logic that state for every problem a solution can be found. Ivy, who was much more aware of Xavier's emotional state than Gabriel, gave my brother a look that suggested he should tread carefully.

"Rest assured, if there's a way, we will find it," she said more encouragingly.

"It won't be easy," Gabriel qualified.

"But not impossible, right?" I could sense that Xavier was clutching desperately to any hope, however slim.

"No, not impossible," my sister said with a small smile.

"I want to help," said Xavier.

"And you can, but right now we need to consider our next move very carefully."

"Rushing in without thinking could make things worse for Bethany," Gabriel warned.

"How could it get any worse?" Xavier demanded.

The more I listened to their deliberations the more frustrated I became. I wanted to be part of their discussions and I wanted to help them. It was strange being talked about in the third person when I was right there in the room. If only I could share with them what I knew, it might help them devise a more effective plan. Being both present and utterly useless grew so maddening that I thought I'd explode. There must be some way to make my presence known to them. How could they not sense my proximity? Those I loved most were a hand's breadth away and yet totally inaccessible.

"We can't act independently of instruction," Ivy tried to placate.

"And how long is that gonna take?"

"The Covenant is aware of the crisis. They will contact us when they see fit." Gabriel refused to disclose more.

"What do we do till then?"

"I suggest we pray."

Suddenly I was worried. It was obvious they couldn't act without first seeking counsel. It was not only standard practice but also the wisest thing to do. I could see that. But what would the Covenant advise? Gabriel had sounded so confident moments ago, but even he did not have the power to contravene their decisions. What if in their infinite wisdom they decided to cut their losses? After all, I hadn't been much of an asset when I was aboveground. I was forever stirring up trouble and creating conflicts for them to solve rather than following instructions. Obedience was not my strong point and while rebellion was expected in a human, in an angel it was inexcusable. Would this trait that had set me apart from my own kind now spell the end of my value in Heaven?

Even if the Covenant was feeling charitable and deemed me worthy of rescue, breaking into Hell would be the greatest challenge my siblings had ever had to face. It was quite likely they themselves might perish in the attempt. Was that risk worth taking? I didn't want to jeopardize their safety, but at the same time my longing to be reunited with them was enormous. As for Xavier, I couldn't bear the thought of any harm coming to him on my account. I'd rather endure the torments of the pit before I'd allow that to happen. I looked at his smooth, tanned arms resting on the tabletop, the familiar cord of soft plaited leather twined around his wrist, and the silver ring I'd given him shining on his index finger. I strained toward him, my fingers seeking his.

"Xavier!" I cried. "Xavier, I'm here!"

To my surprise I heard a faint echo of my own words in the room. Gabriel, Ivy, and Xavier all snapped their heads in my direction like satellites seeking radio signals. An expression of disbelief crossed Xavier's face, as if his sanity had just been cast into doubt.

"Am I losing it or did you guys hear that too?"

My brother and sister looked at each other, uncertainty on their faces.

"We heard it," said Gabriel, his mind already whirring as he contemplated possible explanations for what'd just happened. I hoped he didn't assume it was a demon playing tricks on them.

Ivy closed her eyes and I felt her energy in the room, searching for me. But when she reached the place where I hovered, she passed right through me and I realized that any connection I'd made had lasted only seconds and then shattered.

"There's nothing here," my sister said, but I could see she was unsettled.

Xavier was unconvinced. "No, I heard her voice . . . she was here."

"Perhaps Bethany is closer than we realize," said Gabriel.

Xavier's eyes darted around the room, searching the air. I focused hard and tried desperately to transmit my thoughts to him. Instead the opposite happened and my presence in the room became diluted. I felt my consciousnesses pulling away from the familiar kitchen at Byron. I fought hard against leaving and even tried wrapping myself around the back of a chair, but the room only dissolved around me.

Everything went black, and when the blackness cleared, I saw my body lying by the Lake of Dreams, just as I'd left it. Tucker was there, shaking me by the shoulders.

"Come back, Beth. It's time to come back." I returned to my body with a jolt. All of Byron's warmth was gone, replaced with the cold and damp of the canal.

"Why did you do that?" I protested loudly. "I wanted more time."

"We can't be missing any longer. It's too risky. But don't worry, the magic will stay with you now."

"Are you saying I can project anytime I want to?"

"Yep," Tucker said proudly. "Once a person drinks from the Lake of Dreams, it flows inside you. It shares its power. You can only reverse it by drinking from the river Lethe."

"That really exists?" I asked curiously.

"Sure does," Tucker said. "It literally means 'oblivion.' Some people call it the River of Forgetfulness. It makes you forget who you are."

"That sounds awful. Is it cursed?"

"Not necessarily," Tucker said. "Some people have done things in their lives they don't want to remember. When you drink from the river Lethe, all your bad memories sink to the bottom."

I peered at him closely. "You sound pretty sure of yourself. Do you know someone who's done it?"

"Yeah." Tucker looked at his shoes. "That'd be me."

"What were you trying to escape?" I asked without thinking and Tucker laughed.

"Not much point asking me that now, is there?"

"I guess not," I said, taking his arm. "I'm glad the river made things easier for you."

Tucker squeezed my hand, but he didn't look convinced.

We made our way back to the hotel at twice the speed at which we'd set out, fearful of being discovered. All I could think about was Xavier's hands, not tense as I'd just seen them but stroking my face the way he used to when we felt that all the darkness in the world could not dampen our happiness.

How naïve we were to think as we did then. I knew now how lethal darkness could be. It would take every ounce of courage we possessed to fight it. Even then I didn't like our chances.

12

Hanna's Story

AFTER my first try at what Tucker called projection, it was hard to think about anything else. Now that I'd had a taste of home, Hotel Ambrosia seemed emptier than ever. As the days passed I found myself going through the motions without complaint, eagerly awaiting the next opportunity to return to Venus Cove and keep up with what was happening there. So when Hanna was brushing my hair or fussing over me my mind was conspiring to achieve my only goal: seeing Xavier again. When Tucker was keeping vigil I was counting down the minutes until he finally went to bed and I was free to roam again the place where I belonged, even if it was only as an unseen entity.

Tucker was better at reading my thoughts than I realized.

"It's addictive, ain't it?" he said. "At first you can't get enough." I couldn't deny it. Being transported back to Byron had given me a rush greater than any I'd experienced.

"It felt so real. I was so close I could smell them."

Tucker watched me closely. "You should see your face. It lights up when you talk about them."

"That's because they're everything to me."

"I know, but there's somethin' you need to keep in mind. Every time you go back they've moved on a little with their lives. In time their pain dulls and you become a fond memory. In the end you feel like nothin' but a ghost visiting strangers."

"It would never be like that for me." I glared at Tucker. The thought of Xavier moving on was unbearable and I refused to so much as entertain the idea. "Besides, aren't you forgetting something? I'm not a ghost. I happen to be alive. See?" I gave my arm a decent pinch and watched a blotch of red appear on the white skin. "Ouch!"

Tucker smiled a little at my demonstration. "You want to go again right now, don't you?"

"Of course. Wouldn't you?"

"Have you always been this impatient?"

"No," I replied tartly. "Only as long as I've been human."

Tucker frowned and I wondered whether he doubted my ability to use this new gift responsibly. I decided to try and ease his mind.

"Thanks again for showing me, Tuck. I needed something to help me survive in this place and seeing my family again meant so much."

Tucker, who was unaccustomed to praise, looked abashed and shuffled his feet on the carpet.

"You're welcome," he mumbled. Then his face clouded. "Please be careful. I don't know what Jake would do if he ever found out."

"I'll be careful," I agreed. "But I'm going to find a way to get us out."

"Us?" he repeated.

"Of course. We're a team now."

TUCKER had figured right. I did plan to go back that very night. The taste of home I'd been given had only whet my appetite, not satisfied it. I wasn't lying when I told him I was going to try and get us out, but it wasn't uppermost on my mind at that moment. My impulse was far more self-indulgent than that. I just wanted to see Xavier again and pretend that nothing had changed. Whatever he was doing, I wanted to be there beside him. I wanted to absorb as much of his presence as I could and take it back with me. It would act like a talisman to get me through the interminably long days and nights ahead.

So when Hanna appeared in the doorway carrying my supper on a tray, my first impulse was to send her away. I was anxious to climb into my oversize bed and start the process that would send me home again. Hanna looked at me the way she always did, like she wished there was more she could do to help. Even though she was younger she'd adopted a maternal attitude toward me, as if I were a fledgling that had to be protected and nursed to strength. It was only to satisfy Hanna that I ate hasty mouthfuls of what she'd prepared—crusty bread, some kind of chunky stew, and a fruit tart. Afterward she didn't leave right away but lingered and I sensed she had something on her mind.

"Miss," she said eventually. "What was your life like before you came here?"

"I was in my senior year of high school and living in a small town where everybody knew one another."

"But that wasn't where you came from."

It surprised me that Hanna should make reference to my former home. I was so used to protecting our secret on earth, I kept forgetting that here my true identity was common knowledge.

"I may not have come from Venus Cove," I admitted. "But it became my home. I went to a school called Bryce Hamilton and I had a best friend called Molly."

"My parents were workers in a factory," Hanna said suddenly. "We were too poor for me to go to school."

"Did you have books at home?"

"I never learned to read."

"It's not too late," I said encouragingly. "I'll teach you, if you like."

Instead of reassuring her, as I'd hoped, my words seemed to have the opposite effect on Hanna. She dropped her gaze and her smile vanished.

"There's not much point now, miss," she said.

"Hanna," I began, choosing my words carefully. "Can I ask you a question?"

She shot me a frightened look and then nodded.

"How long have you been here?"

"Over seventy years," she replied in a resigned tone.

"And how is it that someone as gentle and kind as you ended up here?" I asked.

"It's a long story."

"I'd like to hear it," I said and Hanna shrugged.

"There's not much to tell. I was young. I wanted to save someone more than I wanted my own soul. I made a pact, sold myself into this life, and when I realized my mistake, it was too late."

"Would you choose differently if you could have your time over?"

"I suppose I would try to achieve the same outcome but in a different way." Hanna's eyes seemed to mist over, and she stared wistfully ahead, lost in her own memories.

"That means you're sorry. You were too young to know what you were doing. When my family comes for me, we'll take you with us. I won't leave you behind."

"Don't waste your time worrying about me, miss. I made the decision to come freely and there's no backing out of a deal like that."

"Oh, I don't know," I said breezily. "All deals are open to renegotiation."

Hanna smiled, her wariness slipping for a moment. "I would like forgiveness," she said in a small voice, "but there's no one here to offer it."

"Maybe if you tell me about it you'll feel better."

Anxious as I was to return to Xavier's side, I couldn't ignore Hanna's cry for help. She had cared for me and nursed me through some dark hours and I was indebted to her. Besides, I'd only been in Hades a few weeks. Whatever burden Hanna was carrying, she'd carried for decades. The least I could do was set her mind at ease if it was within my power. I shifted my position to make room for her and patted the bedspread beside me. To an ignorant onlooker we might have looked like two girls sharing teenage confidences.

Hanna hesitated and glanced at the door before sitting down beside me. I knew she felt uncomfortable because she kept her eyes lowered and her fingers, red from washing, nervously twisted the buttons on her uniform. She was weighing up in her mind whether she could trust me. Who could blame her? She was alone in Jake's underworld. There was no one for her to turn to for a kind word or advice. She had come to feel grateful for every meal and every night she slept through unharmed. I had the feeling that if anyone were to try to hurt Hanna, she would endure it like a martyr because she didn't believe she deserved any better.

Hanna leaned back and sighed. "I hardly know where to begin. I haven't spoken about my old life in such a long time."

"Start wherever you like," I prompted.

"I'll begin then with Buchenwald," she said softly. She spoke with detachment; her youthful face devoid of feeling, as if she were a storyteller narrating a fable rather than giving a firsthand account.

"The concentration camp?" I asked incredulously. "You were there? I had no idea!" I instantly regretted my interruption as I could see my reaction had halted Hanna's train of thought. "Please, go on."

"In life my name was Hanna Schwartz. In 1933, I had my sixteenth birthday. The Depression hit workers the hardest. We had little money and I had no skills so I joined the Hitler Youth, and when Buchenwald was opened, I was sent to work there." She paused and drew a deep breath. "I knew that everything happening there was wrong. Not just wrong, I knew I was surrounded by evil, but I felt powerless to do anything about it and I did not want to let my family down. All around me people were asking: Where is God in this? How could he let this happen? I tried not to think about it, but deep down I was angry with God—I blamed him. I was planning to apply for a transfer and leave the camp to go home to my parents, when a girl arrived who I recognized. I knew her from home. We had played together as children. She lived in my street and went to the local school. Her father was a doctor. He treated my brother once when he had measles and didn't even ask for payment. Esther was her name. She shared her books from school with me because she knew how badly I wanted to learn. I was too young to understand the difference between us. I knew her life was like mine only she was wealthier, she went to school, and she was a Jew. I knew the SS had evicted and relocated her family, but I didn't see her again until she turned up that day at Buchenwald. She was with her mother and I tried to stay out of sight. I didn't want them to see me there. Esther wasn't well when they brought her in and she seemed only to get worse. There was something wrong with her lungs and she couldn't breathe properly. She was too weak to work and I knew what her fate would be. It was only a matter of time. Somehow, I knew I couldn't let it happen.

"That was when I met Jake. He was one of the young officers overseeing the camp, but he looked different from how he does now. His hair was lighter and in his uniform he was not so conspicuous. I knew he liked me. He smiled at me and tried to make conversation whenever I served food to the officers. One day I was saddened thinking of Esther and he stopped me to ask what was wrong. I made the mistake of trusting him and took the opportunity to tell him about my fears for my childhood friend. When he told me he might be able to help, I couldn't believe my luck. I thought if I could do one good thing I might be able to respect myself again. Karl, that was what Jake called himself then, was so beautiful and so mesmerizing. The fact that someone like him would acknowledge my existence, let alone show interest in my problems, was flattering. He asked me whether I believed in God and I told him that the way my life had played out so far, if there was ever a God, he must have deserted us. Karl told me he had a secret he wanted to share, because he felt he could trust me. He told me he served a higher master, one who repaid loyalty. He said I could help Esther if I swore undying loyalty to him. He told me not to be afraid and that I would be rewarded for my sacrifice with eternal life. When I think back on it, I don't know why he bothered to single me out. I think he must have been bored and looking for someone to play with." Hanna paused as her mind traveled back to her dark past. "It sounded so simple at the time."

"What happened?" I asked even though the answer was obvious.

"Esther was healed. Jake restored her to health so the guards would have no reason to harm her and I came into the darkness. But I wasn't sure Jake had kept his end of the bargain. . . ."

"Did he?" I asked breathlessly.

"He made her well again." Hanna's sad brown eyes flickered up to meet mine. "But that did not keep her from the gas chambers two weeks later."

"He betrayed you!" I couldn't believe what I was hearing. "He tricked you into bargaining away your life. That's despicable, even for Jake."

"It could have been worse," Hanna said. "When I was thrown into Hades, I somehow avoided the pit. I was assigned duties at the hotel and I've been here ever since. So you see, miss, I brought this fate upon myself. I cannot complain."

"But your intentions were good, Hanna. I think there's hope for everyone."

"There is while you are walking the earth. This is a final destination. I don't hope for anything now and I do not believe in miracles."

"You have seen the devil at work," I said. "Why can't you believe in the power of Heaven as well?"

"Heaven has no mercy for the likes of me. I made a pact and belong to Hell now. Not even angels can dissolve those ties."

I frowned and sat on the edge of my bed. Could Hanna be right? Would the laws of Heaven and Hell bind her to this prison? Surely her sacrifice had to count for something. She had well and truly served her sentence. But maybe it didn't work that way. I hoped I hadn't made a promise to her I wouldn't be able to keep. Hanna busied herself tidying the items on my dressing table. They were mainly French perfumes, lotions, and powders—the sort of things Jake thought would make me happy. He really didn't have a clue.

I looked at Hanna, who was now shuffling around the room and avoiding making eye contact.

"You don't believe they'll find me, do you?" I asked softly. She didn't answer but only tidied more energetically. I felt an overwhelming urge to grab her forcibly by the shoulders and shake her into understanding. Because if I succeeded in convincing Hanna then I might convince myself that I wasn't going to be a prisoner for eternity. "You don't get it!" I yelled to my own surprise. "You don't get what I am. Right now I have a whole covenant of archangels plus a seraphim looking for me. They'll find a way to get me out of here."

"If you say so, miss." Hanna gave a perfunctory reply.

"Don't say it like that." I glowered at her. "What are you really thinking?"

"All right, I'll tell you what I'm thinking." Hanna put down her dust cloth and faced me. "If it was so easy for angels to storm this prison, don't you think they would have by now?" Hanna's tone became more tender. "If they could just free the souls in torment, wouldn't they have done so? Wouldn't God have intervened? You see, miss, Heaven and Hell are bound by rules as old as time itself. No angel can enter here uninvited. Think of it this way, could a demon just walk into Heaven?"

"Not a chance," I said as I reluctantly tried to follow her train of thought. "Not in a million years. But this is different. Isn't it?"

"The only thing that works in your favor is that Jake tricked you into trusting him. Your angels will have to find a loophole, just like he did. It is not impossible, but it is very difficult. The entries to Hell are well guarded."

"I don't believe you," I proclaimed as loudly as if I were addressing an audience. "Where there's a will, there's a way, and Xavier has a will stronger than anyone I know."

"Ah, yes, the human boy from your hometown," said Hanna ruefully. "I have heard some talk about him."

"What have you heard?" I asked, fired up by her mention of Xavier.

"The prince is very envious of him," said Hanna. "He has every blessing a human could ask for—beauty, strength, and courage. He is unafraid of death and he is aligned with angels. Plus, he possesses the one thing Jake wants more than anything."

"And what's that?"

"The key to your heart. That makes him quite a threat."

"See, Hanna?" I said. "If Jake feels threatened that means there's hope, after all. Xavier will come for us."

"For you," Hanna corrected. "And even so, he is just a boy with a valiant heart. How can the strength of one man stand against Jake and an army of demons?"

"He can," I countered, "if he has the power of Heaven on his side. After all, Christ was a man."

"He was also the Son of God, there's a difference."

"Do you think they could have crucified him if he wasn't human?" I asked. "He was flesh and blood, just like Xavier. You've been here so long you underestimate the power of humans. They're a force of nature."

"Forgive me, miss, if I cannot hope as you do," Hanna said humbly. "I don't want to raise my dreams out of the dust only to have them cut down. Can you understand that?"

"Yes, Hanna, I can," I said at last. "That's why if you don't mind, I'll hope enough for the both of us."

I thought about Hanna's story for a long time after she left. Although I wanted desperately to go and check on Venus Cove, I couldn't free my mind. It remained stuck on Hanna and the hardships of her young life. I thought about how little I really understood about human suffering. What I knew about the blackest episodes in human history was nothing but cold hard facts. Human experience was so much more complex. There was probably a lot more I could learn from Hanna than I'd realized.

There was one thing I did know; Hanna had made a mistake. But she had expressed regret and she was sorry for her actions. If she was destined to live beneath the ground for the rest of eternity, then there was something wrong with the system. Surely Heaven couldn't stand by and let such corruption go unpunished. *Vengeance is mine, saith the Lord. I will repay.* Hanna was wrong. Heaven would seek justice. I just had to be patient.

13

Speak of the Devil

I had no idea what time it was in Venus Cove, but I kept imagining Xavier's bedroom with its sports paraphernalia and lopsided piles of textbooks on the carpet. For some reason that's where I most wanted to go. The thought of being in his room surrounded by his things made my heart race with longing. Where was Xavier right at this very moment? Was he happy or sad? Was he thinking about me? One thing I knew with certainty was that Xavier possessed the kind of decency that made heroes out of mortals. He had never abandoned his friends in times of need and he wasn't about to abandon me now.

I felt cold and saw that the embers in the grate were dying. I reached for the wine-colored throw draped over the foot of my bed and wrapped myself in it. The candles were burned almost to the wick and cast strange elongated shadows across the walls.

Having decided that I would not be left to languish in Jake's airless kingdom somehow made me feel calmer. As soon as I felt the first waves of sleep, I focused my energy on reconnecting with Xavier in my mind. My body grew heavier and yet I felt an indescribable lightness. It was not possible to pinpoint the exact moment of scission, when matter and spirit chose to follow different paths, but I knew it was happening the minute the details of my hotel room blurred and suddenly the plaster rose on the ceiling was in front of my nose. All I had to do then was allow myself to drift.

As I drifted, like a humming vibration, I travelled through time and space and over water until I reached my final resting place. I was standing in Xavier's bedroom. I didn't land there so much as blow in like a wind under the door. Xavier had thrown himself full length across his bed and was lying on his stomach, face buried in the pillow. He hadn't even bothered to take off his shoes. On the floor a hefty volume of the Princeton Review's *Best 371 Colleges* lay abandoned. His mom, Bernie, had arranged a copy for me too—insisting we both had to make a list of our top ten choices. I smiled at the memory, recalling the conversation Xavier and I had had only days before the Halloween party. We'd been lying on the south lawn taking turns reading aloud the most interesting statistics about our short-listed schools.

"We're going to the same college, right?" he'd asked, but it was more of a statement than a question.

"I hope so," I replied. "But I guess it depends on whether *they* want to station me somewhere else."

"*They* can just butt out. No more ifs, Beth," Xavier said. "We tell them what we want now. We've been through enough to have earned that right."

"Okay," I said and meant it. I took the hefty volume from him and flipped causally through the pages.

"What about Penn State?" I asked, trailing my finger down the index.

"Are you kidding? My parents would have a combined coronary."

"Why? What's wrong with it?"

"It's known as a party school."

"I thought the choice was up to you."

"It is, but that doesn't mean they're not rooting for Ivy League. Or at least somewhere like Vanderbilt."

"University of Alabama?" I asked. "Molly and the girls have applied there. They want to be sorority sisters."

"Another three years with Molly?" Xavier wrinkled his nose teasingly.

"I like the sound of Ole Miss," I said dreamily. "What do you think? Oxford would be just like here, our own little world."

Xavier smiled. "I think I like that idea. And it's close to home. Put it on the list."

The conversation replayed itself in my head as if it had happened yesterday. Now, here was Xavier, slumped on his bed, all plans for the future abandoned. He flipped over to lie on his back, eyes staring blankly at the ceiling. He looked lost in thought and his face showed visible signs of exhaustion. I knew him well enough to be able to read his mood. He was thinking: *What now? What do I do now? What more can I do?* Xavier's rational side was very strong. It was the reason so many people brought their problems to him. Even students he didn't know very well would come to him for advice on which AP class to take or what sport to try out for. Whatever the question they rarely walked away disappointed. Xavier had this uncanny ability to examine a problem from all angles at once. In fact, the tougher the problem, the more determined he was to solve it. Except the one facing him now floored him completely. This time it didn't matter how many angles he considered it from. He had no answers and I knew it was killing him. Helpless was not something Xavier was accustomed to feeling.

I thought of all the things I so badly wanted to whisper to him. *Don't worry. We'll work this out. We always do. We're invincible, remember?* It felt strange, our roles being suddenly reversed. This time it was my job to try and get Xavier through. I willed myself forward so I was hovering just inches away from his face. His eyes were half open, slivers of sky, but melancholy, missing their usual brilliance. His light walnut-colored hair fell across the pillow and his lashes glistened with unshed tears. The wave of emotion that hit me was so strong I almost had to turn away. Xavier was never like this. His eyes were full of life even when he was being serious. He could brighten a room just by entering it. This was the senior class president of Bryce Hamilton; respected and loved by the entire school population. He was the one person nobody ever spoke a bad word against. I hated seeing him so defeated.

A tentative tapping at Xavier's door startled me so much I flew across the room, generating a rush of wind that almost overturned a chair, but Xavier barely seemed to notice. A few moments later, the door opened a crack and Bernie stuck her head into the room. She looked apologetic for interrupting his privacy, but as soon as she saw her son lying listlessly on the bed, concern flooded her face. She covered it quickly with feigned cheerfulness. I could see in her expression her love for Xavier and her intense desire to protect him. He looked so beautiful he could have been an angel himself, but so profoundly sad, it frightened me.

"Can I get you anything?" Bernie asked. "You hardly touched your dinner."

"No, thanks, Mom." Xavier's voice was flat and lifeless. "I just need some sleep."

"What's going on with you, honey?" Bernie inched toward the bed and tentatively sat down. She looked wary; worried that invading the space of her troubled teenage son might not be the wisest idea. Xavier's unresponsiveness told her he wanted to be alone. "I've never seen you like this before. Is it girl trouble?"

I realized his mother had no idea what'd happened. He hadn't told her I was missing. I guessed it was because she'd want to contact the sheriff, demand to know why they weren't investigating my disappearance more thoroughly.

"You could say that," Xavier said.

"Oh, well, these things have a way of sorting themselves out." She laid a hand gently on his shoulder. "And you know your father and I are always here if you need us."

"I know that, Mom. Don't worry about me. I'll be fine."

"Don't take it so hard," Bernie said. "When you're young everything feels a hundred times worse than it is. I don't know what happened between you and Beth, but it can't be so bad."

Xavier let out a short, humorless laugh and I guessed what he was thinking. He wanted to say, "Well, Mom, my girlfriend was abducted by a demon ex-student of Bryce Hamilton and dragged into Hell on the back of a motorbike and right now we've got no idea how to bring her back. So, yeah, actually it is that bad."

But instead he shifted his weight to look across at her. "Just let it go, Mom," he said. "This is my problem. I'll be okay."

I could see in his eyes that he didn't want to worry her. My family was already beside themselves; there was no sense in getting Bernie involved. The less she knew, the better for everyone. My disappearance wasn't an easy thing to explain and not exactly the news you'd want to break to an overprotective parent just before you were due to take your SATs.

"Okay." Bernie leaned down to kiss his forehead. "But, Xavier, hon . . ."

"Yeah?" He looked up but couldn't hold her gaze.

"She'll be back." Bernie gave him a knowing smile. "Everything will work out fine." Then she got up and slipped out the door, closing it softly behind her.

When she was gone, Xavier finally allowed his exhaustion to overcome him. He kicked off his shoes and rolled onto his side. I was glad that soon he would fall into a deep sleep and the torment of feeling so helpless would disappear, at least for a few hours. Just before physical exhaustion took over his body I saw him rummage under his pillow and withdraw something I recognized immediately as one of my cotton knit sweaters. I'd worn it a lot over the summer on cool evenings. It was a pale aqua color and had tiny daisies embroidered around the neckline. He said he liked the way it brought out the auburn streaks in my hair. Xavier pushed his pillow aside and buried his face in my sweater, inhaling deeply. He stayed that way a long time until his breathing changed and became deeper and more regular, and I knew he'd fallen asleep. I sat cross-legged on his bed, watching over him as a mother might over a sick child. I stayed that way until weak beams of pre-dawn light fell over the rumpled bedclothes and Xavier's eyelids began to flutter.

"Rise and shine, doll face!"

Who did that voice belong to? Xavier wasn't awake yet and he hadn't moved or spoken in his sleep. It didn't sound like him anyway. I looked around me, but Xavier's room was empty apart from the two of us. A metallic sound like a door opening made me jump and a doorway materialized in the room, a dark figure leaning against the frame. Suddenly I knew what was happening. My two worlds were blurring, which meant I had to act quickly. I had to get back right now or Jake would wonder why I wasn't waking up. But why was it so hard to tear myself away?

"Sweet dreams, my love," I whispered to Xavier. I bent down to press my specter mouth against his forehead. I didn't know whether he felt anything or not, but he stirred in his sleep and mumbled my name. I saw that his face had cleared and he looked more peaceful. "I'll be back as soon as I can."

I forced myself to return to my body and blinked away the sleep to see Jake watching me intently. He was dressed in a fitted suit jacket over skinny jeans and looked slightly rumpled. The sting of disappointment always followed my return to Hades, but with Jake there it was even worse. I couldn't summon the energy to drag myself out of bed and face another day as bleak as the last. So I decided to stay curled under the covers, at least until Hanna came to coax me out. Jake seemed undeterred by my lack of response.

"I didn't realize you were still asleep. I only dropped by to give you this token of my affection."

I groaned and rolled over.

Jake casually tossed a long-stemmed rose on the pillow.

"Could you be any more clichéd?"

He feigned indignation. "You really shouldn't insult me. That's no way to talk to your other half."

"You're not my other half! We are nothing except enemies," I said.

Jake put one hand across his heart. "Now, that hurts."

"Is there something you want?" I demanded angrily. I couldn't believe I had cut short my visit for this.

"Someone's in a foul mood," Jake commented.

"I wonder why?" Sarcasm was hard to avoid when he was being deliberately obtuse.

Jake laughed softly, his bright eyes boring into mine. He slid closer to me so fast that I barely noticed the movement until he was bent over me, dark hair falling over his shoulders. His face was beautiful in the dim light, his features refined. I was surprised at my ability to register his beauty while at the same time hate him with as much strength as there was left in my body. His bloodless lips parted, and I heard him breathing fast. His black eyes slid over my body, but instead of leering as I expected, he frowned.

"I don't like to see you so sad," he murmured. "Why won't you let me make you happy?" I looked at him with surprise.

Not only did Jake persist in invading my personal space whatever the hour, his insistence on describing the two of us as a potential couple was becoming disturbing. "I know you haven't developed an emotional attachment toward me just yet, but I think we can work on it. I was thinking it might help if we took our relationship to the next level . . . ," he trailed off meaningfully. "We both have needs, after all."

"Don't even suggest it," I warned, sitting up and glaring at him. "Don't you dare."

"Why not? It's a perfectly natural expectation. Besides, it might improve your mood." He rubbed his thumbs in slow circles up and down my arms. "My skills are legendary. You don't even have to do anything. I'll take care of you."

"Are you delusional? I am *not* having sex with you," I said in disgust. "Besides, why do you need that from me? Don't you have your call girls on speed dial?"

"Bethany, my dear, I am not asking for sex. That's not what I'm about. I can have that anytime. I want to make love to you."

"Stop saying that stuff and get away from me."

"I know you find me attractive. That much I remember."

"That was a long time ago, before I knew what you are." I looked away, barely attempting to hide my contempt.

Jake straightened and glared at me. "I'd hoped we could come to a mutual arrangement, but now I see you might need an incentive to help change your mind."

"What's that supposed to mean?"

"It means I need to find a more creative approach." There was an underlying threat in his words that frightened me, but I wasn't about to let him know that.

"Don't bother. It won't make any difference."

"We'll see." My conversations with Jake always seemed to go the same way. He started by propositioning me with something and when I fended him off, he turned vindictive. We seemed to go around in circles. It was time to try a different strategy.

"Too much would have to change for me to even consider it," I added. I hated that I was getting caught up in his manipulative games, but I had no other choice.

Jake's face lit up with anticipation.

"Such as?"

"For starters you'd have to start respecting my privacy. I hate the way you barge in here unannounced whenever you feel like it. I would like a key to my own room. If you want to see me, you need to ask first."

"Fine. Consider it done. What else?"

"I want to be able to move around freely."

"Beth, you don't seem to understand how dangerous it is out there. But I can tell the hotel staff to back off. See? I can compromise." He trailed a finger along my bottom lip and smirked, pleased with the new developments.

"There's one more thing. I want to go back—just for an hour. I need to tell my family and Xavier that I'm all right."

Jake laughed. "What kind of idiot do you take me for?"

"So you don't trust me?"

"Let's not play games. We both know each other too well and you're no good at lying anyhow."

I noticed a shift in his countenance and knew I shouldn't have mentioned Xavier. It always set him off.

"Have you noticed that time's passing and nothing's happening?" Jake asked. "I don't see a rescue team on the horizon. Want to know why? Because it's an impossible mission. It might take them centuries to crack the right portal, if they ever do. By that time, Xavier will be nothing but a maggot-ridden pile in the ground. So you see, Beth, you don't have a choice. If I were you I'd seize the day, make the most of the opportunities in front of you. Everything down here is yours for the taking. I'm offering you a chance to be queen of Hades. Everyone would bow down to you. Think about it, that's all I'm asking."

My stomach twisted into a knot. I didn't know how long I could hold out against Jake. He was so unscrupulous. I had no idea what tactic he'd spring on me next. He'd been around too long for me to have any hope of outsmarting him. I just had to make sure he didn't get into my head. It was my only weapon. I had to stay true to myself and remain spiritually stronger than him. I closed my eyes and focused on inviting positive thoughts.

I tried to visualize how my release from Hades might come about. I imagined Gabriel and Ivy storming through the gates of Hell and carrying me to safety. Their enveloping wings, soft as satin yet powerful enough to crush through walls, would shield me. I imagined Xavier with them, only transformed as an angel so that he had his own beating wings. They reared behind him vibrating with his power. Xavier was glorious in the form of an immortal. Any man who saw him would pledge his undying loyalty. The vision of the three of them, glowing agents of Heaven coming for me, was the only thing that worked to calm my fears.

On the downside, it made me painfully aware of my own wings, bound tight beneath my clothing. I'd been so caught up in my troubles that I'd neglected to think about them. I wriggled uncomfortably, longing to set them free. Jake regarded me with a suspicious gaze.

"You will succumb to me, Bethany," he said, sweeping toward the door. "It's only a matter of time."

14

Messenger

THE next time I managed to project it was raining heavily at Byron. The noise of the rain on the roof drowned out all other sound. It filled the eaves and poured off them in streams. It flattened the grass as if someone had been out there with an iron and turned the garden beds to slush. The noise woke Phantom from his sleep and drew him to the French doors to see what the commotion was about. Satisfied it was nothing that required his intervention he returned to his beanbag and sank down with a prolonged sigh.

Some sort of meeting was taking place. Gabriel, Ivy, and Xavier sat around the dining table. It was littered with pizza boxes and cans of soda—something rarely seen in our house. They must have run out of napkins because they were using a roll of paper towel. It told me that no one could muster the motivation for the usual routines, and cooking and shopping had been the first to go. Gabriel and Xavier sat across from each other, both as immobile as stone. Suddenly Ivy rose from the table and began to stack dishes and put the kettle on, flitting from kitchen to dining room, her white-gold tresses swinging in time with her movements. Whatever they'd been discussing it was clear they'd reached an impasse. They were all waiting for inspiration—for someone to come up with an idea that hadn't yet been considered. But their minds were as exhausted as they were, and it seemed unlikely. At one point, Gabriel opened his mouth, as though a new idea had struck him. But then he changed his mind about sharing it and his face became distant once again.

Everyone froze when the doorbell broke the deafening silence. Phantom pricked up his ears and would have rushed to the door if Gabe hadn't ordered him to stay with a silent gesture. Phantom complied, but not without registering his protest with a low whimper. Still no one moved and whoever was at the door rang again, longer this time and more impatiently. Gabriel bowed his head and sighed when his celestial gift gave him a sneak preview of the visitor.

"We should probably get that," he said.

Ivy gave him a questioning look. "I thought we agreed—no visitors."

Gabriel frowned for a moment as he zeroed in on the thoughts of whoever was waiting on our front porch. "I don't think we have a choice," he said eventually. "She's not planning to leave without an explanation."

Ivy looked as if she weren't entirely comfortable with Gabriel's directive and would have liked time to consider it further, but the tension in the room was so great that she pressed her lips together and went to get the door. My sister still moved with swanlike grace, her feet barely touching the floor. In contrast Molly stomped into the room with her face flushed and her strawberry curls bouncing on her shoulders. When she spoke, it was with her usual direct candor.

"Finally," she said angrily. "Where the hell have you all been?"

I was happy to see that Molly hadn't changed a bit, but the sight of her filled me with sadness. I hadn't realized until that moment how much I missed her. Molly had been my first friend, my best friend, and one of my strongest links to the human world. Now here she was so close and yet so far away. I saw the faint dusting of freckles across the bridge of her nose, her peaches-and-cream complexion, and her long eyelashes that brushed her cheeks. I was horrified at the idea of my earthly memories beginning to blur around the edges and was grateful for the gift Tucker had given me. It would have been too much to bear if all I could remember of Molly was a flash of corkscrew curls and a pretty smile. With my new sight, I would be able to watch over her always. Right now, her blue eyes were full of accusation. She even had one hand on her hip as she looked challengingly around the room.

"It's good to see you, Molly," said Gabriel. He looked as though he meant it. Her liveliness did have the effect of dispeling some of the gloom that had settled over them. "Please join us."

"Can I get you some tea?" Ivy offered.

"I haven't come here to socialize. Where is she?" Molly demanded. "The school told me she was sick, but it's been ages now."

"Molly . . . ," Gabriel began slowly. "It's complicated . . . and difficult to explain."

"I just want to know where she is and what's happened to her." Molly's voice broke at the end, revealing a glimpse of the emotion she was struggling to contain. "I'm not leaving until I get some answers."

Ivy stood stiffly, her long, slender fingers tracing the patterns on the linen tablecloth. "Bethany has gone away for a while," she said. My sister wasn't any better than I was at twisting the truth; honesty was too ingrained in her. Her voice came out sounding too rehearsed and her face betrayed her. "She was offered an opportunity to study abroad and decided to take it."

"Sure she did. And left without telling any of her friends?"

"Well, it was all very last minute," my sister said. "I'm sure she would have told you if there'd been more time."

"What a load of crap!" Molly cut in. "I'm not buying it. I've already lost one best friend; I'm not going to lose another one. I don't want to hear any more lies."

Xavier pushed back his chair and went to stand by the mantelpiece. As he did he took a deep breath and exhaled loudly. Molly's head whipped in his direction.

"Don't think you're off the hook," she snapped, marching over to him. Xavier didn't even raise his head as she berated him. "For months I haven't been able to drag Beth away from your side and now she's suddenly vanished off the face of the earth and you're standing here twiddling your thumbs."

I winced at Molly's words, knowing how much they would hurt Xavier. He was beating himself up enough without her criticism to add to his stress. "I may not be a mathlete, but I'm not a total idiot," she continued. "I know something's up.

If Beth had gone away for a while, there's no way you'd still be here. You'd have gone with her."

"I wish I could have," Xavier said, his voice ragged with emotion. He kept his gaze fixed on the floor.

"What's that supposed to mean?" Molly's face grew pale as she assumed the worst. Fearing he'd said too much, Xavier backed away from her. He looked so overwhelmed by the situation that Gabriel felt the need to take over.

"Bethany is not in Venus Cove anymore," he explained calmly. "She's not even in Georgia anymore . . . but she had no choice in the matter."

"That makes no sense. I asked you not to lie to me!"

"Molly." Gabriel crossed the room in two long strides and took a firm hold of her shoulders. She stared up at him the way you do when someone you thought you knew does something completely out of character. I was standing so close I could almost feel her tremor of surprise. Gabriel had never touched her before in all the time she'd known him and she could see in his eyes that he was shaken by whatever had transpired. "We think we know where Bethany is, but we can't say for sure," Gabriel said. "That's what we're trying to figure out."

"Are you trying to tell me she's gone missing?" Molly asked breathlessly.

"Not missing"—Gabriel hesitated—"more like kidnapped."

Molly's hands flew to her mouth and her eyes widened with alarm. Xavier half raised his head dejectedly, watching her reaction.

"What's come over you?" Ivy was at Gabriel's side in an

instant, positioning herself between him and Molly. Gabriel let his hand drop listlessly from Molly's shoulder.

"There's no point in lying to her," he said firmly. "She's as close to Bethany as any of us. We're not getting anywhere on our own. Maybe she can help."

"I don't see how." Ivy's usually bell-like voice came out sounding sharp and her silver-gray eyes flashed like shards of ice. "She has no business here."

"The hell I don't," Molly cut in vociferously. "If some psycho's taken Beth, what are we gonna do about it?"

"See what you've started," Ivy muttered. "Humans cannot help us now." She threw a resigned look at Xavier. "Especially those who are emotionally involved."

"We weren't there that night," Gabriel retorted. "Humans are the only witnesses we've got."

"Excuse me." Molly stared at them. "Did you just call me a human? I'm pretty sure I'm not the only human in the room." Gabriel ignored her comment and decided to pursue his own line of thinking.

"What's the last thing you remember Bethany saying or doing on the night of Halloween?"

I saw the air around Ivy ripple and shimmer slightly and knew that she was trying to contain her disapproval. She obviously found Gabriel's decision to involve Molly objectionable. She closed her eyes and breathed through clenched teeth. I could read my sister's face. It was as if she were readying herself for a decision she knew would end in disaster.

"Well, she was upset . . . ," Molly began and then hesitated.

"What about?"

"Well, we planned to have this séance at the party. It was just for fun. Beth wasn't happy about it from the start. She thought it was a bad idea and kept telling us not to get involved. We didn't listen and did it anyway. Then things started to get weird and we all got a bit freaked out."

Molly had given her account without taking a breath, trying hard to sound casual. Listening to her, Ivy's eyes flew open and her perfect, pale hands instinctively curled into fists. "What did you say?" she asked in a low voice.

"I said we got all freaked out and . . ."

"No, before that. You said you performed a séance?"

"Well, yeah, but we were just screwing around, it was Halloween."

"Foolish girl," Ivy hissed. "Didn't your parents ever teach you not to play around with things you don't understand?"

Molly looked taken aback. "Just chill, Ivy," she said. "What's the big deal? What does a stupid séance have to do with this?"

"It has everything to do with this," Ivy said, talking almost to herself now. "In fact, I would bet my life that the séance is what began it." She and Gabriel shared a knowing look. She was really only talking to him now. "It must have opened a portal. Without one there's no way he could have returned to Venus Cove after we banished him."

"Huh?" Molly asked blankly. I could almost see the wheels turning in her head as she struggled to put together the cryptic fragments of information being thrown at her. I wanted to shout out and tell them to stop—they were giving too much away. It was unauthorized by Heaven and might end up adding to their problems.

Xavier suddenly came to life. He spun around to face Ivy while shooting Molly a murderous look.

"You think the séance is what raised him?" he asked.

"Raised who?" Molly interrupted loudly.

"They can be a lot more powerful than most people realize," my sister said. "Gabe, do you think this could be a lead?"

"I think all information is worth considering. It's imperative that we find a way to break through."

"Break through what?" Molly demanded. She was looking baffled and hurt at being excluded from the conversation. My siblings were forgetting their manners and would normally never be this inconsiderate. I knew that finding me was the only thing on their minds. It was so all-consuming that they forgot about poor Molly trying to keep up with their discussion.

"But how do we find a gateway?" Ivy murmured. "Do you think we could attempt a séance again? No, that's too dangerous. Who knows what we might let out of the pit."

"What pit? Where?" Molly's voice had gone up several octaves.

"Shut up!" Xavier burst out. I'd never seen him this irate. "Just shut up just for two seconds!"

Molly looked offended for a moment before her eyes narrowed in hostility. "You shut up!" she yelled back at Xavier.

"Great comeback," Xavier muttered. "Do you always have to be so immature?"

"Pretty sure I'm the only sane person in this room right now," Molly said. "You're all out of your freaking minds."

"You don't know what you're talking about," Xavier said darkly. "Isn't there some quarterback you should be chasing around right now?"

"How dare you!" Molly yelled. "Did Tara say something to you? Don't listen to anything she says, she's just pissed because . . ."

"Cut it out!" Xavier threw his hands up in frustration. "We don't care about you and Tara and your petty adolescent disputes. Beth is *missing* and you're not helping so why don't you just leave."

Molly folded her arms. "I'm not going anywhere."

"Yeah, you are."

"Make me!"

"Don't think I won't."

"*Enough!*" Gabriel's deep, stern voice cut through the escalating argument. "This isn't helping anyone." He turned to Ivy. "Do you see? Molly knows things we don't."

"Yeah, well, I'm not telling you squat until I find out the truth," said Molly stubbornly, and Xavier cast a withering look in her direction. Ivy moaned softly and pressed a hand to her temple. Molly was hard work and my sister found her exhausting.

"Bethany's friend or not, this girl could make a preacher cuss."

"Perhaps we should try explaining things to her," Gabriel said kindly.

Xavier raised an eyebrow. "Go ahead, this should be interesting."

"Sit down, Molly," Gabriel began. "And try to listen

without interrupting. If you have questions I'll answer them after."

Molly perched on the sofa obediently while Gabriel paced back and forth as he considered how to begin.

"We are not what we seem," he said eventually, choosing his words carefully. "It's hard to explain, but first it's important that you trust me. Do you trust me, Molly?"

Molly appraised him slowly from head to foot. He was so beautiful that I saw her face become wistful as she took him in. I wondered whether she'd be able to concentrate. Blond hair framed his sculpted face and his silver eyes gazed at her attentively. A faint golden light seemed to radiate several inches around him, trailing after him like a misty haze.

"Of course, I do," she murmured. I could see she liked being the focus of his undivided attention and she wanted it to last. "If you're not what you seem, then what are you?"

"That, I cannot tell you," Gabriel replied.

"Or what, you'd have to kill me?" Molly rolled her eyes, looking droll.

"No," Gabriel replied in an even voice. "But the truth might compromise your safety and ours."

"Does *he* know the truth?" Molly jerked her thumb in Xavier's direction. I got the feeling their relationship was on a downward spiral and wished I could be there to heal the rift.

"He is an exception," Ivy said flatly.

"Really? Why can't I be an exception too?"

"You wouldn't believe the truth if we told you," Gabriel said, trying to placate her. But Molly was defiant.

"Try me."

"Put it this way, how do you feel about the supernatural?"

"I'm fine with it," Molly replied coolly. "I used to watch *Charmed* and *Buffy* and all those shows."

Gabriel winced slightly. "This isn't quite the same thing."

"Okay, well, listen to this. Last week my horoscope in *Cosmo* told me I was going to meet an enchanting stranger and this guy on the bus gave me his phone number. I'm a total believer now."

"Yeah, you've really seen the light," Xavier said under his breath.

"Did you know that Sagittarians have a problem with sarcasm?" Molly snapped.

"That would be very enlightening, except I'm a Leo."

"Yeah, well, everyone knows they're a pack of assholes!"

"My God, you're like talking to a rock."

"You're a rock!"

Fed up with the argument, Xavier scowled and turned away from her, flopping down on the sofa at the far end of the room. Ivy was shaking her head slowly as though she couldn't believe they were wasting time on such trivial matters. I didn't know what to think—was Gabriel really entertaining the idea of letting Molly in on the secret? It seemed unlikely that my brother, who had been so resistant toward Xavier's induction into our little family, would now randomly bring another human into the fold. He must really be feeling desperate.

Gabriel gave Xavier a warning look. Provoking Molly any further wasn't going to help the situation. "Molly, let's talk in the kitchen."

She flashed Xavier a triumphant look as she marched past him, but was all politeness addressing Gabriel.

"As you wish," she said demurely.

Then something happened that took the decision right out of Gabriel's hands. The room began to tremble. The floor shuddered underfoot and the light fixtures began swinging violently. Even in my spirit form, I could feel a tremendous pressure growing in the room.

Ivy and Gabriel moved closer together, not alarmed but somewhat unsettled by whatever was taking place. Xavier sprang up from the sofa, his eyes sweeping across the room, looking for the source of danger. He was tensed to fight, all the muscles in his body at the ready and his feet braced to jump as soon as the signal was given. He looked up in surprise as the glass in the windowpanes rattled and slowly began to crack down the middle. Molly was standing right in the firing line, rooted to the spot. I watched Xavier's head whip in her direction as he quickly calculated the risk in his head. His protective instinct kicked in and he grabbed Molly, pulling her to the ground. His body shielded hers at the same time as the windowpanes exploded, raining splinters across his back like a hailstorm. Molly screamed, but my siblings did not duck or attempt to shield themselves in any way. They stood still as stone as fragments of glass rained down around them, catching in their hair and clothes but causing no injury. They looked so unshakable that I imagined neither fire nor brimstone could have moved them. Whatever was coming, they were unafraid.

"Shield your eyes!" Gabriel commanded Molly and Xavier, who were still sprawled on the floor.

Thunder and lightning came first. Then a blistering white light followed, filling every crevice of the room so that all its occupants were enveloped by it. It looked as though the room had turned into a white-hot furnace, but in actual fact the temperature had dropped at least ten degrees. I felt the chill, even in my intangible form. Even though I was in no danger I looked around for a place to hide and settled for behind the sofa. A high-pitched buzzing filled the air, like static on a television, only louder and so intense you could feel it reverberating in your brain. When the angel finally appeared, he was standing in the center of the room, head bowed and wings fully expanded so they spanned from wall to wall. They seemed to fill the whole space, casting a shadow across every wall, ceiling, and floor. Light shimmered from beneath his luminous skin and dripped from his body, falling in liquid beads onto the ground where they dissolved. When he lifted his head, I saw that his face was as beautiful and cherubic as a child's, and yet behind the exterior one could catch glimpses of something much more commanding and dangerous. In their rightful form, angels were at least several heads taller than even the tallest of humans and this angel's vast and powerful form was evident even beneath the rippling metallic robe he wore. He looked so far from human; it was impossible not to be awestruck. You got the feeling that with the blink of an eye he could crumble the room and its contents to dust at his bare feet.

His boyish beauty contrasted strangely with his marble-sculpted body. His eyes shone and his face was expressionless, as though he were daydreaming alone, rather than standing before a stunned audience. His head moved rigidly, unaccustomed to the atmosphere. His fearsome eyes scanned the room, finally fixing on something the others couldn't see.

He was looking directly at me. I didn't need to look twice to know who he was; I recognized him at once as the Archangel Michael.

15

Can You Keep a Secret?

IT took a while but the blinding light finally subsided along with the roaring in our ears.

"It's safe now," Gabriel announced. Xavier promptly jumped to his feet, but on seeing the archangel he staggered back until he was pressed against the wall. It was as though he needed it for support. But a moment later he drew himself up, stood tall, and confronted the figure before him without flinching or turning away.

Angelic beauty usually proved too much for humans to handle, but Xavier had some experience under his belt. I saw that he seemed to be holding his breath as though his lungs couldn't, or wouldn't, work properly. Something as automatic as breathing had been rendered superfluous in the face of such majesty. Molly had a slightly more dramatic reaction; her eyes widened until I thought they would pop right out of their sockets and her hands fell limp by her sides. Then she let out a strange, strangled gasp and collapsed to her knees, back arched and torso pulled toward Michael as if by some invisible chain. She stared for a moment longer, before her eyes rolled back in her head and she slumped down in a dead faint. Michael tilted his head and observed her calmly.

"Humans," he said eventually in a voice that called to mind a hundred church choirs singing in perfect unison. "They have a tendency to overreact."

"Brother." Gabriel stepped forward. Even in his perfect human form he seemed dwarfed by Michael's splendor. "I am glad you have come."

"It is a dire situation that has arisen here," Michael replied. "One of our own has been captured. Such a transgression must be addressed."

"We are exploring every possibility, but as you know, the gateways to Hell are heavily guarded," Gabriel said. "Has the Covenant got any idea how to break through?"

"Even we are not privy to such information. Only the demons that slither beneath us could know the answer to that question."

Upon hearing that Xavier's anger seemed to override his awe and he stepped forward. "Gather an army," he snapped. "You're powerful enough to do it. Break in and get her out. How hard can it be?"

"What you propose is certainly within our power," Michael answered.

"Then what are you waiting for?"

Michael's eyes slid over to rest on Xavier's face. It was frightening to watch, he seemed to be made up of lots of different parts that were not connected but still functioned as a whole. His eyes, for one, were fathomless and completely devoid of emotion. I didn't like the way he looked at Xavier, like a specimen, rather than a human being.

"The human appears to think nothing of bringing about the Apocalypse," he said.

"Do not blame him," Gabriel answered quickly. "He does not understand the consequences of an ambush and he has strong emotional ties to Bethany."

Michael's slippery, disconnected gaze lingered on Xavier. "So I hear. Human emotion is an irrational force."

Xavier scowled and I knew he resented being spoken about like a stubborn child, incapable of seeing things from a logical perspective.

"I wasn't aware it would result in the Apocalypse," he said drily. "That would be an unfortunate side effect."

Michael raised one delicate, glowing eyebrow at the sarcasm in Xavier's tone. Ivy, who had not spoken a word thus far, hurried to Xavier's side, an outward declaration of her support.

"What are the Covenant's instructions?" she asked.

"We have located a source which may be of assistance," Michael replied distantly. "Her name is Sister Mary Clare. You will find her in the Abbey of Mary Immaculate in Fairhope County, Tennessee."

"How will that help us?" Xavier demanded.

"This is all we can offer for now—we wish you luck." Michael turned toward Xavier. "A word of advice, you would be well advised to develop temperance if you want to be a leader among men."

"I have one more question," Xavier said, ignoring the censuring looks directed at him by Ivy and Gabriel.

"Yes?" Michael said slowly.

"Do you think Beth is okay?"

Michael looked at Xavier with an odd expression. There weren't many humans I could think of who would directly address a member of the Arch, let alone detain him with questions.

"The demon went to much trouble to get her there. Rest assured he would not have done so if he did not value her life."

Michael folded his arms loosely across his chest, bowed his head, and with a flash of blinding light and a crack like thunder, he was gone. I thought he'd leave destruction in his wake, but after the light he left behind waned, I saw that the room had been restored to its original state, apart from a charred ring on the floor where the angel had landed. With Michael gone everyone looked visibly relieved and breathed more easily. Although Michael was batting for our team, his formidable presence had made it impossible to relax. Gabriel stepped around the coffee table to lift Molly into his arms and deposit her gently onto the sofa. Ivy went to get a wet cloth for her forehead. Molly's mouth was open from the shock, but her breathing had returned to normal. Gabriel placed two fingers on the inside of her wrist to check her pulse. Once he was convinced she would revive, he moved away and ran his fingers through his hair as he pondered Michael's counsel.

"A nun?" Xavier asked softly. "How can she help? What could she tell us that the Covenant can't?"

"If Michael has directed us to her, there must be a reason," Gabriel replied. "Humans are more connected to the underworld than we can ever be. Demons make it their life's work to tempt those on earth, especially those who think their faith is unbreakable. It is sport to them. It's possible that this Sister Mary Clare has encountered dark forces. We must find her and see what she knows."

Ivy stood straight and resolute. "I guess that means we're going to Tennessee."

By this time, I was getting sleepy. Too much had happened, most of it stressful. Spending so much time outside my physical dimension was having a strange effect. I wanted to feel my body again, resume the form of flesh, and curl up under the covers; but I forced myself to stick around until Molly woke up. I wanted to see how she would cope with what she'd just witnessed. Would Ivy and Gabriel be forced to tell her the truth? Would she even remember the visit from the glorious stranger or would they get away with telling her she'd slipped and hit her head?

My siblings had disappeared to hastily gather a few belongings for the trip and Xavier was left to watch over Molly. He sat opposite her on one of the deep sofas, lost in his own thoughts, occasionally glancing across to check on her. I watched him sigh wearily and get up to drape a throw across her shoulders. His display of care and attention, even after their recent altercation, was touching and made me long for him even more. Xavier wasn't one to hold a grudge. To protect those more vulnerable was ingrained in him. It was one of the things I loved most about him.

Molly moaned and raised a hand to her head. Now that she was waking up, Xavier was fully alert. He stood up carefully, keeping his distance, not wanting to alarm her. Molly's eyelids fluttered open and she rubbed her eyes with the back of her hand.

"What the hell?" she murmured softly, pushing herself up and blinking groggily. Her face drained of color when her eyes fell on the spot where Michael had been standing. I could almost see the moment when the memory replayed in her mind. Her shock reflected clearly on her face and her jaw dropped again.

"How are you feeling?" Xavier asked tentatively.

"Okay, I guess. What just happened?"

"You passed out," he answered truthfully. "Must be from the stress. I'm sorry for losing it before, I don't want to fight with you."

Molly stared at him. "You have to tell me what happened," she said. "Even with my eyes shut, I could still see the light. . . ."

Xavier's eyes didn't betray the slightest hint of his emotions. He surveyed Molly coolly. "Maybe you need to see a doctor. Sounds like you might have a concussion."

Molly sat bolt upright then and glared at him. "Don't play dumb with me," she snapped. "I know what I saw."

"Really?" Xavier said calmly. "And what might that be?"

"A man," Molly began tentatively and then reconsidered. "At least I think that's what he was; a really big, really bright man. He was all wet with light and his voice sounded like a hundred voices and he had wings—huge wings like an eagle!"

The look Xavier gave Molly would have made even the surest witness doubt their sanity. He pressed his lips together, raised his eyebrows slightly, and drew back a fraction as if Molly were certifiably insane. He was a better actor than I'd given him credit for. But Molly was not taken in.

"Don't look at me like that!" she cried. "You saw him too, I know you did."

"I have no idea what you're talking about," Xavier said bluntly.

"There was an angel standing right there," Molly gestured wildly at the place where Michael had stood. "I saw him! You can't trick me into thinking I'm going crazy."

Xavier gave up. He'd been standing with his arms folded across his chest, wearing an expression of disbelief. Suddenly he just looked exasperated.

"Gabriel," he called out. "You better get in here."

A moment later, my brother was standing in the doorway.

"Molly, welcome back. How do you feel?"

"Why don't you tell Gabriel what you saw?" Xavier cut in.

Molly looked doubtful for a moment. She mightn't care what Xavier thought of her, but she certainly cared about Gabriel's opinion and didn't want to risk him thinking she was unstable. But her doubt was momentary and vanished as quickly as it had appeared.

"I saw an angel," she said with conviction. "I don't know why he came or what he said, but I know he was here."

Gabriel maintained a thoughtful silence. He neither challenged nor acknowledged her story. Instead, he watched Molly with a slight crinkling of his marble brow. Although it would have been hard to tell by looking at his composed face I knew Gabe was thinking about damage control. Molly's discovery spelled disaster for my family. They had been loath to let one human in on the secret and only relented because they had no choice. I'd revealed my true self to Xavier without consulting them. Now two people knowing the truth in a town as small as Venus Cove could pose real problems. But what could they do? Molly had seen Michael with her own two eyes.

I wished I could have been there at that moment to comfort my brother who was facing his own internal struggle. I circled Gabriel in my wraithlike form and tried to transmit my support. I wanted him to know I was behind him whatever decision he made. It wasn't his fault, although I knew he would assume responsibility. Michael had appeared without any forewarning and there had been no time to shield Molly. When the archangels were on a mission, they did not make allowances for human frailty. They served God single-mindedly, delivering His word and His will to those on earth. When Lot's wife had disobeyed their command several thousand years ago, they'd reduced her to a pillar of salt without hesitation. They carried out their mission with fierce determination, obliterating all that stood in their path. Molly had posed no threat to Michael and he had overlooked her, leaving Gabriel to deal with the fallout. I wondered if like me, my brother was changing. Living among human beings made it difficult to maintain divine neutrality. Gabriel was loyal to the Kingdom, but he had seen proof of Xavier's commitment to me and he knew the depth of our attachment. I knew he would never break his allegiance to the Holy Seven, to his rank of arch-angels, but he seemed different than when we'd first arrived in Venus Cove. Then he had been a representative of the Lord, watching the world go by with a detached, measured outlook. Now he seemed to truly want to understand its workings.

Gabriel began to pace, and before I knew it, he'd walked right through me. He stopped abruptly and I knew by the look in his eyes he'd picked up a vibration in the air. I longed for him to tell the others he could sense my presence, but I knew my brother and how his mind worked. There was no point in telling Xavier and Molly I was there. They couldn't see or touch or speak to me in any way. It would only make things harder for them. Gabriel's face returned to normal and he crossed to where Molly was sitting and settled on the arm of the sofa beside her. She instinctively gravitated toward him, but Gabriel made no move to touch her.

"Are you sure you can handle the truth?" he asked. "Please keep in mind that it may affect you for the rest of your life." Molly nodded mutely and kept her eyes fixed on his. "Very well then—what you saw was indeed an angel. In fact, it was the Archangel Michael. He came to offer help so you have nothing to fear."

"You mean he was real?" she whispered, seeming hypno-tized by the idea. "Angels are real?"

"As real as you are."

Molly frowned as she considered the astounding informa-tion Gabriel was offering her. "Why am I the only one who's freaking out?"

Gabriel drew a deep breath and I could see vacillation in

his eyes, but he'd gone too far to back out now. "Michael is my brother," he said softly. "We are one and the same."

"But you . . . ," Molly began. "You aren't . . . how can that . . . I don't understand." Her own lack of comprehension was flustering her.

"Listen, Molly. Do you remember when you were young and your parents told you the story of Christmas?"

"Of course," Molly stumbled. "Doesn't everyone?"

"Do you remember the story of the Annunciation? Can you tell me about it?"

"I . . . I think so," Molly stuttered. "An angel appeared to the Virgin Mary in Nazareth bringing news that she was going to have a child and name him Jesus and he would be the Son of God."

"Very good," said my brother approvingly. He leaned in closer to her. "Now, Molly, can you also remember that angel's name?"

"His name?" Molly looked confused. "He didn't have one. Oh, wait, yes he did. It was . . . he was . . . the angel"—she drew a sharp intake of breath and looked like she might be on the brink of passing out again—"the Angel Gabriel."

"That would be me," my brother said almost unassumingly.

"Don't worry, it took me a while to get my head around it," Xavier added. Molly barely heard him. She was still gaping wordlessly at Gabriel. "Gabriel, Ivy, and Beth are all angels," Xavier added. "A whole other world exists around us that most of us are never aware of."

"I need to know that you understand," Gabriel pressed Molly. "If this is too much for you, I can ask Ivy to wipe your memory. If you are going to be a part of this you need to be clearheaded. We are not the only supernatural creatures here. There are beings out there darker than you can imagine and they've taken Beth. If we're going to get her back, we need to be united."

"It's okay, Molly," said Xavier, reading the fear in her face. "Gabriel and Ivy won't let anything happen to you. Besides, it's not us the demons are interested in." That got Molly's attention.

"What do you mean demons!" she shrieked, leaping off the sofa. "Nobody said anything about demons!"

Gabriel looked across at Xavier and shook his head in disapproval. "This isn't working," he decided. "I think we need Ivy."

"No, wait," Molly jumped in. "I'm sorry, I just need a minute. I want to help you. Who did you say has taken Beth?"

"She was abducted on Halloween by a demon who has been here before," Gabriel said. "We think he was invited back by your séance. You may remember him as Jake Thorn. He attended Bryce Hamilton briefly last year."

"The Australian guy?" Molly asked, scrunching up her face as she tried to tap into the memories that Ivy had deleted from her mind like files from a computer.

"British," Xavier corrected.

"Believe me, he's someone you never want to cross paths with," Gabriel said.

"Oh my God," Molly groaned. "Beth was right about the séance. Why didn't I listen to her? This is all my fault."

"There is no point in blaming yourself," Gabriel said. "It won't help us get her back. We need to focus now."

"Okay, what do I need to do?" Molly asked bravely.

"We're leaving for Tennessee in a few hours," Gabriel said. "You just need to stay here and not breathe a word of this to anyone."

"Hold up." Molly rose to her feet. "You're not leaving without me."

"Oh, yes, we are," Xavier said and I could see the animosity between them flare up again.

"It would be safer for you to stay behind," Gabriel said emphatically.

"No," Molly insisted. "You can't drop a bombshell like that and then leave me behind to stress over it."

"We can't wait," Gabriel said. "You would need to talk to your parents, notify the school. . . ."

"Who gives a stuff about school?" Molly said. "Hello? I ditch all the time." She pulled her cell phone from the back pocket of her jeans. "I'll tell Mom I'm staying at Tara's for a few days."

Before anyone could stop her, Molly was punching in numbers and ducking into the kitchen. I heard her spouting a familiar story about Tara having broken up with her boyfriend, being a mess, and needing her friends around her.

"This is a really bad idea," Xavier said. "I mean it's *Molly* we're talking about. She's the biggest gossip in town. How is she going to keep this to herself?"

But I trusted my brother's judgment completely. While I was worried about Molly being involved I knew that she could be levelheaded when she needed to be.

Ivy didn't appear to share my opinion and for the first time

I witnessed real dissent between her and Gabriel. A door slammed somewhere in the hall and suddenly she was in the room with us wearing an expression like thunder. She threw down the two duffel bags she'd packed. Her ice blue eyes kept flickering toward the kitchen and back to Gabriel. The stress of the situation seemed to have brought out a new side of Ivy. My gentle, patient sister was fading fast and in her place was a soldier of the Kingdom, a seraphim preparing for battle. I knew that seraphim rarely got angry, it took a lot to invoke their wrath. Ivy's behavior told me that perhaps my capture meant more than I realized.

"This is a serious breach of the rules," Ivy said darkly, turning to Gabriel. "We can't afford any more setbacks."

"What rules?" Xavier asked. "There don't seem to be any."

"Demons have never targeted us before," my sister replied. "They go after humans in order to spite Heaven. But this time they've taken one of our own knowing we must retaliate. Unless that's exactly what they want us to do . . . in which case they're trying to start a war." Her gaze fell on Molly. "It's not safe for her."

"Like I said," Gabriel replied. "I don't think we have a choice anymore."

"Just because Molly and Bethany are school friends does not mean we can simply abandon normal procedure."

"There is nothing normal about this situation," Gabriel snapped. "The Covenant is clearly not concerned about another human knowing our identity. If they were, Michael would have timed his arrival more carefully. You may be right in thinking something much bigger is going on here."

Ivy remained skeptical. "If I'm right, think of what we'll be facing. She's a liability."

"She's very insistent. I can't reason with her."

"She is an adolescent girl and you are an arch," Ivy said bitterly. "You've had to deal with much worse in your time."

My brother simply shrugged his shoulders. "We need all the allies we can get." Ivy scowled and pointed a finger at him.

"Fine, but I assume no responsibility for her. She is yours."

"Why are you wasting time arguing about Molly?" Xavier burst out. "Don't we have bigger things to worry about? Like getting on the road and finding this nun?"

"Xavier's right," Gabriel said. "We must put our differences aside and deal with the present. I only hope we get there before it's too late."

As soon as he'd spoken the words, Gabriel seemed to regret them. A pained expression crossed his face while Xavier's flushed with emotion.

"You sound like you've given up already."

"I didn't say that," Gabriel replied. "This is a unique situation. We don't know what we're dealing with. The only angels that ever see the inside of Hell are those that go there of their own volition, the foolish ones that are blinded by pride and turn against Our Father, choosing to follow Lucifer."

"What are you saying?" Xavier said. There was indignation in his tone. "You think Beth did this on purpose? She didn't choose this, Gabriel! Have you forgotten that I was there?"

I could have kicked my brother at that moment. Did he really believe I had chosen a path of darkness?

Ivy crossed the room in a flash and placed a hand on Gabriel's back. "What we're trying to say is that Jake shouldn't have been able to drag an angel into Hell. Either Bethany went willingly or we are on the verge of Armageddon."

16

One Heart

IT was getting harder to hold on. My spirit form seemed to be blurring around the edges, anxious to return to my body. But Ivy's words had me reeling. Could my capture really be a sign that something terrible was brewing?

Unlike Xavier, I didn't blame Gabriel for saying what he did. He was merely calling it as he saw it. It was true, I had accepted Jake's offer. I had done so unwittingly, but that didn't seem to matter. I knew Gabriel hoped for the best, but it was his job to consider all possibilities. I just wished he would soften things a little for Xavier's sake. But my brother could never shy away from the truth. His very creation was intended to embody and protect the truth. Xavier didn't understand that and I could see he was frustrated. He was used to Ivy and Gabriel always having an answer for everything. But this time things were different and their indecision scared him.

Xavier was growing restless. He sat down and then immediately stood up again. His entire body was as taut as a bow and his pent-up energy was almost tangible.

"I saw her," he said after a long pause. He spoke with a quiet intensity. "You weren't there, you didn't see the expression on her face when she realized who she was with. She was terrified once she realized what was happening. I wanted to help her, but I was too late. I tried to save her . . . ," he trailed off, staring uselessly at his hands.

"Of course, you did," Ivy said. She was always more attuned to Xavier than Gabriel was. "We know Bethany; we trust in her. We know that Jake employed the dirtiest tactic of all to win her trust. But it doesn't matter now. Jake won—she's on his turf now. The situation is delicate and the truth is there is no easy way to get her back now."

Gabriel was less inclined to sugarcoat the facts. "If there is a way for us to access the dimension known as Hell, I've never heard of it. No angel has returned to that place since we sealed Lucifer beneath the ground."

"I thought you said we needed to find a portal." Xavier's mouth was a tight line and he was fighting hard to control his emotions. Seeing him like this made my own eyes sting. I wanted so badly to wrap my arms around him, stroke his face and comfort him, whisper that I was alive and even below the earth I'd never stopped thinking about him.

"I did say that," Gabriel conceded. "But that task is easier said than done." He wore his faraway look now and I knew he was no longer present. He was locked in his own private world of contemplation. Despite the doubts I'd just heard him express, I trusted Gabriel. If there was any way to rescue me, I knew he was the one who would find it.

"I don't understand. If Jake broke the rules, why can't we?" Xavier persisted.

"If Jake tricked Bethany into trusting him, then no rules were broken," Ivy said. "Demons have been manipulating souls and damning them to Hell for centuries."

"So we need to play dirty," Xavier said.

"Exactly." Ivy put a hand on his shoulder. "Why don't you stop worrying for a while? Let us figure it out. Maybe this trip to Tennessee will shed some light. What happened to Bethany, an angel of the Lord being taken into Hell, is totally unprecedented. There is no rulebook to consult. Do you see what I'm saying?"

"I think it might be a sign." Gabriel had drifted back to the present.

"What kind of sign?" Xavier asked.

"That Lucifer's powers are growing. This could be an indication of his rising strength, even if it manifested through Jake. We have to think carefully. Rushing in could make things worse. That's why Michael is sending us to this source."

"Look, sitting around drinking herbal tea isn't going to help Beth. You two can think about the big picture all you want, but for me this is about her and I'm going to do whatever it takes to bring her home. If you're not with me, then I'll handle it alone."

Xavier rose to leave and I panicked momentarily thinking he might do something reckless. But Gabriel moved like a flash of lightning to block his path.

"You won't *handle* anything." Gabriel's tone was chilling. "Is that clear? Control your raging testosterone for a minute and listen. I know you want Beth back—we all do—but acting like some comic-book hero isn't going to help."

"And sitting on your butt acting like there's nothing we can do isn't going to help either. Beth once told me your name means 'Warrior of God.' Some warrior you turned out to be."

"Watch what you say," Gabriel warned, his eyes flashing.

"Or what?" Xavier was seething now. At any minute he might lash out and do something he'd regret. I wished I could just reach out to tell him that Gabe was right. Much as I loved him for his loyalty and determination, I knew this wasn't something that could be solved through valor alone. Deep down, I knew Gabriel was hatching a plan, at least I hoped he was. Xavier just needed to give him time to think. Gabriel was still blocking Xavier's path, their eyes locked in mounting tension. To his credit, it was Xavier who backed down first.

"I need to get out of here and clear my head," he said, pushing past Gabriel.

"Okay," Ivy called out after his retreating back. "We'll wait for you."

I trailed behind him as Xavier tripped lightly down the sandy steps leading to the beach. I tried to send out rays of calming energy and hoped he could at least sense them. Xavier seemed to relax a little once he hit the beach. He took deep breaths and exhaled in relief. He walked right down to the dark sand of the shoreline where he stood with his hands deep in his pockets looking out to sea. I watched him shift uneasily from foot to foot, struggling to overcome his restlessness. If only he could stop focusing on his own sense of failure for one minute I might have a chance of making him aware of my presence. He needed to stop mourning my disappearance and just free his thoughts.

As if he could read my mind, Xavier calmly peeled off his sweater and tossed it aside. He pulled off his shoes and left them lying in the sand so he was standing in just his shorts and white T-shirt. He looked down the deserted beach and took a deep breath before breaking into a run. In my spectral form I ran beside him, exhilarated by his accelerated breathing and pumping heart. It was the closest I'd felt to him since our separation. Xavier's movements were graceful, those of a trained athlete. Sports had always been his release and I could feel his tension ebbing. Suddenly his brain had something to focus on other than losing me. The exercise was helping. The expression on his face was less drawn and his body moved with its own rhythm now. I was aware of the muscle definition in his calves and broad shoulders. I could almost feel his agile movements and his weight hitting the sand. I lost track of how long he ran, but when Byron was just a speck in the distance, Xavier finally came to a halt. He bent over, bracing his hands on his thighs. The sun was already setting and tingeing the ocean red. Xavier's chest heaved as he waited for his breathing to slow. I could tell he wasn't thinking about anything right now—for what was probably the first time in weeks his mind was completely clear. I realized there was no time to lose. I had to seize this opportunity. The Crags were behind us, not far from the spot where I'd first revealed my identity to him by releasing my wings and throwing myself from the cliff. I had to wonder now whether I'd done the right thing. From that moment I had complicated his life irrevocably. I had tied his existence to mine and burdened him with problems he should never have had to deal with.

I studied Xavier's face, only inches away from where my own would have been. I could already see his expression clouding as his body resumed normal temperature. The physical exertion had offered him a temporary reprieve; soon he would be agonizing again about what he could have done differently. I was running out of time. I backed up so that I was drifting several meters away from him. I shut my eyes tight and focused on channeling my energy into the spot where my heart would be had my physical form been present. I imagined concentrating this energy into one swirling, powerful ball. The ball held all of my love, all of my thoughts, all of my being. And then I ran. I ran straight toward Xavier, who was staring out at the ocean, his feet half buried in the sand. When I reached him I hit him like a trajectory, the ball of energy breaking over him like a cosmic tidal wave. It was as if his body became liquid and I was able to pass right through him. For a split second, I could feel his very being inside of me, my essence and his fused together. For that one brief moment we shared one heart, one body. Then the moment was gone. Xavier looked stunned as he tried to make sense of what had just happened and instinctively brought his hand up to his heart. I could almost track his thought processes on his face. I hoped I'd gotten it right and hadn't alarmed him into thinking he'd had a heart attack. It took a few minutes for him to process what had happened, but then his expression shifted from confusion to one of pure bliss. When I saw him looking around for me, I knew I'd got it right. I was proud of myself to have broken through on the first attempt! I'd only taken baby steps, but I'd done it—I'd made contact.

Xavier looked straight ahead where I hovered, physically invisible, but spiritually more present than ever. His clear, turquoise eyes seemed to meet mine and the beginning of a smile played around the corners of his mouth.

"Beth," he murmured. "What took you so long?"

{ 17 }

Accomplice

THINGS changed for me after my encounter with Xavier on the beach. What had happened between us was better than kissing him, better than having him sleep in my bed. I had wrapped myself around his beating heart, flowed in his bloodstream, felt the electrical impulses charging to his brain. I knew now what true connection was. And I knew I had to fight for it.

Up until now I had been happy to sit around waiting patiently for my rescue party to arrive. I didn't feel there was much else I could do. Now, like Xavier, I couldn't just wait. I needed to take matters into my own hands. My determination to be reunited with him burned like a flame. I was through with playing the victim. I was through with feeling helpless. Jake scared me; there was no doubt about that, but there was one thing that scared me more and that was being separated from Xavier forever.

A small part of me felt like I'd let Xavier down. Here I was idling in my penthouse suite for the better part of each day, communicating only with Hanna and Tuck and feigning illness to minimize contact with Jake while Xavier did all the work. He was frantically thinking, planning, and putting all else aside while I waited like a damsel in distress. I was better than that. I was capable of pulling my weight and that was just what I'd do. But I couldn't do it alone.

"Tuck, change of plans," I said the moment he walked through my door. "I need your help."

Tucker shuffled his feet uncomfortably. "I don't like the sound of this . . . ," he said.

I wasn't entirely sure I should trust him so soon, but I didn't have much choice. "I want to try and find a portal."

Tucker sighed. "I guess I knew this was comin'," he said. "But, Beth, they're near impossible to find. Only a few high-rankin' demons know where they are."

"I'm an angel, Tuck," I pressed. "I might have a built-in detector or something that could help us. You never know."

"Gotta admire your confidence," Tucker said and paused before adding, "but just so you know, I've been out lookin' for portals a thousand times and I never found jack."

"We might get lucky this time," I said with a smile.

"I'd like to help you." Tucker squirmed. "But if we get caught it ain't you they're gonna string up on the rack."

"So we won't get caught."

"It ain't that simple."

"Yeah, it is," I pressed. "And if we get busted I'll say it was all my idea, I forced you into it."

Tucker sighed. "I s'pose it could be worth a shot."

"Great. Now, where do these high-ranking demons hang out?"

"I know I'm gonna get my butt kicked listenin' to you,"

Tuck said. "But all right, let's do it. Only how are we gonna sneak out? Every inch of this hotel's patroled and they're watchin' you like a hawk."

"I have an idea." I flopped belly down on my bed and reached for the service phone on the bedside table. I'd never had occasion to use it before so the voice on the other end sounded mildly surprised.

"Good evening, ma'am," said the woman at reception. "How may I assist you?"

"Could you put me through to Mr. Thorn's room?" I asked politely. "I need to speak with him."

I heard a brief rustling of papers. "I'm afraid Mr. Thorn is in a meeting," the woman said tonelessly. "He's requested not to be disturbed."

"Could you tell him it's Bethany Church calling," I said.

"Please hold."

Her tone changed dramatically once she returned. This time she addressed me like a VIP. "My apologies, Miss Church," she said in a breathless, fawning voice. "I'll connect you straightaway."

The phone rang twice before I heard Jake's silky voice purring into the receiver. "Hello, sweetheart. Miss me already?"

"Maybe," I said playfully. "But that's not the reason for my call. I'd like to ask your permission for something." Jake wasn't the only one who could turn on the charm.

"Is this a joke, Beth? Since when have you asked my permission for anything? Last time I checked you had quite a will of your own."

I tried to make my voice sound sweet and imploring. "I

just figure there's enough bad blood between us," I said. "I don't want to make things any worse."

"Uh-huh." Jake sounded skeptical. "What do you need?"

"I was wondering if I could maybe visit the clubs," I said in my most unassuming tone. "You know, hang out with the club rats and get to know the place."

"You want to go clubbing?" Jake was taken aback. I knew I'd caught him completely off guard.

"Well, not really," I said. "I just feel like I haven't been out of this hotel room for so long. I think I need to do something before I go stir-crazy."

Jake was quiet while he weighed up my proposal. "Fine. But you can't go alone," he said eventually. "And I'm in the middle of something important right now. Can I pick you up in a few hours?"

"Actually," I said, "Tucker offered to tag along."

"Tucker?" Jake laughed outright. "He won't be much use to you on the dance floor."

"I know," I said. "But he can play chaperone." I lowered my voice, suddenly filling it with disarming familiarity. "I just want to know if you think I'll be . . . you know . . . safe with him? I don't know him all that well, it's not like we're friends or anything." I shot Tuck a repentant look. "Do you think he'll look after me? He won't hurt me or anything?"

Jake gave a low, threatening chuckle. "You'll be perfectly safe with Tucker. He won't let anything happen to you because he knows if he did, I'd skin him alive."

"Okay," I said, trying to disguise my disgust. "If you trust him then so do I."

A new thought crossed Jake's mind. "I trust you're not planning to do anything stupid?"

"If I was, would I ask for permission first?" I let out a long sigh of what I hoped sounded like disappointment. "Look, don't worry about it, I'll stay in. I don't even feel like going anymore."

"No, you should go," Jake urged, anxious not to dampen my mood. "You need to get to know this place if you're ever going to call it home. I'll let security know you're going out."

"Thanks. I won't be back late."

"That's probably best. You don't know who you might run into."

"I'll be fine," I said breezily. "Everyone knows I'm yours by now."

"It's nice to finally hear you say that."

"There's not much point denying it."

"I'm glad you're coming around. I knew you would in time." His voice was low and he sounded so genuinely pleased. It was scary the way he'd built up our relationship in his head—he was completely delusional. I almost wished I could help him, but I knew it was too late for that.

"I'm not promising anything, Jake," I clarified. "Just going out for a while."

"I understand. You have fun."

"I'll try. Oh, and by the way, I'd like somewhere a little more *upscale* than last time. Any suggestions?"

"Bethany, you never cease to amaze me . . . go to Hex. I'll send word that you're coming."

I put the receiver down and flashed Tucker a satisfied

smile. I couldn't have been more pleased with my performance had I just climbed Everest.

"He bought it?" Tucker looked amazed.

"Hook, line, and sinker."

"I've gotta hand it you, you're a better liar than I gave you credit for," he said.

"I was good, wasn't I?" I jumped off the bed and headed straight for the door, eager to get out the stuffy hotel room.

"Uh . . . Beth." Tucker stopped me and appraised my outfit. "You're not gettin' into any club dressed like that."

I looked down at my floral dress and sighed. Tuck was right. I needed to look the part. I rummaged through the other items in my wardrobe. There was nothing that even came close to what I needed.

I was beginning to get frustrated when someone rapped curtly at the door. When Tucker opened it, there stood Asia holding a garment bag in one hand and a designer cosmetics kit in the other. She stepped into the room flashing a savage grin and made no secret of the fact that she was there under duress. She was wearing a leather minidress with a lace-up bodice and red thigh-high boots. Her skin was like milky coffee and she had coated it with something that made it iridescent under the lights.

"Jake sent me," she said in her husky voice. "He thought you might need some help getting ready. Looks like he was right." She threw the garment bag over the nearest chair. "This should be your size. Try it on, then we'll deal with the rest." She looked me over as though I were beyond help. Before I could say anything Asia had followed me into my bathroom. Turning away from her, I hurriedly pulled on the black-and-white bandage dress she handed me and slid my feet into the crystal-studded pumps with bows on the heel. I frowned as Asia resentfully lined up compacts and giant brushes on the marble counter. I knew she wouldn't be wasting her time on me unless Jake had expressly asked her.

"Oh, honey," she drawled. "If you're gonna hit the clubs you gotta look the part. You can't go turning up like some Girl Scout."

"Let's just get this over with," I grumbled.

"Fine by me." Asia grinned and pointed an eyelash curler at me as if it were a deadly weapon.

When I emerged from the bathroom, I was unrecognizable. Every loop and natural kink in my hair had been ironed out, my mouth was a sticky berry-colored pout and silver-blue eye shadow glittered on my lids. Bronzing powder covered my face, giving my naturally pale skin a sun-kissed look. Earrings in the shape of giant fans hung from my ears and the false lashes Asia had glued above my own tickled when I closed my eyes. She had even sprayed my legs with fake tan from a golden bottle and I smelled like a giant coconut.

My transformation appeared to render Tucker speechless.

"Beth, is that you under there?" he said. "You look . . . um . . . very . . ."

"Quit your drooling, farm boy," Asia snapped. "Now let's make tracks."

"You're coming?" he asked.

"Sure. Why not? You got a problem with that?" Asia's eyes narrowed suspiciously.

"No problem at all," Tucker said. He looked at me meaningfully, concluding that this must be Jake's idea of an insurance policy.

When the three of us left the penthouse suite and came down to the lobby, everybody stopped to watch us in unison.

My new attire may not have felt right for an angel, but it did make me feel better equipped to cope with the dangers that might be waiting in the murky tunnels of Hades. I was keen to get going and start my search for the elusive portals. I knew it was dangerous, but for once I wasn't intimidated. I felt as if I'd been kept in the dark, both literally and metaphorically, for weeks.

I purposely ignored the appreciative smiles from the hotel staff as we sailed out of the revolving doors. I was fast learning that manners and friendliness weren't the way to go if I wanted to gain any respect in Hades. Outside a uniformed doorman tipped his hat and signaled to a long black limousine that crawled silently up to collect us.

"Mr. Thorn ordered a car for you," the doorman announced.

"How thoughtful of him," I said grudgingly as I slid into the backseat with Tucker. Even when he wasn't there Jake liked to keep a tight hold of the reins.

Asia sat up front. The driver appeared to know her and they chatted briefly about mutual contacts. From behind the partition of tinted glass, Tucker and I caught muffled fragments of their conversation.

"Stay close at Hex," Tucker advised. "I'm told it draws an interesting crowd." I didn't ask for his definition of interesting. I would soon find out for myself.

The club district of Hades was very different from where Hotel Ambrosia was located. The hotel appeared to be in a more remote area while the club district was a maze of tunnels with metal doors set in concrete walls. The bouncers guarding the entrances looked like clones with their crew cuts and expressionless faces. The way the music spilled out with its rhythmic beat made you feel like the place had a heartbeat of its own. The effect was claustrophobic.

Club Hex was located at some distance from the others, accessible via a separate tunnel. When Asia flashed her pass I realized entry here was by invitation only. Once inside I understood why. The first thing I noticed was the scent of expensive cigars in the air. Hex wasn't so much a nightclub as a gaming room for the Hades' elite to wile away their time. Its main patrons were high-ranking demons of both sexes. They all moved with the agility of panthers and shared a preoccupation with vanity, which was evidenced by their glamorous attire. Not all of them were demons. Some I could see were human—not souls, but flesh and blood, like Hanna and Tuck. I understood without having to ask that they were there for the express purpose of pleasuring their masters.

The club's decor with its baroque flavor was dramatic and suggested the opulence of a long-gone era. There were classical statues, marble pillars, chairs richly upholstered in black velvet, swags of silk curtains and ornate, carved mirrors on every wall. I recognized the song that filtered through the speakers in the ceiling. I'd heard it before in Xavier's car although it seemed much more fitting here: *"I see the bad moon arising. I see trouble on the way. I see earthquakes and lightnin'. I see bad times today."*

Some guests sat at small tables with fringed lampshades, sipping cocktails and watching pole dancers wearing what looked like beaded lingerie. At the central tables the high rollers were engrossed in various games. I recognized the more established games, like poker and roulette, but one called the Lucky Wheel puzzled me at first. Some half a dozen players sat around a table watching small computer screens. The screens showed a mass of people on a dance floor. Each dancer appeared to be represented by a different icon on the wheel. The dealer spun the wheel and the player won if it finished on the icon they'd chosen. It would have struck me as mindless had I not seen for myself the torture that lay in store for the dancers in the pit.

There was nothing secret or clandestine about the patrons of Club Hex. Behavior that might have been deemed objectionable on earth was openly flaunted here. Couples engaged publicly in what could only be described as foreplay as well as unashamedly snorting lines of white powder from countertops and popping pastel-colored pills like candy. Some of the demons were rough in handling their human counterparts and the alarming thing was that the recipients seemed to enjoy being mistreated. The total absence of moral parameters was sickening.

I started having doubts about being there at all let alone seeking out information about portals. The confidence I'd started out with was fast evaporating.

"I'm not sure this is such a good idea, after all," I said, wavering. Tuck said something in response that I couldn't hear above the din of the music. All eyes turned toward me when I entered, despite my attempt to blend in and appear inconspicuous. Some of the demons even sniffed the air as though they could smell that I didn't belong. The ones nearest to us sidled closer, their shark eyes glinting. Tuck wrapped an arm around my shoulder and steered me toward the bar, where I hopped onto a stool, thankful for his protective presence.

Asia ordered us vodka shots. She downed hers in an instant and slammed her glass down while I sipped tentatively at mine.

"It's not cordial, sugar," she mocked. "Are you *trying* to draw attention or what?"

I flashed her a defiant look then tipped my head back and gulped down the contents of my glass. The vodka had no taste but rather coursed down my throat like liquid fire. I followed her example and slammed down my empty glass triumphantly before realizing it was a signal for the bartender to refill it. I left the second glass untouched. My head was already swimming and Tucker was glaring at me. Then Asia said something that came out of the blue and caught both of us by surprise.

"I think I can help you find what you're looking for."

"We're just here to have some fun," Tuck said once he'd recovered.

"Sure you are. I can tell by that look on your face," sneered Asia. "Cut the crap, Tucker. It's me you're talking to. I know what you want and I may have a contact who can offer some advice."

"You're helping us?" I asked bluntly. "Why?"

Asia's tone was condescending. "Well, I'd rather not help you, but his majesty appears to have developed a schoolboy crush, which some would call downright embarrassing. I feel it's my duty as a loyal subject to do what I can to help him get over it. And I figure the best way to do that—"

"Is by getting Beth the hell out of here," Tucker finished for her as if it made perfect sense.

"Exactly." Asia directed her attention to me. "Believe me, I never do anything that doesn't benefit me and right now I'd love nothing more than to see the back of you. Hopefully before any real damage is done to the Third Circle."

I remembered Hanna mentioning the Third Circle back when I'd arrived, but I didn't understand why it was under threat.

"What are you talking about?" I demanded.

"Asia's referrin' to the rebel faction that wants to see Jake brought down," Tuck explained. "They feel he's been neglectin' his duties of late."

"I don't believe it," I said. "How can a faction of demons plot against their leader?"

Asia rolled her eyes. "Jake isn't just a demon, he's a fallen angel. He's one of the Originals, the ones who fell with Big Daddy right from the very beginning. There are eight of them, the Eight Princes of the Eight Circles. Of course, Lucifer himself presides over the ninth . . . the hottest circle of Hell."

"So if there were only eight original demons," I said slowly, "all the others must have been created by them."

"Oh, wow," Asia said mockingly. "Not just a pretty face. Yes, the Originals run the show. The other demons have no real control, they're disposable, nothing but worker bees. The favored ones are assigned to the torture chambers or invited into the beds of the power players. Sometimes they band together to try and overthrow one of the Originals. Course, they always fail."

"What if they were found out?" I asked.

"Jake would slaughter them all."

"There ain't nothing the Originals won't do to protect themselves," Tucker said. "Jake more than anyone."

"So how does this rebel faction plan to overthrow him?" I asked.

"They don't do much," Asia shrugged. "They're idiots mostly, waiting around for a chance to damage his power."

"I thought you were his biggest supporter," I said, trying to keep my voice level. Maybe we could bargain with Asia after all. "Why haven't you told him about this?"

"It never hurts to keep a few things to yourself," Asia said.

"Are the rebels angry with Jake because of me?" I asked.

"Yep." Asia threw up her hands. "They've expressed their concerns but Jake won't listen." She sneered at me. "There's no accounting for taste, I guess."

"Aren't you putting yourself in danger by helping us?"

"Haven't you heard the expression 'Hell hath no fury like a woman scorned'? Let's just say my ego is wounded."

"Can you tell us what you know about the portals?" Tucker asked.

"I didn't say I knew anything. But there is someone out back who might. His name's Asher."

Heavy drapery across a back wall led to an alleyway where a demon in an Italian suit was waiting for us. Asher turned out to be in his mid-thirties. He was tall with dark hair cropped close and a face like a Roman emperor. A cowlick fell across his forehead and there were pockmarks on his cheeks. He was chewing on a toothpick, unaware that he looked like a cliché from a gangster movie. His nose was slightly hooked and he had the same flat shark eyes that identified him as a demon. He was leaning against the wall but moved gracefully forward upon seeing us. He looked me up and down; his curiosity quickly replaced by disapproval.

"That outfit isn't fooling anyone, sweetheart," he said. "You don't belong here."

"Well, at least we agree on one thing," I replied. "Are you with the rebels?"

"Sure am," Asher said. "And I've got exactly two minutes so listen up. What you're looking for you won't find in this district. The portals take many forms, but the one I've heard most about is in the Wasteland, outside the tunnels."

"I didn't know there was anything beyond the tunnels," I said.

"Course there is," Asher sneered at me. "Nothing living of course. Only lost souls roaming until the trackers drag them back."

"How will we recognize it?"

"The portal? Look for the tumbleweed drifting back and forth across the Wasteland. When you leave here head south and keep going. You'll know when you find it . . . if you make it that far."

"How do I know we can trust you?" I asked.

"Because I want to see Jake burn as much as you do. He treats us like dirt and we're sick of it. If he loses his conquest so soon, his power will be challenged and we might have a chance of overthrowing him."

I saw Asia roll her eyes behind Asher's back and wondered how far-fetched his plan really was. It didn't sound like Jake's authority would be questioned any time soon. Tucker nodded his thanks and took me by the arm, steering me back through the club. I assumed he knew how to find the Wasteland and followed obediently.

Before we left Club Hex I caught sight of Asher again. He was at the bar talking to Asia and leaning in close. I saw his tongue dart into her ear as his hand traveled up her thigh and guessed what she must have used to barter the information from him.

It occurred to me how devoid of trust or loyalty this place was. Everything was built on a foundation of lies and deception. It was impossible to tell who was working with, sleeping with, or manipulating whom.

I realized at that moment that even if I lived in luxury as Jake's queen, I was never going to survive here.

Portal

"YOU should go back," I said to Tucker as we trudged through the dingy tunnels. "This was my idea. I shouldn't drag you into it. Tell Jake I ditched you and you lost sight of me. Asia will back you up."

Even as I spoke the words I knew it was too late for Tuck to turn back. If he returned to Hotel Ambrosia without me, Jake would unleash his fury on him.

He must have known that too, but all he said was "You're not goin' out there alone."

"I won't let Jake hurt you," I told him. "No matter what happens."

"Let's not think about that now."

Tucker set off ahead of me at a swift pace. I had no choice but to follow.

We didn't have to go much farther than the club district before the terrain started to change dramatically. The air became suddenly sultry and the landscape barren as a desert. It seemed as if all color and life had been sucked away, leaving nothing but an empty gray husk. Fog swirled overhead, blotting out whatever it was that passed for sky down here. We had left the confining tunnels behind, but we were still trapped in a strange dimension that had no beginning or end. The worst part was the ever-present sound; all around us the air was filled with the muffled wailing of lost and wandering souls. I could feel their presence as they moved past us, like a ripple of heat in the already-stifling atmosphere. I couldn't see them, they were nothing more than a passing shimmer in the air, but I knew they were there and nothing could drown out their preternatural cries. A horrible, suffocating sense of desolation washed over me, as if my soul were being tugged from my body. My heart beat faster and I felt an overwhelming urge to stop. In response Tucker took hold of my hand and picked up his pace.

"I'm tired, Tuck," I heard myself say.

"Don't slow down," he whispered. "This place has that effect on people. We have to keep moving."

The Wasteland didn't seem to affect Tucker in the same way. Maybe it was because his time in Hades had lent him immunity. Or maybe it was because I was an angel and could sense the acute despair of every soul around me.

"If we linger too long the Trackers have a much better chance of picking up your scent," Tucker added.

I'd forgotten all about them. I knew as an angel I gave off the crisp, clean scent of rain that might be camouflaged in the smoky atmosphere of the clubs but would be unmistakable out here in the open.

"Are you going to tell me who the Trackers are?" I was still having problems regulating my breathing. Tuck took one look at my face and shook his head.

"Not right now."

"Come on," I urged. Tucker seemed to have assumed a protective role since leaving the hotel that he wasn't about to relinquish without a fight. "I'll be better off if I know."

Tuck sighed. "Trackers hunt down souls that have wandered off into the Wasteland." He kept his explanation succinct as if there was already too much to focus on without the added effort of conversation.

"Do the souls end up back in the clubs?" I asked naïvely.

"Not exactly."

"They're thrown into the pit, aren't they?" I said. "It's okay, Tucker. I've seen it." I was on the verge of elaborating, telling him to stop trying to spare me from the harsh realities when Tucker stepped lightly in front of me and clamped his hand over my mouth.

"Do you hear that?" he asked.

"Hear what?"

"Listen."

We stood in silence for a moment until I too heard the sound that had made Tucker stop short. It was a voice, breathy and high-pitched, like it belonged to a young girl. It was calling my name. "Bethany!" the voice wailed. "Bethany, it's me." The childlike voice drew closer.

I waited with baited breath as a gust of hot wind swirled around me. Tuck's hand dropped to his side.

"Who are you?" I asked shakily. I felt a presence in the wind, caressing me with long tapering fingers.

"Don't you remember me?" The voice sounded forlorn and yet there was something oddly familiar about it.

"We can't see you," Tuck said boldly. "Come out of the shadows."

"It's okay," I encouraged. "We won't hurt you. We're on your side."

I watched openmouthed as the figure of a girl emerged out of the swirling fog and began to take shape before me. At first she was just an outline, like an artist's rudimentary sketch that hadn't been properly filled out, but as she came into focus and I looked more closely, I knew exactly who she was. The powdery blond hair, the pert upturned nose, the pouting lips were all achingly familiar. Her hair was matted and her cheeks hollow, but there was no mistaking her. Her blue eyes were still luminous, their brightness a sharp contrast against the grime smudged across her face. She stared at me with such despair that I felt all of her sadness seep into me and thought my heart would break.

"Taylah," I whispered. "Is that you? What are you doing here?"

"I could ask you the same thing." She smiled absently. Taylah was dressed, much as she had been in life, in a fitted top and tight denim shorts. She was barefoot and through the dust I could still make out chipped nail polish.

"Were you kidnapped too?" I asked. "Did Jake bring you here?"

Taylah shook her head. "I was judged, Beth," she said softly. "And my soul was sent here."

"But how?" I said in a hoarse whisper. I was having trouble grappling with what she was trying to tell me.

"After I died on the floor of the girls' bathroom, I heard

voices all around me. They were weighing up my sins, calculating my good deeds. And then I was falling."

I wanted to ask what had happened in her past to land her in this place, but I couldn't get the words out. It would have been tactless in the extreme. But I knew it had to be some kind of mistake. Taylah was just a girl. She could be shallow, catty, and competitive sometimes, but those weren't exactly heinous crimes. She was capable of being cruel to those who didn't inhabit her glittering world of tanning and Pilates, but I'd also seen her capable of kindness. I couldn't imagine her doing anything seriously immoral.

"I know what you're thinking," she said, looking shame-faced. "You're wondering what I did to end up here."

"You don't have to say anything, Tay."

"No, it's okay," she said. "I'm here because I was never taught to believe in anything. I didn't understand what was important in life." She hesitated, her blue eyes glazing over. "I only cared about having fun; I never cared about anything real. I sinned and never thought twice about it."

I looked at her expectantly but it took some minutes before she mustered the courage to speak again. "I did something terrible. Well, I didn't exactly do it, but I did stand by and let it happen."

"Let what happen?" I asked.

"A couple of years ago there was a hit and run in Venus Cove and little Tommy Fincher was killed. He was out playing catch in the street. It was all over the papers but they never found the driver. Tommy was only ten years old. His parents never really got over it."

"What's all this got to do with you?"

"I was there when it happened."

"What? Why didn't you report it?" I was confused.

"Because the driver was my boyfriend at the time. He was drunk and I should never have let him behind the wheel. . . ." she trailed off helplessly.

"You covered for him? Why?"

"He was a senior and I was fifteen. He told me he loved me. All the girls in my year were jealous. I was so obsessed with him I couldn't tell right from wrong."

I didn't know what to say to her. The sin of omission was a serious offense. There were some who believed a bystander who allowed an injustice to take place was as guilty as the perpetrator himself. Taylah's only defense was her youth and inexperience. Evidently it hadn't been enough to exonerate her.

"What happened with the guy?"

"Toby and I broke up a few months later when his family moved to Arkansas."

"Why didn't you speak up then?"

"I thought about it but I lost my nerve. It wasn't gonna bring the kid back anyway. I was worried about my reputation and what people would say about me."

"Oh, Taylah," I said. "I wish you'd had someone to help you through it. You must have felt so alone."

She seemed so different from the girl I'd known. The old Taylah had been too busy fussing over her hair to worry about questions of right and wrong. I guess she'd found enlightenment now, only it was too late.

"You know how I knew I was in Hell, or *Hades,* as his royal asshole likes to call it?" she continued. "It wasn't because of the flames or even the torture. I knew where I was because of the total absence of love. You can't stay here, Beth. This place is only about hate. You end up hating everyone but mostly you hate yourself. It'll eat you up."

"Aren't you scared to be out here alone?" Tucker asked.

"I guess so." Taylah shrugged. "But I had to cut and run. I couldn't stand the clubs anymore . . . being mauled by the demons like a piece of meat."

Her words served as a reminder to Tucker, who looked around nervously.

"We need to keep going."

"Walk with us," I said to Taylah, reluctant to part with her again so soon.

We crept on through the barren Wasteland, Taylah trailing beside us, occasionally disappearing and then reemerging from behind the blanket of fog.

As we walked a passage from the Bible floated back to me:

And there came out of the smoke locusts upon the earth . . .
and it was commanded that they should not hurt the grass
of the earth, neither any green thing, neither any tree; but
only those men which have not the seal of God on their
foreheads.

How swift was God's wrath. Youth and lack of under-standing did not preclude one from judgment. Suddenly my purpose on earth had never seemed clearer.

"So you're an angel, huh?" Taylah said. "Should have guessed from all that clean livin'."

"How did you know?" I asked.

"I didn't when I was alive. But I can sense your presence now. And besides, your glow kinda gives you away."

"You don't seem surprised."

"Nothing surprises me anymore."

I didn't know what else to say so I changed the subject. "Molly misses you," I said and Taylah smiled miserably.

"How's she doing? I miss her too."

"She's fine," I said. "Was that really you on the night of Halloween?"

"Yeah." Taylah nodded. "I was trying to warn you. Didn't do much good, though. Here you are."

"You knew what was going to happen?" I asked.

"Not exactly, but I knew the séance was stirring up something bad," she said. "Abby's an idiot; she had no idea what she was messing with."

"Don't be too hard on her; she was sorry once she realized. How did you know to come?"

"I heard on the grapevine that a portal had opened up in Venus Cove. I knew that could only mean trouble so I tried to warn you. Guess I messed that up too."

"No, you didn't," I said firmly. "You tried."

"You'd think an angel would know better than to mess with that stuff," Taylah scolded, sounding a little more like her old self.

"You're right. I should have tried harder."

"Oh, don't get all sentimental," Taylah said. "You know,

you're kind of a legend down here. We've all heard the story of how you broke Jake's heart and your brother banished him underground. He's been waiting ever since for a chance to get you back."

"Does anyone know how the story ends?" I asked croakily.

"Nope," Taylah said. "That's what we're all waiting to find out. I really hope you get back to Xavier."

"Me too," I said.

The expanse of cracked earth before us seemed endless. Only the occasional boulder or solitary cactus plant broke it.

"There's nothin' here," said Tucker, defeated. "I reckon we should head back."

"We can't," I protested. "Asher said there's a portal out here. We need to keep looking."

"We don't have to find it today. It's only one battle we've lost, not the whole war."

"Don't be a pussy," Taylah told him, with her usual candor. "I want you guys to bust out of here."

"When will I get another chance?" I said in a plaintive voice.

"I don't know." Tucker looked apologetic. "But we've been gone too long now, and we're skatin' on thin ice."

The taste of failure was bitter. We'd come so close and ended up getting nowhere. We'd risked everything and achieved nothing. It was only out of concern for Tucker that I was persuaded to turn back. Jake might be angry with me, but the worst he would do was reinforce security so that I'd never set foot outside the penthouse again. Tucker was a different story. Jake kept him around for his own perverse amusement, but I knew he saw him as expendable. We'd already turned to go back when I became aware that something in the air had changed.

"Wait!" I cried, throwing a hand out to clutch Tucker's sleeve.

"What now?" he said. He was growing increasingly uneasy. Perhaps in his mind he'd concluded that we'd been led on a wild goose chase.

"Something feels different." I turned in a slow circle. "Actually, something smells different." This time I had his attention.

"Describe it," he said.

"I think it's salt," I said, suspending thought and allowing my senses to take charge. I knew that smell. It was as familiar to me as my own skin. It was the briny distinctive scent of the ocean and it washed over me like an old friend welcoming me home.

"The portal must be close," I said, detaching from them to scramble feverishly forward. "I think . . . I think I can smell the sea!"

I heard a sharp intake of breath behind me and wasn't sure whether it had come from Tucker or Taylah or both.

"Up ahead!" Tucker's voice was charged. "That's gotta be it. I can't believe you've found it!"

I whirled around to see a mess of tumbleweed drifting back and forth across the dusty red earth, only meters from where we stood. It looked twisted and knotted from its endless journey of being tossed around by the wind across the Wasteland, but there was no mistaking what it was.

I ran forward, half expecting it to dart elusively out of reach, but I was able to grasp it in my hand. It felt coarse and dry beneath my fingers but gave off a compelling energy. I was drawn to it like a magnetic force. Its unobtrusiveness made it the perfect cover for a portal. It was big enough for me to be able to crawl through and on the other side, I was just able to make out a yellow finger of sunlight spilling across white sand.

Tucker and Taylah were beside me in a flash, watching intently. Tuck's face was flushed with anticipation and Taylah's soul practically vibrated with excitement. I reached my arm tentatively through the center of the tumbleweed and felt its dry twigs scratch my arm. At its core the consistency was like dough, malleable but tough to push through. It only allowed access up to a certain point before my arm met with resistance.

"It won't let me get any farther," I complained.

I began to wriggle my arm more determinedly through the opening. I had forced myself into the scrubby tunnel up to my shoulder when I felt a gentle suction tugging on my hand. Panic seized me. What if it was all an illusion? What if the tumbleweed was an elaborate joke being played at our expense? It seemed a pretty far-fetched idea but what if Asia and Asher had been having us on for their own amusement? They were demons, after all. Trapping souls was what they did. What if I came out at the other end of the tumbleweed not in my Georgia hometown but in an even darker recess of Hell? Then I would be completely alone, not even Tucker would be able to find me. I made myself snap out of it. I remembered what it felt like melding with Xavier in my spirit form. How whole and safe I'd felt. The memory of it made me strong. Xavier wouldn't want me bailing on him when I'd come this far. How proud would he be if I actually succeeded in getting out? If I made it through, Xavier would get to see me in the flesh, not as just a vibration in the air. The thought was too tantalizing. I was counting down the seconds in my head before I would feel my feet touch the silky sand.

"Here. Let me try," I heard Taylah exclaim impatiently. I watched as she effortlessly darted above me, a wispy substance floating through the tumbleweed until she was calling out to us from the other side.

"How'd she do that?" I exclaimed, withdrawing my arm and peering through to see her hazy face at the other end. Taylah gave me the thumbs-up before checking out her new surroundings.

"Of course." Tuck slapped his forehead. "A soul can easily slip out!"

"I know this place!" cried Taylah, her voice quavering with excitement. "Beth, you won't believe where I am!" She was crying now. I saw tears of happiness streaming down her face.

"You're in Venus Cove, aren't you?" I guessed immediately. "At the Crags?"

"Yes, Beth," Taylah whispered. "I'm home."

{ 19 }

Sacrifice

"I can see your yard from here!" Taylah cried triumphantly. "The lawn seriously needs mowing."

"Is anyone out there?"

"No, the beach is empty. But the sun is shining and there are no clouds in the sky and someone's out sailing and . . . it's so beautiful here. What are you waiting for? Come on, Beth."

I hesitated. Taylah had gotten through the portal, but what would happen now?

"Taylah," I called tentatively. "Do you think you can stay there? You're still—"

"Dead," she finished my sentence cheerfully. "I know I am. But I don't care. I'd rather be a ghost, free to roam the earth forever than spend another minute in that sewer." A note of panic suddenly crept into her voice. "Oh my God, someone's out here! I can hear them."

"Calm down," Tucker reassured her. His face too was alight with excitement at our discovery. "It's probably just someone on the beach. You're on the other side, remember?"

"Oh, yeah." Then concern crept into Taylah's voice. "I can't be seen like this. What if it's a hot guy?"

"Even if it is, he won't be able to see you," I reminded her.

"Right." She sounded disappointed. I couldn't suppress a smile. Even Hell with all its terrors hadn't been able to entirely suppress the girl Taylah had been in life.

Once Taylah made it through I relaxed a little. There was less urgency now as I knelt by the portal ready to try again. I longed to join her so that I too could look out over the ocean and feel the wind whipping my hair so it streamed behind me. The first thing I'd do after that would be to run home and straight into the arms of my brother and sister. In my enthusiasm I kicked off my heels and sort of jumped headlong into the portal. Suddenly I was inside it, half my body stuck in the Wasteland, the other half looking directly at a shell peeking out of the delicate white sand. I reached out to it. I could almost feel the warmth of the sun on my hands and hear the crash of the foamy waves over the rocks.

I was not a wraith like Taylah and once inside, the portal seemed to tighten around me, like it knew I shouldn't be there. A magnetic force that had first drawn me forward now propelled me backward, but I held on. I soon heard the sound that had alerted Taylah to someone's presence. An energetic sniffing could be heard that was more inquisitive than menacing. My nostrils were suddenly assaulted by an even more familiar scent. It was just the encouragement I needed. I knew who it was even before his silky coat, the color of moonlight, came into view. I caught sight of a pale silver eye and a damp brown nose.

"Phantom!" I gasped in delight. I could only see him in fragments—but it was still my beloved dog. I heard Taylah jump back, alarmed by Phantom's enthusiasm. She'd never really been a dog person, but the emotions that hit me upon seeing him were almost unbearable. I reached out a hand and let it pass right through the portal. Phantom nuzzled his spongy nose into my palm, frantic with the pleasure of recognition. I scratched behind his silky ear and a lump rose in my throat the size of a golf ball. I had to gulp to get my next words out.

"Hey there, boy," I murmured. "I've missed you." My emotion was reciprocated by Phantom, who now began to whimper and scratch furiously at the portal, trying to gain access. Then, like a thunderbolt it struck me that Phantom could not possibly be out on the beach alone. Someone had to be with him. Someone I loved was perhaps only meters away and heading in this direction! It was probably Gabriel, who always took Phantom with him when he went for runs along the beach. I imagined I could even hear his padded footfalls on the sand. His strong, comforting arms might soon enfold me. When that happened every bad memory would be obliterated. Gabriel would know exactly what to say to make everything right again. I repressed the urge to scream out to him just in case something went wrong. I felt as if I were walking a tightrope and needed to tread carefully.

"Tuck," I said urgently. "How do I do this?"

"Slowly," he said, a look of determination spreading over his face. "One bit at a time—don't rush it."

My heart was pounding so loudly I thought everyone could hear it. "Go on now," Tuck said. "Easy does it."

I struggled against the portal, slowly pushing my way

to the other side. Once my hands were through Phantom began licking them relentlessly and I had to swallow back a giggle. The comforting roar of the ocean at Venus Cove and Phantom's familiar panting filled my ears. I pushed forward, feeling the portal first resist and then relax, allowing me to edge through. It was slow work, but I was getting there.

Then I heard the growls.

The sound was so chilling I thought my heart would stop. The low, guttural snarls were coupled with the sound of claws ripping at the earth. Just ahead of me hovered Taylah's face, now drained of color, and Tucker's hands had gone limp on my back. Even before I fully understood what was happening, I knew I had a choice to make. Tuck was still trapped in the Wasteland.

"Keep going!" he said desperately. "You're almost there. Don't turn back." He couldn't hide the terror in his voice.

But I could as much keep going as I could stop breathing. Tucker had been like a brother to me in Hades and I would never abandon him. In the next instant I wrenched myself free from the pull of the tumbleweed and scrambled to my feet beside Tucker. He was riveted to the spot, looking devastated by my decision. I peered into the dusty expanse before me that was broken only by some straggly scrubs. The sound I'd heard was coming from somewhere nearby and it was growing more insistent by the second.

Sheer terror made me duck for cover, but it also made me lose my footing so that I ended up skidding and falling to my knees. Tucker hauled me up, covered in the red dust of this surreal landscape.

"Don't move," he said. We clutched each other as the creatures approached. Finally I could see them clearly; six huge, hulking black dogs stood before us, poised to attack. They were big as wolves, slag dripping from their fangs and a demented look in their eyes. Their faces were mutilated with scars, but their bodies were robust and strong and their claws looked sharp as knives. Their muzzles were stained with blood and the stench of their shaggy fur was overwhelming.

Tucker and I stood frozen on the spot, the portal abandoned. "Beth . . . ," he said in a shaky voice. "Remember the Trackers I was telling you about?"

"Yeah?" I fought to keep my voice from cracking.

"They're here."

"Hellhounds," I whispered. "Perfect."

The lupine creatures knew they had us trapped and circled us leisurely, enjoying their power. When they pounced, I knew they'd move so fast they'd appear only as a blur tearing us to pieces.

The pack closed in, snarling viciously. I saw how rough and matted their coats were, how yellow their eyes. Gusts of dry wind carried their foul odor across to us.

There wasn't much we could do; if we tried to run they would catch us in an instant. We had no weapons, no defense, and nowhere to hide. I wanted to unfurl my wings and carry us both to safety, but they felt like a dead weight on my back—the Wasteland robbing them of their power.

I closed my eyes as the dogs dropped to their haunches in a low crouch, then arched through the air toward us. At the same time, there came a cry from behind and a moment later

Taylah appeared, standing between the hellhounds and us. The dogs were confused and landed with a thud.

"What are you doing?" I cried, trying to clutch at her insubstantial form. "Go back!"

To my despair, I watched the portal close behind her, the glimpses of Venus Cove replaced by nothing but a harsh tangle of weeds. Taylah looked over her shoulder at me, her blue eyes bright with tears. She was so small compared with the hellhounds, her limbs frail, her once-beautiful hair matted and blowing across her face. She gave a small, sad smile and shook her head. "Taylah, I mean it!" I yelled. "Don't do this. You have a chance to be free. Take it."

"I want to make things right," she said.

"No." I shook my head vehemently. "Not like this."

"Please," she said. "Let me, for once in my life, do the right thing."

The hellhounds gnashed their teeth, saliva pooling on the ground. Tucker and I were forgotten as they concentrated on their new target. After all, they were trained to search out souls who had fled into the Wasteland, hoping for escape. Their natural instinct drew them to Taylah.

She spoke quickly. There wasn't much time. "If I go back I'll only wander the earth for the rest of eternity. But you . . ." She fixed me with her intense gaze. "You can make a difference and the world needs all the help it can get. I have to play my part. Besides," she gave a casual laugh, "what can they do to me?"

Before I could object further, Taylah turned to face the creatures.

"Hey, you!" The dogs cocked their heads, grizzly fangs glinting in the dull light. "Yeah, you, ugly mutts," she continued. "Catch me if you can!"

And then she sprinted. It was the signal the hellhounds had been waiting for. All six bolted after her, completely forgetting our presence. I watched in horror as one caught the pocket of her shorts in his muzzle and dragged her through the dirt like a rag doll. Taylah wasn't flesh and blood but that didn't stop the dogs' jaws snapping as they clamored over her lifeless form like vultures. Then the leader of the pack secured her in his teeth before bounding away, Taylah's blond hair trailing in the dust. The pack followed close behind.

I felt my chest heave with violent sobs. Taylah was gone and the portal was already drifting away, no use to us anymore. Then Tucker grabbed my arm so hard it hurt.

"Run!" he said, tearing his gaze away from the bloodied rags on the ground. "We have to run."

And so we did.

WHEN we got back to Club Hex we were so disheveled and out of breath that the bouncer took one look at us and refused us entry. We had to call Asia to vouch for us. When she came to the door she couldn't hide her shock at our return.

"What the hell are you doing here?" she growled between clenched teeth. The bouncer shot her a strange look and she ushered us quickly inside. When the darkness and the pulse of the music enveloped us, she spun around again. "The hounds should have ripped you to shreds."

I looked at Asia closely, the savage look in her black eyes, the hostile, clenched shoulders and realized what she'd wanted all along. She had sent us out into the Wasteland knowing the hellhounds would drag Tuck into the pit and probably dismember me. What she hadn't counted on was Taylah showing up and saving both our skins.

"You really should have mentioned them," I said as breezily as I could. All I wanted to do was cry, but I refused to give Asia the satisfaction. "Running into the hounds kind of tripped us up."

"Why aren't you dead?" Asia stepped forward like she wanted to rip my throat out.

"I guess I'm just lucky," I said defiantly.

"Stop it," Tucker interrupted, too shaken by what'd happened to remember his place. "Let me just take Beth home."

"No." Asia grabbed my arm, digging her talon-like nails into me. "I want you gone."

"Don't touch her." Tucker shook me free and flashed Asia a dark look. She narrowed her eyes viciously.

"Who do you think you're talking to, boy?" she snarled. "Maybe I should mention to Jake the little expedition you just went on."

"Go ahead." Tucker shrugged his broad shoulders. "He'll probably be kinda pissed when he finds out you helped us. I'm just a farm boy, but he really thought he could trust you."

Asia drew back, fury spreading across her feline features.

"C'mon, Beth," Tucker said. "We're leaving."

"Don't think I won't find another way to dispose of you," Asia called after my retreating back. "This isn't over!"

I couldn't worry about Asia's jealousy or her animosity toward me. I couldn't shake the image of Taylah's soul clenched between the jaws of the hellhounds. She was somewhere in the pit right now enduring untold horrors on my account.

Whatever happened from here I would have to make her sacrifice count for something.

WHEN we got back to Hotel Ambrosia I had one objective; get back to the room and talk through my next move with Tucker. If Asia had been prepared to help us once, she might be persuaded into doing it again. I knew how badly she wanted me out of the picture and she'd be willing to do just about anything to make that happen. Asia was well connected and motivated entirely by self-interest.

In the lobby I looked down one of the plush carpeted hallways and caught a glimpse of the boardroom. The door was open just a crack and I couldn't help wondering what was so important that Jake hadn't been able to tear himself away to see me. Normally he leapt at the chance to spend time together. I crept a little closer, despite Tucker's apprehension.

Through the crack I could see the shadows of about half a dozen demons illuminated by the fire burning in the grate. They were sitting around a long table with a decanter of whiskey and empty glasses scattered in front of them. They all had notepads except for one who was standing and presiding over the meeting. A PowerPoint presentation was in progress; its images drawn from the most catastrophic events in human history. I only caught a few as they flashed by; Hiroshima, Adolf Hitler standing at a podium, war tanks, wailing civilians, homes reduced to rubble after natural disasters.

I could make out only a fraction of the presenter, but it was enough to see how different he was from the others. For a start he was much older and wore a white linen suit while the others were in black. On his feet were cowboy boots, the kind with decorative stitching. I couldn't see his face clearly, but I could hear snatches of what he was saying to the group. His voice was gravely and seemed to fill every inch of the room.

"This world is ripe for the taking," he said. "People have never been more in doubt of their faith, more uncertain of God's existence." He seized a fistful of air to emphasize his point. "This is our time. I want to see multitudes falling into the Pit. Remember that human weakness is your greatest asset; ambition, love of money, physical pleasures . . . those are your best weapons. I want you to think big. Don't focus on easy prey. Exceed your own expectations—I want to see a body count like we've never seen before. I want you to take down bishops, cardinals, generals, presidents! Rest assured you shall be richly rewarded."

Then Tucker was tugging at my sleeve, pulling me back into the lobby.

"Enough," he said softly. "We've seen enough."

Hell's Sweetheart

I was hoping to talk things over with Tuck, but once we got back to the hotel there didn't seem all that much to say. We were both too deflated to discuss what'd happened. Not only had we possibly blown our one chance at escape but Taylah had paid the price for it.

I tossed and turned after Tucker left. Soon my pillow was damp with tears as I recalled the sound of the hellhounds tearing at my friend before dragging her into the abyss. To make matters worse, we'd been so close to home. Gabriel had been just on the other side of the portal and I could still remember the feel of Phantom's spongy nose in my hand. Maybe I should have called out—maybe Gabe could have done something. But there was no use wondering about what might have been. The words I'd heard from the charismatic presenter in the boardroom kept replaying over and over in my head: *People have never been more in doubt of their faith*. I cried harder then and not just for Taylah. I wept because I knew it was true. Humanity had never been more vulnerable and there wasn't a thing I could do about it from down here. Finally my tears dried up and I fell into a deep and dreamless sleep.

I woke to the sound of urgent whispering. I blinked groggily, refusing to believe it could be morning already. It seemed like only minutes ago that my head had hit the pillow. Hanna's wide brown eyes came slowly into focus. She was peering at me in her usual fretful manner and shaking my shoulder to rouse me. Hanna's honey-colored hair had been wound into a loose bun at the nape of her neck, but I noticed that a few strands had escaped and fallen loose. They shone like threads of gold in the lamplight. Hanna could hardly be called optimistic, but somehow her presence always had a positive effect on me. Her affection was genuine and amid all the darkness surrounding me I knew her loyalty was something I could rely on. I sat up and tried to look more alert than I felt.

"You must get up, miss!" Hanna said, trying to tug back the covers. I resisted her efforts, pulling the duvet up around my shoulders. "Mr. Thorn is waiting for you downstairs. He wants you to get ready for an important outing."

"I'm not interested in any of his outings," I grumbled. "You can tell him I'm not going anywhere. Say I'm sick or something." Hanna shook her head vigorously.

"He was very explicit, miss. He even gave instructions as to what you should wear."

Hanna lifted a shiny, flat white box sitting on the floor beside the bed and placed it on my lap. I tore off the gold bow and waded impatiently through the layers of tissue paper before lifting out a garment unlike any I had hanging in my closet. Hanna gasped in admiration when she saw it. It was a vivid cherry-colored gown made of the softest crushed velvet. With its dramatic bell sleeves and brocade armbands, it was something you might imagine the Lady of Shalott wearing. With it came a delicate belt made of rings of beaten brass.

"It's beautiful," breathed Hanna, momentarily forgetting where it had come from. I wasn't so easily seduced.

"What's Jake up to now?"

"It's for the parade," Hanna said. She dropped her gaze and I had the distinct feeling she was holding out on me. I folded my arms and gave her a questioning look.

"The prince wishes to present you to the people today," she finally revealed.

"What people?" I rolled my eyes. "This isn't some medieval kingdom."

"*His* people," Hanna explained quietly.

"Why didn't you tell me about this before?"

"Because I knew you would get upset. This is an important event; you cannot refuse."

I hunkered down determinedly under the covers. "We'll see about that."

"Don't be foolish, miss." Hanna leaned toward me earnestly. "If you don't go willingly he will drag you there himself. Today means a lot to him."

I looked at Hanna and saw how fearful she was of Jake's wishes being defied. She'd be horrified if she knew about the trip to the Wasteland. As always it made me wonder what the consequence of my noncompliance might be. No doubt Hanna would be held accountable. My resolve faltered and I threw off the covers, climbed out of bed, and dragged myself into the shower. When I emerged, I saw that Hanna had made up the bed and carefully laid out the gown along with the black satin shoes that went with it.

"He doesn't really expect me to wear that?" I asked. "It's not a costume party, is it?"

Hanna ignored me. Her eyes were still darting nervously toward the door as she hastily helped me into the dress and hooked it up at the back. Despite being made of velvet it felt as delicate and weightless as a second skin. Hanna made me sit while she tugged at my hair to create elaborate side braids, deftly weaving satin ribbons through them, before lightly dusting powder on my face and midnight blue eye shadow on my lids.

"I look ridiculous," I said irritably, examining myself in the cheval mirror.

"Nonsense," Hanna replied briskly. "You look like a queen."

I didn't want to leave my hotel suite to participate in what promised to be another one of Jake's garish events. My room was the only place where I felt halfway comfortable and secure, but a jittery Hanna took me by the arm and ushered me out the door.

In the lobby there was a small party waiting for us, most of whom I recognized from the night of the banquet. When I stepped out of the glass elevator, the cluster of people waiting fell suddenly silent as they examined me. I looked around for Tucker but couldn't find him. Jake, who had been pacing agitatedly up and down the lobby, came toward me looking relieved and approving at the same time. He shot Hanna a vicious look, no doubt blaming her for our delayed arrival.

Jake took my hands and held them up in order to take in

my appearance. A smile of appreciation lightened the usual surliness of his face.

"Perfect," he murmured. I made no move to acknowledge his compliment. Jake himself was dressed so formally in his gloves and tailcoat he could have belonged to an eighteenth-century portrait. His hair was immaculately tied back and his coal black eyes were alight.

"No biker jacket today?" I asked drily.

"We must choose our fashion to match the occasion," he replied amicably. He was relaxed again now that I'd made my appearance. "You forget how much of the world I've seen. I can pick and choose my fashion choices from the last two thousand years, but I find anything preceding the last century to be a little dated."

I spotted Asia in the lobby throwing me toxic looks. She was wearing a slinky copper gown with a plunging neckline and slits that reached the tops of her toned thighs. Her pearly lips shone like mirrors as she sidled up to Jake wearing a sulky pout.

"It's time we got going," she said. "You ready, Princess?" I knew she wouldn't rat us out to Jake for fear of exposing herself, but it still made my skin prickle uncomfortably when she addressed me directly.

A pink convertible limo was waiting for us outside. The driver got out and robotically opened the doors for us. When we were seated, Jake said something to him in a language I didn't understand and he started the engine.

We drove until we came out onto an open road. It was the first time Jake had voluntarily let me venture outside the underground tunnels. At first all I saw was a scarlet sky, lit by ferocious reams of fire. A seething mass crawled across it, marring the horizon. It seemed almost alive, twitching and writhing, until I realized it wasn't a shadow like I thought, but a swarm of locusts. I'd never seen anything like it before. We drove as if in slow motion, steam rising from the pavement. After what seemed an eternity the car finally turned onto a road, flanked by the charred ruins of various vehicles. It was a desolate landscape that called to mind the setting of a sci-fi movie, where the hero finds himself forced to survive the aftermath of a nuclear war.

I couldn't say for certain where we were. Other than my brief and botched excursion into the Wasteland, I had never been beyond the tunnels. I was puzzling over our location when through the haze I started to make out bedraggled figures lining the road. Then I saw the crowd—hundreds, thousands of them—waiting for us, enveloped in smoke and ash. A sea of faces turned expectantly toward us, searching for something. They stared with vacant eyes and waited. What were they waiting for, I wondered. Some kind of sign or signal, but of what? I noticed they must have been wearing the exact same clothes they'd died in. Some wore hospital gowns or shirts smattered with blood and dirt. Others were well dressed in business suits or evening gowns, but they all shared that withered, vacant look of the walking dead.

Within seconds the crowd came to life and began jostling one another for a better vantage point. Their sunken eyes watched me with a burning curiosity. As if in response to an unseen cue, they began cheering and clapping, reaching out to us with skeletal limbs. I shrank back in fear, for once thankful that Jake was with me. Though I resented him and knew this hideous parade was his doing, I found myself drawing closer to him. Ironically, he was the closest thing I had to a security blanket in this place and right then his presence was the only thing keeping me sane.

As the limo crawled along the road the crowd swarmed around it. I had no idea where we were headed or what event these souls had gathered to witness, but I did know that Jake was parading me through the streets like some kind of trophy. I knew I represented a triumph over the forces of Heaven. My capture was a coup for Jake and I could see in his face that he was enjoying every moment.

Suddenly Jake was on his feet in the limo, pulling me up to join him. I tried to wrestle free, but his grip was so tight that when he took his hands away he left two red welts behind. The crowd seemed to go wild now, clambering over one another to scramble onto the hoods of cars or hang out of the charred windows.

"You should wave," Jake said. "Get some practice in."

"At least tell me where you're taking me?" I said.

Jake gave me one of his trademark looks, half smile and half sneer. "And spoil the surprise?"

The driver made a left off the main road and pulled up in front of what appeared to be a junkyard with pylons of twisted metal. An area had been cleared to erect a makeshift stage complete with microphones and speakers. Jake's bodyguards, wired so they could communicate with one another, patroled the area. Jake offered me his arm and I was so overwhelmed by the commotion happening around me that I actually took it. He looked smug but I was too nervous to care. Together we climbed the red-carpeted steps as if we were A-listers at some Hollywood party. Waiting for us onstage beneath a canopy of twisted black roses were two silver thrones, draped with black mink. Perhaps in a different setting they might have been striking, but today they seemed like dead weights, iron manacles binding me to this subterranean world. I wasn't feeling too steady on my feet so when Jake escorted me to my seat, with a great show of gallantry, I sank into it with relief. A hush now fell over the amorphous crowd as they waited for Jake's address. Even the bats I'd seen flying soundlessly overhead stopped mid-flight.

"Welcome, everyone," Jake began. He didn't seem to need a microphone. His powerful voice reverberated through the crowd. "Today marks a momentous occasion, not only for me but for the entire kingdom of Hades."

The cheering rose in volume and only died down once Jake raised his hands to call for silence. Below us I noticed the elite of Hades seated in order of rank. Each wore the same condescending and somewhat sadistic expression but at the same time managed to be utterly mesmerizing. The souls seemed terrified and yet unable to tear their gazes away. I felt a burning hot wind against my cheeks and wished I were back in the penthouse; imprisoned but safe from the prying eyes of the damned.

Jake stood tall as he lifted one hand in a grand, sweeping gesture and like dominoes the watching souls fell to their knees one by one. I tried to keep my focus on the crimson sky and not look directly at anyone in the crowd. I was too afraid of what I might see in their eyes. I had a sick feeling in the pit of my stomach that told me something terrible was about to happen. I saw a bent and bearded old man haul himself up the steps with the aid of a staff and approach the microphone. He was dressed in the daily vestments of a priest, black cassock and white collar. His face was lined and weathered looking. His eyes were red-rimmed and bloodshot and the skin beneath them was pouching; soft pockets of purplish flesh that reminded me of used tea bags.

"Please welcome Father Benedict," Jake said, sounding like a talk-show host. "He will be conducting today's ceremony." Jake smiled indulgently as the older man bowed his head in reverence. I was taken aback to see something so sacrilegious—a man of God bowing before a demon like Jake.

"Don't look so shocked," Jake said casually, returning to his seat. "Even the most devout can fall."

"You're despicable," was all I said.

Jake looked at me in surprise. "Why me?" He jerked his head in Father Benedict's direction. "If you want to point the finger at someone, point it at him."

"What is he even doing here?"

"Let's say he failed to protect the innocent. He works for us now. I'm sure you can appreciate the irony." I glared at him furiously. "Or not."

It occurred to me that Jake was being deliberately cagey. Despite the heat, I felt my blood run cold, as though someone had injected shards of ice directly into my bloodstream. I knew I was Jake's conquest, a souvenir of his victory over the agents of heaven. But what else was going on?

"Whatever you want me to do, I won't do it," I said.

"Calm down," Jake replied. "Your presence is all that's required." Suddenly the pieces seemed to fall into place. The gown, the parade, and now a ceremony—it was starting to make sense.

"I won't marry you," I said, gripping the throne so hard my knuckles turned white. "Not now, not in a million years from now."

"This isn't a wedding, darling," Jake said, laughing softly. "That part comes later. As a gentleman, I would never push you into something you weren't ready for."

"Oh, but kidnapping's okay?" I asked sarcastically.

"I needed to get your attention," Jake replied in a blasé tone.

"Do you really want to be with someone who can't stand the sight of you?" I asked. "Don't you have more self-respect than that?"

"How about we save the domestic spat for a more private time? Right now you're everybody's sweetheart. Just enjoy the moment."

Jake gestured toward the audience, who were waiting with baited breath for something to happen. "They've made a long journey to welcome their new princess."

Then, quick as lightning, he pushed back his chair and was behind me, propeling me forward so I was now center stage. There rose a collective flutter of excitement and thousands of eyes watched me with a fanatical eagerness. "This," Jake whispered seductively from behind, "is an induction.

Look around you, Bethany. This is your kingdom and *these* are your people."

"I'm not their princess," I spat. "I never will be!"

"But they want you, Beth. They need you. They've been waiting such a long time. Just think of the difference you could make around here."

"I can't help them," I said feebly.

"Can't or won't?

The conversation was interrupted by the sound of someone loudly clearing her throat. It was the redhead named Eloise from the banquet. "Can we please get on with it?" Jake responded by motioning Father Benedict forward.

"Let's begin."

I had no idea what their "induction" involved, but I knew I couldn't go through with it. I had to get away. I bolted for the steps and even managed to scramble down a couple before being met by Jake's entourage below. Soon they were swarming around me. Their hot hands grasped at me from every direction. Their faces contorted with pleasure, flashing between masks of beauty and their true grotesque forms. A few moments later, I was forcibly returned to my seat. Jake sat beside me looking serene. The priest placed a silver crown of vine leaves on his head and it shimmered against his smooth dark hair. In his gnarled hands, Father Benedict held an identical crown intended for me. When he spoke, his throaty voice resounded through the space.

"We are here today to welcome a new member into our family. The prince has searched for her for many centuries and we share in his happiness now that he has found her at last. She is no mere mortal who succumbed to the lure of power and immortality. She comes from a much higher place—a place known as the Kingdom of Heaven." There was a collective gasp from the spectators. I wondered if their tortured minds could even remember such a place as Heaven. Somehow, I doubted it. "You shall worship her," Father Benedict intoned, his voice rising in fervor. "You shall serve her and bow to her will." I wanted to get up and contradict every edict coming out of his mouth, but I knew I would only be silenced. Father Benedict concluded, "I present to you, the new Princess of the Third Circle, the Angel Bethany!" With that he turned and placed the crown on my head. As soon as he did a flash of lightning illuminated the red sky and a storm of ash blew up around us, forcing the souls to duck for cover and shield their faces. The demons seemed to enjoy the crowd's reaction.

Then as quickly as it had started the ceremony appeared to be over. The priest hobbled off the stage and the crowd began to disperse. Just as we were getting back into the car a ragged child tore through the crowd toward us. He was small and frail with an urchin's face. He reached for me, arms outstretched in supplication. Diego noticed him first. He leapt out of the procession and grabbed him, his cruel fingers coiling around the child's throat. I watched in horror as the child began to gasp for breath, his eyes wild with terror, his small hands scrabbling uselessly at his sides. Then Diego looked suddenly bored and tossed him aside as if he were a crumpled paper bag. A strange gurgling sound came from the boy's throat. Every instinct in my body urged me to run to his aid. I tried to move forward, but Jake's vise-like grip pulled me back.

"Show some dignity!" he snarled.

Then, without thinking, I kicked him hard in the shins to free myself. It distracted him long enough for me to rush to the boy's side. I lifted up the little limp body, the train of my gown dragging in the dirt. The child's eyes were shut, and I gently brushed the dust from his gaunt cheeks, laid my hand against his chest, and willed whatever healing energy I had left to restore the life force that had been stolen from him.

When the color returned to his lips and his eyes flickered open, I smiled down at him reassuringly. It was only then that I noticed how quiet everything around me had become. Every face was turned in my direction. I saw Jake standing only feet away, but his face was fixed in an expression of dismay. Before I could move Jake's party enfolded me, guiding me protectively back to the car. Only once I was seated next to him did I feel Jake's hot breath at my ear.

"Never do that again," he said. "What do you think this is? We are children of Lucifer. Our purpose is to inflict suffering, not relieve it."

"Speak for yourself," I told him boldly.

"Listen to me," Jake hissed, grabbing my arm. "The Seven Virtues in Heaven are Seven Sins in Hell. An act of kindness here is a capital offense. Even I won't be able to protect you."

I wasn't listening to Jake anymore. Suddenly I felt very calm. I knew now I had the potential to make a difference, even in Hell. My entire body rippled with this new awareness.

I had only done what came naturally to me, tried to offer comfort where I had witnessed pain. I focused on my powers of healing, felt them gather momentum under my skin. My wings tingled, but I repressed the urge to unfurl them. Light began to emanate from me. It spilled out of the car, into the dusty clearing and over the heads bobbing in the crowd. It rose and bleached the fire in the sky to a milky white. All the while I could hear Jake's voice in the background. . . .

"What are you doing? Stop that right now! I forbid you!" He didn't sound angry now, only alarmed. Then the light ebbed and finally vanished, leaving in its place a solitary white butterfly. It hovered in the air just above the crowd, a tiny fragment of hope in a sea of despair. Some tried to grasp it, but every face was now turned upward, either in wonder or in horror. Jake became rigid as stone. With him temporarily incapacitated, it was Asia who stepped forward and took charge.

"Kill the bug," she snapped. "And get her outta here."

{ 21 }

Big Daddy

BACK at Hotel Ambrosia, Jake's demons gathered for a crisis meeting. They refused his offer of the boardroom and stood in the lobby arguing loudly like schoolchildren in the playground. I was largely ignored, but I heard my name bandied around along with phrases like *massive screwup* and *we're cactus*. The dispute continued to swell until I felt Jake grab hold of my elbow and steer me toward Hanna, who watched from the wings and nervously wrung her hands.

"Get Beth upstairs," Jake said, propeling me into her arms. "Don't stop and don't speak to anyone."

"I didn't mean to cause so much trouble," I stammered. I couldn't bring myself to say I was sorry . . . I wasn't. I just hadn't expected this kind of pandemonium. "It sort of just happened."

Jake ignored me. "Now, Hanna!" he roared.

"I don't understand why it's such a big deal," I said, resisting Hanna's attempts to bustle me away. "At least tell me what's going on."

Jake lowered his voice and fixed me with his smoldering gaze. "Things are about to get ugly. I'm trying to save your skin and my chances of doing that are much better if you get out of the way."

Looking around I saw the tar black eyes of every demon present blazing with bloodlust. My presence was no longer being viewed with the customary amusement or curiosity. The faces around me looked manic, like they wanted nothing more than to dismember me limb by limb. I watched as Jake turned to face my jurors. He looked tall and formidable in his black tailcoat with his hair unbound and falling free around his shoulders. I could see by his aggressive stance that he was bracing himself for a fight.

"Come away, miss." Hanna was becoming flustered. This time I didn't argue but hurried after her. Even inside the elevator, fragments of the raging argument floated over to us.

"This is a travesty!" someone was shouting. "You should never have brought her into the Third Circle."

"She's young," I heard Jake growl defensively. I felt a little guilty for leaving him to face the music alone. His own kind was turning on him because of me. "She's new to this life. She needs more time to adjust."

"How much time? She's upsetting the balance here," someone countered. "You wanted a kitten to play with—now teach it the house rules."

"She isn't some animal I can train to do tricks." Jake was seething now.

"What do you want with her anyway?" someone else chimed in. "Is it worth jeopardizing our reputation for a little private amusement? The other Circles are laughing at us."

"I do not answer to you." Jake's voice was low and throaty.

"Perhaps not, but you are not the highest authority here."

"You really want to disturb him? Over *this*?"

"No, but I will if you can't keep your little bitch under control."

The room seemed to go deathly still. I watched Hanna hit the button for our floor in rapid succession as the elevator stalled.

"What did you just say?"

"You heard me."

"You might want to consider retracting that comment," Jake said. It was hard to miss the underlying threat in his voice.

"Bring it on, big shot. Let's see what you got."

TUCKER was already waiting for us when Hanna let us into the room. He immediately flipped on the chrome security lock even though we all knew it wouldn't be much use in keeping demons out.

I sat cross-legged on my bed, hugging a pillow for comfort. "What do you think is happening down there?"

"You mustn't worry, miss," Hanna replied dutifully. "Mr. Thorn will talk them round. He always does."

"I hope you're right," I said. "I didn't realize they'd get so worked up."

"They're demons, they always overreact." Tucker shrugged, trying to make me feel better.

JAKE stayed down in the lobby deliberating for what seemed like hours. In the end, just after midnight, both Tucker and

Hanna went to bed. I was getting sleepy and about to change out of the velvet gown when I heard Jake outside my door, calling my name. It was the first time he'd knocked rather than just let himself in.

"I'm glad you're still up," he said as soon as I let him in. "We've got to go."

He sounded apologetic rather than commanding, and a garment was bundled under his arm. There was a strange look in his eyes and if I didn't know better, I'd have said it was fear. He hadn't looked like that even when Gabriel had wrapped him in tongues of fire and commanded the earth to swallow him alive. He'd only looked defiant in defeat. What could have happened to rattle him so badly?

"Where are we going?"

Jake pressed his lips together and tried to repress his mounting anxiety. "They've called a hearing."

"What? Why?" I was fully awake now.

"I didn't expect it to go this far," Jake said. "I'll explain on the way."

"Can I change first?"

"No time."

Outside the lobby, Jake's motorcycle waited for us, purring with a life of its own.

"Why the bike?" I asked.

"I want to avoid drawing too much attention," he said. "Here, put this on." He tossed me the brown cloak he'd been carrying.

"I thought attention was just what you wanted," I said, recalling the humiliating parade of only hours before.

"Not this time."

"Why should I listen to anything you say?" I said.

"Beth." Jake sighed as if he were in pain. "Hate me as much as you like but trust me . . . tonight I'm on your side."

For some reason I believed him. I slipped on the cloak and pulled the hood over my head. Jake helped me onto the bike and we sped soundlessly through the tunnels that unspooled and interweaved before us, as intricate as a spiderweb. I pressed my face into his back to hide from whatever horrors lurked in the dark.

Before long Jake pulled up abruptly in front of what appeared to be a derelict warehouse at the end of a narrow alley. We dismounted and stood facing the ruins of a building that was several stories high despite the fact that it was underground. Vandals had smashed most of the windows and they'd been boarded up with cardboard. Graffiti was scrawled across the external walls. Jake hesitated for just a fraction before moving forward. The look on his face suggested he was trying to come up with a game plan.

"This is it," he said looking at me with uncharacteristic seriousness. "You get an audience with Big Daddy himself. There aren't many dead or alive that can claim that honor."

"Whoa, what?" I cried. "You've taken me to Lucifer? Are you crazy? I'm not going in there!"

"We have no choice," Jake breathed. "We've been summoned."

"Why? Is this about the butterfly?" I asked desperately. "I won't do it again, I swear." Whatever confidence I'd regained by the end of the parade deserted me then.

"You're not the one they're angry with," Jake said. "They have assembled to judge me and decide my punishment for bringing you here."

"Well, good," I snapped. "You *were* wrong in bringing me here. It'll serve you right when they send me back."

"I hope it's that simple," Jake murmured, his eyes distant. "But we'd be getting off lightly."

"What's that supposed to mean?"

"Nothing, let's go inside." Jake drew himself up. "We've kept him waiting long enough. Remember, don't speak unless spoken to. Got it? This isn't the time to get fresh."

Jake had barely got the words out when a black-suited bouncer much like the others I'd seen in the underground clubs pulled open the heavy doors. There was the grinding sound of metal sliding on metal as he motioned for us to step inside.

"C'mon in," a voice that reminded me of smooth, rich whiskey called from inside. "I don't bite."

Inside, the warehouse had been set up to look like an improvised courtroom. Seven dark, shadowy figures were seated in a semicircle on what appeared to be upturned crates. Some had their arms crossed like they'd been kept waiting too long. I knew instinctively that they were the Originals and Jake's equals. As I scanned the faces I saw Diego, Nash, Yeats, and Asia lurking in the dim light. I assumed that they too had been summoned—perhaps as witnesses.

When my eyes adjusted to the dim light I saw that presiding at the head of the group was a significantly taller figure. He was seated in a high-backed Tudor-style chair that had seen better days. He wore a white linen suit with a red silk tie and his feet were encased in white cowboy boots. Although his face was still in shadow, I was sure he was the rousing speaker I'd overheard in the boardroom. He held an ivory-topped cane that he tapped softly on the cement floor, as if he were already bored. When Jake and I entered all conversation died on the spot and for some minutes no one spoke. It gave me a brief opportunity to assess the derelict space and those who occupied it.

Apart from the shattered panes of glass there were cobwebs hanging in sheaths from dust-coated machinery. The rustling of wings overhead suggested that bats had made their home in the timber rafters. Like Jake, the fallen angels surrounding me were images of faded beauty. The gender of some was indeterminate, but they shared the same chiseled features; fine lips the color of peaches, slightly aquiline noses, and strong jaws. They had the wasted, vacant look of those who had devoted their lives to idle pursuits. They were incapable of feeling surprise yet I knew my presence surprised them. There was something about the way they held themselves and the air of superiority they radiated that distinguished them as the Originals. They were the equivalent to royalty in this world. Only now they regarded Jake coolly, as though he were no longer one of them but an outcast who had wandered from the pack.

When the face of the white-clad man came into view, I saw he was older than others and more weather-beaten. His skin was tanned and leathery and his eyes were a pellucid blue but devoid of any expression. He was immaculately groomed and wore his silver hair tied back loosely with a gilded clasp. Even I had to admit, he was extremely beautiful. Angels were not supposed to age, but I guessed that the constant propagation of evil was bound to take its toll. Despite having aged some, Lucifer's face was radiant, his eyes sharp and every angle perfectly sculpted. His brow was broad and his eyes held such electricity it made the hairs on my arms stand on end. I knew that in Heaven, he had once been among the most revered of our kind, elite in beauty and intelligence. When he spoke, his voice rang out, slow and musical.

"Well, hello there, little angel," he said. "How's this for a family reunion?" Some of the Originals tittered in response.

"Father." Jake stepped forward in a business-like way. "This is all a misunderstanding. If you would grant me the opportunity to explain . . ."

"Oh, Arakiel, my dear boy," Lucifer crooned in a paternal tone. "You have much to answer for."

It took me a moment to realize that he was addressing Jake by his angelic name. As always, I found myself startled by the reminder of Jake's former life. It was so strange to think that long ago, before I'd ever come into existence, they had all dwelled in Heaven. Gabriel would remember it with clarity and in his mind it wouldn't feel like so much time had passed. I knew he'd witnessed the uprising of the rebel angels and their ultimate expulsion from the Kingdom. I knew the evil they had perpetrated since, yet one word kept ringing in my mind: *brothers*. And look what had become of them now. For a moment all my fear and anger dissolved and I felt only a deep sense of sadness. Lucifer's voice drew me back to the proceedings at hand.

"You owe this court an explanation, Arakiel," he said. "This little escapade of yours has caused much dissension among our ranks. Some fear it may undermine all we have worked to achieve. We must, at all costs, preserve what is ours."

"Father." Jake bowed his head. "I mean no disrespect, but it was you who sanctioned this assignment to begin with."

"Indeed," Lucifer agreed. "I applauded your boldness in bringing her here, but it seems your emotions have since gotten the better of you. I fear this is no longer strictly business for you." His eyes narrowed mischievously. "In fact, I suspect it never was."

"Excuse me, I have a question . . ." I stepped forward and the glowing eyes of the demons flashed in unison as they fixed their gazes on me. I dug my nails into my wrist to keep from trembling and continued. I was in way over my head, but at the same time I needed answers and ironically, I had a feeling Lucifer would tell me the truth. "I'm a little confused. I understand it was you who wanted me here, but what I don't understand is why."

Lucifer's lip curled up in a smile. "It's true," he said. "It was with my consent that Arakiel brought you to us."

"But I'm no one important. Why me?"

Lucifer leisurely drummed his fingers together over the top of his cane. "You're a pawn, my dear," he said. "As you know, Heaven has launched another one of its pathetic little heal-the-world schemes." Lucifer rolled his eyes. "The whole thing is incredibly tedious—we make a mess, they clean it up and so on and so forth. And we're bored of the whole thing, which is where you come into it." His pale eyes watched me lazily. "I used you to send out a message."

"What message?"

The swarthy Diego suddenly stood up, taking it upon himself to clarify. "That it's game on."

"What does that mean?" I asked weakly, struggling against the rising panic in my chest.

"Well, I guess it's safe to let you in on the secret now that you're here," Lucifer drawled. "Let's just say it's time this little family feud was brought to a head."

Jake, who had so far remained silent for the duration of this conversation, chose this moment to speak. "Dragging an angel into Hell against their will is a sign," he said. "It marks the beginning of the war."

"There's going to be a war?"

"There was always going to be a war," Lucifer said, "ever since my self-righteous prick of a brother had me evicted."

"We've been waiting a long time," Diego added in his clipped Spanish accent. "To show them who's boss, to let them know just how fragile their precious little planet really is."

I swallowed hard and shook my head. "No," I said. "It's not true."

"Oh, yes," Nash piped up, enthused by the turn the hearing had taken. "We're talking about the final showdown, the face-off between your daddy and ours."

"You better believe it, little angel," Lucifer added. "We're on a one-way road to Armageddon. And what a show it promises to be."

I stood rooted to the spot, hardly daring to breathe. Part of me hoped the demons would suddenly burst out laughing and reveal I was the butt of some cruel joke. But deep down, I knew it was no joke. They were deadly serious and the world was in dire trouble. I couldn't believe what I was hearing. They believed my capture was going to work as a catalyst, the final straw that would tip the angels over the edge. Would it really work? Hell had lashed out, would Heaven now have no choice but to retaliate? Lucifer had condoned my abduction to rally against My Father and stir things up to trigger a final confrontation that would be bloodier than ever. He knew it was a step too far, but that was the point. He was throwing down the gauntlet and waiting for Heaven to take up the challenge. He was opening the gates and inviting war in.

The hearing seemed to have gone off on a tangent. Jake brought it back to what was uppermost in his mind.

"So will you leave us be?" he asked. "Father, the angel has served her purpose and poses no threat. I ask that she be entrusted to me."

"Oh, dear," said Lucifer with an exaggerated sigh. "I'm afraid I can't do that." He lifted his cane and pointed it directly at me. "Not after the little show Miss Church put on for us yesterday."

"She belongs to me!" Jake's voice was too strident in the lofty warehouse. I was no strategist, but even I could see that he was losing ground. He needed to curb his emotions if he wanted to get anywhere here.

Lucifer sat up straighter and Jake dropped his head humbly, showing regret for his outburst.

"When I put you in charge I wasn't aware you had *invested emotionally* in the project." Lucifer spoke these last words as if they left a bad taste in his mouth.

"I . . . I haven't," Jake said. "I knew she would be a prize, and I thought only to add to our conquests—"

"Don't lie to me, boy!" Lucifer roared so unexpectedly that those assembled jumped. "You have coveted her right from the start. I would never have trusted you with this had I known the extent of your obsession."

Jake looked up to meet his father's gaze. His jaw was twitching now. "It's what you taught me to do: Reach out and take what I want."

Lucifer gave a hollow chuckle and his tone softened. "To *want* is different than to *need*," he said. "You *wanted* the boy with the lame leg and the brat from Buchenwald. But Bethany . . . you *need* her and your attachment is weakening you, siphoning your strength. It disturbs me to see one of my strongest fall like this."

"I will redeem myself, Father," Jake said.

"You will indeed," Lucifer replied. "I will see to it personally that you do."

"What can I do?" Jake bowed his head and Lucifer clicked his tongue softly.

"You are my child, one of my most accomplished children.

Don't worry." He smiled indulgently. "Daddy will fix everything."

"He's not one of your children," I cut in, unable to stop myself. My mouth appeared to have made a decision independently of me and kept moving even though I knew with every fiber of my being that I should shut up. "If you recall it was My Father who created him . . . and *you*, by the way."

Jake spun on his heels and flashed me a deadly glare. Lucifer only cocked his head to one side and regarded me with mild amusement.

"Look around you, little angel," he said. "The world is in ruins and you are in Hell. Where is your father now? Why doesn't he come and save you? Either he doesn't care or he isn't as powerful as you seem to think."

"He had the power to cast you out of Heaven," I said brazenly.

"And why do you think he did that?" Lucifer flashed me a brilliant smile. "Why do you think he built this underground cage to contain me? It's because he was scared. One does not need to lock up that which is not dangerous."

"If you're so dangerous why don't you bust out?" I challenged.

"Can't." Lucifer shrugged and waved a hand around him. "But I can breed an army and send them out in my place. It's called a loophole, darlin'." He turned his attention to Jake.

"I admit I can see the attraction. She's quite spirited, isn't she?"

"I'm sorry, Father," Jake implored. "She doesn't know what she's saying, do not take offense."

"I'm not offended," Lucifer said, "but I'm afraid you cannot keep her."

Jake's eyes filled with alarm despite his efforts to appear composed.

"Is it true what your brothers tell me . . . did she conjure life?" Lucifer asked.

"Yes, but it was an accident. It won't happen again, I'll make sure of it," Jake insisted.

"You're not following me, boy. Her presence has raised hope. You introduce hope in Hell and everything we've worked for goes up in smoke."

"I'll keep her under lock and key. I'll do whatever it takes. You have my word."

"I can feel the righteousness rolling off her in waves. It's nauseating. Is it just me or can anyone else feel it? She's already infected our world with her compassion and that dreary love-thy-neighbor attitude. Her very presence here is an aberration."

"But, Father, think of the gains."

Lucifer looked dismissively at Jake. I could see he was ready to bring the proceedings to a close. "I gave you permission to bring her here; I never said she could stay."

"You cannot take her from me!" Jake sounded like a petulant child and even stamped his foot.

Lucifer leaned forward and rested his elbows on his knees. "There is nothing I cannot do if I so desire," he replied. "You are at my mercy here and don't you forget it. I could strip you of your powers for this. Lucky for you, I don't like to see my sons downtrodden." He gave an exaggerated sigh. "I can't help my paternal instincts."

"So you're going to send her back?" Jake sounded crushed.

"Send her back?" Lucifer arched an eyebrow. "This ain't some fairy tale, boy. We don't work that way down here, you of all people should know that." He shook his head in dismay. "See the damage she has done to you already."

Jake turned to me, his eyes wild with panic.

"Do something," he mouthed fervently.

I stood numb with confusion and a penetrating fear. First he had instructed me not to speak and now he wanted me to react. What did he think I could do?

Lucifer stood in one fluid movement. "I'm sorry, Arakiel, but this plan of yours has been very poorly executed. From the moment she descended into Hades you knew it would come to this. Never love that which you cannot keep. Your angel was always condemned to die."

Suddenly an idea came into my head. "It won't work," I stammered. "I can't die here. Those are the rules. Killing me will only send me back to Heaven."

"No, my dear." Lucifer shook his head. "Your death on earth would send you back to Heaven. It's a whole different ball game down here. Hellfire is strong enough to annihilate an angel for good."

"What if she agrees to convert," Jake said desperately. "What if she becomes one of us?"

"Highly unlikely," Lucifer said languidly, inspecting his manicured nails. It was evident he was bored with the whole discussion. "She's shackled to the A-Team, I can tell."

"At least offer her the choice."

Lucifer gave a heavy sigh. "My dear Bethany, would you

like to consider the option of renouncing Heaven and using your powers to assist us?"

"No," I said. "A thousand times no."

"Satisfied?" Lucifer said to Jake.

"Father." One of the unfamiliar Originals stepped forward. It was a woman with coils of glossy raven hair that fell to her waist, ruby lips, and brilliant hazel eyes. She had a face like a porcelain doll's and her skin was so milky pale she looked as though she had never seen the sun. Maybe she hadn't, I thought absently. I wondered why I wasn't filled with panic, why I wasn't crying or begging for leniency. I felt like time had stopped, the seconds were crawling by and my emotions seemed to have shut down as if someone had pulled out a plug. The female demon continued, "I think we could make an example of her."

"How so, my lovely Sorath?" Lucifer asked.

"If we are to undo her influence and restore the balance of power we must show the people that we mean business," Sorath swiveled her swanlike neck to look me in the eye. "We must punish her publicly."

Lucifer tapped his chin and looked pensive. "Interesting idea. What do you suggest?" He smiled at the seven demons like an indulgent parent. "I will let you decide the method."

I watched in silent dismay as the Originals scampered out of their seats like a swarm of vultures to form a huddle. They conversed together in hushed voices. Diego and Nash cast sly glances in my direction and Asia looked smugger than a cat that had just stumbled upon a saucer of cream. Lucifer waited patiently while Jake paced compulsively, looking like he wanted to say something. He kept opening and closing his mouth, the perfect argument eluding him. Eventually, Sorath stepped out of the circle.

"We have decided," she said with a satisfied grin.

"And you are all agreed?" Lucifer sounded almost disappointed. "There's no need for lively debate?"

"No, Father," she said.

"Then by all means, declare your verdict!"

Sorath turned to face me and the others slunk forward to flank her. Her eyes gleamed like blades and her lips pulled back into a smile of delight.

"Burn her," she purred.

Lucifer clapped his hands in approval. From behind me, I heard Jake let out an agonized moan.

22

Vigil

I stood helplessly as the demons filed out of the warehouse. Now that my fate had been decided, they didn't deem me interesting enough to acknowledge. Only Asia paused, long enough to mockingly blow me a kiss as she sashayed past.

"Arakiel, at dawn you will surrender your angel to us," Lucifer called nonchalantly over his shoulder. "You have what is left of tonight to say your good-byes. Can't say I'm not big-hearted."

I knew the enormity of what had just happened hadn't sunk in because I was so calm. Jake was saying something reassuring to me, but I barely heard him.

"You're in shock," he said, guiding me to the chair Lucifer had occupied. "Sit down here. I'm going after my father to try and talk him out of this madness."

I knew Jake was wasting his time. The decision was irrevocable and nothing Jake said was going to change it. I didn't want to waste time pleading or bargaining. I had one thought and one thought only. If Lucifer was right (and there was no reason to doubt him), I only had a few hours of existence left and I had no intention of spending them with Jake. It was his selfishness that had gotten me into this fix to begin with. I had to make it back to Venus Cove one last time to say good-bye to Xavier and my family.

I knew that if I saw Xavier once more whatever happened to me in the morning would be a lot easier to bear. But I wasn't going back just for me. Somehow I had to let Xavier know that it was okay for him to go on with his life, give him my blessing to move on. There was no way I was going to try and tell him what lay in store for me. I'd never want to cause him that much pain. I wanted Xavier to accept that I wasn't coming home and stop searching for answers. I knew from my time in the Kingdom that people never really got over the loss of a loved one, but their lives did continue, eventually offering them new joys to compensate for their losses.

I didn't know how long Jake would be, but I figured negotiating with Lucifer was bound to take a while. I'd never attempted projection from anywhere other than my room before, but it was easier than I expected because this time I didn't care who found out.

I found Xavier in his room sitting on the edge of his bed. He looked distracted and a little disheveled from lack of sleep. A half-packed gym bag lay open beside him. His gaze was fixed on the feather sitting on his bedside table. It was the one he'd found on the seat of his Chevy after our first date. He picked it up, lightly brushed his fingertips across it and inhaled its rainy scent. I watched him place it between the folds of a pressed shirt in the sports bag. Then he reconsidered and returned it to its place on top of the leather Bible on his bedside table. I knelt in front of him and saw him shiver as if from a draft. Goose bumps appeared on his arms, but he continued to sit very still.

"Xavier?" I knew he couldn't hear me, but the expression on his face changed to one of concentration. Could he sense my presence? Could he also sense how wrong things were? He leaned forward as if to catch a sound in the air. I thought about making contact with him the way I had that day on the beach, but somehow it didn't feel right anymore. And I wasn't sure I could pull it off in my current state of mind.

"Hey, baby," I began tentatively. "I've come to say good-bye. Something's happened and I'm pretty sure it means I won't be able to come and see you again. So I wanted to come one last time to tell you not to worry about me anymore. You look so tired. Don't go to Tennessee—there's no point now. Try to forget you ever met me. I want you to have an amazing life. You need to focus on what's ahead of you now and let go of the past. I wouldn't take back a single second of the time we had, but . . ."

"Beth," Xavier spoke suddenly, interrupting my train of thought. "I know you're here. I can feel you. What are you trying to tell me?" He waited a moment and then added, "Can you give me a sign like last time?"

He looked so hopeful that an idea popped into my head. I had a way of telling Xavier exactly what I wanted him to know without the need for words. The room was in semi-darkness. I focused my energy and used it to throw open the drapes and saw Xavier blink as the room flooded with light.

"Good one, Beth," he said. I drew closer to the window

and blew hard on it so that a patch of glass fogged up. Then I stretched out a ghostly finger and used it to draw a heart on the windowpane. In it I simply wrote, X + B.

Xavier smiled at my handiwork.

"I love you too," he said. "I won't ever stop."

My tears came in a flood then and I couldn't stop them. If only I knew I would see him in the next life, maybe I could stand it. But I wasn't going back to Heaven. I didn't know where I was going. All I knew was that an eternity of nothingness awaited me.

"You have to stop loving me," I said in between sobs. My entire body was wracked with the sorrow of giving him up. "You have to move on. If there's any way back after death I promise I'll find it. But only to check up on you and the extraordinary life you'll be having."

"There you are!" I jumped at the voice, but it was only Molly letting herself into the room. "Gabriel and Ivy are waiting outside. They want to get going. What's the holdup?"

Xavier closed the curtains protectively over my sketch.

"I'm on my way," he said. "I just need a minute." Molly made no move to leave.

"Before we go, can we talk? I need some advice."

Xavier turned his face to the window where I still stood. I knew he didn't want me to leave. "I'm kinda busy right now, Molly. Can it wait?"

"Kinda busy staring into space? No, it can't wait. My whole life is falling apart and you're the only person I can talk to."

"I thought we were fighting."

"Build a bridge," Molly snapped. "I need advice and nobody else will understand."

"This is about Gabriel, right?" I noticed then that Molly's face was tear stained. She had been crying too. The corners of her mouth quivered and her shoulders shook now that Xavier had broached the subject of my brother.

Talk to her, Xavier, I thought. *Molly needs you and she's your friend. You're going to need your friends around you.* I didn't know whether Xavier received my silent message or the sight of Molly in tears tugged at his heartstrings, but he sat down and patted the bed beside him.

"Come on then," he said. "Spit it out but make it quick, we don't have much time."

"I don't know what to do. I know this thing with Gabriel isn't good for me, but I can't seem to let it go."

"What's stopping you?"

"I know how amazing we could be together. I just don't understand why he doesn't see it."

"So you still feel the same?" Xavier asked. "Even though you know he isn't human?"

"I always knew he was special somehow." Molly sighed. "And now I know why. He's not like any guy I've met because he's not just a guy . . . he's a freaking archangel."

"Molly, you've got so many guys chasing you, you practically have to beat them off with a stick."

"Yeah, but they're not him. I don't want anyone else and he doesn't want me. There are times when I think he feels something, but then he just shuts it off."

"You're going to have to learn to do the same. I know it's hard, but you have to look after yourself. Think about what you want long term. If Gabe doesn't want to be part of your life, it's doesn't mean yours is over."

"How am I ever gonna replace someone that perfect? No one will ever measure up which means my life is pretty much over at seventeen. I'll end up like Mrs. Kratz at school—a dried-up old prune reading romance novels and supervising study hall."

"I don't think you'll end up like Kratz—you need a college degree to do her job."

"You suck at giving advice!" Molly's face cleared as she let out a peal of laughter. Then her face became suddenly serious.

"Do you think we'll find Beth?"

"Yes." Xavier didn't blink.

"How do you know for sure?"

"Because I'm not stopping until we do, that's how. Now, are we heading to Tennessee or what?"

Before following Molly out the door Xavier moved to the window and put his palm over the outline of the heart enclosing our initials.

"I'm coming, Beth," he murmured. "I know you're feeling lost right now, but I want you to be strong for both of us. Just remember who you are, what you were created to do. No one can take that away from you, no matter where you are. I feel your presence with me all the time so don't go giving up now. There's no way I'm staying here without you. If Heaven couldn't separate us, Hell's got no damn chance. Hang in there. I'll see you soon."

When Jake returned I knew my last hope of escaping death had expired. I looked at his face as he leaned against the door frame and saw that it was whiter than parchment. He pressed his head into his hands in frustration. I waited to feel something like anger, fear, or even despair, but I felt none of those things. Maybe it was because the idea of not existing didn't make sense in my head yet. Part of me didn't even think it was possible. I had always existed, if not as a human on solid earth, then as an essence in Heaven. I still existed now even though I didn't know how to define myself anymore. I couldn't imagine no longer being able to think or feel or yearn for my family. Was it really possible that by morning I would disappear forever, lost not only to those around me, but lost to myself as well? Where would I go? I was barred from earth, not permitted back to Heaven, and not accepted in Hell. I would simply cease to exist and it would be like I never lived at all.

With a movement as quick as a tiger pouncing, Jake was by my side.

"I suppose saying I'm sorry doesn't really cut it," he said, looking down at me with real pain in his coal black eyes. If he had one redeeming feature it was that he genuinely didn't want to see me go.

"I played a part," I said numbly. "I used my powers in the wrong place."

"I should have known you'd react that way, I should have warned you!" Jake slammed his fist into a timber post so hard that an explosion of dirt and timber fragments rained down on us from above. Jake brushed the debris from my hair and I didn't recoil because I found myself unable to react to anything right now. I couldn't move; it was as if I'd forgotten how.

"I guess we both misjudged," I said with a tight smile. "Rookie mistake, right?"

A car drove me back to Hotel Ambrosia, Jake speeding ahead of us on his motorbike. He drove recklessly, almost swerving the bike off the road several times. I imagined him turning over new ideas in his head as he rode, locked in his own world of plotting and scheming. I didn't argue when he accompanied me up to my suite. All of this might have been his fault, but I didn't want to spend my final hours alone.

Hanna was waiting for me with a tray of supper. For once, I didn't push the food away or tell her to leave it for later. For the first time in Hades, I took notice of the food offered to me: thin slices of rye bread, goat cheese, smoked salmon curled in waves around the rim of the plate, shiny olives, and ruby colored wine that tasted of plums. I ate slowly, making sure I tasted every mouthful. For me the food was reminiscent of my memories of being on earth. It was something I'd never experience again and I wanted the moment to last.

Hanna had never seen me eat with such focus or tolerate Jake's company without complaint. She watched me, her face crumpled in pain. There was no way for her to help me now and she knew it.

"Everything will be okay, miss," she said eventually. "Perhaps things will have changed in the morning."

"Yes," I murmured vacantly. "Everything will be better in the morning."

Hanna took a few tentative steps toward me, conscious that Jake was watching her every move.

"Is there anything I can do for you?"

"Just get some rest, Hanna. Don't worry about me."

"But . . ."

"You heard her," Jake said in his most chilling voice. "Clear this away and leave us in peace."

Hanna nodded subserviently and hurriedly cleared the dishes, throwing me a final look of distress over her shoulder.

"Good night, Hanna," I called softly after her as she slipped out the door. "Thank you—for everything."

When she was gone, I went through the motions of washing my face and brushing my teeth. I paid meticulous attention to each routine. Everything felt different to me now. I was acutely aware of the warm water running in rivulets over my body, the feel of the clean cotton towels against my skin. Every movement felt new, as if I were experiencing it for the first time. It occurred to me that I might be in Hell, but I was still alive. I was still a living, breathing, talking person. Not for much longer.

I stepped out of the bathroom to find Jake half sitting, half slumped on the sofa, staring into space with his chin pressed into his hand. The black tailcoat lay discarded on the floor along with the white bow tie. He had his shirtsleeves rolled up to the elbows as if in preparation for strenuous work. The room smelled strongly of cigarettes. Jake had poured himself a large tumbler of scotch, and it seemed to have steadied his nerves. He held the bottle up to see if I wanted to join him, but I shook my head. I didn't want my thoughts muddled by alcohol. I moved around him, straightened the cushions on the sofa, tipped out the contents of the ashtray, and rearranged the items on my dressing table. Eventually, I ran out of things to distract me and there was nothing left to do but climb into the vast bed, huddle into a corner, and wait for morning. It was clear neither of us would be getting any sleep. Jake didn't try and talk to me; he was like a statue, locked in his own world. I hugged my knees and waited patiently for the terror I expected to finally break over me like a tidal wave. But it refused to come. I had no idea what time it was. There was a digital clock by the phone, but I tried not to look at it. I couldn't help sneaking a look once and saw that it was three forty-five A.M. The minutes seemed to stretch for an eternity because when I looked again only a few minutes had passed. Jake and I remained lost in our own private thoughts.

I hoped my last thoughts before I lost consciousness would be of Xavier. I tried to imagine a fairy-tale ending for him with an adoring wife and five children. Phantom would live with them and the house would be full of music and laughter. On Sundays he would coach the local Little League team. Xavier would think of me from time to time, usually in moments of solitude. But he would think of me only as a distant memory, as the high school sweetheart who'd left a mark on his heart but was never destined to be part of his future.

"You're thinking about him, aren't you?" Jake's voice cut through my reverie like a blade. "I don't blame you. He would never have done anything so stupid—he at least protected you. You must despise me now more than you ever did."

"I don't want to spend my last hours being angry, Jake," I said. "What's done is done—there's no point blaming you now."

"I promise I will fix this, Bethany," he said fiercely. "I won't let them harm you." His refusal to accept the reality in front of us was becoming irritating.

"Look, I know you're used to calling the shots and all," I said. "But even you can't change this."

"We could run," Jake muttered, talking rapidly as his mind desperately searched for solutions. "But all the exits here are guarded. Even if we managed to outsmart the guards we wouldn't get far. Maybe I could bribe one of them to let us into the Wasteland . . ."

I wasn't really listening. I didn't want to hear his far-fetched ideas and I wished he would just be quiet for a while.

"We still have time before dawn," Jake continued, talking to himself now. "I'll come up with something."

23

Blood Sports

WHEN the Hades' dawn broke, I wasn't prepared for it and neither was Jake. Voices outside in the hall blasted through the silence and jolted us both out of our trance-like states. I was surprised to find I hadn't closed my eyes all night. I was still sitting stiffly under the covers, with my knees drawn up to my chin. Jake sprang up from his position on the couch, glaring at the door with a venomous expression.

"They're here," he announced in a voice full of doom.

When the door opened it revealed an entourage that included Diego, Asia, and several other demons I only vaguely recognized. No less than four hulking bodyguards accompanied them.

"Sure you've got enough backup there?" Jake growled, his dark eyes flashing with fury.

"Big Daddy anticipated you might put up a fight," Diego gave him a lopsided grin and flicked his head in my direction. "Take her."

The tank-like guards stormed into the room and soon I felt their vast hands close around my forearms, hauling me easily out of bed like a rag doll. I was still barefoot and in my nightgown. I stumbled when they tied my wrists roughly together with rope and used it to pull me unceremoniously across the room.

"Don't manhandle her!" Jake took a step toward me and the other demons sprang, immediately closing in on him. It was appalling to see his brothers and sisters turn on him so quickly. In the chaos, he disappeared from view and all I could hear was a chorus of vicious snarling and spitting. The fear was beginning to well up in me now and I couldn't stop myself from shaking.

"Beth!" I could hear Jake calling to me, his voice filled with desperation. "Beth, I won't let them go through with it!" But I didn't believe him and I could tell he didn't either. All conviction was gone from his voice.

The guards pushed me roughly down the passage and headed for the lobby. The others followed, casually chatting among themselves. When I caught her eye, Asia winked at me. In the lobby, Tucker appeared out of nowhere, his face a mask of distress. I could tell from the haunted look in his eyes that he'd heard the news. I tried not to look at him as we passed. I didn't want to make him feel any worse.

"Beth!" he yelled as the procession passed him. He lunged forward, trying to fight his way through the throng of demons to reach me. Nash snapped his fingers, and with a sickening crunch, Tuck's legs buckled beneath him. He cried out and I heard the sharp crack of bones breaking as he crumpled to the ground. I craned my neck to look back at him as I was shoved through the revolving glass doors.

"It's okay, Tuck," I called. "I'll be okay!" I glared furiously at Nash, who was striding casually alongside me. "Fix him," I said in a thin voice. "Your vendetta against me has nothing to do with him."

"You're really not in a position to be making demands," Nash replied pleasantly.

A fleet of black Escalades was waiting for us in the tunnel outside the hotel. I was bundled brusquely into the front one, sitting between Asia and Diego. Up close, they reeked of cigarette smoke, hard liquor, and pungent perfume. I slid down in my seat and tried to regulate my breathing, telling myself I wasn't truly going to die. Something would happen; someone would come to my rescue. They had to.

"Take us to the Ninth Circle," Diego told the driver. "And take the back route."

"At least you get to check out from Big Daddy's pad," Asia told me. "How's that for VIP treatment?"

I bit my lip and didn't respond. I focused on the gliding of the car as it sped through the pockmarked underground tunnels of Hades. The fear had crept from my belly into my chest now and was snaking its icy fingers up my throat, cutting off my air supply. I swallowed hard, determined not to give them the satisfaction of seeing me lose control.

To get to the Ninth Circle we had to travel deeper underground and when the cars stopped I saw that we were in a vast and ancient amphitheater at the very core of the earth, its center strewn with red sand. The stands were packed as if the entire populace of Hades had been invited to witness this momentous event. Lucifer and the seven other Originals occupied the sheltered seats in the highest tier, where they watched the proceedings with zeal, as if they were expecting a show. Human servants refilled their goblets and offered platters of food. On a raised platform in the center of the arena rose a tall wooden stake. Its base had been driven into the ground. A pile of dry sticks and straw had been arranged in a pyramid around it. The flammable material reached halfway up the stake, around where I calculated my waist would be.

The executioner was not a hooded medieval figure as I'd expected but a man in a business suit, his clothes so understated he might have passed for a bank clerk. It was only his sunken gray cheeks and colorless lips that made him look like death personified. When his scabby hands reached for me my skin crawled at his cold touch. Although he was withered looking I was no match for his wiry strength. He untied my wrists and pinned my arms behind me so that I was pressed against the stake. I remained motionless as he used even thicker ropes to bind my arms, waist, and feet to the stake. He pulled the ropes so tight they chafed and cut into my skin. The sticks and straw bit at my bare feet and ankles, but I couldn't move an inch. The crowd watched the proceedings with a sense of mounting excitement. I tried to keep my eyes turned upward and to dissociate myself with what was happening to my body. But I couldn't keep my thoughts from taking a gruesome turn. How long would it take for a victim to burn—minutes or hours? Did the body burn in sections from the feet up? Would I pass out from the pain before my skin began to melt? Would physical burning or asphyxiation be the actual cause of death?

When he was satisfied that I was securely tied, the executioner stood back to survey his work. Someone in the crowd passed him a rusty can of gasoline and he began to douse the straw with it. The caustic smell wafted up and burned my nostrils. My heart was beating so fast, I thought it would explode through my rib cage. The metallic taste of fear filled my mouth, but I didn't cry out, scream, or beg for mercy. My mind and body were churning relentlessly, but I didn't let the terror show on my face.

"This," the executioner croaked in my ear, "is what happens to those who serve the wrong master. Heaven's gone bankrupt, haven't you heard?" He jumped off the platform.

Lucifer rose to his feet and the crowd fell instantly silent. He looked around for a moment, his eyes seeming to absorb everything, down to the last minute detail. He didn't speak, just slowly raised his hand as a signal for the execution to begin.

It was the simplest, most casual gesture, but it resulted in the crowd letting out an uproarious cheer. His power over them was absolute. It was frightening to watch how they both feared and adored him. When he motioned for silence the result was instantaneous and every sound was extinguished as if someone had flicked a switch. A deep hush fell over the crowd as the executioner struck a long match, held it aloft for a moment, and then dropped it with a theatrical sweep of his arm onto the gasoline-doused construction. The flames roared up with lightning speed. From his seat, I saw a smile of satisfaction cross Lucifer's face while Jake thrashed desperately against the demons restraining him. Asia was biting her lip, but only to keep her excitement in check.

The flames rose around me like a hundred hungry mouths, quickly devouring the sticks and straw at the base of the stake. I squeezed my eyes tight shut, waiting for the suffocating heat, the inevitable agony to start. I sent a quick prayer to My Father, not in the hope of being spared but seeking forgiveness for all my failings. Then I waited for the flames to do their work.

I felt nothing. Had the torture begun but I was in too much shock to notice? Several more moments passed without any change. I looked around to see coils of flame leaping in every direction . . . only they weren't touching me. The flames rose and seemed to part around me so that two columns of fire burned on either side of my body. But I was not burning. Not even a strand of my hair was singed. All I felt was a warm prickling sensation as the fire snaked around me. My flesh should have been melting from my bones, but the fire refused to harm me. If it chanced to touch my skin it seemed to bounce off and veer in a new direction. It was as though I were wearing invisible armor. For one fleeting moment, I thought I heard a choir of angels singing. The sound was gone in an instant, but it was long enough for me to know I hadn't been abandoned.

It took a while for the spectators to realize what was happening. Once they did the cheers changed to howls of disappointment. Some shook their fists to indicate how cheated they felt. In the VIP stand Jake had stopped struggling and stared at me in open wonder. Lucifer looked momentarily confounded and then rose slowly to his feet, eyes flashing. Speculative whispers broke out all around the amphitheater.

I couldn't believe what was happening. Could this be the work of Heaven protecting me? Had someone enchanted the flames or was it my own powers keeping me safe? I had no idea, but I murmured hasty thanks to whatever higher power had chosen to spare my life. One look at Lucifer's face told me how humiliated he felt before all those assembled. He'd intended my death to demonstrate his power and I had unwittingly shown him up. The flames seemed to be subsiding around me now.

"Cut her loose," he commanded in a voice like steel.

The executioner obeyed, climbing the platform and wielding an axe to hack through the ropes, which were too hot to touch. Once free, I stepped out of the fire completely unmarked. As soon as I did, the flames rose up to devour the wooden frame, which was quickly charred to cinders.

"What the hell is going on?" Asia leapt forward, looking wilder than ever. She whipped around to face Jake. "She should be fried to a crisp! What did you do?"

"Nothing . . ." I thought I heard Jake's voice tremble. "I . . . I don't know what happened."

"Liar!" Asia screamed.

"Silence." Lucifer held up a ringed finger. "Arakiel had no hand in this. It seems the angel has been holding out on us. Her powers are greater than we know."

"What now?" someone asked.

Lucifer's listless blue gaze met mine and this time I didn't flinch away.

"Arakiel," he said tonelessly. "Kindly escort Miss Church to the chambers until we decide what to do with her."

As it turned out the "chambers" were Hell's version of a prison cellblock and they made Hotel Ambrosia look like paradise. The bodyguards hustled me out of the arena into a car and before I knew it I was being thrust into a space in the wall barely large enough to contain me. It was made of rough, cracked stone and rusted iron bars secured the entrance. When I sat down, my elbows scraped against the walls and my legs began to cramp after five minutes. There was total darkness in the chambers, but strange noises like the shuffling of feet and the clanging of metal pipes filtered through, along with mute cries of despair. The smell of damp was overwhelming.

Once the bodyguards left I heard Jake's voice through the bars. Although I could barely see him I could hear the mixture of relief and confusion in his voice.

"How did you do it?" he asked in a hushed tone. I heard his rings clink as he wrapped a hand around the bars. "Tell me the truth."

"I don't think it was me."

"Well, don't admit that to anyone, got it?" Jake said sharply. "It's the only bargaining chip we've got left."

"What are you going to do?"

"I don't know yet, but I'll speak to my father—try and persuade him to let you go. Maybe things will be different now he's seen how special you are."

I didn't respond—I was too drained from the day's ordeal. "Leave it to me," Jake said.

A few moments later I heard his retreating footsteps and I was left alone in the darkness.

24

Tennessee Blues

WITH Jake gone, there was only one way to take my mind off my physical discomfort. I shoved all troubling thoughts out of my head and focused on projection. I squeezed my eyes shut, willing my thoughts to shift away from this nightmarish place. The transition happened easily, like flipping a channel in my head. There was a rush of wind and then I had the feeling of my body dropping away like a stone as I rose in my spectral form. Before the darkness cleared, a voice reached me, distant at first but growing clearer. I could feel the familiar chug of an engine beneath me and smell leather mixed with sandalwood. I would have known that smell anywhere. It belonged to a certain 1956 Chevy Bel Air convertible. I felt the knot of tension in my chest instantly unravel and I breathed a deep sigh of relief. I was in Xavier's car.

As my astral form took shape, I realized I was hovering in the backseat of the Chevy between Xavier and Molly. They seemed to be angled as far away from each other as was physically possible, both gazing sullenly out the windows at the passing landscape. Any rift mending that had occurred in the last few hours had evidently been only temporary. Ivy and Gabriel were sitting tight-lipped up front, clearly relieved to be at some distance from whatever dispute was in progress. As I watched the highway speeding by, I realized that we were in unfamiliar territory. My family must have already left Venus Cove far behind them. They sure weren't wasting any time.

"We're almost there," Gabriel said sounding like a parent hoping to placate restless children. His voice, deep and resonant, reminded me of a low chord strummed on a guitar. Hearing his voice triggered a sharp pang of nostalgia for the way life used to be before Jake showed up and shattered everything. "We're about to cross the Tennessee state line."

"I don't see why we couldn't have gone by plane like all normal people," Molly grumbled.

"We weren't going to fly to cross one state," Ivy replied calmly, though I could sense that her patience was wearing thin. Molly shifted and her elbow went right through my rib cage. The sensation was uncomfortable like a bar of heat spearing through my side. I guessed it was the life force of her human body colliding with my spectral form. I automatically wriggled away from her.

"Ugh, I knew I shouldn't have eaten all those Junior Mints on the way over here," Molly complained rubbing her stomach. I noticed she was wearing pink sweatpants and a matching cropped hoodie. Her auburn curls were pulled up into a high ponytail on top of her head and a hot pink duffel bag had been shoved under the seat in front of her. I couldn't suppress a smile, knowing that Molly would claim she'd dressed sensibly for the occasion. Nobody responded to her comment. I supposed there wasn't much to say about Junior Mints when your mind was preoccupied with demonic kidnappings and apocalyptic signs. The Chevy coasted along the highway and Xavier laid his forehead against the window. He looked edgy, like he needed to be doing something more than lounging in the back of a car.

I peered through the window and watched the Georgia countryside fly by. I was struck by how scenic it was. The earth seemed to have a life of its own and lush forestland spread out before us like a cloak. Vivid red maples grew thick and fast, forming shady canopies where their branches interlocked. I caught sight of butterfly weed and delicate purple prairie clover among the velvet greenery. As we traveled I watched as the earth became carpeted with sycamore twigs. The sky above us looked vast and open, only a handful of clouds scudded lazily across it, like lilies drifting across a clear blue pool. Things seemed simpler out on the open road and I felt close to the natural world. I was reminded of my old home in the Kingdom. Something about this place made me feel more connected to it than I had in a long time. I let out a heavy sigh and Xavier, who'd been resting against the window, sat up straight and glared at Molly.

"What?" she demanded when she noticed him staring at her.

"Please don't do that," Xavier said.

"Do what?"

"Breathe in my ear like that."

Molly looked insulted. "What kind of freak do you think I am? Why would I want to blow in your ear?"

"I said *breathe*."

"Oh, I see, so I'm not allowed to breathe now?"

"That's not what I meant."

"You do realize, I'll suffocate if I'm not allowed to breathe."

Xavier leaned forward. "Seriously, guys, let me drive," he implored. "Someone else can sit back here and be tortured."

"I'm not even talking!" Molly protested angrily.

"You're talking now," Xavier groaned.

"We'd be there already if we'd gone by plane."

"The pilot would have crashed after five minutes of listening to you talk."

"It'd still be safer than driving around in this old bomb."

"Hey!" Xavier could not have looked more offended had someone insulted his manhood. He always got worked up when people took shots at his car. "It's vintage."

"It's a vintage pile of crap. I don't know why we couldn't take the Jeep."

I'd been wondering that myself. I got the feeling that taking the Chevy had been Xavier's idea. Maybe it made him feel more connected to me. We'd shared plenty of memories in that car, and maybe he'd wanted to take those with him when he left his old town and his old life completely behind. But Xavier wasn't about to share that information with Molly. Instead he said, "You wouldn't know a classic car if you fell over one."

"Jerk," she muttered.

"Airhead."

Ivy whipped around and glared at them both. "Were you two born in a barn? Knock it off."

Molly looked sheepish while Xavier sighed loudly and sank down in his seat once again. A few minutes of blissful silence followed until Gabriel pulled into a gas station. Xavier couldn't get out of the car fast enough and vanished inside, almost before my brother cut the engine. I considered following him, but I knew he was only going to fill in the time sulkily inspecting packs of gum and dated magazines until it was time to pile back into the car. Molly threw him a dirty look as she trotted off to find the restrooms.

I followed as my siblings made their way over to a man in oil-stained overalls, squinting beneath the hood of a rusted pickup truck. I noticed that beneath the smudges of grease on his face he had a twinkle in his eye and a cheerful demeanor. He was chewing tobacco and an old Hank Williams tune crackled from a portable radio nearby.

"Hello," Ivy introduced herself. "It's beautiful weather you're having."

"Hi there," the man replied, dropping his tools to give Ivy his undivided attention. "Sure is." He thought about shaking her hand, but reconsidered when he glanced down at his grime-caked fingernails. Up close, he had gentle blue eyes and a crooked smile. "How do you do?" His husky voice was made melodic by his flowing Southern accent. It was beautiful to listen to and of all the voices in the world I thought none sounded quite so musical.

"What's your name?" Gabriel asked and Ivy shot him a

look. His way of skipping over small talk sometimes made his style of conversation sound like a flat-out interrogation.

"Earl," the man replied, wiping a hand across his brow. "How can I help you?"

"We're looking for the Abbey of Mary Immaculate in Fairhope County," Ivy told him. "Do you know it?"

"I sure do, ma'am. It's near on seventy miles from here."

Xavier, who had sauntered out of the shop to join the discussion, did a quick mental calculation and sighed.

"Great," he muttered. "That's another hour on the road."

Ivy gave him a dismissive glance. "Is there a place to stay near the abbey?"

"There's a motel on the highway," said Earl. He looked Ivy up and down from her fawn trench coat and riding boots to her immaculately groomed blond hair. "It's none too flashy though."

"That's not a problem," my sister said demurely. "Can you tell us anything about the abbey itself?

Earl cleared his throat softly and averted his gaze, which immediately drew Gabriel's attention.

"We would be very much obliged if you could tell us what you know," my brother said in a voice suddenly full of charm. It had the usual hypnotic effect.

"Yeah, I know a thing or two 'bout that place," Earl said hesitantly. "But I ain't sure you wanna know."

My brother and sister leaned forward eagerly.

"Trust us," Ivy encouraged, flashing the man a smile that made him wobble on his feet. "We'd appreciate anything you can tell us. We haven't been able to find out much ourselves."

"That's 'cuz everythin's been locked up there for a spell," Earl said, mopping his brow again.

"What do you mean?" Ivy frowned.

"When you work at a gas station for a livin' you hear things," Earl continued in a conspiratorial voice. "A lot of folk come through here and they talk. I don't mean to eavesdrop, but I sometimes hear things without meanin' to. That abbey you're talkin' about—I got a bad feeling about it. Something ain't right there."

"What makes you say that?" Gabriel pressed, his voice low and intense.

"It used to be a real nice place," Earl continued. "We used to see the sisters 'round town all the time, visitin' folk and teachin' Sunday school. But 'bout two months ago we had a nasty lightnin' storm, worse than we ever seen. After that, the sisters didn't come out no more. They said one of them fell sick from the storm and couldn't be disturbed so they shut themselves up inside the abbey. Not a soul's been in or out since."

"How could a lightning storm make anyone sick?" Xavier asked. "That's not possible, unless the woman was physically struck by lightning."

"Sure, it don't make a lick of sense," Earl replied, shaking his head sadly. "But I drove past the abbey one night when I was a makin' a delivery out that way. I tell you, ain't nothing natural 'bout what I saw."

"Can you tell us what you saw?" Gabriel had stiffened and his expression told me he already knew the answer and he didn't like it.

"Well." Earl frowned and looked embarrassed as if the others might be on the verge of questioning his sanity. "I was headin' back into town when I passed by the place and I thought I heard someone screamin', only it didn't sound like no noise a human could make. It was a howlin' like some kind of wild animal. So, I got out of my car, wonderin' if I should call the sheriff and I saw all the top floor windows had been boarded up and there was scratches on the front porch like somethin' was tryin' to get in . . . or out."

Ivy twisted her head to look at Gabriel. "He could have warned us," she said in a low voice and I knew she was talking about Michael. "We are underprepared for this." I saw her gaze fall on Molly, who was applying a coat of lip gloss, using the car window as a mirror.

"I'm sorry, ma'am, I didn't mean to alarm you," Earl added as an afterthought. "I might just been an old coot losin' his mind."

"No, I'm glad you told us," Ivy said. "At least we know what to expect."

"Perhaps you can help us with one more thing," Gabriel said gravely. "The sister who fell ill on the night of the storm . . . what was her name?"

"I believe it was Sister Mary Clare," Earl said solemnly. "Shame—she was a real nice one too."

THE rest of the trip was more subdued as Gabriel made his way to the motel. Even I knew they couldn't barge into the abbey guns blazing until they'd thought of a strategic plan of action. To Ivy and Gabriel the source of disruption at the abbey was painfully clear, but Molly's and Xavier's confusion showed on their faces.

The motel was called the Easy Stay Inn and was situated just off the main highway, too far from the township to attract many tourists. As a result it was fairly shabby and badly in need of some maintenance. The parking lot was empty and the neon sign only flashed every few minutes, the rest of the time emitting a whining, static hum. The brown bricks had been painted white, but exposure to the elements had left them peeling and weathered. Inside the motel was only a small improvement, with dark paneled walls and brown carpet. A TV was blaring in one corner and a woman sat behind the reception desk, painting her nails and snickering at a *Jerry Springer* rerun. She was so stunned by the group's arrival she spilled her nail polish, but recovered quickly and stood up to greet the visitors. She wore tight stonewashed-denim jeans and a tank top. Her red hair was curly and scraped away from her face with a floral headband. Up close, I saw that she was older than she first appeared. A crookedly pinned name tag told us her name was Denise.

"Can I help you?" she asked uncertainly, clearly thinking they had lost their way and were looking for directions. My brother and sister stepped forward to deal with the formalities. I realized how they must look; like a golden couple, too perfect to be real. I had to admit the four of them looked strangely out of place in this setting. They stood close together, forming a secure unit, like a barricade against the rest of the world. It struck me that Xavier was starting to act more and more like one of us. He used to be more relaxed in the company of people, interacting with them easily, charming them as if it were second nature. Now he looked detached and reserved; every so often a frown creased his brow as though he were agitated by something unseen. My family had all made an effort to dress like average travelers, Gabriel and Xavier in dark jeans and black T-shirts and Ivy in her fawn trench coat. They all wore dark sunglasses to keep from drawing attention. Unfortunately, it had the opposite effect. The woman behind the desk stared at them as though she had suddenly found herself in the company of some rather gloomy film stars.

"We require two twin share rooms for the night," Gabriel said stiffly, handing the woman a shiny gold credit card.

"Here?" Denise asked in disbelief before realizing she wasn't helping business much. She gave a nervous laugh. "It's just that we don't get many folks through this time of year. Are y'all here on business?"

"We're on a road trip," Gabriel explained hastily.

"We're hoping to visit the Abbey of Mary Immaculate," Ivy said. "Is it walking distance from here?"

Denise wrinkled her nose. "That old place?" she said disdainfully. "It gives me the creeps; no one's been out there in a long time. It ain't far though, other side of the highway, just down a dirt road. You won't see it straight off on account of all them trees."

As she spoke, she inspected Ivy with an envious gaze and I tried to imagine how things must look from her perspective. Ivy's tumble of golden hair reached halfway down her back and her face was glowing and radiant despite the gravity of her expression. Her skin was translucent and her perfect, sculpted features barely moved when she spoke. She was like a stunning illusion you felt might fade away if you got too close. Denise turned to Gabriel, a hint of bitterness in her voice. "So, are you wantin' a honeymoon suite for you and your wife?"

I heard Molly snort from the green vinyl sofa and knew she was wondering what the motel classed as a "honeymoon suite," seeing as it resembled a highway shack with as much atmosphere as a toolshed.

"Actually, we're not . . . ," Gabriel began, but stopped himself just in time when he saw the sudden gleam of hope in Denise's eye. The last thing he needed was to waste time fending off the clumsy advances of another infatuated female. "We're not fussy," he finished carefully. "A simple room will be fine."

"And for you two?" Denise asked, inclining her head toward Xavier and Molly.

"Ew!" Molly burst out. "No way am I sharing a room with him."

Denise looked sympathetically at Xavier. "Lovers' tiff?" she asked. "Don't worry, honey, it's the hormones. They'll pass."

"He's the hormonal one," Molly replied. "Moody as all hell."

"Do you need any extras?" Denise asked. "Towels, shampoo, Internet access?"

"How about a gag?" Xavier muttered, casting a dark look at Molly.

"Oh, that's real mature," she said tartly.

"I'm not going to talk about maturity with a girl who thinks *Africa* is a *country*," Xavier countered.

"It so is," Molly insisted. "Like Australia."

"The word you're looking for is *continent*."

"If I hear one more word out of you two . . . ," Ivy warned.

Denise shook her head, mildly amused. "I wouldn't be a teenager again for all the money in the world." Her attempt at lightening the mood was met with blank stares from both parties. She waited for the tension in the room to ease or at least for someone to express some kind of normal sentiment like exasperation, exhaustion, irritation. But they all just stared vacantly at her; too caught up in their own private worries to pay her much attention. "Well, enjoy your stay," she said falteringly.

Gabriel leaned forward to take the keys and credit card Denise was holding out to him. I saw his fingers accidentally brush her hand and watched her body react to his touch. She seemed to lean involuntarily toward him and her hand flew to her mouth. Then she sagged against the desk as though that one bolt of intoxicating energy had left her thoroughly exhausted. She looked up into his eyes like molten silver and shivered. Gabriel brushed away the white blond hair that had fallen into his eyes and took a step back. "Thank you," he said politely and strode from the lobby, Ivy floating alongside him like a fairy. Xavier and Molly followed wordlessly.

A diner adjoined the motel and seeing as it was nearly evening, they all found themselves gravitating in its direction. The diner was empty save for a lone trucker sitting in the back corner and a surly waitress chewing gum and lazily wiping down the countertops. Both looked up in surprise when the door jangled and Gabriel and the others entered. The trucker looked disinterested, too worn-out to study them properly and the waitress looked first shocked and then distinctly annoyed at having four new customers to attend to. Like Denise, she was clearly used to having time on her hands.

I took a moment to look around the diner; it was simple but clean and welcoming. A counter ran along the length of one wall where plump round stools were arranged in a line. The floor was black-and-white linoleum and the booths were upholstered in a burgundy vinyl. A blown-up poster of Elvis Presley was displayed on the wall above the counter; he smirked down at us wearing an upturned collar and a wicked gleam in his eye. The far wall was papered with a collage of newspaper clippings relating to local Fairhope news. The four chose a booth farthest away from prying ears and settled down.

"So are you going to tell me what's going on?" Xavier asked immediately.

"Michael didn't tell us much." Ivy sighed. "We're going into this blind so we really need to focus now."

"There's something in that convent," Gabriel spoke almost to himself. "Something he expects us to find. He wouldn't send us all this way unless it was a surefire lead."

"Are you saying there could be a . . ." Xavier hesitated and lowered his voice. "A gateway we don't know about?"

"Even if there was, there's no way to get it open without a dem—" Gabriel broke off as he cast a glance around the deserted diner. The waitress was busy chatting to a friend on the phone. "Without a demon. They're the only ones who know how."

"But we're going to hit up the abbey tonight?" Molly asked, sounding like a character in a spy movie. It was clear she felt left out and wanted to make some kind of contribution, no matter how inane. Xavier rolled his eyes at her choice of words, but made no comment. I could see he wanted to avoid another sparring match.

"We'll go after dark," Ivy replied. "We don't want to be seen."

"Won't it be kinda creepy at night?"

"Feel free to stay at the motel," my sister said calmly. "Though the convent is probably less frightening."

"Can we please try and stick to the topic?" Xavier was growing exasperated. "You still haven't told me what the guy at the gas station was going on about." He leaned forward and rested his elbows on the tabletop. "What did he mean about the lightning storm?"

Ivy and Gabriel exchanged glances. "It might not be the best time to discuss it," Ivy said, looking pointedly at Molly. "In fact, it might be better if you both stay at the motel tonight. Let Gabriel and I deal with this."

"Like hell I'm staying behind," Xavier said. "What are they hiding?"

"You don't have to worry about me," Molly said in a practical tone I'd never heard her use before. "I've seen enough freaky supernatural stuff by now. I can handle it."

Gabriel pressed his hands flat against the table and regarded them both with a measured look.

"This is definitely not something either of you have encountered before."

"Gabe . . . ," Xavier said earnestly. "I know you're worried, but we're in this together now. I've got more riding on this than you understand. You gotta trust me . . ." He glanced across at Molly and grudgingly rectified, "Trust *us*."

"Fine," Gabriel said quietly. "The lightning storm, the howling, the scratches on the porch . . . it all points to one thing."

"No human could cause that sort of damage on their own," Ivy added grimly. "We're talking about nuns here, sisters who've devoted their lives to servitude. Think about it, what could possibly make these women lock themselves away from the world? What would be the worst thing imaginable in their eyes?"

Molly stared vacantly, but I could almost see the wheels turning in Xavier's head. His clear, turquoise gaze widened when the pieces finally fell together. "No," he said. "Seriously?"

"Looks that way," Gabriel replied.

"Then, we *have* dealt with this before," Xavier said. "Isn't that exactly what Jake did last year?"

Gabriel shook his head. "That was mild compared to this. They were just spirits; temporarily harnessed to cause damage. This is the real thing and it's a hundred times stronger . . . and more vicious."

"Can somebody please tell me what you're talking about?" Molly demanded, clearly fed up with being treated as though she were invisible.

Gabriel sighed heavily. "What we're dealing with here is a case of demonic possession. I hope you're ready."

A weighty silence settled over the table, broken only by the soft tapping of a pencil against a pad as the waitress waited to take their order.

"What can I get for y'all?" she asked. She was pretty in a nondescript way with limp blond hair and too much foundation. Her expression told me she dreamed of a more glamorous life than being stuck in a dead-end diner with nothing to do but watch traffic on the highway.

The somber mood of my family failed to lift, and the waitress raised her eyebrows impatiently.

Molly was the first to snap back to normality and plaster a fake smile across her face.

"I'll have the fried chicken and a Diet Coke," she said sweetly. "Can I get ketchup with that?"

25

Get Thee to a Nunnery

I was surprised when Gabriel and Ivy decided to change and head straight to the abbey after dinner with Xavier and Molly in tow. It was close to ten o'clock and I'd assumed they would call it a night and wait until morning. But something must have made them feel they shouldn't delay any longer.

Outside, the night air was crisp and the sky was a cape of royal blue velvet scattered with stars and wispy clouds. If it wasn't for the threat that lurked behind the woods opposite the highway, I would have felt entirely at peace. The sound of cicadas filled the air and a mild breeze played gently with Ivy's hair before drifting off to ruffle the treetops. There was something about this place, a quiet dignity and a grace from a forgotten time. It held an air of mystery, as if the weeping willows knew something we didn't.

Molly shivered as they crossed the highway and let themselves meld with the shadows dancing among the trees. She pulled her jacket tighter around herself and drew instinctively closer to Xavier. He slung an arm around her shoulders and gave her a reassuring squeeze. I was relieved to see a flicker of his former self beneath the brooding exterior. I knew the stress was getting to him more every day, eroding his usual easygoing manner. It was part of the reason he and Molly were always at each other's throats. He was at odds with himself, I realized. Half of him saw Molly as a connection to me as well as a reminder of our old lives at Bryce Hamilton. The other half couldn't help but let his concern for my safety overwhelm him. At times like these I knew he both resented Molly for the séance and blamed himself for not being able to change the turn of events.

"You'll be all right," he told her. "We'll all be all right." I saw the faraway expression in his eyes and knew he was thinking of me. He had to believe I'd be okay in order to keep going. I needed him to believe it too. It was his faith that was keeping mine alive. I wondered if I should try and make my presence known to him, but I was too drained from the recent ordeal to be anything other than a passive spectator.

The woods grew thick and fast, but Gabriel's finely tuned senses managed to quickly locate the dirt road Denise had mentioned. It was just wide enough to allow cars to pass through, but had been neglected over the last few months and bordering shrubs were already weaving their way across it. Tree branches hung low, drooping over the road, and clumps of sodden leaves muted the footsteps of visitors. The moonlight shining through the trees bathed the path in a milky gray light. A crescent moon dipped periodically behind the treetops plunging the path into occasional darkness. It was a good thing Gabriel and Ivy radiated light from their skin. It was faint, like the glow of a cell phone in a darkened room, but better than nothing. When an owl hooted from somewhere above, Molly stumbled and cursed under her breath. Almost imperceptibly, Gabriel dropped his pace so he fell into step with her. Although he didn't say a word, she seemed soothed by his presence.

Soon the trees thinned and the looming shadow of the old convent became visible. The Abbey of Mary Immaculate was a three-level, whitewashed Gothic Revival building. It had an adjoining chapel with spires rising to pierce the night sky, a reminder to onlookers of the Lord's lofty presence. There were rows of pointed windows across every floor, cast-iron gates and a gravel path leading to the front door. A lamppost illuminated the front garden with its grotto housing a statue of Our Lady as well as kneeling saints positioned among the tall grass. What was most disturbing was the derelict air of the place—the weeds that had sprouted up and overtaken the entrance to the chapel, the leaves that clogged the path and the boarded-up windows on the attic floor.

"I wonder how many sisters live here," Xavier murmured.

Gabriel closed his eyes and I knew he was reaching out and tapping into the history of the place, its life before recent events. He was always careful not to intrude too deeply on the private thoughts or feelings of individuals; he only brushed the surface to ascertain their identity. "There are twelve sisters in total," he said eventually. "Including the one who is afflicted."

"How did you know that?" Molly asked. "It looks like no one lives here at all."

"Now is not the time to ask questions," Ivy said patiently. "You will witness many things tonight that cannot be explained."

"I find it's easier if you don't overthink it," Xavier advised.

"Just how am I supposed to do that?" Molly complained. "I feel like I'm waiting for someone to jump out and tell me I've been punk'd."

"I think they only punk famous people," Xavier said under his breath.

Molly looked annoyed. "That's not helpful!"

"Look." Xavier turned to face her. "Let me try and help you out here. You know when you're watching a horror movie and the character always decides to go into the dark room where the killer's waiting?"

"Yeah?" Molly said blankly.

"Do you ask why the character's dumb enough to go into that room?"

"Well, no, it's a movie. You just go with it."

"Exactly," Xavier said. "Think of this like a movie and don't ask questions. You'll only make things harder on yourself if you do."

Molly looked like she wanted to argue, but a moment later she bit her lip and nodded hesitantly.

The locked gates opened easily at Gabriel's command and the group slowly approached the steps of the abbey's front porch. I saw the concern on Ivy's face intensify—deep, uneven grooves were etched into the timber boards, at least half an inch deep. They extended along the front and veered sharply off toward one of the windows as if someone had been dragged back inside after putting up one hell of a fight. My mind immediately thought of the poor human who had been possessed to act in such a way. The scratches in the porch were deep enough that shards of wood must have been driven beneath her nails. I shuddered to think what other damage had been done to the afflicted sister.

The wraparound porch was long and sheltered with pretty white awnings and posts. A pair of wicker rocking chairs sat beside a table still set for afternoon tea. Insects had laid claim to the biscuits on the plate and the tea in the china cups had grown moldy. A string of rosary beads lay on the ground as if someone had dropped them in a great hurry. The screen door looked scratched and the mesh torn as if someone had tried to rip it from its hinges. Xavier and Gabriel exchanged uncertain glances.

"Here goes," Xavier said with a heavy sigh. He reached out and lightly pressed the brass doorbell. Immediately the sound of chimes echoed dimly from within. For several long minutes they were met with nothing but silence.

"They can't ignore us forever." Ivy folded her arms across her chest. "Ring again."

Xavier obliged, holding the bell down longer. The chimes reverberated more loudly this time, sounding almost ominous as if heralding a message of impending disaster. If only the sisters knew that help was waiting outside. There was a rustling sound in the foyer, but the door remained unopened. Ivy or Gabriel could have blown it apart in a heartbeat, but I supposed that wasn't the best impression to make when trying to convince a nervous nun that you're on the same side.

"Please open the door." Gabriel leaned against the fly screen, his words coaxing. "We've come to help." The door opened a crack, the security chain still on. A face appeared and surveyed my brother with caution.

"My name is Gabriel, this is my sister and these are our friends," he continued soothingly. "May I ask your name?"

"I'm Sister Faith," the nun replied. "Why are you here?" She was soft-spoken, but I could hear her voice was distorted with fear. Ivy decided to step forward and declare their intentions.

"We know about Sister Mary Clare and the cause of her illness," she said in a voice filled with compassion. "You don't have to hide anymore. The creature that has overtaken her—we can send it away."

"You can do that?" Hope crept into the nun's voice, but only for an instant before she became suspicious again. "I'm sorry I don't believe you. We've called on every priest and minister in the county. They're powerless against it. What makes you any different?"

"You have to trust us," Ivy's said solemnly.

"Trust is somethin' we're a little short on these days." The nun's voice broke off with a quiver.

"We know things," Ivy pressed. "We have knowledge others cannot possess."

"How can I be sure you're not one of *them*."

"I take it you believe in God, Sister," Gabriel said.

"I've seen things . . ." Sister Faith's voice faltered, as though she were unsure what to believe anymore. Then she remembered herself. "Of course I do."

"Then believe that He is here now," Gabriel said. "I know your faith has been tested in the extreme, but it is not without cause. You have been touched by darkness, but you have not been broken. Now you shall be touched by light. Blessed are the pure in heart for they shall see God. Blessed are those who are persecuted for righteousness' sake for theirs is the Kingdom of Heaven. Let us in, Sister; let God return to your home. If you turn us away you are succumbing to darkness."

Molly stared openmouthed at my brother and there was a dead silence from inside the house. Then, slowly, the security chain was released and the front door of the abbey swung open. Sister Faith stood in the doorway, her eyes filled with tears.

"Oh my stars," she whispered. "So He has not forsaken us."

Sister Faith was a robust-looking woman in her sixties with pale skin and a fresh-scrubbed face. Faint wrinkles were etched around her eyes and mouth and I wondered how many of those she had accumulated over the last few months. A lamp on the hall table illuminated the wide foyer and curved staircase, but there was a stale smell in the air.

While Gabriel and the others made their introductions I moved away to study the framed black-and-white photographs on the wall. The glass in every frame had been shattered so the images were blurred, but I saw they recorded the official opening of the convent in 1863. Originally the convent had been built to house a group of Irish nuns who ran it for half a century as an orphanage and refuge for young women who'd fallen into disrepute.

Sister Faith led us silently past a parlor where rows of thin mattresses had been lined up on the floor—the sisters were clearly too afraid to sleep upstairs. As we climbed the sweeping staircase I caught a glimpse of the storerooms, infirmary, and a rustic-looking kitchen all located on the ground floor. The place would have been beautiful once; cozy in winter, bright and airy in the summer, but now it was a broken home. The kitchen floor was littered with broken utensils as if someone had thrown them around the room. Broken chairs were stacked in a corner and torn linen lay in a heap by the door. I guessed from these observations that the sisters had tried to expel the demon on their own with little success. I looked away from the shredded pages of a Holy Bible. The sight made something deep inside me churn. It was strange to visit an earthly location so damaged by demonic activity. Something fierce and terrible had shaken the house to its very foundations, knocking over ceramic vases and toppling furniture. It was also stiflingly warm, and even in my spirit form I felt the heat crawling across my skin as though it were alive. Molly immediately tore off her jacket, but the others didn't move, despite their discomfort.

On the second floor we passed the sleeping quarters with rows of cell-size bedrooms now stripped of their mattresses and the communal bathrooms. Finally we stopped at a winding mahogany stairwell leading to the attic where Sister Mary Clare had been isolated for her own safety as well as the safety of others. Sister Faith hovered uncertainly at the foot.

"Can you really return Sister Mary Clare to the hands of God?" she asked.

"We'll need to assess her condition before we can answer that," Gabriel replied. "But we will certainly try."

Ivy touched Sister Faith gently on the arm. "Will you take us to her?"

The nun peered worriedly at Xavier and Molly. "All of you?" she asked in small voice. "Are you sure about that?"

Gabriel gave a tight smile. "They're tougher than they look."

At the top of the stairs was a single locked door. I could sense the evil pulsing behind it even in my astral form. It was like a physical force, trying to repel the presence of Ivy and Gabriel. In addition to the mustiness there was another smell seeping from under the door, the smell of rotting fruit when the flesh has turned saggy and gray and insects have begun to burrow into it. Xavier flinched while Molly coughed and covered her nose. My siblings showed no reaction. They stood together, shoulders touching in a gesture of complete unity.

"I do apologize about the smell," Sister Faith said self consciously. "But there's only so much air freshener can do."

Outside the door, only a candle lit the tiny landing. It sat on an antique dresser dripping wax onto its silver holder. Sister Faith dug into her deep pockets to produce an old-fashioned brass key. Behind the door we could hear muffled thumps, ragged breathing, and the screech of a chair being dragged across timber boards. A sound like grinding teeth and a sharp crack like snapping bone followed. Sister Faith crossed herself and looked desperately at Gabriel.

"What if you can't help her?" she whispered. "What if the Lord sent us his messengers and that fails too?"

"His messengers do not fail," Ivy said calmly. She produced a black hair tie from her pocket and methodically pulled her curtain of golden locks into a ponytail. It was a small gesture, but I knew it meant she was preparing for a violent struggle.

"There's so much darkness in there." Sister Faith's face was creased in pain. "Living, breathing, tangible darkness. I don't want to be responsible for the loss of life—"

"Nobody is dying tonight," Gabriel said. "Not on our watch."

"How can I be sure?" Sister Faith shook her head. "I've seen too much now . . . I can't trust . . . I don't know how I'm supposed to . . ."

To my surprise, Xavier stepped forward. "With all due respect, ma'am, there's no time to waste." His voice was gentle but firm. "You've got a demon tearing apart one of your sisters and we're on the brink of an apocalyptic war. These guys will do everything they can to help you, but you need to let them do their job."

His gaze went blank for a moment as if he were remembering something that happened a long time ago. Then he refocused and put a hand on Sister Faith's shoulder. "Some things are beyond human understanding."

If my spirit form had allowed it, I would have cried at that moment. I recognized those words as my own. I had spoken them to Xavier that night on the beach when I'd taken a blind leap of faith and thrown myself from a cliff, letting my wings break my fall and revealing my true identity. When I had convinced Xavier it wasn't all a bizarre prank, he'd been full of questions. He'd wanted to know why I was there, what my purpose was, and if God really existed. I'd told him: *Some things are beyond human understanding.* Xavier hadn't forgotten.

I remembered that night as if it were yesterday. When I closed my eyes, it all came flooding back to me like a tidal wave. I saw the cluster of teenagers around the crackling bonfire, embers spitting from the flames like fiery jewels until they sank into the sand. I remembered the sharp smell of the ocean, the fabric of Xavier's pale blue sweatshirt beneath my fingers. I remembered the way the black cliffs had looked like looming puzzle pieces against the mauve sky. I remembered the exact moment I had tilted my body forward and left gravity behind me. That night had been the beginning of everything. Xavier had accepted me into his world and I was no longer the girl pressed up against the glass looking in on a world I could never be a part of. The memory of it made me ache with longing. We had thought facing Gabriel and Ivy after I'd exposed our secret was a challenge. If only we'd known what lay in store for us.

The sound of the key turning in the lock drew my attention back to the present. Xavier's words had encouraged Sister Faith to reveal what lay behind the closed door. Everyone seemed to hold their breath as the smell of rotting fruit grew stronger and a ripping snarl shot though the air. It seemed that time stood still as the door swung open in slow motion.

The room was rather ordinary; sparsely furnished and only somewhat larger than the cubicle-size bedrooms on the second floor. But what we found crouched inside the room was anything but ordinary.

26

See No Evil, Hear No Evil

AT first she looked like an ordinary woman, tense and wary of the strangers standing in her doorway, but a woman nonetheless. She was wearing a cotton chemise that reached her knees and would have been pretty had it not been torn, blackened, and stained with blood. Her long, dark hair was a tangled mess around her shoulders and she crouched by the grate of the fireplace grabbing fistfuls of soot and spilling it onto the bare boards. Her knees were scuffed and cut as if she had dragged herself across the floor. Had I been physically present my first instinct would've been to go to her aid, help her to her feet, and comfort her. Instead I looked to Ivy and Gabriel, but they didn't move. I realized why when I focused on the eyes looking back at us and saw that they no longer belonged to Sister Mary Clare. The others saw it too, and Molly let out a stifled cry and edged behind Xavier, whose face reflected mixed emotions. His expression shifted from pity to disbelief to disgust and back again in a matter of seconds. This was something he'd never had to deal with before and he wasn't sure what the appropriate response was.

The young nun, who couldn't be more than twenty, was

crouched on the floor, looking closer to an animal than any kind of human. Her face was twisted grotesquely, her eyes huge, black, and unblinking. Her lips were cracked and swollen and I could see the points where her teeth had pierced right through the flesh. A row of intricate symbols had been branded into the skin on her arms and legs. The room itself was in no better shape. The mattress and linen had been torn to shreds and scratches were gouged into the floor and ceiling. Words were scrawled on the walls in an ancient script I couldn't decipher. I wondered for a moment how the walls had come to be smeared with coffee until I realized it wasn't coffee, but blood. The demon cocked its head to one side like a curious dog, and its gaze lingered on the visitors. There was a long, deep silence, until the demon snarled again, gnashing its teeth. Its head darted rapidly from side to side, looking for a point of escape.

Ivy and Gabriel moved in tandem, ushering the others back and sweeping into the room. The demon's eyes widened as it spat viciously at them. The saliva was tinged red from having bitten its tongue. I noticed that it didn't need to blink and could focus with frightening precision. Ivy and Gabriel joined hands and the demon screamed as if this gesture alone caused intense pain.

"Your time on this earth is over." Gabriel fixed his steel-like gaze on the creature, his voice full of righteousness and authority. The demon stared for a moment before recognition dawned and its face cracked into a hideous smile. I saw that Sister Mary Clare's teeth had been ground into uneven stumps.

"What are you going to do?" the demon jeered, its voice singularly high-pitched and scratchy. "Vanquish me with holy water and crucifixes?"

Ivy's demeanor did not change. "Do you really think we need toys to destroy you?" she asked in a voice like water flowing over river stones. "The Holy Spirit is alive in us. It will soon fill this room. You will be cast back into the abyss from which you sprang."

If the demon was alarmed, it didn't show it. Instead, it deftly changed the subject. "I know who you are. One of your kind belongs to us now. The little one . . ."

Xavier looked as if he were about to step forward and take a swing at the creature, but Molly gripped his arm and with some effort, he turned his face away. "It knows our weaknesses," I heard him murmur to himself like a mantra. "It plays on our weaknesses." Xavier may not have had any direct experience with possession before, but he'd learned enough from Sunday School to know how the Devil worked.

"It's funny you should mention that," Gabriel said to the demon. "It's exactly what we wanted to talk to you about."

"You think I'm a whistleblower?" the demon hissed.

"You will be," Ivy replied pleasantly.

The demon glanced over her shoulder and its eyes flashed. Suddenly, a blast of wind lifted Xavier off his feet and threw him against a wall. He slid onto the ground and to my horror an invisible force began to drag him across the floor.

"Stop it!" Molly screamed, reaching for him.

"Molly, no!" Xavier yelled and gritted his teeth as he was flung against the steel bed frame. "Stay there."

"You threaten, I threaten," the demon taunted as Xavier struggled against its hold.

"Enough." Gabriel thrust his palm forward in a pushing motion and the demon cried out and seemed to crumple in pain. It was obvious whose power was dominant. "We're not interested in playing games," he said darkly. "We want to find a portal."

"Are you out of your mind?" the demon growled. "Do you have a death wish?"

"We have come to reclaim our sister," Ivy said. "And you will tell us how to find her."

"Make me!" the demon spat.

"If you insist." There was a sound like muffled fireworks and then streams of white light began to pour from Ivy's fingertips. As she flexed and twisted her fingers the strands of light seemed to enter into the body of the demon like electric shocks. It let out a feral howl and clawed at its torso.

"Stop!" it screamed. "Stop! Stop!"

"Will you tell us what we seek to know?" Ivy asked. She turned her palm slowly from side to side so the beams of light twisted inside the demon and it shrieked even louder. Ivy was choosing her method carefully. I knew the Holy Light would sear the demon, but leave Sister Mary Clare's body completely unharmed.

"Yes," it screeched. "I'll help you. Stop!"

Ivy snapped her hand into a fist and the light vanished. The demon collapsed on the floor exhausted.

"Easily convinced, aren't they?" Gabriel muttered.

"No sense of loyalty," my sister replied with disdain before rounding on the creature. "Where is the nearest portal?" she demanded.

"It doesn't matter," the demon croaked. "You'll never get through it."

"Answer the question," Gabriel said. "How did you get here?"

"Why don't you just send me back?" the demon tried to stall. "That's what you've come to do, isn't it? Are you really willing to let me fester inside this poor girl just to fulfill your own agenda?" It clicked its tongue as if to indicate disappointment. "Some angels."

Gabriel made the Sign of the Cross very slowly and deliberately, and when he finished, he seemed to catch something in his hand. He drew back his arm and launched it at the demon. Although it was invisible, the thing collided with the demon with incredible force and it yelped, spraying foam from its mouth across the floor.

"There's a place called Broken Hill down in Alabama," it gasped. "There's a train station there. Years ago there was a train wreck. Sixty people died. The closest portal is there."

"Shouldn't there be a portal in Venus Cove?" Xavier snapped. "The one Jake took Beth through?"

"Powerful demons can conjure portals at will," Gabriel replied. "That one was only temporary to serve Jake's purpose."

Xavier glanced at the demon on the floor. "But how do we know it's telling the truth?"

"If there was a train wreck in Broken Hill it could be true," Ivy said. "Traumatic events causing loss of innocent lives can result in the formation of a portal." She hesitated. "Still, it could be lying. Gabe, can you get inside its mind—see if it's telling the truth?"

A look of repulsion crossed Gabriel's face as he contemplated reaching inside the mind of such a creature. He'd told me once that a demon's mind was thick and clogged with a sticky black substance like tar. That's why exorcisms were so draining for the afflicted human beings. Once that stuff got inside of you, it stuck. It clung to you like glue, infecting you and spreading like a fungus until every inch of you belonged to them. Some humans didn't survive the separation. It was like tearing apart two souls; only one half didn't want to be separated. It was a vicious tug-of-war with the human body as the rope. I knew that once the demon had surrendered the information my siblings needed, they would have to tear it out of Sister Mary Clare. I didn't want to watch, but I couldn't bring myself to turn away. Gabriel closed his eyes and the demon clutched the sides of its head as if a sudden migraine had come on. A few moments later, my brother withdrew, disgust written all over his perfect features.

"It speaks the truth," he said.

"So if we find the portal we'll be able to get Beth back?" Xavier asked.

"If only it were that easy," the demon cackled. "You'll never get through it."

"There is always a way," said Ivy in a level voice.

"Oh, yes," the demon snickered. "Though I wouldn't try and trick your way in. You may find you're not able to get out."

"We don't resort to tricks," Gabriel said.

"You could always bargain her back," the thing suggested,

its lip curling maliciously as its empty, black eyes fell on Xavier. "Trade him for her. And you'd do it, wouldn't you, boy? I can see it in your eyes. You'd sacrifice your soul to save her. It's a high price to pay for something that isn't even human. How do you know she even has a soul? She's just like me— except working for a rival corporation."

"I'd shut my mouth if I were you." Xavier scraped his walnut-colored hair away from his face and I caught a flash of my promise ring on his hand. In his black T-shirt and jeans he didn't look celestial like my brother and sister, but he looked tall and strong and thoroughly pissed off. I could tell he wanted to wipe the smirk off its face, but Xavier could never bring himself to hit a girl, even one who was possessed.

"Hit a nerve, have we?" the demon crooned.

I thought Xavier might snap, but instead, his tense posture relaxed and he leaned against the wall, surveying the creature coolly.

"I feel sorry for you," he said slowly. "I guess you wouldn't know what it's like to be loved or wanted by anybody. You're right, though; Beth isn't human, because humans have a soul that they struggle all the time to stay in touch with. Every day is a battle for them to listen to their conscience and do the right thing. If you knew Beth at all you'd know that she doesn't have a soul, she's *all* soul. She's filled with it, more than any human possibly could be. You wouldn't know that because emptiness and hatred is all you've ever known. But that won't win out in the end—you'll see."

"You're very cocky for a mere human," the demon replied.

"How do you know fate won't tempt your soul to become as black and twisted as mine?"

"Oh, I don't think that's going to happen," Ivy said with a smile. "His soul is already marked as one of ours. Xavier's got a reserved seat in Heaven."

"Now, if you don't mind," my brother cut in smoothly. "We're done making small talk."

The demon seemed to know what was coming and leapt up, arching its back like a cat and hissing furiously. Molly, who was hovering in the doorway, ducked as if she expected objects to begin flying around the room.

"Is this the part where you start chanting in Latin?" she asked tremulously.

Gabriel's gaze flickered toward her. "Get under the bed, Molly. You don't need to witness this."

"It's okay," Molly shook her head. "I've seen *The Exorcist.*"

My brother gave a humorless laugh. "This is a little different," he said. "Humans need prayers and rituals to send a demon back to Hell. But we're stronger than that."

He held out his hand and Ivy entwined her dainty, peach-colored fingers with his. At exactly the same moment their wings opened, spanning the width of the room and casting long shadows on the walls. The others watched in astonishment as light began to blaze from their outstretched wings to form a cloud around them. Their bodies seemed to hum and vibrate and then ever so slightly levitate off the ground. Then Gabriel spoke.

"In the name of Christ Our Lord and all that is Holy, I command you be gone. Return this earthly body to the hands of God and slither back into the pit of fire where you belong."

The demon's head began thrashing back and forth like a whip, as though it were having some sort of seizure. The cloud of muted, golden light crept forward, beautiful to the human eye, but a mark of death for any agent of darkness. The demon tried to dart past my siblings, but the light was like a force field keeping it back. It struggled violently, but to no avail. The misty cloud had almost reached it and I watched the demon throw itself to the floor. As the light surrounded it, descending like a fog, Sister Mary Clare's body began to emit smoke from her nose and a sizzling sound like meat on a barbeque filled the air. Molly's jaw dropped in horror and she backed away from the scene before her, covering her ears against the demon's strangled screams. Xavier too went pale and swallowed hard, watching with a pained expression. The body on the ground had gone rigid, its torso lurching upward in shuddering convulsions. I saw a bulge appear in Sister Mary Clare's abdomen, it seemed to be shifting upward, through her chest, like a hideous tuber-shaped growth. Xavier winced as the sharp crack of a snapping rib was heard amid the grunts and gasps. The bulge distorted the woman's throat until suddenly her mouth flew open and she began to choke and gurgle. My siblings concentrated harder, their light constricting around the nun's throat and sure enough, a steaming, thick black substance came pouring through her open mouth and flopped onto the floor like a dead fish.

Ivy dropped her hand, retracted her wings, and sank to

her knees in exhaustion while Gabriel knelt beside the body on the floor. Free at last from the poisonous creature that had been holding her hostage, Sister Mary Clare looked very different. The vicious expression was replaced by one of liberation, despite the pain she must have been in. Her face was still bruised and battered, but as her eyelids fluttered open I caught sight of a pair of pale blue eyes. The young woman seemed to sigh in relief and her head lolled to one side. Gabriel looked concerned and bent low over her, his fingers pressed lightly against her neck, searching for a pulse.

He looked up at Ivy. "It's not good."

My sister floated across to join him and together they began to work on Sister Mary Clare. Gabriel seemed to be healing the physical wounds while Ivy went deeper, trying to reach Mary Clare's soul and restore it to health and to God. I couldn't imagine the state her soul must be in after sharing a body with a demon for months. It would be shredded almost beyond recognition, but if anyone could help her, it was a seraphim. I watched as Gabriel touched her cheeks and the bruising and swelling began to subside. His fingers traced across her lips and they were whole once again. Sister Faith hurried to bring a wet cloth and gingerly wiped away the dried blood that caked her lips and chin. When Gabriel moved his hands, I saw that Sister Mary Clare's teeth had been restored as well. My brother had left her with no physical reminder of the torment she'd endured. Although her body was returned to full health, her chest was still. Ivy remained hunched over her, eyes tightly shut. My sister's body trembled with the effort and Gabriel put his hands on her shoulders to steady her. Bringing a soul back from the brink of death was tiring work even for an angel as strong as Ivy and I could see that Sister Mary Clare was almost beyond help. A soul, once taken by Death, was almost impossible to get back. The soul belonged to him until it was claimed by either Heaven or Hell. If no one wanted it, it was tossed into Limbo like garbage.

I knew Ivy had to travel down the tunnel of Sister Mary Clare's subconscious and coax her back before she slipped away forever. I imagined her mind was like a mess of crawling vermin, contaminated by the evil that had inhabited her body for so long. Death was close, anybody could see that. She was probably teetering on the edge, unwilling to return to life lest it be full of the agony she remembered. The tunnel of death sucks the life out of you, it wants you to give in. It wants you to surrender. Of course, the darkness could never touch my sister, but it could still deplete her strength and being inside Sister Mary Clare's infected mind was bound to take its toll.

Eventually, after what seemed like forever, Ivy released the nun's hand and watched as her eyes blinked and then opened. She immediately took a deep, gasping breath like someone who had been held underwater too long.

"Oh praise the Lord!" Sister Faith cried. "Thank you, bless you." She seized Mary Clare in a tight hug as the bewildered woman sat up and looked around in confusion. I saw her properly then and realized just how young she was—no more than early twenties with a clear face and a sprinkling of freckles across her nose.

"What . . . what happened?" she stammered. Her hand reached up to touch her knotted hair, which was caked with blood. Sister Faith's mouth fell open.

"She doesn't remember?"

"She's in shock," replied Gabriel. "Over the next few days it will come back to her through flashes and nightmares. She will need your support."

"Of course." Sister Faith nodded frantically. "Whatever she needs."

"Right now she needs a shower," my brother said. "And then you should get her into bed." He looked around the trashed room. "Is there somewhere she can stay while this mess gets cleaned up?"

"Yes, yes," Sister Faith was muttering to herself. "I'll have Adele set up a bed." She looked at Gabriel and Ivy. "I don't know how to thank you," she said, her eyes welling up again. "I thought we had lost her forever, but you have given us our sister back and reaffirmed our faith like I never expected in this lifetime. You have our unending gratitude."

Gabriel only smiled. "It was our pleasure," he said simply. "Now take care of your sister. We will see ourselves out."

Sister Faith gave my siblings one final look of rapture and then hurried the frail Mary Clare out of the room. I heard her calling through the house to the others. I wondered if they would believe the story of the mysterious visitors and the heavenly retribution they'd delivered.

When they were gone, Ivy, who had been uncharacteristically quiet, let out a soft sigh and seemed to sway for a moment on her feet.

"Easy there," Xavier said, taking a step toward her. "Are you okay?"

With a resounding swish Gabriel's wings retracted, folding behind his muscular back. He wrapped a strong arm around Ivy's waist to support her and she leaned against his shoulder, regathering her strength.

A moment later her wings also retracted, but I could see the effort it cost her. She took a deep breath and gave Xavier a faint smile.

"I'm just drained," she said. "I'll be fine in a minute."

Gabriel began to usher the little party toward the door. "Come," he said. "Our business here is finished, we should leave."

Outside on the porch, Gabriel caught sight of Molly. Clearly, the full impact of what she'd witnessed had just hit her. She clutched the porch post, her hands shaking. She looked as if she could hardly support her own weight and took one wobbly step forward, stretching out her hands to regain her balance. Gabriel slipped an arm around her waist to help her down the steps, and when they reached the bottom, he wordlessly sank down beside her as she knelt on the ground and threw up into the flower beds. One hand still on her shoulder, he gently lifted her hair away from her face and held it back—not speaking, just patiently waiting for her to finish.

27

He Loves Me Not

IT was the early hours of the morning by the time the four of them made it back to the Easy Stay Inn. Although some color had returned to Molly's face, she seemed overcome with exhaustion. Xavier looked equally worn-out and badly in need of sleep. Only my siblings remained as composed and poker-faced as always. The only indication of the stress they'd just undergone was their rumpled clothing. Ivy's strength seemed to have replenished by the time they got back, but I knew it had been a tough night for her. It must be frustrating, I thought. Her strength and power in the Kingdom was boundless. But from what I could see, the longer angels lingered on earth and mingled with humanity, the more finite their powers seemed to become.

At the first opportunity, Xavier disappeared to his room without saying a word to anyone. I wanted to follow him so we could be alone for a while. I imagined myself lying down beside him on the bed and pressing my head against his chest the way I used to do. I wanted to focus every shred of energy on letting him know I was there; to offer him what little comfort I could and let his presence comfort me. But Ivy and

Gabriel were the ones planning the next move and I needed to stay put if I wanted to be kept in the loop.

"What's with him?" Molly muttered as soon as Xavier shut the door behind him.

"I imagine he's disturbed by tonight's events," Ivy said drily as she fitted her key into the lock. "He needs some time to process it." I knew Molly's naïveté irritated her sometimes.

For some reason, Molly was still purposelessly hovering beside my siblings. They both had the good grace not to ask what she wanted. Maybe she wanted out of the whole rescue mission. Maybe she'd taken on more than she bargained for and was ready to go home.

The bedroom door was painted a murky maroon color. With a heavy sigh Gabriel pushed it open and flicked the switches on the wall. The room was filled with a harsh amber light and the rattle of a defective overhead fan. The twin beds were covered in thin floral duvets with matching bedside tables and fringed nightshades. The carpet was a faded salmon color and curtains on a metal rod covered a single rectangular window.

"It has a certain charm," Ivy said with an ironic smile. Although my siblings had grown used to the luxury of Byron, their surroundings were immaterial to them. They could've been in a luxury suite at the Waldorf Astoria for all the difference it made.

"I'm going to take a shower," Ivy said, scooping up a bag of toiletries and disappearing into the bathroom. Molly watched her go, biting her lip and shifting anxiously from foot to foot. Gabriel's penetrating eyes watched her patiently.

They reminded me of a snowstorm—clear and pale and so full of depth that you could easily lose yourself in them. He removed his jacket and hung it on the back of a chair. The tight white T-shirt he wore accentuated his impossibly perfect physique. Molly couldn't seem to tear her gaze away from his rippling body and the way the fabric strained across his defined chest. He looked superhuman, as if he could shoulder a car with minimal effort. That was probably because he could if the situation called for it.

The sound of water running through the old pipes filtered out from the bathroom and Molly immediately seized it as an opportunity to strike up a discussion.

"So, will Ivy be okay?" she asked awkwardly. It was clear she wasn't there to talk about Ivy, but a more effective opening eluded her.

"Ivy is a seraphim," Gabriel replied as if that settled the matter.

"Yeah," Molly said. "I remember. And that's pretty cool, right?"

"Yes," said Gabriel slowly. "It is *cool*."

Taking this as encouragement, Molly edged her way into the room and perched on the bed, pretending to examine her fingernails. Gabriel leaned against the doorway opposite her. If he'd been human he would have looked awkward or uncomfortable, but he was composed in every way. No matter what environment he found himself in, my brother always gave off an air of self-possession, as if he'd been there all his life. He stood with his hands folded behind his back and his head tilted slightly to one side as if he were listening to a silent internal melody. His attention seemed far from Molly, although I knew he was waiting for her to speak. He could probably hear her heart thumping in her chest, smell the sweat on the palms of her hands—even read her mind if he wanted to.

Molly raised her eyes nervously. "You were amazing today," she said. Gabriel looked at her, perplexed by the compliment.

"I was doing my job," he replied in his low, compelling voice.

I could tell by the expression on Molly's face that his voice affected her in ways I couldn't understand. It seemed like each word he spoke entered her body on a physical level. Molly shivered slightly and wrapped her arms around herself.

"Are you cold?" my brother asked. Without waiting for her answer he chivalrously lifted his jacket from the back of the chair and draped it around her shoulders. The thoughtful gesture seemed to move Molly to such an extent that she struggled to keep her eyes from misting up.

"No, really," she insisted. "I always knew you were amazing, but today was different. You were like something out of this world."

"That's because I'm not from this world, Molly," Gabriel replied evenly.

"But you're still connected to it, right?" Molly pressed. "To people, I mean. Like Xavier and me?"

"My job is to protect people like you and Xavier. I wish you only health and happiness . . ."

"That's not what I'm saying," Molly cut in.

"What *are* you saying?" He looked at her with the piercing intensity of someone determined to understand a way of reasoning that was not his own.

"It's just that I think you could want more. These last few days I've been sensing that like . . . maybe . . . you might have felt . . ."

I sprang onto the bed and knelt beside Molly. I tried to send out a message of caution, but she was too absorbed in Gabriel's presence to notice I was there with her.

No, Molly, don't do it. You're smarter than this. Think about it. Gabriel isn't what you want him to be. You're about to make a huge mistake. You only think you know him. You've imagined there's more to it than there really is. If you're hurting now, this will only make things worse. Go and talk to Xavier first. Wait a while—you're tired. Molly, listen to me!

Gabriel turned his head slowly to look at her. The movement was almost robotic. His face was cast in shadow from the dim motel light, but his hair still glowed as it fell gently around his cheekbones like strands of gold and his eyes were a forever-shifting haze of silver and ice blue.

"Maybe I felt what?" he asked curiously.

Molly sighed in exasperation and I knew she'd had enough of dropping hints. She stood up so she was standing directly in front of him. With her mermaid tumble of curls, wide blue eyes, and dewy skin she looked as enticing as ever. Most men would not have had the willpower to resist her.

"You act like you don't have feelings, but I know you do!" she said confidently. "I think you feel a lot more than you let on. I think you could love someone, even fall in love with someone if you chose to."

"I'm not sure what you're trying to say, Molly. I value human life," Gabriel said. "I wish to defend and protect My Father's children. But the love you speak of . . . I know nothing of that."

"Stop lying to yourself. I can see through you."

"And what exactly do you think you see?" Gabriel raised an eyebrow and I realized he had an inkling of where the conversation was headed.

"Someone's who's just like me," Molly cried. "Someone who wants to be in love but is too scared to let it happen. You care about me, Gabriel—admit it!"

"I've never denied caring for you," Gabriel said gently. "Your well-being is important to me."

"It's more than that," Molly insisted. "It has to be! I feel something incredible between us and I know you must feel it too."

Gabriel leaned forward. "Listen to me carefully," he said. "You have somehow gotten the wrong idea about me. I'm not here to . . ."

Before Gabriel could finish, Molly leapt forward and closed the distance between them. I saw her arms reach around his waist and her fingers close over his T-shirt. I saw her stand on the tips of her toes and strain up toward him. I saw her eyes close in a moment of pure ecstasy as their lips met. She kissed him fervently, longingly, intoxicated by him. Her body ached for his touch and she pressed herself against him. She trembled with the intensity of it, her whole body straining to get closer to him. The room became charged with a strange energy, and for a moment I thought something would ignite between them that would blast through the walls of the motel room. Then I saw Gabriel's face.

While he hadn't moved away from Molly, he wasn't returning her kiss. His arms remained rigidly by his sides, his mouth unresponsive, refusing to meld with hers. Molly might have been kissing a waxwork for all the response she drew from him. Gabriel let her continue for a moment before gently disengaging himself from her grasp. She fought him for a second then staggered back and sank down on the bed.

"No, Molly. This can't happen."

Gabriel only looked saddened by her display of affection. He wore a thoughtful frown, looking at Molly the same way he looked at all mortal dilemmas he needed to solve. He'd worn the same expression when they'd stopped to talk to Earl at the gas station and again when he'd inspected the grooves on the front porch of the Abbey. His clear eyes were serious as he grappled for a solution to a problem he had not before encountered. A strange look crossed Molly's face as his indifference finally dawned on her. Her forehead creased as she tried to make sense of the overpowering attraction she felt that seemed to be strictly one-way. I could tell she couldn't quite believe it and I noted the exact moment when humiliation replaced her passion. Blood rushed to her cheeks and she squirmed under Gabriel's inquisitive gaze.

"I can't believe I got it so wrong," she murmured. "I never do that."

"I'm sorry, Molly," Gabriel said. "I apologize if I've said or done anything to mislead you."

"Don't you feel anything?" she asked more angrily. "You must feel something!"

"I do not possess human sentiment," Gabriel said and then thought to add, "nor does Ivy." Maybe he hoped it'd make Molly feel better to know that her advances would be lost on my sister as well. If so, it didn't have the desired effect.

"Quit acting like you're a robot or something," she snapped.

"If that's how you'd prefer to think of me . . ." Gabriel trailed off.

"It's not!" Molly burst out. "I'd prefer to think of you as real, not some tin man who doesn't have a heart."

"My heart is nothing but a vital organ pumping blood around this body," Gabriel explained. "I lack the capacity to give the love you speak of."

"What about Beth?" Molly asked. "She loves Xavier and she's one of you."

"Bethany is an exception," Gabriel conceded. "A rare exception."

"Why can't you be an exception too?" Molly insisted.

"Because I am not like Bethany," Gabriel said in a matter-of-fact voice. "I am not young and inexperienced. There is something in Bethany's makeup, a flaw or a strength, that allows her to feel what humans feel. I do not have that in my programming." I was too caught up in the mounting tension to wonder whether or not I ought to be offended.

"But I'm in love with you," Molly whimpered.

"If you think you love me, then you don't know what love

is," Gabriel said. "Love has to be reciprocated for it to be real."

"I don't understand," Molly said. "Am I not hot enough for you or something?"

"Now you're just proving my point," Gabriel sighed. "A body is merely a vehicle. The deepest emotions are experienced through the soul."

"So it's my soul that isn't up to your standards then?"

"Don't be ridiculous."

"What's wrong with you?" Molly exploded. "Why don't you want me?"

"Please try to accept what I'm saying."

"Are you saying no matter what I do, no matter how hard I try, you'll never feel that way about me?"

"I'm saying you're behaving like a child because that is what you are."

"So it's because you think I'm too young," Molly said desperately. "I can wait. I can wait until you feel ready. I'll do whatever you need."

"Stop," Gabriel said. "This discussion is over. I cannot give you the answer you want to hear."

"Tell me why." Molly's hysteria was rising. "Tell me what's wrong with me that you won't even consider me!"

"You should leave now," Gabriel's voice had gone flat. He was no longer trying to console her.

"No!" Molly shouted. "Tell me what I did!"

"It's not what you did." Gabriel's tone became harsher. "It's what you are."

"What's that supposed to mean?" Molly choked out.

"You are human." My brother's eyes flashed. "It's in your nature to be lustful, greedy, envious, deceitful, and proud. All your life you will fight against those instincts. My Father gave you free will, He chose you to rule His earth and look what you have done with it. This world is in ruins and I am here only to restore His glory—I have no other purpose and no other interest. Do you think I am so weak as to be seduced by a doe-eyed human who is barely more than a child? I am different from you in every possible way. I can only try to understand your ways and never, not in a thousand years, will you come close to understanding mine. So that is why, Molly, your efforts here are useless."

Gabriel watched impassively as tears began to flow, mingling with Molly's mascara and smudging her cheeks. She wiped them away furiously with the backs of her hands.

"I . . ." Her hiccups caused her to stutter. "I hate you."

She looked so vulnerable then I wished I could have done something to show her she wasn't alone. If I'd been there, I would have also liked to kick my brother in the shins for his lack of sensitivity.

"For your sake," Gabriel said distantly, "perhaps hate is better than love."

"It doesn't matter to you, either way," Molly sobbed. "I don't matter."

"That is not true," Gabriel said. "If your life is being threatened, that is my concern. If you are in danger, if anyone is ever harming you, you may depend on me to protect you. But in matters of the heart, I cannot help you."

"You could at least try. You could challenge your so-called

programming the way Beth did and see what happens! How can you know what you might feel?"

She was so passionate in her conviction that I almost hoped Gabriel's heart would melt. But he only lowered his eyes as if he had committed a grievous sin.

"For your information God wants people to be happy," Molly went on defiantly. I had the sense that she was trying to build a case like she'd seen in school debates. "Go forth and multiply, right? I remember that much from Sunday School."

"Those directions were given to man," Gabriel said very quietly.

"So you don't get to be happy? You can't want a life?"

"It's not question of wanting. It's more a question of design," Gabriel said, and Molly looked defeated. "You need someone to love you the way you deserve. I promise to watch over you every day of your life." His voice was tender. "I'll make sure you're always safe."

"No!" Molly was yelling like a spoiled child now. "That's not what I want." She shook her head vehemently, causing some of her copper curls to come loose and fall across her pale face. Molly was too caught up in her whirlwind of emotions to notice, but Gabriel's expression seemed to shift as he watched her. On his face, I read a compulsive desire to reach out to her—this strange, tumultuous creature that he did not understand. His hand twitched and he slowly lifted it, like he might be about to brush away her tears.

Then Ivy stepped into the room wearing a bathrobe. She looked surprised by the commotion and Gabriel quickly dropped his hand, his face returning to its usual impassive mask. A moment later Molly bolted from the room, silent tears still streaming down her face.

Ivy shot him a sympathetic look. "I wondered how long it'd be before that conversation happened."

"You knew? Why didn't you say something? It might have helped me handle it better."

"I doubt that," said Ivy with quiet insight. If there was anyone who could hope to understand Gabriel it was her. While he remained complex and unreadable to people and angels alike, Ivy had always had the uncanny ability to read his thoughts.

"What should I do now?" It was rare for Gabriel to seek counsel on any matter, but the nature of teenage love was a complete mystery to him.

"Nothing," Ivy replied. "These things happen. She'll get over it."

"I hope so," my brother replied in a voice that made me wonder if it was only Molly he was thinking about.

Ivy lay down and turned out the light. Gabriel sat on the edge of his bed, chin cupped in his hand, staring into the darkness. He sat there, unmoving, long after Ivy had fallen asleep.

28

Misery Loves Company

RETURNING to the constraints of my physical body came as a rude shock to me. Being with my family and feeling like part of their lives again had made me forget my current predicament. Now I was back in my cramped cell in the reeking chambers of Hades, where the space was so tight I couldn't stand up. As if to add to my woes, the air around me was filled with the acrid stench of sulfur and continuous lamentations for help. I had no idea how long I'd been projecting, but I knew it must have been a while because all my joints were stiff and my muscles ached when I moved.

Someone had thrust some dry crusts and a tin cup of water into my cell. I sat in my nightgown, so besmirched by muck that its original color was almost undetectable. I tried to slow my breathing to fend off the escalating panic in my chest. I huddled in the corner with my head tucked up against my shoulder. Several times a shadowy warden walked past to further torment the captive souls. He was identifiable only by the fiery embers of his eyes and the metal prongs he rattled along the bars. For some reason he didn't stop at my cell. Once I was sure he'd gone I pushed myself over to the tin cup and took a long gulp of water. It had an unpleasant metallic taste. My whole body was sore, but the sharpest pain was coming from behind my shoulder blades. Now that I couldn't even stretch anymore, my wings ached worse than ever. I thought if I didn't release them soon I would go insane.

To distract myself I thought about Molly and Gabriel. My heart went out to them both. Whatever strange connection existed between them had no hope of developing. Molly didn't fully grasp the concept of divine love. This was love in its purest form, unaltered by human interpretation and encompassing all living creatures. It was a celebration of creation. Although he might be confused by the intensity of Molly's emotions, I knew Gabriel would be fine. He would not deviate from his purpose. He wouldn't even need to think about it. Molly on the other hand would suffer badly from the perceived rejection. I hoped Xavier would help her through it. He'd grown up in a household full of sisters—he'd know what to say.

I knew Jake would show up eventually and sure enough, his silhouette appeared a moment later, hovering in the darkness. His face emerged from behind the bars lit by the long torch he carried. I could smell his spicy cologne and I noticed that his presence no longer had the usual alarming effect on me. In fact, it was the first time I was actually relieved to see him.

I inched forward, scraping my skin on the concrete floor of the tiny enclosure. I would have liked to send him away, but I couldn't. I would have liked to express my anger, but I wasn't strong enough. We both knew I needed his help if I didn't want to perish in this hole in the wall, buried alive until my body wasted away and my spirit was crushed.

"This is an outrage," he hissed under his breath when the torchlight revealed my condition. "I'll not forgive him for this."

"Can you get me out of here?" I asked, hating myself for my lack of stoicism. But seeing as I'd survived a burning at the stake, maybe I wasn't meant to be a martyr.

"Why do you think I came?" he said, looking pleased with himself. He touched the lock on the cell and it turned to ash and crumbled to the ground.

"Won't Big Daddy find out about this?" I asked, surprised to hear myself casually using his nickname.

"Only a matter of time." Jake sounded unconcerned. "There are more spies down here than there are souls."

"And then what?" I needed to know what the future held. Was Jake only offering a temporary reprieve? He seemed to read my thoughts.

"We'll worry about that later."

He tugged at the cell door and it shifted a little, enough for me to squeeze through.

"Hurry," Jake urged, but I didn't move. Moving in any direction was difficult.

"How long have I been here?"

"Two days, but I hear you slept through most of it. Here, give me your hand. I'm sorry things turned out like this."

His apology caught me off guard. Jake was not in the habit of accepting responsibility for the damage he'd caused. He looked at me intently and I could see he had something on his mind. His brow was creased and a look of preoccupation had replaced his usual expression of scornful detachment. His hawk-like gaze didn't leave my face.

"You're not well," he observed at last. I wondered what made him think I'd be well given the circumstances. Jake was like a chameleon; he could change his manner to suit his own agenda. Right now his solicitous behavior was unsettling me and I couldn't resist a sarcastic reply.

"Being kept in a cage doesn't do much for the complexion," I muttered.

"I'm trying to help you here—you could at least show some appreciation."

"Haven't you helped me enough?" I said, but when he offered me his hand again I took it.

Slowly and by using his arm to support my weight I managed to wriggle out of the compartment. I found that although I could stand I couldn't take more than a step or two without my legs giving way. Jake took one look at me before handing me the torch and lifting me into his arms. He strode out of the chambers with a regal confidence and although I was sure I saw eyes like burning coals watching us through the gloom, no one made any attempt to stop us.

Outside the chambers Jake's motorbike was waiting. He deposited me carefully on the back before mounting and switching on the ignition. Seconds later I was pressed against him as the suffocating chambers of Hades disappeared behind me.

"Where are we going?" I whispered, seeing unfamiliar surroundings.

"I have an idea I think might make you feel better."

Jake drove without stopping until we reached the entrance to a deep gorge with steep cliff walls and black running water that seemed to flow into a channel underground. Jake dismounted lightly, watching me with growing agitation.

"Are you in pain?"

I nodded mutely. There was little point withholding information from him now. There was nothing he could do with it that could possibly worsen my situation. Jake seemed to have anticipated what was happening to me and seemed more informed than I was.

"Tell me," he continued. "How do your wings feel?"

The directness of the question caught me off guard and I felt myself blush suddenly. There was something about it I found objectionable. My wings were one thing that defined my very existence. I had worked hard to keep them from prying human eyes. They were an intensely personal part of me and I wasn't sure I wanted to discuss their condition with Jake Thorn, Prince of Hades.

"I haven't given them much thought," I said evasively.

"Well, think about them now."

Once Jake had drawn my attention to them I became aware of how they were throbbing beneath my shoulder blades, burning to be released. Every so often they sent shooting pains down my back. I felt irritated with him for drawing my attention to the problem. I had deliberately chosen to ignore the issue of my wings. What was the point of doing otherwise in Hades?

"We need to do something about them," Jake said decisively. "If you want to keep them that is."

I didn't like his use of the plural *we* rather than *you*. It made me feel as if we were working as a team, as if we had shared problems we could tackle together. I gave him a blank stare.

"Perhaps what I'm trying to say might be better demonstrated." Before I knew it Jake was peeling off his black leather jacket and flinging it to the ground. He turned his back to me and pulled his shirt up over his head. Then he stood with his back straight and his head slightly bowed, a humbling pose that looked distinctly out of place on him.

"What do you see?" he asked in a muted voice. I scanned the contours of his back. Jake's shoulders were slender but well formed and not unathletic. He didn't have bulging muscles, but every tendon was taut and lean and rippled when he moved. He looked fast on his feet and dangerous.

"I don't see anything," I replied, averting my eyes.

"Look closely," Jake urged, taking a step backward so he was even closer, his back bent in front of me in a white arc. Something caught my eye then and I looked with open curiosity. The skin on his back was smooth and unblemished except for two rows of tiny pea-size nodules that ran like an extra set of vertebrae under each shoulder blade. The row of little beads under his skin, only a centimeter or two apart, looked like scarring from wounds that hadn't properly healed. I didn't need to ask what they were the remnants of.

"What happened to them?" I asked in a hoarse whisper,

the true meaning of what he was showing me suddenly jelling in my mind.

"They wasted away over time and eventually fell off," he said bluntly.

"From lack of use?" I asked in disbelief.

"Yes, but more as a result of retribution," he said. "The point is that I had them too once and, believe me, they were spectacular."

Had I caught a note of regret in his voice?

"Why are you telling me this?"

"Because I want to avoid the same thing happening to you."

"But how can I stop it?" I asked my eyes filling with tears. "I'm always locked up. Unless . . . are you saying you're going to let me fly?"

"Not exactly," Jake said, before I could start to imagine what seemed like an incomprehensible thought. "It would be more like supervised activity."

"What does that mean?"

"I *am* going to let you fly but on two conditions. I have to make sure you're safe . . . and that you're not seen." Suddenly I knew why we were there. The gorge was concealed yet perfectly designed for flight.

"You don't trust me?" I asked.

"It isn't a question of trust. You couldn't go far even if you did try to escape. It's more a matter of what you might run into out there on your own."

"So how are you going to ensure my safety?" I asked. "It's not like you can fly with me."

"That's where my idea comes in," Jake said. "It might seem odd to you at first but try to be open-minded. It really is the only way for you to survive as an angel."

"What's your idea?" I asked curiously. My wings seemed to know we were talking about them and strained to burst open. It took all of my self-control to restrain them. I didn't know if I could do it for much longer.

"It's no big deal," said Jake lightly. "It simply involves you wearing a restraint."

"You want to put me on a leash!" I was outraged now that his meaning had become clear.

"For your own safety," he qualified.

"You've got to be kidding me! I'm not going to let you fly me like some kind of weird pet! That's just sick. Thanks but no thanks."

I sounded so resolute in knocking back his offer, but at the same time, I was all too aware of my wings, which were itching for freedom and pushing up against my back. The dull ache behind my shoulder blades was beginning to intensify.

"So you'd rather let them wither? You know you don't have much time before they start to crumble and fall away like old plaster. Are you sure that's what you want?" Jake asked.

"Why are you so keen to help me?"

"Let's just say I'm protecting my investment. Think about it, Beth. You don't have to decide now although we are in an ideal position."

"If I agree I don't want an audience," I said suddenly self-conscious.

"There's only the two of us here. That's not an audience. I don't want to see you lose your wings and you don't want to lose them. It's a win-win situation, don't you think?"

"If I do it," I warned, "it's only so that I can fulfil my *God-given* purpose."

"Always the optimist," he smiled.

"It's called faith," I said.

"Whatever it's called I think we should do everything we can to keep your angelic essence intact, don't you?"

Jake's offer was both insulting and tempting. If he was right and I was at risk of losing an essential part of who I was, did I really have a choice? My wings were one of the things that distinguished me from him and his kind. My wings were a precious gift bestowed by my Father. If I made it out of Hades, what would I do without them? And how would Xavier feel if I came back with such a vital part of myself missing?

I brushed away the tears that were already snaking down my cheeks and took a deep breath.

"Okay," I said. "I accept."

Jake lifted my chin with his thumb, his strange but beautiful eyes scanning my face. "Good decision," he said before steering us to a nearby rock ledge. "Put your right foot up here," he instructed before upending the contents of a small, carved box he withdrew from under the bike. A shimmering chain made of fine silver links, attached to a manacle pooled onto the rock. It looked like a magical object from a mythological world. I wanted to ask about its origins but held back. Jake wrapped one end of the chain around his wrist and fettered the manacle around my ankle. Being made of mesh meant it was remarkably flexible, melding around my flesh as if it were a part of me.

I looked around at the ravine in which I was permitted to take flight. The rock face rose steeply on both sides and ended in a pervasive darkness. The black waterfall flowed silently. It was like a rocky void, a strange, ghostly abyss illuminated only by the headlights of Jake's motorcycle, which cast a pool of opaque light around us.

"Knock yourself out," Jake said.

Although I'd been reluctant about revealing my wings to Jake, they now seemed to have a will of their own. They were so desperate for release they didn't even wait for a trigger or a signal from my brain. I didn't try to restrain them and a moment later my linen nightgown hung in ragged shreds from my back. The thought of flight had energized me and my wings seemed to creak from lack of use as they rose up behind me. They emitted a pale silver light of their own and I felt them humming with power. My other muscles were also coming back to life now that my circulation had returned.

Jake watched me in silent fascination. I wondered how long it had been since he'd seen an angel's wings up close. Did he still remember the intoxicating feeling? I didn't have time to stop and consider it. My wings arched like a feathered canopy over us both. Jake studied them with a wistful longing and I felt suddenly proud of them. My wings were the one physical feature that separated us despite our common origins. They were a tangible reminder of who I was and where I'd come from. I would always be different from Jake. My flight through the darkness would be a reminder of all that he and his kind had relinquished for the sake of pride and power lust.

I rolled my ankle from side to side, testing the strength of the shackle. Then I dropped my head to my chest, sprinted forward a few paces, and let my wings lift me into the air.

The moment my feet were swept off the ground, I felt an instant relief, as if something dry and withered inside of me had sprung to life again. I threw myself against the enveloping darkness without grace or rhythm. I dived through it, fanning it with my beating wings and it seemed to part a little to let me through. When a firm tug at my ankle told me I'd gone too high, I didn't dwell on my captor below but simply swooped down again, making sure to stay lower. I let my thoughts switch off and my body take over. I didn't feel the same exhilaration I did when I flew with my family at Venus Cove, but the deep physical release was worth it. Jake stood on the ledge below, face upturned and the chain leash wound around his wrist.

From where I was he looked very small and irrelevant. In that moment I was all that existed—not my worries or fears or even my love for Xavier. I was stripped back to my very core, nothing but energy, darting and looping through the airless ravine.

I flew until my wings were begging for rest and even then I didn't stop. When I finally descended Jake was looking at me with undisguised awe. Wordlessly he tossed me a helmet and swung himself onto the bike.

"Come on," he said. "You can spend the night at the Ambrosia—our secret."

"You can't keep secrets from Lucifer," I said. "You must know there'll be repercussions."

"True." Jake shrugged. "But right now, I don't really care."

29

Sweet Revenge

I woke the next day feeling more like myself than I had in a long time. I stretched and arched my back, pleased to find the muscles feeling light and relaxed rather than as heavy as concrete. It was a relief to be back in the luxurious surroundings of Hotel Ambrosia even though I knew it could only be temporary.

I'd just thrown off the covers and slipped out of bed when I heard the sound of a key card in the door of the suite. I tensed up for a second expecting trouble, but it was only Hanna and Tuck poking their faces through the door. I assumed they were the only ones allowed to know about my return. Jake had ordered a lavish cooked breakfast and Hanna almost dropped the overladen tray in her enthusiasm to rush to my side.

"I'm so glad to see you," she said, embracing me tightly. "I can't believe you're alive." I breathed in her now-familiar smell of freshly baked bread.

Tuck, who was more guarded with his emotions, crossed the room to give my shoulder a fraternal shove.

"You had us worried for a while," he said. "What happened back there in the arena?"

"I'm not actually sure," I replied, accepting the glass of orange juice that Hanna thrust into my hand. "I didn't do any of it on purpose, the fire just parted around me."

"How did you manage to get out of the chambers?"

"Jake came last night and let me out. I'm guessing there's going to be trouble."

"He defied his father's orders?" Hanna's eyes bulged. "That's a first."

"I know," I said. "I hope he knows what he's doing."

"Everyone's been talkin' bout you and your powers," Tuck said. "They reckon Big Daddy was gonna let you out himself, see if he could cut a deal with you."

"Maybe when Hell freezes over," I said under my breath, but I couldn't keep myself from feeling just a little bit hopeful. If Lucifer came up with terms I could agree to, then maybe there was a slim chance I wouldn't have to return to my prison in the earth. On the other hand if Jake setting me free made Lucifer angry, I could end up in worse trouble. "I need to find something to wear," I said, glancing at the dirty undergarments on the floor. I was still in the oyster silk pyjamas I'd found folded on the bed when I arrived.

I started riffling through the wardrobe, eager to change into clean clothes. Jake had added jeans and a sweater among the showy dresses and silk shirts. Perhaps he finally understood the importance of flying under the radar. I'd just slipped on the sweater and was tying my hair back in a ponytail when the door buzzed again and Jake waltzed in, forgetting to knock.

"Didn't your mother teach you any manners?" I snapped. I

expected him to be anxious after last night's escapade, but he looked so unconcerned that I wondered what bargain he'd managed to negotiate overnight.

"Never had a mother," Jake replied breezily, before waving a dismissive hand at Hanna and Tuck. "Get out."

"I want them to stay," I protested.

Jake gave an exaggerated sigh. "Come back in half an hour," he instructed them in more pleasant tones before turning his attention back to me. "So, how are you feeling?"

"Much better," I said truthfully.

"So I was right," Jake crowed. "The solution was staring us in the face."

"I guess," I muttered. "What's going to happen now? Should I be worried?"

"Relax, I'm working on it. My father prides himself on making sound business decisions and right now I'm plugging you as an asset rather than a liability. It's got him thinking." Jake looked at me, expecting a response, but I remained silent. "You can thank me anytime you're ready."

"Just because I might not have to go back to that infested hole doesn't mean I'm any less miserable," I explained.

"That's a slight exaggeration," he said flippantly.

"No, it's not," I said, annoyed by his attitude. "I may not be in pain anymore, but this place is still my worst nightmare."

Jake spun around suddenly, his dark eyes on fire. "What's it going to take with you, Bethany?" he said in a low voice. "It seems nothing I do for you is ever good enough. I'm all out of ideas."

"What did you expect?"

"A little gratitude wouldn't go astray."

"For what? Did you really think rescuing me and then flying me like a kite would change anything? I'm still here and I still want to go home."

"Get over it," Jake snarled.

"I'll never get over it."

"Well, that proves you're an idiot because I know for a fact that pretty boy is already over you."

"He is not!" I retorted hotly. Jake could talk about whatever he wanted and most of the time it didn't bother me, but Xavier was off-limits. Jake had no right to mention his name let alone presume to know what was happening in his life.

"Shows how little you know." Jake was taunting me now. "Hormonal teenage boys don't wait around forever. In fact, they're short-term thinkers. Didn't they teach you that in Sex Ed? It's out of sight, out of mind with them."

"You don't know anything about Xavier," I said, determined not to let him get to me. "You have no idea what you're talking about."

"What if I told you I get regular updates about life on earth?" Jake smirked. "What if your brother and sister have given up looking for you and Xavier has moved on? He's with another girl as we speak . . . the pretty redhead in fact. What's her name again? I *think* you know her. . . ."

I could feel my temper growing. Did Jake honestly think he could trick me into doubting the people I loved? How naïve did he think I was?

"I'm telling the truth," he added. "They've accepted they can't help you. They tried and failed and sadly now they have to move on."

"Then why are they going to Alabama to try and find a . . ." I swallowed my words immediately, realizing my mistake seconds too late. I bit my lip and watched as Jake's brows lowered darkly and his eyes glittered with rage.

"How could you know that?" he said.

I hoped my face didn't betray me as I tried desperately to repair the damage. "I don't know. I'm just guessing."

"You're a very bad liar," he observed, approaching with the slow stealth of a panther. "You spoke with total certainty just then. I'm betting you've seen them . . . maybe even communicated with them."

"No . . . I haven't . . ."

"Tell me the truth! Who showed you how?" Jake swept a crystal vase off a table so it smashed on the floor, scattering long-stemmed roses. I wished he would calm down. I wished he hadn't dismissed Tuck and Hanna. I didn't like being alone with him when he was this worked up.

"No one showed me anything. I figured it out by myself."

"How many times have you done this?"

"Not many. A few."

"And every time you were with *him*, right? It's as if you never left! I should have known you were up to something. I was a fool to trust you!" He raised his hands and clawed at his temples like someone deranged.

"That's priceless—you talking about trust." But Jake was no longer listening.

"You've been playing me, making me think we were growing closer, trying to keep me in the dark about what was really going on. I thought if I gave you space and treated you like a queen you might forget about him. But you didn't forget, did you?"

"That's like asking me to forget who I am."

"You still think like a schoolgirl. I thought Hades might help you mature a little, but I see now the experience has been wasted on you."

"It's an experience I never asked for."

"You've had your last happy reunion—of that you may be sure." He'd resumed his usual cynical tone, but the threat beneath it was real. I knew I should say something to dispel rather than exacerbate the tension between us.

"Why do we always have to fight?" I ventured. "For once can't we try to understand each other?"

Jake shook his head and gave a rueful laugh.

"Well played, Bethany. You're quite the actress, but you can stop now. The game's up. You had me going for a while, though. I almost believed you were making an effort. I should have known better. I should have left you to rot in the chambers. You've put me in a very bad temper."

"I don't care," I said. "Do whatever you like with me, send me back or hand me over to Lucifer."

"Oh, you misunderstand me. I'm not going to harm a single hair on your head," Jake leered. "But I will make you sorry you treated me with so little respect."

The implication behind his words sent chills through me.

"What's that supposed to mean?"

"It means travel plans of my own are in order. I think it's time I saw firsthand what you're missing so badly."

ALTHOUGH Jake had been deliberately vague about his intentions I knew him well enough to know he didn't waste time making idle threats. He was headed to Tennessee to get even with me. I didn't know what he planned to do once he got there, but I knew he wouldn't stop until he succeeded. Being passed over for Xavier just when he thought he stood a chance must have been a bitter pill for him to swallow. Anyone else would have accepted it with greater dignity. But exacting revenge was the only thing that was going to satisfy Jake and what better way was there than targeting the people I loved? There was no way Jake's demonic strength was any match for my powerful siblings and there was little point in him going after Molly. So that just left Xavier. My Achilles' heel. Exposed and vulnerable. Especially if Jake caught him alone. And that would be easy enough to achieve.

If Xavier was in danger there was no time to waste. I needed to get back to earth and warn him before Jake got there first.

I couldn't project right away because my mind kept filling with images of Xavier in trouble and the agitation threw my focus. In the end I jumped in the shower and turned the cold water on full blast. The shock of it cleared my head and settled my thoughts long enough for me to focus my energies. The projection happened effortlessly after that.

A moment later I was outside Xavier and Molly's room at the Easy Stay Inn. The window was open a crack so I slid in like a trail of smoke and hovered below the ceiling fan. All was silent apart from the sound of their regular breathing and the wind chasing some dead leaves around in the parking lot outside. Molly was sound asleep in her bed, the previous drama of the evening erased from her face. Her resilience never ceased to amaze me. Xavier was much less comfortable in his sleep. He kept changing position and even sat up once to thump the pillows. Before lying down again he rested on his elbows to check the time on the digital clock. It read 5:10 A.M. Xavier cast a look around the room, his turquoise eyes bright in the darkness. When he finally did drift off to sleep his face stayed troubled, as though he were fighting battles in his dreams.

I wished I could reach out to comfort him even though I knew I was the primary cause of his distress. I had turned his life upside down and now his safety was being threatened. So far Jake had not disturbed them and for a fraction of a second I entertained the hope that he might have been bluffing just to rattle me. But I'd seen the look in his eyes and I knew better.

The room turned suddenly cold and Molly pulled the covers up over her head. I could hear the sound of wolflike breathing. I saw it then: A shadow slid into the room with us. It crept across Molly's sleeping form under the duvet and danced across Xavier's features.

Sensing the presence, Xavier's eyes snapped open, and he swung himself out of bed. His whole body was poised for a fight. I saw a vein throbbing in his neck and could almost hear his heart racing.

"Who are you?" he said through gritted teeth as a figure began to take shape before him. I recognized the curly hair and baby face even before he had fully appeared. It was Diego, dressed formally in a black suit and tie as though he were going to a funeral.

"Just an acquaintance," Diego replied in a lazy voice. "Jake said you were pretty—he wasn't lying."

"What do you want?"

"You're not very polite for someone I could kill with my little finger," Diego said in his slimy, slightly effeminate voice.

"You do know there's an archangel and a seraphim next door, right?" Xavier retorted. "Think maybe they can take you down?"

Diego gave an empty chuckle. "They were right about you, just like a lion cub. Killing you would be too easy."

"So do it then," Xavier hissed and I felt my stomach plummet to my feet.

Diego cocked his head to one side. "Oh, that's not why I'm here. I've come to deliver a message."

"Yeah?" Xavier said without a hint of fear. "Then go ahead and deliver it."

"Our sources inform us that you and your angel squad are trying to pull off a rescue mission," Diego said, a smirk in his voice. "I'm here to tell you not to waste your time. You might as well call off the chase. The angel you're searching for is dead."

There was a long silence. Xavier's heart, which had been

racing just minutes before, seemed to slow down and thud like a pound of concrete in his chest. But when he opened his mouth to speak, he didn't betray a hint of emotion.

"I don't believe you," he said in a level voice.

"Had a feeling you might say that," Diego replied, his smiling face framed by dark curls. He reached behind him and produced a rough burlap sack. "So I brought along some evidence."

From the sack he withdrew something feathered and folded. When he shook it loose I saw it was a section of broken, blood-stained wings. *My wings.* "You can have this as a keepsake if you like," he said. What he held up was twisted and bent and the blood had congealed in parts causing the feathers to stick together. Diego waved it like a fan and droplets of blood spattered onto the floor. I saw Xavier draw a sharp intake of breath and lean forward as if someone had punched him in the stomach, knocking the wind out of him. His turquoise eyes darkened, like clouds rolling across sky and blotting out the sun.

"Hellhounds," said Diego, nodding his head in commiseration. "At least it was quick."

"Don't listen to him!" I cried, but my words were lost in the void that separated us. The desire to be with him filled me so strongly that I thought I would explode through the confines of my spectral form.

At that moment the door burst open and my brother and sister appeared. For the first time, a look of true fear flashed across Diego's face. I guessed he hadn't counted on running into them.

"Did you think we wouldn't pick up your scent?" Gabriel

asked, his voice drenched with anger. His eyes fell on Xavier's face and then the mangled, bloody wings that Diego's had dropped on the ground. Ivy saw them too and an expression of disgust settled on her face.

"You really are the lowest of the low," she said.

"I try my best," Diego said, chuckling.

"Tell me it isn't true," Xavier said, his voice choked.

"Nothing but cheap tricks," Gabriel replied, kicking the wings aside, as though they were a theater prop.

Xavier let out a low moan of relief and pressed his back against the wall. I knew how he felt. When I thought Jake had run him down with the motorcycle, the grief had been crippling and the relief made me giddy.

"What are you doing here?" Gabriel demanded.

Diego stuck his bottom lip out in a mock pout. "Just trying to have a little fun. Humans are so gullible—dumb beasts."

"Not as dumb as you," Ivy said, while Gabriel moved to position himself on Diego's right-hand side, pinning him between the wall and the doorway. "Looks like you've got yourself trapped."

"A bit like that little angel of yours," Diego snarled, though I could tell by the way he curled his fingers that he was nervous. "She's trapped in the pit burning as we speak and there's nothing you can do about it."

"We'll see about that," Gabriel said.

"We know you're trying to find a portal." Diego's attempts to stall or distract them were poorly disguised. "You'll never find it and if you do, good luck getting it open."

"Do not underestimate the power of Heaven," Ivy said.

"Oh, I think Heaven has forsaken Bethany by now. Have you considered that our daddy may be stronger than yours?"

Ivy looked up and a hot blue fire seemed to blaze in her usually cool gray eyes. She raised her chin to match her opponent. She opened her mouth and a language flowed out that sounded high and sweet like a hundred children singing or wind chimes in the summer breeze. The air around her started to shimmer, like heat rising off the pavement. Then, without speaking, she thrust her hand out toward him. To my shock, her hand disappeared straight into his chest, as though he were made of nothing but clay. Diego seemed just as surprised as I was and grunted loudly. Something began to glow in his chest and I realized that Ivy was literally gripping his heart. The light shone brighter, making his skin papery and transparent. I could see the outline of his rib cage and Ivy's hand, encasing his heart in a scalding prison of light. Diego seemed to be completely paralyzed, but he managed to open his mouth and let out a strangled scream. Through the screen his chest had become, I saw the heart begin to swell and pulse in Ivy's hand, as if it were going to rupture. Then with a *pop*, like a bursting balloon, it disintegrated and Diego vanished in a flash of light.

Ivy drew a deep, shuddering breath and then brushed her hands together as though she had touched something contaminated.

"Demons," she muttered.

The noise of the explosion woke Molly, who sat upright, scrambling to smooth down her curls.

"Huh . . . what . . . what's going on?" she mumbled, her voice slurry. I was amazed that she'd managed to sleep through the drama.

"Nothing," Gabriel said quickly. "Go back to sleep. We just came in to check on you."

"Oh." Molly stared at him wistfully for a moment before remembering the events of the previous night. Then her face darkened and she turned her back, wriggling down under the covers.

Gabriel sighed and shrugged at Ivy while Xavier picked up the car keys on the bedside table.

"Uh . . . thanks for taking care of that," he said. "If it's all right I'm gonna go for a drive. I need to clear my head."

I followed him, eager for us to spend some time alone, even if he didn't know I was there.

"Hey, baby." He patted the hood of the Chevy out in the parking lot and gave a sad smile. "Things are getting pretty crazy, hey?"

I slid into the passenger seat as Xavier started the familiar purring engine and pulled out onto the highway. His body seemed to relax behind the wheel of the car, flowing more easily. He looked so beautiful with the worry wiped from his face. I could stare at him for hours—his strong arms, the outline of his sculpted chest, his hair falling across his eyes, strands glowing golden in the predawn light. His brilliant turquoise eyes were half closed as he let the Chevy leach the tension from his body. His foot nudged the accelerator and the car responded with an obedient growl. Xavier never drove fast with me in the car; he was too conscious of my safety. But in this moment he was completely free and I knew he needed this time to himself in order to regroup. The car glided around a bend in the road, shadowed by the cedar trees that lined the highway. Up ahead the left side of the road fell away, with nothing but jagged cliffs below. Picking up speed on the open road, Xavier rolled down his window and flicked the radio on. The station was playing the biggest hits of the eighties and the chords of "Livin' on a Prayer" rang out into the air. The song about a couple whose struggle to survive hard times was especially relevant to us.

> We've got to hold on, ready or not
> You live for the fight when it's all that you've got.

Xavier's mood seemed to lift a little as he mouthed the words and tapped the steering wheel in time with the beat. But outside, an unnatural wind was blowing up, scattering leaves across the highway and down the cliffs on the opposite side. I knew something was wrong—the presence of evil had followed us. I had to warn Xavier to go back. It wasn't safe for him out here alone. He needed to be close to Ivy and Gabriel so they could protect him. But how could I let him know that?

When the song ended an idea suddenly hit me. I focused my energy and used it to interfere with the radio frequency. The sound broke up until it was just an irritating hum. Xavier frowned and fiddled with the dials, trying to tune the channel. I concentrated on gathering my strength and called out his name. Then out of the blue it was my voice he heard crackling through the speakers.

"Turn back, Xavier! You're not safe out here. Find Ivy and Gabriel. Stay with them. Jake is coming."

The shock of hearing my voice almost caused Xavier to swerve the car off the road. He recovered in time and slammed on the brakes. The Chevy screamed to a halt in the middle of the deserted road.

"Beth? Is that you? Where are you? Can you hear me?"

"Yes, it's me. I want you to turn back." My voice was insistent. "You have to trust me."

"Okay," Xavier said. "I do. Just keep talking."

Xavier shifted the car into gear and made a U-turn. I breathed a little easier as I sat curled in the passenger seat with my knees up. Once he was back at the motel he would pass my message on to Ivy and Gabriel and they'd know what to do. As Xavier drove my attention was drawn to the discarded gum wrappers and an empty soda can on the car floor. It was so unlike him—he was usually obsessive about car maintenance. I remembered once how the new GPS he'd installed in the Chevy had left a ring on the windshield. It bothered him so much that he dragged us to the auto shop to find a plastic holder to stick on the dashboard. The memory made me smile.

"Beth, you still here?" Tapping into the radio waves had left me drained, but I summoned whatever remnants of energy I had left to create friction in my fingertips, which I ran lightly over his cheek, a feather-soft caress. I saw the hairs on his arms stand on end.

"Do that again." Xavier smiled.

We weren't far now from the Easy Stay Inn. The landscape was becoming more familiar and we had almost left the sharp cliffs behind. I had just given myself permission to breathe easy when something unexpected happened. The Chevy lurched and then accelerated straight past the turnoff, leaving the low rectangular façade of the motel behind.

"What the hell?" Xavier looked around. "Beth, what's going on?"

The car seemed to take on a crazed purpose of its own. Xavier's foot slammed repeatedly on the brakes, but they refused to respond. The steering wheel was locked. I slid over to the driver's side to help him but my attempts to will the car to stop were in vain. Suddenly, I glanced up and saw in the rearview mirror two eyes like glowing embers staring from the backseat.

"Don't do this, Jake!" I pleaded. The car was now veering crazily from one side of the road to the other. Xavier's efforts to steer it back on course were futile. The car continued to crash forward, branches lashing out across the windshield, stones crunching under the wheels.

My heart stopped when I saw what we were heading for. Jake was maneuvering the car away from the woodland and toward the rocky escarpment. A couple of times the Chevy teetered so close to the edge I was sure it would tumble right over and smash against the cliffs. Dust rose in clouds impairing Xavier's vision, but there wasn't much he could do other than press his back against the seat and wrestle ineffectually with the wheel.

I turned and saw Jake sitting calmly in the back. He was smoking a French cigarette and blowing smoke rings out the window.

He was playing a game with us.

30

Guardian Angels

"STOP!" I begged Jake. "*Please* stop!"

The accelerator hit the floor and the car lurched drunkenly as if it were being steered by a blind man. The cliffs fell sharply away to the right and there was nothing but a fine metal railing separating the road from the devastating drop. I needed to manifest—even if only to tell Xavier what was happening, to see if there was some way I could get him safely out of the car. But fear crippled my concentration. It'd require every scrap of energy I had left to appear to him and even then I wasn't sure I could do it.

Suddenly I caught sight of his hands gripping the steering wheel. I saw my promise ring and the trademark leather wristband he always wore. I knew the feel of both by heart. Those hands had held mine so many times; they had comforted me, fought for me, protected me, and anchored me to the world of the living. I remembered the moment I first saw Xavier sitting on the pier. He'd looked up at me, the light of the setting sun picking up the golden strands in his honey brown hair. I remembered thinking his eyes held so much depth. I'd wondered then who he was and what he was like, not expecting I'd ever see him again. The memories flooded back to me. The two of us sharing chocolate cake in a booth at Sweethearts—he'd looked at me as though I were a puzzle he was determined to solve. I remembered the way his voice deepened when he was roused from sleep, the way his lips felt against the back of my neck. I remembered his smell, his fresh clean scent like the woods on a summer day. I remembered the way the crucifix around his neck glinted when the moonlight caught it. I knew everything about him and every little detail was sacred to me. I realized then that our subliminal connection could transcend any physical barrier.

Without any warning I manifested right there in the passenger seat. Xavier nearly yelled out in shock, and his ocean eyes widened while Jake pushed his face between the two front seats.

"Hello, darling," he said darkly. "Thought I'd find you here. Bit of car trouble I see."

"Beth," Xavier whispered. "What's happening?"

I realized suddenly that he couldn't see Jake. He had no idea what was going on.

"It's okay," I told him. "I won't let anything happen to you."

"Beth, I can't do this much longer." His voice almost broke. "Where are you? I don't know what to believe anymore and I need to get you back."

"Oh, boo hoo!" Jake whined from the backseat. "She's mine now, tough break."

"Shut up!" I snapped and Xavier looked surprised. "Not you," I clarified quickly. "Jake's here with us."

"What?" Xavier swung around, but to him the backseat looked empty.

"Just trust me," I said as the Chevy lurched violently close to the edge of the cliff. Xavier gasped and lifted an arm to shield his face, expecting a collision, but the car swung back onto the road at the last minute.

"Xavier," I said. "Look at me."

I didn't know how much time we had together, but I needed to let him know he wasn't alone. A familiar Bible verse floated into my head. It was an old favorite of mine and came from Genesis 31. It spoke about the Mizpah, the Meeting Place. It was a place that could be anywhere and nowhere at the same time. A place that didn't exist in this dimension but held more power than anyone could understand. It was a place where a reunion of spirit could occur without any physical presence. I remembered the day at Bryce Hamilton when I'd run into Xavier's arms, terrified that one day we'd be separated. The words from that afternoon came back to me clear as day: "Let's create a place. A place that's just ours; a place we can always find each other if things ever go wrong."

"Do you remember the white place?" I whispered urgently.

Xavier's body unclenched a little as he looked directly at me. "Of course," he murmured.

"Then close your eyes and go there," I whispered. "I'll be waiting for you. And don't forget . . . it is only space that separates us."

Xavier drew a deep breath and in his eyes I saw an understanding that hadn't been there before. He closed his eyes, let go of the steering wheel, and sat very still.

I heard Jake's harsh voice from the backseat. "I've had just about enough of this sentimental crap for one day."

"Listen . . ." I whipped around to try and reason with him, but it was too late. I felt a sickening jolt in my stomach as the Chevy skidded to the side of the road, smashed through the flimsy iron railing as if it were made of matchsticks, and plummeted over the cliff face.

"No!" I screamed.

Xavier didn't react. He was still in the white place, indifferent to whether he would live or die.

I watched the Chevy plunge over the cliff in what seemed like slow motion. I heard a sickening metallic screech as the underbelly of the car scraped across the rock ledge. It seemed to teeter for a moment; its body tilting precariously as it balanced on the edge. Then gravity took over and with a deep shudder and a cloud of dust, the car fell. At the sight of it, nearby birds squawked and fled the trees, vanishing into the sky as they sounded their warning. I saw Xavier's body get thrown forward and collide with the steering wheel. The moment seemed to last for the longest time. My vision tunneled and I noticed the strangest things. The sunlight through the windshield hit Xavier's hair, making the strands glow copper and gold. Xavier's hair had always been a soft shade of brown like honey or walnuts, but today, in this moment, I could have sworn he wore a halo of golden light. Xavier had made no effort to protect himself. Anyone else would have thrown his hands up to shield himself, but Xavier remained unnaturally calm and still. He showed no signs of panic, as if he were resigned to accept his fate. When his hair shifted out of the way, I caught sight of his face and it struck me how young he looked. I could see in him the schoolboy he would have been not so many years ago. His skin was smooth and unmarked, without even a wrinkle to mark his years on earth. *He's hardly lived*, I thought to myself. There were so many things he could have been, and now he'd never get the chance to really grow up . . . to be a husband . . . to be a father . . . to make a difference in the world.

I realized then that I was screaming, screaming loud enough for all the town to hear me, but nobody did. The Chevy was still nosediving toward the rocks below where it would smash and crumple like tinfoil. I'd never felt more powerless in my entire life. My body was still imprisoned deep underground in Hades and my soul was trapped between the dimensions. But as I caught sight of Jake's smirking face in the rearview mirror, I realized I wasn't as powerless as I thought. I spun around and grabbed him by both wrists. He looked surprised, but didn't shake me off.

"Don't hurt him," I pleaded. "I'll do whatever you want. Name your terms."

"Is that so?" Jake smiled. "A trade . . . how interesting."

"This isn't the time for games!" I begged. The car was only seconds from the rocks and dusty ground below. "If Xavier dies, I'll never forgive you! Please . . . let's make a deal."

"Okay," Jake said. "I'll spare his life in exchange for you granting me one wish."

"Done!" I cried. "Just stop the car!"

"Do I have your word?"

"I swear on my life."

The Chevy lurched to a stop in midair, completely frozen. It was a sight to behold and it was lucky there were no humans around to witness it.

"I'll see you back home, Bethany."

"Wait—you can't just leave him here!"

"He'll be taken care of," Jake said and with a snap of his fingers he vanished from the backseat. After a few seconds, I became aware of the presence of Ivy and Gabriel. They screeched to the edge of the cliff in a borrowed Range Rover and bolted out. Seeing the Chevy suspended in the air, Gabriel didn't hesitate, he ran to the cliff's edge and jumped, his wings bursting out to hold him up as he descended toward the rocks below. I'd forgotten how majestic Gabriel's wings were and the sight made my breath catch in my throat. They reared up ten feet in the air, blazing white and powerful beyond belief. They were heavy and feathered and yet seemed to ripple with a life of their own. Ivy followed suit, graceful as a swan, her feet skimming the edge of the cliff as she swooped down. Her wings were a different color from Gabriel's. His were ice white and flecked with brass and gold. Ivy's on the other hand were more of a pearly gray like a dove's and dappled with rose petal pink. Xavier had opened his eyes and was staring incredulously at the angels now hovering in front of the windshield of his airborne Chevy. He blinked hard, uncertain whether to trust his own eyes.

"What the hell . . ." he breathed.

"It's okay," I told him. "You're okay."

But Xavier could no longer hear me. He just watched in

amazement as Gabriel looped his hands through the front window, gripping the roof of the car. On the other side, Ivy did the same. Then they began to slowly lift it back onto the road. The muscles in their arms didn't even strain, just flexed ever so slightly as they guided the car back to solid earth. It landed so smoothly that Xavier didn't even shift position in his seat. Ivy's and Gabriel's wings, which had been beating rhythmically to hold them up, retracted in a flash as soon as their feet connected with the ground.

Xavier threw open the door and jumped out at the first opportunity. He leaned against the hood and exhaled loudly.

"I don't believe it," he murmured.

"Neither do we." My sister glowered. "What were you thinking?"

"Hold up." A look of surprise flitted across Xavier's face. "You think I did this on purpose?"

Gabriel fixed him with his penetrating gaze. "A car doesn't drive itself off a cliff."

"Guys." Xavier threw up his hands. "Jake was controlling the car. What kind of an idiot do you take me for?"

"You saw him too?" Ivy's eyes widened. "We sensed his presence, but we didn't think he'd have the nerve to show himself."

"He didn't show himself exactly." Xavier frowned. "I couldn't see him . . . but Beth told me he was there."

"Beth?" Gabriel looked as if he thought Xavier might be losing his mind.

"She spoke to me through the radio . . . and then she appeared when I thought I was going to die." Xavier twisted his face into a grimace, aware of how far-fetched his story sounded. "It's true, I swear."

"All right," Ivy said grimly. "Whatever happened, we have to remember that Jake is pulling some dirty moves. At least we got here in time."

"That's the thing," Xavier said, crossing his arms. "The car was gonna smash, I know it was. Then suddenly it stopped, and Beth and Jake were gone."

"What are you saying?" Gabriel asked.

"I'm not sure—but I know Jake was trying to kill me. Something or someone stopped him."

Ivy and Gabriel exchanged worried looks. "Let's just be thankful you're all right," said my sister.

"Yeah." Xavier nodded, but he still looked concerned. "Thanks for helping me out. Jeez, I hope no one saw you."

A faint smile played around Gabriel's lips and he pushed back the lock of golden hair that had fallen loose from his ponytail.

"Look around you," he said. "Do you see anyone?"

Xavier looked and a thoughtful frown appeared on his face. His eyes fell upon a snake in the long grass. It seemed to have stopped mid-slither, locked in place. He turned his face upward and his mouth fell open in surprise to see the fleeing birds frozen in the sky, as if the whole world had become trapped inside a painting. Only then did the dead silence become apparent. All the sounds of the world had stopped. There was no buzzing of crickets in the air or the sound of vehicles on the road. Not even the wind could break through the silence.

"Wait . . ." Xavier passed a hand over his eyes. "Did you guys do this? No way, it's impossible."

"You of all people should know that nothing is impossible," my sister said.

Xavier's brilliant blue eyes met Ivy's cool, steel gaze. "Tell me you didn't stop time."

"We didn't stop it exactly," Gabriel said casually, inspecting the Chevy for signs of damage. "We may have put it on hold for a few minutes."

"Are you serious!" Xavier cried. He was struggling to process what they were telling him. "Are you even allowed to do that?"

"That's beside the point," Gabriel retorted. "We did what we had to do. Can't have civilians watching two angels carry a car out of the sky."

My brother closed his eyes for a moment and lifted his palms upward. A moment later signs of life burst out all around us. I jumped, having never realized how noisy life was until I heard the world without it. It was strangely comforting to see the trees swaying in the breeze and watch a beetle shuffle across the dry earth.

Xavier shivered and shook his head as if to clear it. "Won't people notice what just happened?"

"You'd be surprised what slips under the human radar," Ivy said. "Stranger things happen every day and nobody pays any attention to it. People constantly catch glimpses of the supernatural, but they turn a blind eye, they blame it on too much coffee or not enough sleep. There are hundreds of excuses to disguise the truth."

"If you say so," was all Xavier said.

"What about Bethany?" Ivy asked. "You say she was physically present?"

"I saw her." Xavier scuffed his shoe against the ground. "I've sort of . . . communicated with her a few times now."

Ivy pursed her lips. "Thanks for sharing that piece of information with us," she said and then a crease appeared in her forehead. "I wouldn't have thought it was possible."

Gabriel frowned. "Astral projection?" he asked dubiously. "From Hell?"

"Perhaps Bethany is more powerful than the demons realize . . . than even she realizes."

"What they don't know," Gabriel said, "is just how connected to the earth Bethany really is." He cast a sidelong glance at Xavier. "*You* tie her to this place more strongly than anything they understand." He drummed his fingers against the hood of the car and a thoughtful expression crossed his face. "From what we've seen so far, it's like a magnetic pull drawing the two of you together. The bond is so strong that Bethany is able to reach you even from where she is."

Even though my heart was still throbbing in my chest from the shock of what had just happened, I still managed to feel proud of my relationship with Xavier. If I could reach him, even from my underground prison, if my love for him could break through a barrier of evil, it was truly saying something about the strength of our connection. The phrase *how good are we?* floated into my head and I smiled to myself, thinking this would be an appropriate time to give him a high-five.

Gabriel's words seemed to have touched Xavier in a different way.

"This is crap," he said eventually. "Jake's playing us and we're letting him." He passed a hand over his face and the silver promise ring on his index finger glinted in the new morning light. "Does he really think we're just gonna lay down and die?" His expression was so hard I thought I could see silver lightning bolts in his ocean eyes. He dragged a hand through his hair and squinted into the horizon. "Well, I've had it. I want her back and I'm sick of these games. Come hell or high water, I'm going to find her. You hear that, Jake?" Xavier opened his arms and yelled at the open sky. "I know you're out there somewhere and you better believe me. This is not over."

Gabriel and Ivy remained wordless. They stood together like one entity, their pale eyes grave and the rising sun setting their hair ablaze. I could see something different in their eyes and realized with a start that it was anger. Not just anger; but a deep, unbridled fury toward the demonic forces that had claimed one of their own.

When Gabriel spoke, his voice was like a rumble of thunder. "You're right," he said to Xavier. "We're through playing by the rules."

"We need to act now," Xavier said.

"What we need to do is get back to the motel and pack our things," Gabriel said. "We're leaving for Broken Hill in an hour."

31

Deal with the Devil

I wasn't hopeful. Even though I knew my family would find the train station in Alabama where the fatal collision had occurred, I had no idea how they planned to get the portal open. Portals were engineered to repel angelic power; only agents of darkness knew how to use them. Gabriel was a high roller in Heaven, and even he couldn't wrangle them open. As far as I knew, the angels had never had any reason to break into Hell. They were unconcerned with what went on underground—that was Lucifer's domain. It was only when Hell's inhabitants snuck up to wreak havoc on the earth that they got involved. A small part of me wanted to believe that Xavier's stoicism would be enough to save me, but I pushed aside the tiny kernel of hope that threatened to blossom inside me. If I let myself wish for salvation, I wouldn't survive the blow should they fail.

I was so caught up thinking about Gabriel's plan that I almost forgot what had led them to take such extreme action. Xavier had almost died. If it weren't for the deal I'd struck with Jake, he'd be gone by now, joining the millions of souls in Heaven where I might never see him again. Jake had tried to kill Xavier; he had sent Diego as bait to confuse him and push him over the edge. The flutter of hope I felt in my belly turned into something fiercer, something seething and dark. The hatred I felt toward Jake was like nothing I'd experienced before. He had me completely cornered, at his mercy, separated from my loved ones with no hope of returning to them . . . and still he wasn't content.

I flung open the door of my hotel suite and ran down the passage toward the VIP lounge where Jake spent most of his time when he wasn't tormenting me. I needed to find out what he wanted in exchange for Xavier's safety. I found him reclining on a leather sofa, deep in conversation with Asia, who gave a nasty smirk when she saw me.

"Your brat is here," she said, downing the contents of her shot glass and standing up. "I'll see myself out."

"You," I said when I was within inches of Jake, "are the most repulsive, despicable creature to ever slither out of the ground!" I was literally vibrating with anger. Jake sat up and watched me with a bemused expression. I wanted to punch him right in his smug face, but I knew that wouldn't do any good. I'd only end up hurting myself.

"Hello, cupcake," he drawled. "You seem upset."

"I can't believe you tried to hurt him!" I yelled. "This was supposed to be between me and you. Why do you always have to go one step too far?"

"No harm, no foul, right?" Jake waved his hands as if nothing had happened. "Now, if I remember correctly I am a repulsive, despicable creature that *you* made a deal with."

"Only because I had no choice!"

"The circumstances aren't really important," he said.

I gritted my teeth and glared at him. "So what do you want, Jake? What's the trade for sparing Xavier's life?"

Jake regarded me lazily with a stare that was like ice and fire at the same time. His bottomless black eyes reminded me of a deep, cold well, the kind in which you drop a stone and never hear it hit the bottom. But when he looked at me, they blazed with an uncomfortable intensity that made my skin itch. He pressed his long, white fingers together and frowned, looking as if he wanted to say something but couldn't find the right words.

"Just spit it out."

He gazed at me long and hard before leaning forward and spreading his hands flat on the table in front of him. "Oh, I know exactly what I want from you."

"Go ahead," I said boldly. "Let's hear it."

Jake sighed. "I've spent some time considering how to best use my little bargaining chip in order to bring us closer."

I narrowed my eyes. "Go on . . ."

"I think I've come up with the perfect deal," he stood up and moved closer to me. "The one thing you want most is to protect your polo-wearing pretty boy and keep him alive. The one thing I want most is simple. I want you—though regrettably you have never reciprocated those feelings despite proof of my devotion."

I swallowed back the urge to snort at his use of the word *devotion*.

"Okay . . . ," I said stiffly. I didn't like where this was heading. I wasn't exactly sure what he had in mind, but knowing Jake, it couldn't be anything fair or reasonable.

"I'll promise not to harm him," Jake said. "I'll even promise not to interfere in your little projection adventures. But I want you to give up something in return."

"I can't imagine what I've got that you would want," I said in confusion.

"Maybe you're not thinking hard enough," Jake smiled humorlessly. "There's something I want very much indeed. Think of it as a gift, in return for my clemency."

"Quit beating around the bush and tell me what you're asking," I said impatiently, trying to keep my emotions under control.

"I'm asking you to give yourself to me," Jake said, his dark eyes glinting.

I had an inkling of what he was alluding to, but I didn't want to accept it. I needed to hear him say it aloud to confirm my suspicions. "You're going to have to spell it out," I said defiantly.

"Oh, you're so adorably naïve," Jake smirked. "I mean it quite literally. I will never go near your precious Prince Charming again if you agree to surrender yourself to me for just one night. I want you to give me your virtue."

"Wait . . . you want me to . . ." I faltered as the true meaning of his words sank in and I stared at him in disgust. "You want me to have sex with you?"

"That sounds so transactional. I'd prefer it if you used the term *making love*," he said.

I stared at him, grappling to find an appropriate response. There were so many things I wanted to say, so many ways of expressing my repugnance for him and my unmitigated refusal to touch him.

"You have serious issues," was the first thing that made it past my lips.

"There's no need to be rude," Jake said pleasantly. "If my ego weren't the size of the Northern Hemisphere, I might be wounded right now. There are plenty of women falling over themselves for a chance to spend a night with me. Consider yourself privileged."

"Do you even realize what you're asking?" I spluttered.

"It's sex, the satisfaction of a carnal appetite. No biggie," Jake said.

"It is a big deal!" I yelled. "You're supposed to have sex with the person you love, the person you trust, the person you hope will one day be the father your children."

"That's true," Jake conceded. "Sex can sometimes have nasty side effects in the form of small children, but I'll arrange everything so there are no complications. You'll be in expert hands."

"Are you even listening to me?" I said. "This is as bad as selling my soul."

"Don't be ridiculous," Jake scoffed. "The purpose of sex is pleasure not procreation. All you have to do is relax and let me do what I do best. Remember, every compromise has a price."

"The purpose of sex is to create life," I corrected him. "In sleeping with you I'd be committing to you, making a statement that I trust you, that I *want* to create life with you. *With you* . . ." I repeated for emphasis. "You're a liar and a cheat and a murderer. I would never give myself to you!"

Jake didn't even have the good grace to look offended. "We made a deal," he said tonelessly. "You agreed to do anything

I asked. If you refuse now, I'll make it my personal mission to make sure Xavier doesn't live to see another sunrise."

"You stay away from him."

"Hey." Jake stabbed a finger in my direction. "Don't deal with the devil if you can't handle it."

I shook my head. I couldn't believe what he was asking. He'd chosen the one thing I couldn't deliver. It would be like inviting his darkness to enter my physical body, allowing our two violently opposite souls to merge.

"I suppose Xavier doesn't mean that much to you after all," Jake said lazily. "If you're willing to let something so insignificant threaten his life."

I stared at him as my mind struggled to come to terms with what I'd just heard. Would it really be the ultimate betrayal or the ultimate sacrifice?

"I just always imagined it would be with him," I murmured almost to myself.

"I know," Jake said, his voice drenched with exaggerated sympathy. "And usually I'd be more than open to the prospect of a threesome, but under such circumstances I think it might be a little *awkward*."

I didn't bother trying to come up with a response. I felt sick to my stomach. Jake had the power to kill Xavier—he'd proved that this morning. If I reneged on the deal, there was nothing stopping him from heading straight back to find him. I knew Ivy and Gabriel were on the alert, but all he had to do was find Xavier alone and in a moment of weakness. He wouldn't care if it took him days or weeks, he'd find a way. I knew what I had to do before my mind fully grasped the concept. Xavier's words floated back to me then: "Beth, a relationship isn't only based on the physical . . . I love you for you, not for what you can offer me." Did that mean he'd want me to accept Jake's offer? I didn't know and I wished I had someone to guide me. All I knew was that the prospect of sleeping with Jake, horrible as it was, was easier to imagine than the prospect of losing Xavier. The truth was I'd do whatever was required of me to keep him safe.

"All right," I agreed, my eyes brimming with tears. "You win. I'm yours."

"Good," said Jake. "You've made the right decision. I'll send Hanna up to help you get ready. I want to make good on this deal tonight . . . just in case you should change your mind."

WHEN Hanna came up to see me her face was ashen and she was clutching a garment bag under one arm.

"Oh, Beth," she said softly. It was the first time she'd called me by my name and it struck me by surprise. "I wish it hadn't come to this."

"How'd you find out?" I asked in a dull voice.

"Word spreads quickly around here. I'm sorry."

"It's okay, Hanna," I said, swallowing hard. "It's no more than I expected from Jake."

"I hope that after all this . . . someday . . . you're reunited with Xavier," she said. "He must really be something."

"He is."

Thinking of Xavier was the only way I could get through this ordeal without breaking down. If Xavier lost his life because of me, it would be worse than an eternity in Hell.

"Come on," Hanna said, patting me gently on the back. "Jake is expecting you in an hour." She unzipped the garment bag and withdrew what looked like a long bridal gown.

"Do I really have to dress up?" I asked dejectedly. I didn't want any fuss. This was going to be horrible enough without the accompanying theatrics.

"The prince has picked out a dress specially," Hanna said. "You know what he's like, he'll be offended if you don't wear it."

"Do you think I'm doing the right thing, Hanna?" I asked suddenly, compulsively smoothing the threads on my duvet. My mind was already made up, but I wanted reassurance from someone so I didn't feel quite so alone.

"What does it matter what I think?" Hanna busied herself, picking invisible lint off the dress as she tried to avoid the question. I knew she hated to think her opinion counted for anything, for fear it might get her into trouble.

"Please?" I asked. "I really want to know."

Hanna sighed and stopped what she was doing. When she looked at me her wide brown eyes were full of sadness.

"I made a deal with Jake too once," she said. "And he betrayed me. Demons will say anything to get what they want."

"So you think he's lying to me? That he'll hurt Xavier anyway?"

"It doesn't matter," Hanna said. "What you're about to do will haunt you forever . . . but you will never forgive yourself if you don't. You need to know you did everything you could to keep Xavier safe."

"Thank you, Hanna," I said.

Hanna nodded and helped me into the virginal white gown and satin shoes. Then she wove tiny pearls into my hair. Jake had done this deliberately, it was his own twisted form of irony. In his head he'd probably built this up to be some kind of romantic reunion instead of the business arrangement it really was. The dress was as tight as a corset around my waist and fell in undulating waves down to the ground. It had a décolletage that showed off my alabaster white skin. Well, I thought bitterly to myself, it was the right dress for the occasion . . . just in the wrong place, with the wrong person.

While Hanna was fastening a pearl necklace around my throat, Tucker came up to the suite and his face fell when he saw what I was wearing.

"So it is true," he said softly. "You sure y'know what you're doin'?"

"I don't have a choice, Tuck," I replied.

"Y'know, Beth." He sat hesitantly on the edge of my bed. "I know things seem pretty bad at the moment . . . but I've never admired you more than I do right now."

"How do you figure?" I asked. "Not much to admire if you ask me."

"No," Tuck said, shaking his head. "You might not see it now, but you're real strong. When Jake first brought you in, nobody thought you'd last a day. But you're tougher than you look. Despite everythin' you've seen, despite everythin' they've done to you—you still got faith."

"But I'm letting Jake win," I said. "I'm giving him what he wants."

"Naw," Tuck said in his husky voice. "Givin' him what he

wants would be refusin' . . . puttin' yourself first. You're givin' up somethin' real special and Jake knows you're doing it outta love. You hate him more than anythin' and yet you're gonna give yourself to him to protect the person you love. That's gotta be eatin' him up."

"Thanks, Tuck." I wrapped my arms around him and buried my face into his neck, which smelled of warm hay. "I never thought of it that way."

As I stared at my reflection in the mirror, I thought maybe Tucker was right after all. Maybe I needed to stop thinking of this as an act of sordid unfaithfulness, but rather as the ultimate act of love.

32

The Sword of Michael

I had a few minutes to myself before it was time to go. Hanna and Tuck left me alone, figuring I needed some time to gather my thoughts. I couldn't help myself and started projecting almost before they'd closed the door behind them. I wanted to see Xavier one last time; I wanted his face to be the last thing I saw before I gave away a precious part of myself. I knew if I could hold on to the memory of him in my head, I'd be able to get through this.

My family had already arrived in Alabama. It would've only been about a two-hour drive, but I was still surprised to find they'd gotten there so quickly. As far as I could tell, Broken Hill was a sleepy little town much like Venus Cove. The train station was no longer in use. The wooden benches lining the brick walls were littered with rubbish and the old-fashioned ticket booth was unattended. Weeds sprouted from between the tracks and crows pecked uselessly at the dry ground. I imagined it would have once been a charming little place, brimming with life. It was clear that since the train crash that had claimed so many lives the residents had steered clear of it and now it was nothing but a derelict shadow of its former self. The Chevy pulled up beside the rusted tracks and my family stepped out. Ivy sniffed the air and I wondered if she could smell sulfur given off by the portal that had to be close by.

"This place gives me the creeps," Molly said, still lingering in the car.

"Stay where you are," Gabriel told her and for once she didn't argue.

"So what now?" Xavier asked. "Any idea what we're looking for?"

"It could look like anything," Gabriel said, bending down and holding his right palm above the earth. "But I think it's embedded here in the tracks."

"How do you know that?"

"The earth is always hotter above a portal into Hell."

"That figures," Xavier sighed. "All we gotta work out now is how to open it."

"That's the problem," Ivy said. "Our combined power isn't enough. We need back up."

"Damn it." Xavier kicked the ground with the toe of his boot, sending pebbles flying. "What was the point of coming here?"

"Michael wouldn't have sent us on a wild goose chase," Ivy murmured. "There must be something he wants us to do."

"Or maybe he's just a douche."

"Indeed," said a disembodied voice behind them.

They all spun around in time to see the archangel materialize before them, his towering form shadowing the tracks.

He looked exactly the same as the first time we'd seen him, fair-haired and glowing, his powerful limbs much larger than the size of an average human. His wings were retracted.

"Not again," I heard Molly groan from the car and she put her head between her knees.

Gabriel and Michael acknowledged each other as equal warriors by bowing their heads in recognition. "We have followed your instructions, brother," Gabriel said. "What is it you would have us do now?"

"I have come to offer you my help," Michael replied. "I bring with me the most powerful weapon throughout Heaven and Hell. It can open a portal as easily as popping a cork."

"Thanks for sharing that vital piece of information earlier," Xavier muttered ill-humoredly.

"It was for me to decide when the time was right," Michael said, fixing his eyes on Xavier. "The Covenant met to discuss this unforeseen predicament. Lucifer knows the power of the angel he holds hostage and he plans to use her to achieve his own ends."

Michael's words struck a chord with me. For him to know that, it meant that all this time I hadn't been alone. Heaven had been watching all along. Did I dare to hope that all was not lost?

"How does he plan to do that? Bethany's no puppet," Ivy protested.

"That we cannot know," said Michael. "But divine essence in the hands of any demon is dangerous. Lucifer's aim is to bring about Armageddon—the final battle—and he hopes to use the angel to his advantage. The forces of Heaven must retaliate."

"How exactly does Beth fit in?" Xavier asked.

"She's a catalyst, if you like," Michael explained. "The demons want to trigger a full-scale war, but we will not descend to their level. We will show them the might of Heaven without the need for bloodshed."

"You were always going to help us, weren't you?" Xavier said suddenly. "Why couldn't you have done that right from the start?"

Michael inclined his head slightly. "When a child breaks a toy and his parents immediately buy him a new one, what lesson is learned?"

"Beth is not a toy," Xavier began hotly, but Gabriel put a restraining hand on his shoulder.

"Do not interrupt an angel of the Lord."

"Heaven can always intervene," Michael continued. "But He chooses the appropriate time. We are merely His messengers. If Our Father righted every wrong in the world, nobody would learn from their mistakes. We reward faith and loyalty and you have demonstrated both. Besides, your journey is not over. Heaven has plans for you."

"Plans for me?" Xavier repeated, but Michael only fixed him with his powerful glare.

"Let's not ruin the surprise."

It was a shock to hear what Michael had to say. He ran with the big guns in the Kingdom and I had doubted my rescue was high up on his agenda. But it seemed that Lucifer was playing a more dangerous game than I'd realized. Michael seemed to think we were on the brink of war and that Heaven needed to reaffirm its dominance. I still had no idea how he planned to break through the portal, but he seemed confident in his abilities.

"The portal?" Ivy gently reminded him, anxious not to lose any more time. "We are here for a reason."

"Very well," Michael said, and from beneath his flowing robes he withdrew an object so bright and glorious that Xavier had to turn his face away.

The long, flaming sword pulsed in Michael's hand ready to do his bidding. It burned blue at the edges and looked almost too elegant for its purpose of destruction. Along the golden hilt were etched letters in a language no human could possibly understand. The letters seemed to ripple and glow with a soft blue light. The sword was alive—as if it were blessed with a spirit of its own.

"The Sword of Michael," said Gabriel in a strangely reverential tone I'd never heard him use before. "It's been a long time since I've seen it."

"It actually exists?" Xavier asked.

"It's more real than you know," Gabriel replied. "Michael has gone up against them before."

Xavier thought for a moment. "Of course," he said finally. "It's in Revelation. 'And there was war in Heaven. Michael and his angels fought against the dragon, and the dragon and his angels fought back.' The dragon was Lucifer, right?"

"Correct," Gabriel replied. "Michael was the one who cast him into Hell at Our Father's command."

"Good job," Xavier said and Michael raised an eyebrow. I smiled at how informal his manner was compared to my siblings'. "And you reckon you can bust back in?"

"Let's see, shall we?" was all Michael said.

He drew himself up to his full height in the middle of the tracks. The sword in his hand vibrated so loudly it caused the nearby birds to take flight. "Hey, man," Xavier called out, sounding uncomfortable. "Sorry for calling you a douche. My bad."

Michael nodded delicately to indicate there were no hard feelings. He raised the sword above his head so the sunlight poured off its silver surface in streams.

"In the name of God I command you . . ."

His voice started off booming and then began to peter out. I was fading away, back to my Hades. I tried to linger. I needed desperately to stay and see whether Michael's sword would unlock the portal. But the jarring sound of a hotel phone ringing tugged me mercilessly back to my body.

"HELLO?" I asked, fumbling for the receiver and almost dropping it.

"Mr. Thorn is waiting in the lobby," said the receptionist. I noticed her tone had changed from last time we spoke. Then it had been respectful. Now it was smug.

"Tell him I'll be right down."

I hung up and flopped back onto my bed, exhaling loudly. I didn't know what to think. Could Michael really be about to burst through the portal and rescue me? I didn't dare believe it. I dithered helplessly for a few moments, wondering what to do. I knew one thing for certain: I couldn't let Jake find out what I'd just witnessed. I needed to go along with the deal as if nothing had happened. I hoped my skills as an actor were up to the challenge.

I met Jake in the lobby of Hotel Ambrosia. He'd shed his customary biker jacket and replaced it with tailcoats and silver cuff links, probably in a bid to play the romantic hero. But we both knew that despite the lavish dress-ups there was nothing romantic about the arrangement we'd made. Tuck and Hanna stood just inside the revolving doors looking forlorn as I was bundled into the back of Jake's limousine and we sped off down the tunnels of Hades. I waved at them through the back window, trying to convey the same message of hope I'd been given.

The car finally pulled up at the mouth of what appeared to be a cave. I climbed out and glanced around.

"This is your idea of a romantic location?" I asked dubiously. "Why didn't you just choose a broom closet?"

"Just wait." Jake smiled secretively. "You haven't seen it yet. Shall we?" He held out his arm and escorted me into the dark. I held on to him as he glided us through a short tunnel that opened as if by magic onto an expansive stone chamber. It had been arranged especially for the occasion. For a moment all I could think about was how strangely beautiful it looked. I stopped on the spot and stared openly.

"You organized all this?"

"Guilty as charged. I want to give you a night to remember."

I looked around in amazement. The floor of the underground cave was filled with shallow milky water the color of opals. Rose petals and candles floated on the surface, casting a soft flickering light against the fissured stone walls and sending shadows dancing across the water. Candelabra hung in midair, enchanted by Jake's dark power. At the far end of the cave was a flight of broken stone steps that led to dry land. In the center sat a vast bed lavishly covered in gold satin and fringed pillows. The stone outcrop was decorated with intricate hanging tapestries and portraits from a forgotten world. Gilded mirrors covered every bare space, reflecting the murky light in a spectacular glittering pyramid. The notes of an operatic aria filtered from hidden speakers. Jake had transformed this dank, dark space into a fantastical subterranean world. Of course, the setting didn't change anything.

My eye caught sight of something, half concealed by the water. It was a marble statue of the armless Venus de Milo. Through the fog, I could see a dark liquid trickling down her stone cheeks and landing with a rhythmic drip into the water below. It took me a moment to realize that the statue was crying tears of blood.

Before I could say a word, Jake softly clicked his fingers and an ornate gondola appeared before us.

"After you," he said, gallantly offering me his arm for support. I stepped cautiously inside the waiting vessel and Jake slid in beside me. The gondola steered itself across the glittering water until it nudged against the stone platform. I stepped out, not bothering to gather up the hem of my dress, which dragged up the stone stairs. Jake drifted over to the bed and let his fingers trail across the coverlet. He beckoned me to his side.

Now we stood facing each other in silence. I could see a hunger in Jake's face that made me shiver. I didn't feel anything other than hollow. My emotions had completely shut down; my body was running on autopilot. I knew I needed to stay calm and detached while I waited for help to come . . . if it came. I didn't allow myself to consider what would happen if Michael's plan didn't come to fruition. I knew if I did that I would scream or try and fling Jake away from me. So I stood still and waited. Jake reached out and ran his long, slender fingers down my arms. They worked skillfully and a few moments later the strap of my gown fell down exposing my shoulder. He leaned down and pressed his hot lips against my skin, moving along my collarbone and into the hollow of my throat. His hands came up and tightened around my waist, pulling me toward him. When he brought his lips to mine, his kiss was urgent. I tried not to think about the way Xavier used to kiss me—softly and slowly, as if the kiss were its own reward, not a prelude to anything more. I felt Jake's tongue forcing my lips apart and pressing into my mouth. His breath, as hot as molten lead, was suffocating. As his hands began to crawl over my body, he seemed not to notice how unresponsive I was. Then, in one fluid movement, his hand reached out and opened the zipper on the back of my dress. It crumpled to the floor before I even realized what was happening and I stood before him in nothing but a transparent silk undergarment.

Jake drew back for a moment, breathing heavily as if he'd just run a marathon, then he pushed me down onto the bed and crouched over me, watching me with a curious expression.

He shimmied down the bed and slipped a hand against my inner thigh rubbing his thumb in slow circles. He began to kiss a path from my neck down my breasts and stomach as he lowered his body over mine.

Where were Michael and the others? A sickening thought occurred to me. There was every chance that the sword had failed to open the portal, or maybe Michael had changed his mind. It only took minutes to alter the course of destiny; anything could have happened in the time I'd missed. I felt my heart begin to beat faster and a sheen of sweat broke out across my chest. Jake ran a finger lightly across it and smiled with satisfaction. He lifted one of my fingers to his mouth and sucked gently on it.

"Enjoying yourself after all?" he asked. My mouth felt too dry to speak, but I forced out an answer.

"Can we just get this over with?"

I thought it was a pretty safe bet that Jake would want to draw out the experience as long as possible, but his answer caught me off guard.

"We can do it however you like." He tore off his shirt and threw it to the ground so his bare chest was looming over me, his chocolate hair falling over his blazing eyes. He dipped his head and I felt his teeth graze my ear. "This is just the beginning," he whispered, moving down and running his tongue along my breastbone. "You think this is intense? Just wait, I'm going to push you over the edge. You'll feel like you're about to explode."

I trembled with fear beneath his touch. There were a hundred things I wanted to say, but I willed myself to keep quiet.

At the back of my mind a voice was screaming out. *What if they're not coming?* And as the minutes ticked by it became more and more apparent that they weren't going to come. I tried stalling.

I reached up and let my finger travel lightly down Jake's chest. He shivered and pressed against me more heavily.

"I'm nervous," I whispered, making my voice sound as innocent as possible. "I've never done anything like this before."

"That's because you've been with an amateur," Jake said. "Don't worry, I'll take care of you."

I couldn't think what else to say to delay the inevitable. There was no sign of Xavier or my family. It was too late now; there was nothing else I could do. I lay back and closed my eyes, accepting my fate.

"I'm ready," I said.

"I've been ready for a long time," Jake purred and I felt his hands shift and travel up my thighs.

Suddenly there came a sound like a deep groan from the bowels of the cave. It was as if the very rock itself were being torn apart. The sound echoed off the walls, causing Jake to sit bolt upright, suddenly fiercely alert, his black eyes darting. The sound suggested the ceiling above us might be on the verge of caving in. I sat up, straining to hear a comforting sound.

I heard Jake let out a vicious stream of curses right before the far wall exploded in an ear-splitting shower of dirt and stone, and a familiar 1956 Chevrolet Bel Air convertible plunged through the jagged hole. The car seemed to soar through the air almost in slow motion as it plowed into the cave and landed meters from us with a sound like a thunder-clap. Its body was long and sleek, just like I remembered; its headlights blazing and its sky blue paint scuffed from the dive it had just taken.

"Xavier?" I whispered.

The windshield was coated with dust, but a moment later the driver's door creaked open and a figure stepped out. He was just as I remembered him, tall and broad shouldered with eyes of liquid blue. The honey-colored strands of hair that fell across his forehead were still streaked with gold and around his throat, I could see the crucifix winking in the gloom. Behind him, Ivy and Gabriel stepped out from the passenger doors, looking like pillars of gold in the dark chamber. Their expressions were hard and their steel gray eyes were fixed on Jake. A wind blew up and their golden hair fanned out behind them. It took me a moment to realize that their wings had emerged, as they always did in preparation for conflict. They reared up behind them, like the wings of an eagle, casting shadows ten feet high against the stone walls. They looked as strong and majestic as always, but I could sense that just being in this place weakened them. They didn't belong here and soon their powers would begin to diminish. There was no sign of Michael—I assumed he had opened the portal and disappeared. But his sword glittered in Gabriel's hand. Molly too was nowhere to be seen. She must have been left behind in Alabama—this part of the mission would prove too dangerous for her.

Xavier's face flooded with relief. He stepped forward and reached out to me but stopped when he registered my state of undress. His gaze traveled over the bed, the flowers, and the rumpled sheets. Our eyes met and the pained expression in his made me feel like someone had slapped me across the face. He looked confused at first, then angry, and then strangely blank, as if the roller coaster of emotions that hit him was too overwhelming to manage.

It was Jake who first broke the silence.

"No!" He lunged toward me and grasped me so tightly I cried out in pain. That seemed to spur Xavier into action.

"Take your filthy hands off her!" he growled. He went to run forward, but Ivy and Gabriel appeared by his side in an instant, holding him back. Jake glared at them like a ferocious animal, his black eyes wide with rage and panic.

Gabriel's lip curled in an expression of mockery I'd never seen him wear before. "Did you really think you'd get away with this?" he asked in a soft voice that was all the more menacing.

"You shouldn't be here," Jake hissed. "How did you get in?"

Gabriel stepped forward and swung the sword in an arc, casually testing the weight of it in his hands.

"Let's just say we had unexpected reinforcements."

Jake hissed like a serpent, spraying spit through the air.

"You wouldn't understand, but we take care of our own," Gabriel said.

I felt Jake's fingers dig harder into my shoulder. "She's *mine*," he spat. "You can't take her from me. I won her fair and square."

"You cheated and you lied," Gabriel said. "She is ours and we have come to claim her. Release her before we make you."

For a moment Jake stood completely still. Then suddenly

I felt myself lifted off my feet, his fingers wrapped around my neck. I was dangling in midair and the pressure around my throat was almost unbearable. My feet kicked helplessly and I struggled to suck in whatever wisps of air I could.

"I could break her neck in an instant," Jake taunted.

"To hell with this," Xavier said and before anyone could stop him he charged forward and rammed into Jake with his right shoulder, as if he were on the football field. Taken by surprise, Jake released me and I sank onto the bed, gasping for breath. They tumbled backward into the water. Jake seemed taken aback by the passion behind Xavier's attack. Xavier swung, his fist connecting solidly with Jake's jaw. They tackled each other again, rolling over rocks in the shallows as they struggled for control. I heard Jake grunt repeatedly as Xavier's fist thudded into him. It was evident who was physically superior. But Jake wasn't one to play fair and as soon as he regained his composure for a moment, he swept a hand through the air and Xavier was flung across the cavern and crashed onto the bed beside me. Jake snapped his fingers and iron chains materialized around us both, binding us to the spot. Jake approached like a predator, waiting for the kill. He loomed above us for a moment and then his fist shot out and punched Xavier square across the left eye. Xavier's head snapped to the side and I saw him wince, but he didn't give Jake the satisfaction of knowing he was hurt. I screamed and struggled against the restraints as Jake's fist smashed into Xavier's jaw and a trickle of blood ran from his lip.

Then a force lifted Jake clean off his feet and threw him

across the cave. The chains that bound us dissolved. Xavier groaned and rolled onto his side, facing me.

"I'm sorry," he said. "I'm so sorry I let this happen. I swore to always protect you and I let you down."

I stared at him for a moment before throwing my arms around him and burying my face in his neck. "You're here," I whispered. "You're really here. Oh God, I've missed you so much."

We stayed locked in our embrace for several long moments before we sat up to see my brother and sister squaring off against Jake. He had transformed from a dapper gentleman into something that looked barely human. His dark hair was mussed, his nose was bleeding, and his eyes were glistening with rage.

Ivy and Gabriel together looked like unassailable opponents.

"Let Bethany go, Arakiel," Gabriel warned in a low voice. "Before this gets out of hand."

"You'll have to kill me," Jake spat. "And you did a bang-up job of that the first time."

Gabriel pointed Michael's sword directly at Jake. "We do not come unprepared."

"You think I don't know what this place does to you?" Jake asked. "Every second you spend here, you grow weaker."

"There are four of us," Gabriel pointed out.

"Including one human and one angel so easy she was about to surrender herself to a demon."

Xavier slid off the bed and fixed Jake with a dark look. "Don't talk about her that way."

"What?" Jake taunted. "Can't handle the idea that your little girlfriend was about to let another man enjoy her? Give her something you never could?"

Xavier shook his head. "That's not true."

"Ask her yourself," Jake said smugly.

Xavier turned his head an inch to look at me. "Beth?"

I didn't know what to say. How could I break the news to him that I had been on the verge of committing an unforgiveable betrayal? I opened my mouth and then closed it again, twisting the bedsheets in my hands.

"I think her silence speaks volumes," Jake said, sounding pleased with himself.

Xavier flinched and drew back. "So it is true." He waved a hand around him. "That's what all this is?"

"You don't understand," I said. "I was doing it for you."

"For me? How exactly do you figure that?"

Jake clapped his hands in delight. "Oh, come now, this isn't the time for a lover's tiff."

"I made a deal," I blurted out. "If I slept with him, he said he wouldn't try and hurt you again."

Gabriel's silver eyes flickered across to Jake. "You really are the vermin of the earth," he said in disgust. "Don't blame Bethany, Xavier—she didn't know he was lying."

"You were lying?" I cried. "I was going to give myself to you and you were lying to me the whole time!"

"Of course I was," Jake scoffed. "Never trust a demon, sweetheart. You of all people should know that."

Before I could respond, Xavier let rip with a steady flow of cursing. I'd never heard him cuss before and even Gabriel raised his eyebrows in surprise.

"My oh my, it seems pretty boy has some bite in him after all," Jake said.

"When will you stop screwing with us?" Xavier hissed. "Is this the only way you can get a kick out of life? Are you really that pathetic?"

I took the opportunity of Jake's distracted state to jump off the bed and run to my brother and sister, positioning myself safely behind them.

"You can hide, Bethany," Jake called lazily. "But you're not getting out."

"Actually, brother," Gabriel said darkly. "It's you who isn't getting out."

Suddenly Gabriel's wings lifted him off his feet and in a flash he soared over Jake—Michael's sword poised above him. It all happened so quickly, it was almost a blur. I heard the swish of metal slicing through the air, a ragged gasp, and when Gabriel's feet touched solid earth, the sword was embedded deep in Jake's chest. Xavier's mouth fell open in shock and he ran to me, wrapping an arm around my shoulders. Jake screamed then and gripped the hilt, tearing it from his body and tossing it to the ground with a clatter. The blood that stained the blade was thicker than normal and black as night. It spurted from the gaping wound to pool around him, his demonic power leaking out with it. Suddenly blood bubbled like froth from Jake's mouth. A spasm jolted his body as he collapsed, twitching to the ground.

Before Jake's face became a mask he raised his head and reached out to me. His eyes were pleading as he mouthed something soundlessly. At first I couldn't make out the words but I caught fragments in between his ragged breathing.

"Bethany, forgive me."

Pity made me move toward him. I was driven by a desire to offer what comfort I could.

"What are you doing?" I heard Xavier's voice behind me, but I was too distracted by the misery in Jake's black eyes. He may have been my tormentor in Hades but I knew it all stemmed from a twisted desire to win my affection. Maybe deep down Jake just wanted to be loved. At the very least, he shouldn't have to die alone. A strange part of me wanted a chance to say good-bye.

"Bethany, no!"

My fingers had almost closed over Jake's withering hand when I was suddenly yanked back. I toppled onto the ground and saw a pair of luminous wings beating over my head. Gabriel, understanding what I was about to do, had swooped across the cavern to stop me.

"Stay back! If you touch him now he takes you with him into death."

I curled my fingers into a fist and pressed it against my chest. So I had misjudged again. It seemed Jake had remained true to himself till the bitter end.

He was still staring fixedly at me as his body jerked one last time and then was still. We watched the fire go out of his eyes until they glazed over and stared dully into space.

"It's over," I whispered, needing to say the words aloud in

order to believe them. Ivy and Gabriel closed around me in a tight embrace. "Thank you for coming for me."

"We're family," Gabriel replied as if it were the only explanation necessary.

I found Xavier's face and took it in my hands. His eyes were wet with tears and when he touched my cheek, I realized I had been crying silently too.

"I love you," I said simply, stating an unassailable fact. There was plenty more I could have said, but in that moment it was all I needed to say. It was all that mattered.

"I love you too, Beth," Xavier said. "More than you can ever know."

"We need to move quickly," Gabriel said, shepherding us toward the Chevy. "The portal won't stay open much longer."

"Wait." I resisted as they tried to usher me into the car. "What about Hanna and Tuck?"

"Who?" Ivy asked in confusion.

"My friends, they looked after me while I was here. I can't just leave them."

"I'm sorry, Bethany." My sister's eyes were full of genuine sorrow. "There's nothing we can do for them."

"It's not fair," I cried. "Everyone deserves a second chance."

"The demons are coming." Gabriel took my hand. "They know we're here and the portal is starting to seal. We must leave or we'll be trapped."

I nodded silently and followed them, hot tears trickling down my cheeks. Gabriel took the wheel while I leaned against Xavier in the backseat. I looked over my shoulder one last time and saw Jake's body floating in the water. What he'd put me through would probably haunt me for the rest of my existence, but he could no longer hurt me. I wanted to feel anger, but I felt only pity for him. He died as he had lived, alone and without ever having known love.

"Good-bye, Jake," I whispered and turned my face away, burying it in Xavier's chest. I felt him kiss the top of my head and his strong arms held me close as the Chevy roared to life and sped toward the gaping hole in the cave that had already begun to close over.

I had only one thought as the blackness closed in, drawing me back to my beloved earth. I was going back to the life I'd known before, the life I'd missed and longed for . . . but there in Xavier's arms, I was already home.

Epilogue

ON the manicured lawns of Bryce Hamilton the seniors loitered under the bright June sunlight in their royal blue caps and gowns, faces glowing with excitement. Somehow, they didn't look like teenagers in need of direction anymore; they were young people ready to make their own way in the world. College was still several months away and everyone was looking forward to the summer break. I knew Xavier had received offers from several colleges eager to recruit him into their ranks, especially those with all-star football teams.

Even though graduation wouldn't impact on my future in the same way, I couldn't help but get caught up in the flurry of nervous excitement. We were waiting for the signal for the procession to begin. Outside the auditorium I spotted Gabriel and his middle school choristers warming up for their closing performance of "Friends Forever," a popular if clichéd choice as valedictory song.

Among the seniors the buoyant mood was contagious. The girls adjusted their caps and pinned back one another's hair so it didn't fall over their eyes and ruin the photographs. The boys were less concerned about appearance, focusing instead on vigorously shaking hands and thumping one another on the back. We were all wearing the class rings that had been delivered only days before. They were simple silver bands engraved with the school motto: LIVE. LOVE. LEARN.

Bryce Hamilton loved pomp and pageantry. Inside the auditorium invited guests and parents were taking their seats and fanning themselves with folded copies of the program. Ivy was sitting beside Dolly Henderson from next door, feigning interest in the neighborhood gossip. Waiting in the wings was Dr. Chester and the teaching staff in full academic regalia, the color of their hoods denoting their individual branch of expertise. The principal would give the opening address, and then as class president, Xavier would deliver the valedictory speech. He hadn't had much time to prepare, but Xavier was a natural orator and I knew he'd be able to deliver an inspirational speech with just a few scribbled notes to guide him. From outside I spotted Bernie in the audience, trying to keep her youngest from clambering over each other and telling Nicola off for playing Peggle on her iPhone.

After the ceremony high tea would be served in the cafeteria, which had been transformed with white tablecloths and flower arrangements to befit the occasion. A professional photographer was already clicking away behind his camera lens, and I watched Abby and the girls apply fresh coats of lip gloss and make sure their caps were straight. I was looking forward to the part where we'd all throw our caps into the air—I'd seen the scene in several movies and wanted to experience it firsthand. Ivy had taped my name to the inside of mine so I'd be able to find it easily afterward.

The whole school was buzzing with a strange energy. But amid the excitement was an underlying wistfulness. Molly and her friends would never sit out in the quad again; this position would be passed on to the next group of seniors who could never be quite the same. The days of skipping class, cramming for exams, and flirting with boys at the lockers in between periods were over. School had united us; we were expected to pursue our own lives now, and chances were, we'd never all be in the same place again.

I wanted the ceremony to hurry up and start. I was so caught up in the excitement I almost forgot I was a mere onlooker in all of this. I felt entirely human, like I should be worrying about college applications and my future career prospects. I had to remind myself that this life was not meant for me. The best I could do was share in the experience through Xavier and my friends.

Molly appeared by my side and threw her arms around me.

"My God, it's so sad!" she cried. "I've spent the last four years complaining about this place and now I don't want to leave."

"Oh, Molly, you'll be okay," I said, tucking a wayward corkscrew curl behind her ear. "It's ages till college."

"But I've spent thirteen years of my life at this school," Molly said. "It's weird to think I'm never coming back. I know everybody in this town; it's my home."

"And it always will be," I said. "College is going be an amazing adventure, but Venus Cove will still be here when you come back."

"But I'll be so far away!" she wailed.

"Molly." I laughed and hugged her. "You're going to 'Bama—it's one state away!"

She giggled and sniffed. "I guess so, thanks, Bethie."

I felt a hand wrap around my waist and then Xavier's lips were at my ear.

"Can I talk to you?" he murmured. I turned and looked up at him. The blue of the graduation gown emphasized the color of his eyes and his silky walnut hair wasn't even mussed by the cap.

"Sure, what's up?" I asked. "Are you nervous?"

"No," Xavier said.

"Is your speech ready? I haven't heard any of it!"

"We're not staying." Xavier delivered this earth-shattering statement with surprising equilibrium.

"Excuse me?" I said. "Why not?"

"Because it doesn't mean anything to me anymore."

"Don't be ridiculous."

"I've never been more serious in my life."

I still didn't believe him. "I think today is turning everybody weird," I said. "Don't you want to graduate?"

"I'll graduate whether I attend the ceremony or not."

I saw then that his eyes were bright and his smile made his whole face radiant. He was actually serious about leaving.

"You're giving the valedictory speech!"

"It's taken care of. Wes is stepping in for me. Wasn't cheap though."

I stared at him. How could he make jokes when he was about to walk out on one of the most momentous events of his life? Everybody expected him to lead the ceremony—it wouldn't be the same without him.

"Your parents will never forgive you," I said. "Why don't you want to stay? Aren't you feeling well?"

"I feel fine, Beth."

"Then why?"

"Because there's something much more important I want to do."

"What could be more important than you graduating?"

"Come with me and you'll find out."

"Not until you tell me where we're going."

"Don't you trust me?"

"Of course I do." I nodded ardently. "But I've never seen you do anything this . . . you know . . . reckless."

"Funny, I don't feel reckless," he said. "I've never felt more in control."

Bryce's marching band started up the procession and the students began filing into the auditorium to take their places on the stage. A teacher on duty was counting them in by tens. I could see Molly searching for me in the crowd as we'd planned to sit together. The school captains always filed in last because their seats were in the front row. I looked over at Gabriel. He was escorting his choir backstage, but he must have sensed something was up because he threw me a questioning look over his shoulder. I smiled and gave him a feeble wave in return, hoping I gave off the signal that everything was under control. Xavier was looking at me expectantly.

"Come and sit with me under the old oak for five minutes

and I'll explain everything. If you don't like the plan we'll come back and go in together. Agreed?"

"Five minutes?" I reiterated.

"That's all I'm asking."

I stood under the dappled light of the old oak tree in the middle of the school's sweeping circular driveway knowing this would be our last tryst here together. A wave of nostalgia hit me. The oak had been a reliable friend to us during our time at Bryce Hamilton, its gnarled branches providing refuge and serving as our secret meeting place whenever our desire to be together overcame any sense of responsibility. I wrapped my arms playfully around its wide trunk while Xavier continued to look as though he'd just made the discovery of the century.

"Okay," I said. "Your time starts now. What's this great idea that warrants skipping out on graduation?"

Xavier took off his cap and gown and flung them onto the grass beside us. Underneath he was wearing a white shirt and tie over dress pants. Seeing his athletic chest under the flimsy cotton stirred in me the usual deep, visceral yearning.

Xavier was gazing at me dreamily. He bent his head and kissed my hand. "I've been thinking about us."

"Good thinking or bad?" I asked immediately, the yearning giving way to fear.

"Good, of course."

I was able to breathe easily again. "So let's hear it."

"I think I've found the answer."

"That's great," I said lightly. "What's the question?"

But Xavier was deadly serious. "The question is how do we make sure no one comes between us again."

"Xavier, what are you talking about? You need to relax. We're together now. I'm back. Jake won't bother us again anytime soon."

"If it's not Jake it'll be someone or something else. It's no way to live, Beth. Always looking over our shoulders, wondering how much time we've got left."

"So let's not do that. Let's just focus on what we've got right here and now."

"I can't. I want this to be forever."

"We can't have that expectation. You know that."

"I think we can." I looked into his brilliant, fathomless eyes and saw something I hadn't seen before. I couldn't put my finger on exactly what it was, but I knew something had changed.

Then in the next minute Xavier had firmly taken hold of my hands and dropped to one knee by the base of the oak, the crinkled leaves on the ground crunching under his weight. My heart started racing like an express train. An internal tug-of-war began between joy and devastation at what he was about to do.

"Beth," he said simply, his flawless face lit up with anticipation. "There is no doubt in my mind that we belong together, but to spend the rest of my life with you would be an honor and commitment I would cherish." He paused, his clear, blue eyes luminous. My breath caught in my throat, but Xavier only smiled. "Beth," he repeated. "Will you marry me?"

The look on his face was one of pure happiness.

I was dumbfounded. I could honestly claim that Xavier was an open book to me by now, but I certainly hadn't seen this one coming. Involuntarily I glanced up at the sky for guidance, but none was forthcoming. This was something I would have to deal with on my own. A number of possible responses tumbled through my mind, one more rational than the next.

Xavier, are you delirious? Have you completely lost your mind? You're not even nineteen and in no position to get married. Don't you think we need to think this through? I can't let you throw all your dreams away . . . after college maybe we can talk about it. We don't have the authority to make this kind of decision alone. Your parents are going to disown you. How will Ivy and Gabriel take it?

But only the least rational found its way to my lips.

"Yes."

We moved quickly away from the old oak, fearing someone would come looking for us. As soon as I'd given Xavier my answer he scooped me up in his arms and charged off toward the school gates, not stopping until he got to the street where his Chevy was parked. Xavier deposited me carefully on the curb to open the passenger door, then jumped behind the wheel and headed straight for town.

"Where are we going now?" I said breathless with exhilaration.

"We have to do something to celebrate."

A few minutes later the Chevy pulled up outside Sweethearts on Main Street. Inside the café was almost empty. I figured most of its regulars must be at Bryce's graduation ceremony. I stole a quick glance at my wristwatch when Xavier wasn't looking. We'd been gone at least half an hour by now.

Our absence would have been well and truly noticed. The principal was probably halfway through his opening address. There would be whispers and questions among the teachers backstage as to who had seen us last and where we might have gone. Someone would volunteer to look around the grounds. Ivy and Gabriel would notice our empty seats and know something was amiss, while Xavier's parents would be totally confused by their model son's disappearing act. Thinking about all this was sobering and certainly tempered my elation. I had to at least confirm that Xavier had made his decision with a clear head.

"Xavier," I began tentatively.

"C'mon, Beth, you can't have changed your mind already?"

"No, of course not. I just have to say one thing."

"Okay. Shoot."

"You have to think about your future."

"I have. It's sitting right in front of me."

"But what will your parents think?"

"I thought you only wanted to say one thing."

"Please, Xavier, be serious."

"I don't know what they'll think. I'm not planning to ask them. This *is* the right thing to do. I've thought about it long and hard. It's what I want and I know it's what you want too. If circumstances were normal we might approach things differently, but we don't have that luxury. This is the only way to protect what's ours."

"But what if it makes things worse."

"Doesn't matter because we get to face it together."

"Have you thought about *how* we're going to do this?"

"It's all taken care of. Father Mel has agreed to help us out. In fact, he's waiting for us right now down at the chapel."

"Right now?" My jaw dropped. "Shouldn't we tell someone first?"

"They'll only try and talk us out of it. We can tell the whole town afterward. Once our families get over the initial shock we'll all go out and celebrate. You'll see."

"You make it sound so easy."

"That's because it is. Marriage is a holy sacrament. Even God will have to be satisfied."

"I was thinking more about your mom."

"What's she got to complain about? At least we're getting married in a church!"

"That's true."

Xavier raised his milkshake to propose a toast.

"To us," he said as our glasses clinked. "What God hath joined together let no man put asunder."

What could I do but return his optimistic smile? I wanted nothing more than to be his forever. How could I tell him it wasn't the interference of man I was worried about?

I remembered the anguish Xavier had endured during the time I'd languished in Hades. Now the crisis was over, the boy I loved was back, ready to declare our commitment to the world. He was prepared to risk everything for happiness. The old Xavier had returned to me, perhaps even stronger than ever. I couldn't risk losing him again, even if it did unleash the wrath of heaven.

Xavier must have read uncertainty in my face.

"You can still back out," he said quietly. "I'll understand."

I hesitated a moment, all the possible consequences flooding into my head. But when Xavier took my hand, everything cleared and I knew exactly what I wanted.

"Not a chance," I replied. "I can't wait to be Mrs. Xavier Woods."

Xavier slammed his hand down on the tabletop, frustration momentarily clouding his face.

I jumped. "What did I say?"

"Damn it, I forgot about the ring!"

"We can worry about that stuff later," I placated.

"No, we don't need to," he said with a smile.

He reached into his trouser pocket and teasingly withdrew a closed fist. When he opened it a round antique ring box sat neatly in the palm of his hand.

"Open it," he suggested.

I gasped when I lifted the tiny metal clasp and the lid sprang open. The box contained a rose-cut diamond ring so perfect it took my breath away. As soon as I set eyes on it, I knew it was my ring and I was never going to part with it. I'd never felt such a strong connection to a material possession before. The ring seemed made for me. I didn't even stop to consider it might need resizing. I just knew it would fit. There wasn't anything showy or ostentatious about it. I'd been with Molly and the girls when they'd admired the displays in the local jewelry store. I'd always feign interest to be polite, but the gaudy modern diamonds they gushed over left me cold. They looked so colorless and harsh. My ring was as delicate as a flower. Its design could not be improved. The multifaceted central stone was set in a platinum band and peaked like a tiny dome. Encircling it were smaller diamonds that recessed down the shoulder of the ring.

"It's perfect for you," Xavier observed.

"It's so elegant," I breathed. "Where on earth did you find it? I've never seen anything like it before."

"My grandmother left it to me in her will. My sisters were pretty pissed off that she wanted me to have it. It's a ring made for an angel. Aren't you going to try it on?"

I nodded and reached hesitantly for the ring, still struggling to believe that something so intricate and so precious was to be mine. But I never got the chance to try it on. Just as Xavier's words were spoken, the very earth beneath us began to shake as if Heaven itself were in revolt.

The ring slid off the table and tumbled onto the trembling floor.

{ Acknowledgments }

Thank you, Mom—for everything. I don't even know where to start.

Thank you, Liz Kerins, for being my adopted big sister and dear friend. Our Texas road trip was epic.

Thank you, Janna, Gail, and all the Memphis girls, for making me fall in love with the South.

Thank you, Christopher, for understanding that "creative" is pretty much code for "crazy."

Thank you to each and every one of my fans. Without you, none of this would have been possible. I love y'all!

Thank you to everyone at Feiwel and Friends, for their commitment and dedication to this series.

Thank you to my agents, Jill and Matthew, for believing in me.

Thanks to my dear friend Lisa Berryman—your intelligence, grace, and insight have helped shape me as a person, as well as a writer.

Lastly, thanks to my country music heroes: Hank Williams, Johnny Cash, Willie Nelson, Kitty Wells, and Alan Jackson, for being my constant inspiration.

ALEXANDRA ADORNETTO was fourteen when she published her first book, *The Shadow Thief*, in Australia. The daughter of two English teachers, she admits to being a compulsive book buyer who has run out of shelf space, and now stacks her reading "in wobbly piles on my bedroom floor". She lives in Melbourne, Australia.